MW00345272

Secret Service Journals
Assassination and Redemption in 1960s Detroit

A NOVEL

By Bob Morris

PathBinder
Publishing LLC
COLUMBUS, INDIANA

Published by PathBinder Publishing
P.O. Box 2611
Columbus, IN 47202
www.PathBinderPublishing.com

Copyright © 2022 by Bob Morris
All rights reserved

Edited by Doug Showalter and Paul J. Hoffman
Covers designed by Paul J. Hoffman

Cover photos courtesy of Walter P. Reuther Library, Archives of Labor and Urban Affairs, Wayne State University.

Main photo: A nighttime view of the Detroit skyline, 1970, Tony Spina Photographs. From left: Walter P. Reuther, Walter P. Reuther Photographs; John F. Kennedy in front of Cobo Hall during the American Legion Convention, October 1960, Tony Spina Photographs; Lyndon Baines Johnson, undated, Walter P. Reuther Photographs.

First published in 2022
Manufactured in the United States

ISBN: 978-1-955088-44-2
Library of Congress Control Number: 2022913798

All rights reserved. No part of this book may be reproduced or transmitted in any form whatsoever without prior written permission from the publisher except in the case of brief quotations embodied in critical articles and reviews.

To the love of my life:

Terry Ahwal Morris

Table of Contents

Introduction

This book is a work of historical fiction. The key figures in the book are fictitious. There are many real people who play a part of this story. Some are recognizable. Several others are real people that, in most cases, were known by the author. In each case, the author has done his best to represent these characters accurately, both in their words and actions. President Kennedy and members of his administration are real. President Kennedy's speeches, press conferences, and TV statements are accurate.

In the cast of characters listed below, the author has indicated which are real and which are creations of his imagination.

Cast of Major Characters
R - Real characters. F - Fictitious characters

Simpson Family - *F*
Bill Simpson
Annie Simpson – Bill's wife
Jimmy Simpson -Bill's dad
Jenny Simpson – Bill's mother

Secret Service Detroit Office - *F*
Reed Clark – Office Director
Joe Kowalski – Bill's partner
Joe Bishop – Agent

Secret Service National Office - *F*
Jim "Mac" Macalister – SS Director

Chicago Investigation - *F*
Bob Montague – Office Director
Larry McRae – Secret Service Agent
Daniel Kranz – Chicago Police Department

FBI - *F*
Fred Fry – Detroit Office
Elliott Glenn – FBI Headquarters

United Auto Workers Union (UAW) – *R*
Ken Morris – UAW regional director
Walter Reuther – President UAW
Victor Reuther – UAW leader
Emil Mazey – Secretary Treasurer UAW
Irving Bluestons – Aide to Walter Reuther
Paul Schrade – UAW West Coast regional director

Others - *F*
Bill Eaton – Sue Monroe's grandson
Rita Gray – Key witness against Simpson
Bernie Levine – Simpson's attorney
Mike and Kathy Paxton – Simpson's neighbors after prison
Sam Starr – Simpson's best friend after prison
Sue Monroe – Simpson's girlfriend

Preface ~ 2019

Bill Eaton was driving from Lansing to Birmingham, Michigan, to see his grandmother. In the past few years, he had made the trip less often than he should have. But now, at twenty-seven, he was going just about every weekend. Susan Eaton, his grandmother, was dying. At seventy-eight, she had developed ovarian cancer and had only a few months to live.

Bill's grandmother was determined to live her final months in her 1928, two-story home she and her late husband, Tom, had purchased in 1975. Bill's grandmother and grandfather were married in 1973 and raised two children: his father, Tom Jr., and their daughter, Annie. Tom Jr. followed his father's footsteps by having a successful career with General Motors. His Aunt Annie taught high school at a nearby school system. The divorced and retired Annie now cared for her mother as much as possible with the assistance of outside help.

Bill pulled into the driveway in his Chevy Camaro. Pulling his nearly six-foot body out of the driver's seat, he entered the two-story home he had known all of his life. He felt a cold and heavy atmosphere—he didn't like it.

"Hello!" he called as he walked into the living room.

Aunt Annie appeared, "*Shhh!* Your grandma just fell asleep," she said, giving Bill a hug.

After getting a brief update of his Grandma's latest trip to the doctor, Bill told his aunt to take a break and he would sit with his grandmother.

He climbed the stairs to his grandmother's bedroom, observing the new lift that had been installed along the stairwell wall. Though the curtains of her room were pulled, the dim light filtering through could not hide the happy surroundings: a place full of bright colors and many framed photos of family gatherings and trips on the walls, dressers, and nightstand.

Bill looked at the sleeping woman: her breath was heavy, but steady. He sat down in the comfortable chair next to the bed and began reading his book, a political biography.

Soon his eyelids grew heavy, and he began to snooze. A few minutes later he was awakened by his grandmother's weak voice: "Billy, is that you?"

He sat up. "Yep, Grandma, I'm here." He was surprised at how tired and drained she sounded. For the first time, Bill realized her days were numbered. She coughed a cough that shook her frail, thin frame.

"Grandma, what can I do for you?"

"No," she said when she regained her composure. "No, I'm fine. Just stay with me; it's so good to see you." She reached for his hand, looked down at the book he was reading, and then began to drift in and out of sleep. As the day moved forward, she at times released his hand, but they were never separated by more than a few inches. Occasionally, Annie checked on them to see if they needed any help.

Around four o'clock, his grandmother tightened her grip, and he closed his book. She looked at him, and a smile formed on her wrinkled face, the once blonde hair having long ago changed to a striking gray. Her eyes opened. She seemed to be studying him. "Billy," she said in a voice just above a whisper, "would you do me a favor?" Her voice was somber, her blue eyes looking into his.

Thinking she wanted him to open the drapes or some other task, Bill said, "Of course, whatever you want."

"Now, this is serious. I have a ... a story that no one, not even your father or Anne, knows about. Even your grandfather never fully understood what happened."

Bill leaned in, adjusted his chair a bit, and looked into the woman's eyes. *What on earth could she be talking about?* He continued holding and massaging her hand as they talked.

"Now, you just know me as your grandmother. I've tried to be a good parent and a better grandmother." He started to protest her observation, but she waved him off. "Dammit now, let me finish. Now, I've always loved your grandfather. He was the kindest, most affectionate man." A tear came down the corner of her right eye, and Bill wiped it off with a tissue. He had no idea where she was going with this. His curiosity was mounting.

She continued, "Before your grandfather, I had deep, deep affection for a man. In many ways more powerful than even for your grandfather, although your grandpa was the best and couldn't have made my life better. Still, my relationship before your grandpa changed me forever, and before I die, I don't want my first love's memory and the history he lived, forgotten. It's very important and," her voice broke a bit, "people need to know. Can you understand?"

"I will try ... I'll do my best," he said, wondering where in the hell she was going with this.

"Okay. Now, while I'm alive, I don't want your aunt or your dad to know this story. After I'm gone, it will be entirely up to you what you do with my little piece of history. You can throw out the material or whatever. Frankly, almost everyone involved with this story is either dead or very old. Still, it could have some serious consequences. Now, after we are done here, I want you to go up into the attic. In the far northeast corner, over your dad's bedroom, under some boxes, you will find an old wicker basket. It's fairly heavy, so be careful of your back. It contains some boxes of photos and other stuff. Most importantly, it contains some journals and other writings by him." She paused. "Take them home. Don't let Anne or anyone else see the contents, at least not now."

"Grandma, why are you being so mysterious? It's okay if you knew someone before Grandpa."

"Oh, Jesus, I know *that!*" she said, showing some of her old feistiness. "This is far more than the romance of a young schoolteacher. You will see. Just take the basket home. Don't open it now. Just go home tonight, and come back next week—we can talk more then."

With that, she talked about some other subjects, then fell into a deep sleep. Bill covered her with the light blanket and went to the stairwell that led to the attic. He turned the button of the old pre-code light switch and walked up the stairs. Once on the third floor, he moved to the corner as instructed, ducking to avoid hitting his head as the ceiling that angled down.

There were four boxes of books stacked up that had a thick layer of dust on them. Behind them, underneath some additional boxes, lay the wicker basket, thickly woven and strong, more like a small storage locker than the flimsy container he envisioned.

Pulling the basket out of the corner, he set it underneath the naked light bulb. He couldn't resist defying his grandmother's instructions and opened the lid. There were two shoe boxes on top. One box was full of photos, and on top of the images was an old Wilson tennis ball. He took a quick look and blinked with surprise. There was a 5x7-inch black and white photo of his grandmother playing tennis. *Wow, Grandma was hot back then.* He looked at the back of the photo and read the inscription, written in black ink: "Great backhand! Sam."

He continued looking through the photos and found an old postcard. The photo on the card was of a theater's front arcade: "Sid Grauman's Chinese Theatre." On the back side, a note was scrawled, "Hi Babe! Great trip to LA. Much to talk about! Love, Bill." He saw the faded postmark that said "Hollywood, California, July 13, 1970." The postcard was addressed to Susan Monroe, his grandmother's maiden name. *Shit, who was this man?*

He closed the shoe box, replaced the wicker lid, and carried the basket downstairs. Aunt Annie was with grandma, so he quietly moved downstairs and out the front door, squeezing the basket onto the Camaro's passenger seat.

***

That night, back at his modest East Lansing condominium, Bill turned on the television to catch the Michigan State University football game. He set the basket down on his carpeted living room floor and carefully began to unload the contents. Underneath the two boxes were several spiral notebooks, wrapped in ancient plastic covers from a dry cleaner. The journals were labeled: "The White House," "The Assassination," "Prison," and "Reuther." The other shoe box contained faded newspaper clippings, primarily about the death of a man named Walter Reuther. Also included were additional journals with no dates or markings on the covers, and an envelope labeled, "The Chicago Assignment." On the very bottom of the basket was a carefully wrapped photo in a frame, a wonderfully candid photo of two men talking by a limousine. One was clearly President John F. Kennedy in a golf shirt; Bill didn't recognize the other man. He looked to be in his early thirties and was dressed in a button-down shirt. The man seemed to be listening intently to what the president was saying.

What remained in the basket were a few faded, brown articles, dated 1964, from the *Detroit Free Press* and *The Detroit News* about a trial. The man on trial was someone named William Simpson.

Bill opened a beer and began reading the journals in chronological order. He deduced that they were written by this man, Simpson.

***

Bill never had a chance to discuss the material in the wicker basket with his grandmother. She died four days after his visit. His family and close friends gathered for the funeral. That evening, after the mourners had all gone, Bill asked his mother how she came up with his name.

His forty-six-year-old mother, Jenny, adjusted her black pillbox hat. "Well now, that's an appropriate story for your grandmother's funeral. You know, when I was about six months pregnant with you, Grandma came to your dad and me and asked very politely that, if we had a boy, could we name him William and call him Bill? You know, she never asked us for anything. And, of course, your father and I were very young when we married, and she always supported our decision. Anyhow, she said she always liked the name Bill. We agreed. Your dad, being the smart-ass that he is, said, 'Mom, if it's a girl, should we call her Billie?' When you were born, we honored you grandmother's request."

***

Bill spent the next couple of months reviewing and trying to understand the documents, which basically amounted to diaries. In time he began to realize the story they told. It seemed to him the story started at the White House, when this man, Bill Simpson, started the first day of a new assignment.

PART I ~ 1962
Chapter One
The White House

Bill Simpson felt like it was his first day of kindergarten. Everything seemed new and different from all he had known. Walking from the Old Executive Office Building to the White House was the thrill of a lifetime. A Secret Service agent for five years, based in the Detroit office, Simpson was on a special assignment occasionally offered to agents: a four-month tour of duty on the presidential detail. It was Monday, March 5, 1962, and Bill was walking on air.

Reality set in as Jeff Peters, the agent escorting him to his assignment, spoke to him in a soft, Virginian accent: "Simpson, take a good look around and a deep breath, okay? Then, let's get to work. I'm going to walk you through to our desk in the West Wing. Agent Ford is there and will break you in. Remember, we are here for one reason, and one reason only, and that is to protect the president first, then the first lady, and then the vice president. Whatever you see or hear is none of your business—in one ear and out the other. That's the way it has to be. Got it?"

Bill had already been told this during his briefings, but he didn't have a problem with Peters repeating the instructions. Soon they were at a desk placed strategically so that several halls in the West Wing could be observed. He was introduced to John Ford, a pleasant man, who began showing him the ropes. Like Peters, Ford spoke with a syrupy, southern accent.

Ford started the conversation by asking Simpson about his background. As he responded, Bill looked around the office area and studied some of the people moving around the bustling, business-like area. Some of the men he knew from television news stories, but most he did not recognize. Then, suddenly, walking out of the Oval Office's outer office was the president's brother, Bobby Kennedy, the attorney general. Something about him seemed standoffish. Bill could not quite put his finger on it; he could only call it a sort of "regal aloofness."

Ford asked him about his previous work in Detroit, which he pronounced as "DEE-troit." Simpson told him he'd broken up a couple of counterfeiting rings, and that the Detroit office occasionally worked with Canadian law enforcement to track down counterfeiters, often located in Windsor, directly across the Detroit River. "For over thirty years, a bunch of Detroit underworld gangs have used Windsor to skirt us. Some mobsters find it easier to recruit in Windsor than the US."

"Kids?" Ford asked, surveying Simpson's wedding ring.

"Yep, a two-year-old girl and one on the way."

"Good for you. Now, let's watch, and I'll give you the lowdown about who these people are and what we should be watching for. It's important to understand that inside the White House the ushers and other White House staff take care of the president and first family. We are to observe and stay with him as necessary, but the White House staff handles all personal issues. On the road, it's different; we are in charge."

Bill learned a great deal and felt more comfortable in his new role as the day progressed. He still could not get over being part of the White House experience.

The next day, he was assigned to stand directly outside the Oval Office. He replaced a fellow agent, Jim Carr. The young, clean-shaven man introduced Bill to the president's secretary, Evelyn Lincoln. Mrs. Lincoln was welcoming and seemed genuinely happy to have him as a new member of the detail.

Minutes later, the door to the Oval Office opened and several people came out whom Bill did not recognize. The last to emerge was easily recognizable: Pierre Salinger, the president's press secretary.

From inside the Oval Office, Bill heard the famous Boston accent: "Pierre, Kenny! Hang on for a moment." Salinger and another man, whom Bill guessed was the appointment secretary Kenny O'Donnell, paused just inside the doorway and, suddenly there was President John Fitzgerald Kennedy speaking quietly to the two men. He was dressed in a dark suit, his silk tie casually pulled up around the collar of his shirt, his thick hair parted left.

After a moment, the men left the outer office, and Kennedy's piercing, green-grey eyes met Bill's. He walked up and said, "Ah, are you, ah, new to the detail? I don't think I remember you around."

"Yes sir, Mr. President. I started yesterday," Bill responded.

Kennedy nodded and smiled. "Where're you from?"

"Detroit."

"Ah, Detroit is one of my favorite cities. The Motor City and the, ah, UAW."

"Yes, sir. My father works for Ford in one of the auto plants."

"Very good." The president looked Bill up and down, sizing up his 5-foot, 10-inch frame. "So, ah, looks like you might have played some football."

"Yes, sir. I played a little in high school, before Korea." Bill had been an all-city, third-team receiver and defensive back in high school.

"Good, I, ah, thought so. Well, good to have you on board," the president said, returning to his office.

Bill Simpson stood there in the West Wing foyer, mesmerized.

***

That night, Bill was resting in the small, furnished apartment the Secret Service used for men rotating from the field to DC. He called his wife, Anne, collect to tell her the news of the day. She was excited over his brief exchange with President Kennedy. Yet, he detected an undertone of frustration, perhaps because she could not be with him. She was a housewife, at home with a toddler with another due in five months, plenty of time for Bill to return from DC for the birth. Taking this assignment was important for his career, Bill knew, but he was leaving her at a bad time. Thankfully, her parents and his folks lived nearby.

Next, he called his parents. His mother answered and, after a few casual words, put his dad on the phone. Bill could not hide the excitement in his voice as he talked about his first two days. "And Dad, the president could not have been more gracious. When I told him I was from Detroit, he responded by mentioning the Motor City and the UAW. Then, I told him you worked in a Ford plant."

"That's great. Of course, I don't see how Jack Kennedy could have beat Nixon without Walter Reuther and the UAW behind him. But son, you should have said I'm an active UAW man."

"Yeah, I didn't think of that, but hopefully I can fix that with him down the road."

"And remember, Bill, we talked about keeping a journal. This will be historic stuff, something your grandkids will enjoy reading." Bill complied with his father's suggestion. It was a good one and something he worked on during major projects for the rest of his life.

***

On March 10, Bill was on Air Force One headed to Miami. President Kennedy was scheduled to speak at a fundraiser and then spend the rest of the weekend at his father's Palm Springs mansion. The fundraiser was a political event for one of the president's closest friends, Florida Senator George Smathers.

On the way, Jeff Peters told Bill that while every agent had to constantly focus on his job of protecting the president, there were times when it was worthwhile to listen with half an ear to some of Kennedy's comments. "Especially at the beginning of his speech," Jeff added, "because Kennedy is just so damned funny."

During the fundraising dinner, Bill was in the back of the packed hall, keeping an eye on people. He did, however, follow Peters's suggestion and listen a bit to the president, who started ribbing Smathers by saying he, Kennedy, always asked Smathers for his advice on political matters, especially in moments of personal conflict. The president continued:

"In 1952, when I was thinking about running for the US Senate, I went to Senator Smathers and said, 'George, what do you think?' He said, 'Don't do it. You can't win. Bad year.'" The crowd howled in laughter knowing Kennedy had beaten a strong incumbent senator.

Kennedy went on: "In 1956, ah, I was at the, ah, Democratic National Convention and didn't know if I'd run for vice president or not, so I said, 'George, what do you think? This is it—they need a young man.' George said run. So, I ran … and I lost." The crowd again roared with laughter.

"In 1960," Kennedy said, "I was wondering whether I ought to run in the West Virginia primary. 'Don't do it. That's a state you can't possibly carry.'" The crowd roared again knowing that Kennedy beat Hubert Humphrey in the crucial primary.

"And, actually, the only time I got nervous about the whole matter was in Los Angeles at the Democratic Convention, when George came up and said, 'I think it looks pretty good for you!'" People laughed to the point of tears.

From that point on, the president had the crowd eating out of his hand. After the event, they went to his father's estate. The detail worked out of a small, but functional shack, located in front of the mansion, for the rest of the weekend. By Sunday afternoon, Bill was back in Washington.

***

While in Palm Beach, Bill noticed the cliques on the president's Secret Service detail. The regulars did not let guys like Bill too close to the president, especially when they traveled outside Washington. It seemed most of the regular detail were southerners, all had military or police experience, and all were white men. One thing bothered Bill in particular: the men drank—and drank hard—when they were off duty.

Bill was no prude and certainly no angel, but the binge drinking disturbed him. The alcohol-soaked orgies often took place at the detail's house near the Palm Beach residence. At times, after a long day, when the president had a motorcade through a major city, the guys felt it was their right to relax. The only problem was that technically, the detail was always on duty when the president traveled. Bill never said anything. Occasionally, to be part of the team, Bill had a drink or two, but that was it. He never got tipsy and certainly not drunk as some of his colleagues did.

Some agents were bad drunks. They occasionally uttered racial slurs or made tacky comments about Mrs. Kennedy, as well as extremely negative comments about "Volunteer"—the detail's code name for Vice President Lyndon Johnson. There were, however, never any critical comments about the president—only smiles, winks, and knowing looks.

***

Because of his father's activities in the Michigan labor movement, Bill always kept an eye on battles between big labor and major companies. The United Auto Workers, the United Steel Workers, and the Teamsters unions were big players in the nation's economy. They had the power to shut down major employers and put millions of people out of work during a strike. Bill felt that labor unions generally handled their power responsibly. Since the Great Depression, union membership had risen dramatically, followed by better wages, health care, and pensions negotiated between unions and the companies they represented. When unions negotiated these benefits, the non-union and white-collar employees often received the same.

In late March, Bill read numerous stories in the papers that the United Steel Workers were in tough negotiations for a new contract with the top steel companies. The United States Steel Corp. was the biggest of the bunch—like General Motors in the auto industry. If steel prices dropped or rose, the entire country's economy could be affected. From time to time, he heard some of the administration staff discussing the contract talks. The gray-haired Labor Secretary, Arthur Goldberg, was personally keeping the president posted on the negotiations. The industry had signaled to Kennedy that, if it had to capitulate to high wage demands, it would have to pass the costs to consumers. This was the last thing Kennedy wanted. The year 1962 was a precarious time for the US economy, and Kennedy was concerned that any significant changes in steel employee wages could have a huge negative impact on the country's inflation rate. Kennedy put his administration and his personal prestige on the line to convince labor to seek modest gains in their negotiations. Labor unions were furious. As a result, Kennedy had several meetings on the subject and invited non-steel labor leaders to the White House to seek their counsel.

On one particular weeknight, such a meeting was scheduled. Bill was on the security desk and reviewed the list of invitees. Among the names was Walter Reuther, the UAW president, and the man to whom Bill's father had referred in their phone call a few weeks prior. When Reuther entered the secured area inside the West Wing, Bill asked a fellow agent to cover for him.

"Mr. Reuther, do you have a second?" he called out.

Reuther turned around with a startled expression. He was a handsome man, about five-eight with red hair, easily in his mid-fifties. He gave off an air of power and energy. Bill had heard him speak before while accompanying his father, but they had never met.

"What can I do for you?" Reuther replied.

"My name is Bill Simpson. I'm with the president's Secret Service detail. I wanted to introduce myself to you. You might know my father."

Reuther looked at him curiously. "Really?"

"Yes, Jim Simpson from Local 400."

"Jimmy Simpson!" Reuther said as a smile erupted on his face. "Of course I know Jimmy. He's a great union brother. How long have you been with the Secret Service and the president?"

Bill quickly explained his role in Detroit's Secret Service office and his newly assigned detail.

"My God, I should have been informed you were here. It's always good to know where our friends are," Reuther added, glancing at his wristwatch.

Bill put up his hand. "I know you have to go. I just wanted to introduce myself. When I was young, my dad took me to several meetings where I had a chance to hear you speak."

"I wish Jimmy had introduced us. Hopefully, we will get a chance to talk more in the future." With that, Reuther turned and headed to Kenny O'Donnell's office.

Two days later, Bill was stationed in the White House foyer, just inside the main entrance to the building. He had gotten word that "Lancer," the president's Secret Service code name, was going to be coming down from the second-floor residence and heading to a waiting car. About one-thirty, President Kennedy descended the stairs from the residence, followed by a White House usher and agent John Ford.

When he spied Bill at the desk, the president walked over to him. "Ah, Simpson, right?"

Bill, standing for the president, said, "Yes sir, Mr. President."

"Walter Reuther and I talked about you the other night. He said good things about you and your, ah, father."

Not knowing what to say, Bill uttered, "Thank you, sir."

"Yes," the president said. "I think we will be seeing more of you." He turned and walked out the door.

Bill looked over at Ford, who had overheard the exchange and now sported a dark frown.

***

As April commenced, the steel crisis was coming to a head. Just as Kennedy hoped, the steel unions agreed to modest increases, then, four days later, eleven of the twelve major steel companies decided to raise the cost of steel by three and a half percent. This was a huge, inflationary increase, and the decision made Kennedy look like a fool to organized labor. The president was furious.

One early morning, Bill was standing at his post outside Mrs. Lincoln's office, where the president and Kenny O'Donnell were talking. The president suddenly spoke in a loud voice, driving his index finger at O'Donnell: "You know, ah, my father always told me that all businessmen were sons of bitches, but I never believed him."

Bill suppressed a laugh. It was just what his father or Walter Reuther might have said.

As the days passed, Bill had a good idea what the Kennedy Administration was up to. He noticed Secretary of Defense Robert McNamara meeting with Kennedy, his staff, and Secretary Goldberg. Keeping his ear to the ground, Bill learned that McNamara was directed to review all steel contracts being handled by the Defense Department. McNamara was then to turn as much business as possible to smaller steel firms that had not raised their prices.

Bill noticed Bobby Kennedy attending more meetings about the steel crisis. Later, Bill heard the president say the Justice Department ought to investigate the potential of a monopoly by US Steel, which controlled nearly twenty percent of all steel produced in the United States. "Perhaps US Steel should be broken up," Kennedy suggested to his brother.

A day later, Bill overheard Bobby Kennedy say to Kenny O'Donnell, "Jesus Christ, Kenny! We're going for broke. I'm going to have the IRS investigate the head of every goddamned steel company! We'll see if their expense account deductions will hold up under scrutiny. When they travel, is it purely for business purposes or are they taking their secretaries with them for some fun? Then, the FBI is going to interview them. We're going to scare the living shit out of those bastards. We can't lose this."

On April 10, the president addressed the country in a televised speech. He talked about the excessive new costs that the Department of Defense faced if this increase went through. He then focused on the economy, fragile and just starting to move out of recession. He added that the country's economy could go under if such an increase continued. He essentially said that it was un-American for these eleven steel companies to increase costs first without seeking new ways to economize, just like the steel workers had done.

The next day, Kennedy held a press conference at the State Department auditorium, the only nearby room that could handle all the White House reporters and the heavy TV equipment. Bill was assigned to be part of the team to cover it. The president was still angry. While Bill was surveying the crowd, he heard the president say, "Some time ago, I asked every American to consider what they would do for his country. And I asked the steel companies the same thing. In the last twenty-four hours, we have their answer." He attacked each of the steel presidents for their selfishness.

A day later, the steel industry capitulated and rescinded the increases. The White House was jubilant.

That weekend, the president and his family went to Hyannis Port, Massachusetts, to celebrate, with Bill as part of the detail. Just after his election, President Kennedy had issued instructions to the Secret Service that, when they were in Hyannis Port, Palm Beach, or other "casual" locations, he wanted the detail members to dress casually, no suits. Bill packed just one suit along with a supply of casual wear.

The detail had a trailer that served as its headquarters. In addition, a modest cottage was secured for the agents spending the weekend. During the day, the president moved from the main house, his parents' place, to his home next door. President Kennedy tossed a football around with his brother, Ted. Both men had surprisingly good arms. Later, he watched as Ted boarded a sailboat. Minutes later, the boat disappeared over the deep, blue horizon. Though he never saw the boat return to shore, Bill noticed Ted and his wife heading to the main house for dinner.

The president lounged around, played with his kids, and took phone calls. Bill walked the grounds, his attention focused on the perimeter. Word spread fast when the president was visiting, and hundreds of sightseers drove slowly down the Hyannis Port Road to the Kennedy compound, hoping to get a look at the president and, perhaps more significantly, the first lady, Jacqueline. From time to time, Bill waved tourists along if he felt a car had stopped too long for a photo. Back in December 1960, when President-elect Kennedy was at the family's Palm Springs residence, an older man named Richard Pavlick had strapped dynamite to his body, with the intent of killing himself and Kennedy. Pavlick, ready to detonate the bomb, was walking up the driveway but held off exploding the bomb when he saw Jackie Kennedy and her children with JFK. Jackie and the kids were not part of his assassination plan, and he did not detonate the bomb. The hesitation allowed the Secret Service detail to quickly apprehend him.

On Saturday night, Bill's duty was over, along with several of the other guys. The main house had sent down some dinner. Most of the guys, including Bill, drank a beer or two. A few of the guys drank hard liquor, in some instances to excess. The room was a blue haze of cigarette smoke. Bill indulged in his favorite brand, Lucky Strike.

After dinner, the men relaxed around a coffee table in the small living room. John Ford, who had been drinking copious amounts of scotch, said in a slightly slurred voice, "So, Simpson, you and the president have become buddies, eh?" The three other men looked at Bill.

"I don't think so," Bill responded, surprised by Ford's tone.

Ford chuckled condescendingly. "Oh yeah, the president does not just go out of his way to greet a member of the detail. That's unheard of around here, isn't it guys?"

The other men nodded their heads. Bill realized Ford was referencing the moment in the White House foyer, when Kennedy stopped by Bill's station.

Not wanting to sound defensive, Bill said, "The president simply wanted to acknowledge the fact that Walter Reuther knows my dad, and he wanted me to know they had talked about it. No big deal."

"No big deal?" an agent named Watkins repeated. "It's always a big deal when a President singles out a member of the detail for personal reasons—very unprofessional."

Another agent muttered under his breath, "And a commie, too," referencing Reuther.

Bill didn't take the bait. He stood up, grabbed his freshly opened bottle of beer, and walked out of the room. He didn't want to be around people getting drunk on the job. In his mind, the president's detail had to always be prepared. Excessive drinking on the road was a disgrace.

***

Soon Bill found out that he was assigned to accompany the president to the biennial UAW convention in Atlantic City, New Jersey. Much to both Bill's pleasure and dismay, the president wanted him to serve as one of his body men, directly escorting him into the convention hall and onto the stage, where he would deliver his speech.

To Bill, the idea of being with the president at a UAW event, with his own father watching from the audience, was gratifying. Yet, he knew the detail would use it against him. It was receiving special treatment from the president for political reasons, something Bill didn't want to believe or even think about. Since the Hyannis Port confrontation, he was getting the cold shoulder from many of the veteran agents—not something he wanted to encourage.

Bill was with the president as they entered the huge Atlantic City convention hall on a cool day in early May. The advance team had worked with the UAW to provide a secure route when Kennedy entered the hall and headed to the podium. Per the president's request, Bill was with him as he worked the lines of enthusiastic UAW delegates—working people from throughout the United States and Canada.

These delegates represented more than one million people who worked in auto, aerospace, farm implement, and other industries. Walter Reuther and the UAW had been early supporters of Jack Kennedy, and the president wanted to show his appreciation. UAW members screamed their approval as Kennedy took his time working the crowd and greeting as many as possible. Bill's job was to move the president along toward the podium.

Once on the podium, the president relaxed, greeted Reuther, and took a seat. The crowd settled down, while Reuther provided an inspirational introduction, and then Kennedy faced a huge standing ovation from thousands of eager faces. Bill was stationed on the stage's right steps, surveying the crowd, both nearby and in the far corners of the hall. He spied his father, Jimmy, working his way through the throng. Jimmy grinned and waved, and Bill responded with a discreet wink and nod. He would call his father later that night.

President Kennedy began his remarks with references to the recent battle with the steel industry. Humor never far away from his key points, he began, "Last week, after speaking to the chamber of commerce and the American Medical Association, I began to wonder how I got elected. And…" He stopped for a long pause for emphasis and gazed over the room before finishing, "now I remember."

The crowd went nuts, eating up the president's comments like he was speaking to each of them personally.

"I said last week to the chamber that I thought I was their second choice for president by a majority of the chamber members—anyone else was a first choice."

The crowd loved it.

"Harry Truman once said there are fourteen or fifteen million Americans who have the resources to have representatives in Washington to protect their interests," Kennedy continued, "and for the interests of the great mass of other people, the hundred and fifty or sixty million, it is the responsibility of the president of the United States. And I propose to fulfill it."

After the speech, as the president's motorcade returned to the airport, Kennedy could not hide his pleasure. Bill sat in the shotgun seat of the Lincoln. The president seemed to enjoy speaking to working people—the same type of people he once represented in his Boston congressional district. He and Kenny O'Donnell were in the backseat, laughing and talking. It had been a good day.

"Kenny, it was so much, ah, fun coming here after the steel thing."

"Mr. President, they were eating out of your hand."

"Simpson, what did you think?"

Bill was not expecting such a direct question. He paused before replying, "Well, Mr. President, I couldn't focus too much on your speech, but I can tell you that was one very happy and excited crowd."

"Yes, sir!" O'Donnell added.

"Yep. Good job, Bill."

The president asked O'Donnell what was on the schedule for the rest of the day. After getting briefed, the president mumbled, "Christ, my back is killing me." Soon they were on the flight back to the White House.

***

Throughout his tour, Bill managed to get home once during a weekend in mid-May to see his wife and family. Anne was feeling the pregnancy, and Bill felt guiltier with each week he was away. He normally enjoyed being at their home on Detroit's east side, but he sensed Anne was upset with him the entire weekend. At one point, he said the assignment would be over soon.

Anne glared at him. "*Soon?* Jesus, Bill, it's six more goddamned weeks! You won't be home until almost the Fourth of July. You don't know how hard it is with Debbie and carrying around all this damned weight."

"Sweetheart, I'm doing what I can."

"No, you're doing what you want. You always have."

Rather than respond, Bill left the room, his daughter in his arms.

On Sunday night, Jimmy took Bill to the Detroit Metropolitan Airport in Jimmy's 1960 Ford Galaxie by way of the Ford Freeway. Jimmy reached over and pushed in the cigarette lighter. When it popped out a minute later, he lit a Camel.

Exhaling smoke from his nostrils, he said, "Bill, I have some good news. Our local vice president is moving to the UAW international staff. I'm being appointed to replace him."

"Dad, that's great! You'll have new responsibilities, and you'll be out of the plant."

"Yeah," his dad answered. "But more importantly, I can really help spread the need for unions and the UAW. Too many of the younger guys don't seem to care anymore. They think their benefits, good pay, and safety improvements are gifts from the company. They don't know how hard the UAW had to fight for those things."

Bill, following his father's lead, lit his own cigarette. "Dad, you're a great communicator and you'll be able to get through to these guys. I know you."

"Thanks, son. I hope so."

Later, as the Northwest Orient four-engine, propellered Electra rumbled down the runway, Bill thought about Anne. He probably should have refused the assignment. It would have cycled up again in a few years.

Immersed in the loud hum of engines and enjoying his second cigarette of the flight, Bill thought back to his early days. He had graduated from high school in 1949 and was headed to Army boot camp that September. His dad had told him not to worry about a summer job, that he should enjoy this time and have fun since it might be the last time in his life he'd have so few responsibilities. Bill had an entire summer to enjoy before he began his tour of duty.

He picked up a 1938 Dodge jalopy and paid for the gas by working part-time at a filling station. In July, he and a bunch of guys worked up baseball games at one of the Chandler Park ball fields. One Saturday, he noticed an extremely attractive girl in the bleachers watching the game. He did some checking and found out that her brother played ball on the opposing team and that they lived in the East English Village area, a higher-end neighborhood about a mile or so from his parents' house. Soon, he and Anne were dating and, by the time he entered boot camp, they were going steady.

***

By June, Bill felt he had finally developed a routine with the detail. His assignments were near the president, but not so close that they made verbal contact very often. His relationship with the detail members was still cool, but both he and the other agents seemed more relaxed and did their jobs. Bill kept to himself.

One Friday afternoon, the president went to the Congressional Golf Course for a round of golf with Navy undersecretary Red Fay, who had served in the Navy with Kennedy; Florida Senator George Smathers; and Peter Lawford, the Hollywood actor and the president's brother-in-law. Lawford, much to the dismay of club members, played barefoot.

Bill was part of the detail walking in advance of the group. He made sure that the group in front of the presidential foursome did not linger. He also served as a forecaddie. The president's group played slowly. Kennedy, despite the back pain that Bill observed just about every day, was the best golfer of the bunch and had a natural, athletic swing. After the group finished its round, the members moved to the clubhouse for cocktails. Bill was stationed at the front door, and other members of the detail were outside the small dining room that had been reserved for the special guests.

The president's group did not stay too long, which was not a surprise to Bill since Kennedy was not a drinker. JFK occasionally enjoyed a cocktail, but beyond that Bill did not see any abuse of alcohol. On his way out through the lobby, Kennedy saw Bill and waved him over to the presidential limousine.

"So, Simpson, did you, ah, enjoy your day?"

With a smile, Bill responded, "Well sir, it was fine, but you were the one playing. We were working."

"Ah, but not too hard," the president said with a grin.

"Very true, Mr. President."

"Bill, right?" the president asked. Bill nodded. "Listen, it might take a while, but I'm going to see if we can get you stationed permanently on the detail. We'll move your family here. Does that sound all right?"

Bill was dumbfounded. "Well, yes sir."

"Well, ah, don't say anything yet. We'll see if it can be worked out." The president turned and climbed into his Lincoln limousine. As Kennedy started to sit, Bill heard him groan, followed by an "ah" of relief once the president settled into the leather seat. Bill closed the limo door, moved quickly to his car, and the motorcade was on its way back to the White House.

About a week later, Bill was told to report to Jim Macalister's office. "Mac," as he was called, was a legend in intelligence lore. He had been part of the Office of Strategic Services during World War II. In 1944, Mac was caught on a mission inside Germany. Bill had no idea why he was not immediately executed. Some said he was being saved for potential prisoner swaps as the war ended. The Germans sent him to an old prison in Prussia, where the Nazis held special political prisoners. When the Allied troops entered the prison in 1945, the German guards had all deserted their posts, and all that remained were emaciated prisoners; Mac was one of them. Upon Mac's return to the United States, Gen. George Marshall wanted to help the sick and shaken soldier. In time, Mac recovered physically and was assigned to the Secret Service. There, he used his uncanny and creative mind to help track down counterfeiters and eventually served on the White House details for Presidents Truman and Eisenhower. Ike appointed him as the SS director in 1958.

Mac's office was in the Treasury Building. Bill arrived early for the eight-thirty meeting. He was not sure what the meeting was about, but thought it might have something to do with his tour coming to an end in a few weeks. He waited anxiously in the director's outer office for about twenty minutes before the secretary told him the director was ready.

Macalister looked up from his mahogany desk, stood and walked around to greet Bill with a quick and firm handshake. He was a surprisingly short and thin man about 5-foot-6 and could not have weighed more than 150 pounds. He had a receding hairline with bushy eyebrows. This, added to the way his face was lined with wrinkles, gave him a harsh and unpleasant look. Bill noted his physical stature did not meet Secret Service standards, so there had to have been some push from the top during the hiring process.

Bill saw three framed, black-and-white photos of Mac, one each with Presidents Truman, Eisenhower, and Kennedy. Each photo had a signed comment scrawled on it from the president. There were no personal effects on his desk. *This guy is no nonsense.*

"So, you're Bill Simpson," Mac said, motioning Bill to sit in a chair across from his desk. His voice was scratchy, like sandpaper. The smaller man returned to his chair and opened a file. "Has your White House tour been good for you?"

"Yes, sir," Bill responded. "I've learned a lot. It's a lot different being on the detail than working out of the Detroit office."

"I bet it is. Listen, I'm going to keep this brief."

Bill nodded, a bit surprised by the man's tone.

"Simpson, you would not have been selected for the White House detail unless we felt you are a very good agent and someone with great potential. So, you feel you've had a good experience. Well, perhaps you have, but that is not what your colleagues and superiors tell me."

Bill was stunned. He had never had a bad evaluation in his life, and if he had done something wrong, why hadn't anyone told him? "Sir, this is the first I've heard of any negative comments about my performance."

Mac looked him square in the eye, sizing him up, then he looked down at his file. "Well, let's see here. It says here you are aloof, not a team player, promoted socialist-leaning labor leaders and, most importantly, you have gone out of your way to develop a personal relationship with the president. What do you say about these statements?"

"Sir, let me try to explain. First, I never tried to develop a personal relationship with President Kennedy. When I was first assigned, I had duty in his office. The president came to me. He recognized I was new and seemed interested in getting to know me." Thinking rapidly, Bill added, "And, I should add that every interaction I've had with the president has been initiated by him, not me. Yes, I was accused by Agent Ford of trying to create a personal relationship, but it's just not true."

"What about Reuther? You sought him out. Right?"

"Well, there is truth in that. I did recognize him when he entered the building to meet with the president. He is someone who has had a long-standing relationship with my father, and I thought I'd introduce myself. We couldn't have spent more than two minutes talking."

"And now the president wants you to be a permanent member of the detail."

"Sir, I did not initiate that discussion. I was extremely surprised when President Kennedy made the suggestion."

"But you didn't reject the suggestion, did you?"

"No, sir. The first thing I was told when I started on the detail, by Agent Ford, was 'don't make waves' and just focus on protecting the president, which is what I've done. In addition, my wife is seven months pregnant and, believe me, I just want to get home."

"Okay, Simpson," Mac said, closing the folder on his desk. He met Bill's gaze. "I'm not surprised by any of this. The detail veterans feel like they are part of a special club. But what you have done, whether by plan or by accident, is unforgivable for a member of the Secret Service. You've become political. You have moved from an agent in the service to someone who now has the persona of a man with political contacts—not good. People will assume you are someone who can achieve his ends through political relationships. Considering your wife's situation, I'm ending your assignment here at the end of the week, a little early. Be back in Detroit by next Monday."

Bill was not sure if he should be relieved or not.

Mac continued, "Simpson, I'm not going to add anything to your personnel file on this matter. You will return to Detroit, and I will be watching your performance there. Regardless of what the president wants, you are not going to be a member of his detail."

"That's fine with me, sir," Bill said. He could tell by Mac's body language that the interview was over, so he got up from the chair. Before turning to the door, he said, "I appreciate the fact that you chose to listen to my side of the story." Mac nodded and Bill walked out of the room.

Walking back to the White House, Bill was in deep thought. *What the hell just happened?* Was he set up? Probably. Was it by Ford or the majority of the detail? He didn't know. One thing was clear: every move he made was being observed and recorded by someone.

He completed his White House assignment and was back in Detroit five days later.

Chapter Two
The Case

It was good to be back in Detroit. Bill had missed his day-to-day work assignments and going after bad guys. He wanted to get the bad taste of the Macalister meeting and the petty detail agents out of his mind. He looked forward to being out in the field and developing his work routines again.

Working out of the Secret Service office in the downtown federal building, Bill felt at home again. He had not been the only agent in the Detroit office to serve on the president's detail. Three of the eighteen-person office had been part of that rotation in previous years. While people were happy for Bill's assignment, the office staff saw it as a routine step for an up-and-coming agent. Almost all the agents and secretaries greeted his return with a lot of ribbing over hanging out with JFK and, most importantly, the president's glamorous wife, Jackie. One agent got a bunch of laughs when he quipped that Bill had probably spent his three months permanently assigned to watch the president's children, Caroline and John-John.

Protecting the president, the first lady, and the vice president was the Secret Service's best-known responsibility. Congress had, by 1948, reauthorized the Secret Service Act, reaffirming these duties, along with the continued counterfeit violation investigations. The legislation also added the investigation of crimes against the Federal Deposit Insurance Corp., federal land banks, joint-stock land banks, and national farm loan associations. As a field agent, Bill primarily covered counterfeiting. Occasionally, he assisted agents investigating some of the other responsibilities. Upon his return, he met with the office director, Reed Clark, a competent and easy-going man in his mid-forties. After some brief updates, Clark assigned him new files. Bill was back to work and relieved to be away from the president's detail and all the politics.

On the home front, things were still rocky with Anne. Her due date was mid-August, and this pregnancy had been more difficult than the first. Bill tried to be as supportive as he could. On weekends, he worked on several deferred maintenance issues at their house. He enjoyed spending time with Debbie. He was amazed at how much the little girl had grown and learned during his months away. Even with the difficulties with Anne, being home was relaxing, and he felt like life was getting back to normal.

They saw family and, when Anne felt up to it, took in a movie, a drive to Belle Isle, or a full day's outing to Metropolitan Beach on Lake St. Clair. About every other weekend, Bill and his father joined some of Jimmy's friends for a round of golf at either the nearby Chandler Park Golf Course or the gem of public golf courses on the east side, Maple Lane Golf Course in Macomb County. Ever the natural athlete, with some practice, Bill's golf game dramatically improved, and he was shooting in the low eighties for eighteen holes—far better than Jimmy or his friends.

Even if Bill was just hanging out around the house, there was nothing like watching a Tigers baseball game on TV after cutting the grass on a Saturday afternoon. Listening to George Kell and Ernie Harwell calling the games was a pleasant reminder of being home. Lying on the couch, sipping a Stroh's beer, and maybe catnapping a bit, was a great way to spend a lazy Saturday afternoon. Sometimes, Debbie took her afternoon nap and they both stretched out on the couch or on the carpeted floor.

On Monday mornings, Bill typically jumped into his green, 1959 Ford Galaxie four-door and headed downtown on Gratiot Avenue, which was less congested than the Edsel Ford Expressway, and took the same amount of time during rush hour. As he headed into the city, he passed several neighborhood shopping areas, noticed airplane activity at Detroit's City Airport, and then cut through the traditional Black Bottom/Paradise Valley neighborhoods. Soon after that, he drove into the parking structure adjacent the Federal Building on Lafayette Street.

By late July, Bill was deeply involved in a counterfeiting investigation regarding what he believed was a small-time mobster bringing in fake money from Windsor. The counterfeiters seemed to use the Hazel Park raceway as one location of distributing the bad bills. There were other distribution locations, too, but the thoroughbred track had long had links to the underworld, so this seemed like the best place to start his investigation.

Bill and his new, twenty-six-year-old partner, Joe Kowalski, drove out to the raceway in the agency's pool car, a stripped-down black 1961 Plymouth Fury. A first-generation immigrant, Kowalski was from the deeply Polish community of Hamtramck. Much like Bill's, Kowalski's father had worked in factories around Detroit's industrial center, and Joe was able to go to college at night while working his way through school at the nearby Dodge Main Plant. Joe wanted to become a lawyer, but saw an advertisement for the Secret Service at Wayne State University's law school administration office. He still planned to go to law school, but that had been deferred as he focused on his early career in the agency. He was single, but engaged to be married soon, and Bill wondered if Joe's dream of becoming an attorney would become a reality.

They walked through the Hazel Park Raceway's innards to the facility's administrative offices. They entered the spartan office and walked up to a counter that separated the public from the office staff. Bill flashed his Secret Service credentials and told the clerk he was looking for the head of the track.

"You want to talk to Mr. Harmon. Hold on." The woman disappeared down a corridor. A few minutes later, she returned and said, "Boys, just go down the hall. You want the last office on the right."

A short, stocky man in shirtsleeves and suspenders greeted them at the door, introducing himself as Charlie Harmon. He motioned the men to two hard metal chairs, then sat behind his desk. "Okay, so how can I help you boys?"

Bill removed a three-by-five pocket notebook from inside his coat. "Well, Mr. Harmon—"

"Ah, call me Charlie. Everyone does." Harmon pulled out a cigar and offered stogies to the agents. They shook their heads no, but Bill pulled out his pack of Lucky Strikes and offered one to Joe, and they lit up. Harmon repeated, "Now, what can I do for you boys?"

"Okay, Charlie, it's pretty simple. We've received reports of counterfeit money in five-, ten-, twenty-, and fifty-dollar denominations entering circulation here. This money is probably coming through your betting windows, and we are going to need to interview you and your betting window employees and any other men who handle money. Is this a problem?"

"Well, ah, I don't think so," Harmon responded, not sure how to answer the question. "Can you give me some more details of what you want to do … and will it affect our business?"

"We have no plans to stymie your business at this point," Bill said. "We're hoping for your full cooperation. We'd like to begin interviews as soon as possible, like, tomorrow."

"Can we work around our racing schedule?"

"Sure." Bill looked at Kowalski. "Joe, we can be here before or after the races, right?"

"No problem," Joe said.

"Alright. Charlie, what time can we come tomorrow? Is eight-thirty okay?"

"Well, I need to talk to my boss and our lawyer, but I don't think it will be a problem. Give me your phone number, and I'll call you before five this afternoon."

Bill gave the man his business card, and the two agents left the building. Around five-thirty that afternoon, Bill heard the switchboard office phone ringing. It was Harmon.

"We are set to go," he said. "Sorry for the delay. About eight-thirty?"

"We'll be there," Bill answered. He hung up and looked at Joe. "It looks like we gave Harmon's bosses something to think about," Bill said with a grin.

***

That was the beginning of some grinding weeks. The agents interviewed all the appropriate people at the track. No leads developed. The guys at the betting windows and those behind the scenes, the ones who counted and recounted money, didn't have much to offer. Rarely did they see any bills that were fresh, either from a bank or some other source. They counted the money at the window and again later in the back offices. The money was transferred to armored cars and taken to a local bank.

Some of the track employees' responses did not ring completely true with Bill and Joe. They knew they were dealing with pros, people who had handled currency on an everyday basis for years, if not decades. They should have detected any irregularities in the currency, but hadn't. Was it because there was something crooked going on or perhaps they did not want to get involved? Both were violations of the law, but with different consequences.

At the same time, more tips began trickling in regarding counterfeit currency being circulated. Fake currency was showing up in several unsavory areas involving some of the city's most unpleasant characters. Bill and Joe had their hands full. The agents contacted Detroit and suburban police departments, local banks, savings and loans, and credit unions. The guys reached out to major retailers. They also provided mimeographed copies of material that gave instructions to front-line employees who handled cash on what to look for and what to do if they suspected something.

After about ten days, their outreach proved fruitful, and some useful tips came in. Bill and Joe checked them out. Their plan was to find someone spreading bad money and see if they could trace it back to the counterfeiters. As with all investigations, most of these tips were not worth the paper they were written on and, after a quick call or interview, were disregarded. Some, however, deserved serious examination.

The Detroit police informed the agency's investigators, which had increased from two agents to four, that counterfeit currency was found at the Gotham Hotel in Paradise Valley. The Gotham was the best hotel in the black section of the city. Detroit, like many northern cities, practiced a form of Jim Crow segregation, and the need for quality hotels for African Americans was great during the 1920s through the 1950s. Segregation generally forced top black entertainers like Duke Ellington, Louis Armstrong, Ella Fitzgerald, Billie Holiday, and Sammy Davis Jr. to perform in "colored" clubs, mostly in Paradise Valley. The hotel of choice for these black superstars was the Gotham.

As the sixties dawned, things began to change in this black community. Integration slowly increased at most white-only downtown hotels and clubs, so that big-time black entertainers could perform and stay at all locations throughout Detroit. Additionally, with the growth of television, some people stopped going out to nightclubs for entertainment. They watched top-notch performances from their living rooms, eating their dinner in front of the TV set. This meant that once fine establishments like the Gotham had seen their best days. To add insult to injury, the state was planning to build an expressway through Paradise Valley, and the hotel lay directly in its path. This all meant that the once great Gotham Hotel was struggling to make ends meet, and seedier elements had expanded their presence at the hotel. It was no great surprise to Bill that counterfeit currency might be spreading around the Gotham, but how?

Bill and Joe climbed in a pool car and headed toward Paradise Valley. Once on Woodward Avenue, Bill said to Joe, "You know, we would be a hell of a lot more efficient in these cases if we had a black agent."

"A colored agent?" Joe replied with a note of skepticism.

"Yeah. We need to better communicate with these people, people who live with crime and violence more than we ever see. These folks just want a safe neighborhood, good schools, and a decent place to live, just like us."

"I don't know, Bill. I don't know that a Negro agent would be accepted in the service."

"Well, my friend, it's coming. I know that President Kennedy specifically told the Chicago office to integrate and apparently recruited a very good agent. We will be integrated soon. Who knows? We might even have women agents someday."

"Bullshit," Joe said as Bill parked the car.

Bill went to the front desk inside the Gotham's tired lobby and asked for the owner, John White. After a few minutes, an older black gentleman wearing a suit emerged from the offices in the back. He motioned Bill and Joe to come to the lounge, where they could have coffee. The Secret Service agents followed him into a walnut-paneled, well-appointed bar. Photos of top black entertainers and sports figures across the years lined the walls.

"We don't see Secret Service agents around our establishment—what on earth could we have done?" White asked.

Bill looked White square in the eyes. "We are not sure you've done anything. We're just following up on some leads regarding a case we've developed. Part of our responsibility is detecting counterfeit currency, and we've identified a ring we think is bringing counterfeit money into Detroit from Canada. Some of these bills have been tracked to the Gotham."

White raised his hands. "We don't have nothin' to do with that kind of stuff."

"Hold on, let me finish," Bill said. "What we'd like to do is sample some of the cash that comes in and out of the hotel. We have some staff that can come in. Our assumption is that the bills are being passed through the hotel, but we need to know from where."

"And, if I don't agree, sir?"

"Look, if you guys are innocent, which I assume you are, our guys are not looking for anything except bad bills. We're asking for your cooperation. If you don't provide it, there are other, more painful ways we can get it. I can always get a court order, so how about it?"

White frowned. "You're going to bring some white men in here to go through our safe and cash registers?"

"Yep. We can come in randomly or focus on the mornings if that's easier for you."

"That would help. Look, I try to run a clean hotel here. I suspect I have guests that are not the most reputable of people, but they pay their bills."

Bill waved him off. "We are not looking for other problems. Now, if someone commits an infraction in front of us, we will report it to the proper authorities. We're not going to go anywhere in your hotel except where money is handled. Is that alright?"

The older man sighed in resignation. "Listen, having a bunch of white cops coming through our doors could really screw our business. Could we meet them at our back door and escort them to the appropriate office, so they are less likely to be detected?"

Bill smiled at the irony. "You don't want white guys coming through your front door? I get that, and I'm sure we can work something out. Joe, you will work these details out, right?"

"No problem," Joe responded.

As White studied him closely, Bill considered that the man typically expected threats from white law enforcement officers. Still, White didn't seem threatened, and that was what Bill wanted.

"Okay, man. Come any time you'd like. We'll be here."

"Thanks. This helps a lot. Joe will call you before he heads out here," Bill said as they stood up. The three men walked through the bar to the lobby.

Bill paused near the exit. "I understand they're going to put an expressway through here?"

A pained expression appeared on White's face. "Yeah, in a few years the government's taking almost all of Paradise Valley and Black Bottom for a damned highway. They're going to ruin us. I just don't know what people around here are going to do. Hell, we're all going to go out of business. The state ain't going to give me enough cash for this old place, so I'm screwed. Same with most others. Man, it's bad for the city."

"Yeah, progress is a bitch," Bill replied as he headed out the door.

He wondered for a moment on his way to the car what the future held for area business owners and professionals once the expressway went through. Still, the people from the suburbs will have an easier time getting to the city. Then Bill thought about the Gotham and smiled to himself. There had to be more vice and other crap going on in there than he could imagine. If his guys looked, he knew they would find something.

As they made a left onto Woodward Avenue, Joe said, "Jesus, Bill. Why were you so nice to that guy? You know that place is full of all kinds of shit."

"Look," Bill said. "These guys have been on the bottom of the totem pole forever. They aren't doing the counterfeiting. Almost everyone we are talking to is cooperating. I can't assume these guys won't either. He hardly blinked when we asked to audit his cash. It's okay to treat people with dignity, Joe."

Joe huffed to himself and said nothing more.

Bill began thinking how glad he was to have more staff on the job, people who could spend time identifying bad bills and helping with leads. As he headed down Woodward, red lights flashed in the rearview mirror. An unmarked Ford sedan with a portable flasher attached to the roof was closing in on him. Bill pulled over.

He glanced over at his partner. "Joe, don't say a word. I'll handle this."

A plain clothes officer got out of the vehicle and walked briskly toward his car. Another man walked toward the passenger side. Bill already had his window down by the time the officer got to the window. "Who the hell are you, bub?" he barked. "Let's see some ID."

Bill said, "I know who I am, but who the hell are you? Are you a cop?"

"Yeah, I'm Detroit undercover and I need some ID, fast."

Bill figured he was the real deal and pulled out his wallet. Joe did the same.

The officer's eyes grew wide. "Secret Service. Jesus H. Christ. Okay, I'm Officer Connor, we've been talking to headquarters. We knew by your license plate you were the feds but didn't know who. They want you to come down to headquarters. Eddie here will go with you, and I'll take your partner downtown. You," he said to Joe, "come with me. Oh, man," the officer added, "this is one big fuck-up."

Bill asked if he could contact his office, since the Secret Service cars in Detroit did not have radios. "Wait until we get downtown," Connor replied calmly.

A few minutes later, they were at the police headquarters near Greektown. Much to Bill's surprise, they were taken to the police commissioner's conference room. *This must be a big deal.*

After about ten minutes, a group of men, some in uniform and some not, came into the room. An older man with wavy, salt-and-pepper hair and horn-rimmed glasses stepped forward. Bill recognized him immediately.

"Hi, I'm George Edwards. What the hell is going on here? Why are you trying to screw up our stakeout?"

Edwards, the Detroit Police Commissioner, was Harvard educated, a lawyer, judge, city councilman, and former union organizer. He had helped organize the UAW in the thirties with Walter Reuther and others.

Bill introduced himself and Joe, then explained the case they were working on. "We don't know anything about a city investigation at the Gotham," he said. "In fact, we were tipped off by the Detroit police that counterfeit money was floating through there."

Edwards looked at an officer sitting across the table from him. "Clancy, I thought we cleared all of our actions on the Gotham and the other mob operations with the feds, state, and other jurisdictions."

Clancy, a square-jawed man who looked to be in his early forties, replied, "Yes, sir. We have. We've been working with the FBI, Customs, Immigration, the State Police, and the County Sheriff's Office—"

"You didn't say Secret Service!" Edwards barked. "Did you contact them?"

"Well, sir," a flushed Clancy stammered, "I don't believe I did. I must have missed those guys."

"Must have missed those guys!?" Edwards exploded. "Christ!" Turning to Bill, "Simpson, I guess I owe you guys an apology."

Bill, feeling a bit more relaxed, said, "Well, Mr. Commissioner, having just spent about a half an hour in the Gotham, it's pretty clear it's a property that's passed its prime and now, God knows what's going on there."

"Well," Edwards replied, "We know there's a significant numbers operation going on and sometime later this year, we are going to bust it wide open."

"Sir, I think I actually got the owner to cooperate with our investigation," Bill said. "I told him our job was to look for counterfeit bills, which I don't think the hotel knows are being distributed. If there's a numbers operation going on, that might explain why bad money is flowing through there. It seems to me that if we simply stop the investigation, it might raise all kinds of red flags to White and the racketeers. What if we played dumb and continued our investigation? That might actually deflect any focus on your activities."

Edwards thought for a moment. "That might work." He looked around the room and asked his men what they thought. There were murmurs of approval and a few other comments. "Okay, Simpson. We'll consider your plan, but just stay on the ground floor. I don't want you going upstairs and messing around with our work. Agreed?"

Bill nodded. "Our plan is to just do our job in their back offices during morning hours. They know we are going to check for bills randomly, but we will check with you before we go in. Just let us know whom to work with. Joe here will be a contact with the department. Also sir, when you do bust the numbers guys, could you keep track for any counterfeit money? If they are pushing that stuff, you could add a federal charge to their illegal activities, too."

"Yep, we can do that."

"Great," Bill replied. "Finally, could you call my boss and let him know why were detained and how we resolved things?"

Edwards smiled. "Of course. Give all the information to Clancy here. He will be your contact, and he will make sure we are coordinating with the Secret Service." The commissioner left the meeting, and soon Bill and Joe were on their way back to the office.

***

On August 16, Anne gave birth to a healthy son. They named him John James Simpson. The boy had the names of both Anne's and Bill's fathers.

In mid-September, Bill took the family on a much-needed vacation out west. With the summer tourist season over, they had a great time. They drove through Rocky Mountain National Park, then to Yellowstone National Park, stopping at Mount Rushmore on their way home.

Traveling with kids was tough, but most hotels had porches or balconies with their rooms, allowing Bill and Anne time to enjoy a quiet relaxing evening after the kids were put down.

Overlooking the Rockies one evening, Anne said, "Bill, I'm glad we made this trip. I know the kids are way too young to ever remember this, but I will."

"Me too," Bill said.

"It's been good for us, hasn't it?"

"Absolutely," Bill said as he leaned over and kissed his wife.

It was a hectic ten days, but good to be spending time with Anne and the family. It was also tough on the pocketbook, with hotels, restaurants, and other travel expenses. But seeing so much of America was breathtaking. To save money, they had borrowed a propane cooking stove and made lunches at roadside parks along the way, which was fun for all. Bill hoped there were many more road trips as the kids grew older. He and Anne returned to Detroit feeling refreshed. The trip had been great for their marriage, and they seemed to know each other again.

The return to work was not what Bill expected.

Chapter Three
JFK in Detroit

As soon as Bill returned to work, everything in the office was turned upside down. Word came that, on October 5, President Kennedy was coming to Detroit and Flint for a campaign swing to stump for the incumbent Governor John Swainson and the rest of the Democratic Party ticket. The Detroit office did much of the advance work for the president's detail, including scouting all the locations on the president's schedule. It also coordinated activities with the Detroit and Flint police departments and the Michigan State Police.

Bill was assigned to check out the Book Cadillac Hotel, where Kennedy was booked in the presidential suite. There was also to be a rally on the street adjacent to the hotel followed by a meet-and-greet session with VIPs from Michigan's Democratic Party. Bill and the other local agents spent hours preparing for the daylong event.

The day before the event, Bill was out of the office most of the day. Upon his return, Jeff Peters, his fellow agent from his DC assignment, had left a phone message. Bill dialed the White House number and asked the receptionist if Peters was available. After a moment, the line clicked, and Bill heard the familiar southern accent: "Bill, is that you? How are you doing, boy?"

"I'm great. How about you? Am I going to see you tomorrow?"

"Absolutely. In fact, I know I'm going around protocol, but since we're buddies, I thought I'd check in and find out what's going on."

"Well, outside of being overworked and all of our case work being put on hold for the president's day in Michigan, everything is normal."

Peters laughed at the sarcasm.

"I'm assigned to the Book Cadillac," Bill went on, "and will be overseeing the rally on Washington Boulevard, the reception in the hotel, and available for the president's downtime before they head to Flint."

"You're not going to be at the airport?"

"No. Reed Clark is. Do you know Reed?" Peters asked.

"We've met once or twice, but I don't know him."

"Reed thought it best if I were nearby while the president was relaxing at the hotel and meeting some of the local politicians, since I have a sense of who they are. After the morning rally, I can make sure the president is in the hotel and ready for his reception."

"Okay, that makes sense. You know," Peters said, his tone suddenly changing, "I'm not quite sure what happened, but I know there were some uncomfortable bumps in the road while you were assigned to the detail. Don't let it get you down. I know the president thinks highly of you, so I'm sure he will be glad that you are nearby."

"Thanks, Jeff. That means a lot."

Bill didn't have time to think about why his fellow agent had raised the awkward subject of his time at the White House—he had to get back to work.

***

When October 5 arrived, word came that President Kennedy had arrived, and his motorcade was working its way downtown. Bill stationed himself outside the hotel, standing with the event coordinator, a staffer for the local AFL-CIO. They stood by a crude but sturdy platform built for Kennedy's speech and about twenty dignitaries. The Detroit labor movement had turned out a good crowd. On top of that, the president was popular in Michigan, and men and women of all ethnicities and colors were in attendance.

When the motorcade pulled up to the designated parking area, the president stepped out of his limousine with Governor Swainson and Detroit Mayor Jerome Cavanagh. Other dignitaries were exiting cars, including Michigan's relatively new Attorney General Frank Kelley, the UAW's Walter Reuther, the leader of the state AFL-CIO Gus Scholle, and others.

Swainson introduced a few speakers, including Reuther. After about twenty minutes of firing up the crowd, the governor introduced the president. Kennedy spoke for thirty minutes to an exuberant crowd that cheered their president. After the speech, Bill escorted the president to the reception room in the Book Cadillac.

The reception was orderly, with a lot of politicians talking excitedly about local elections. A line formed, and the president greeted each person, with photos taken to remember the occasion.

Near the end, Bill saw the president looking around for someone. When Kennedy's eyes locked with his, the president waved him over. "Ah, Simpson, good to see you."

"Yes sir, Mr. President."

"Listen, as this is winding down, ah, get me to my suite. Also, where the hell is my staff? I want them to invite the governor and attorney general to join me for lunch. If you don't see them, do you mind doing it for me?"

John Ford, Jim Carr, and Jeff Peters led the president to his suite on the hotel's top floor. Bill found Swainson and Kelley and escorted them to the suite. Upon entering the hotel room, Kennedy pulled in his guests, and much to his surprise, invited Bill into the room. Bill glanced over at John Ford, who was scowling.

The president addressed the agents: "Boys, I ah, need Simpson here for a few minutes." And added, "This is, after all, his ah town." Soon, the door was closed, and Bill was in the room with the president, the governor, and the attorney general.

Swainson and Kelley were watching Kennedy's every move. Kennedy addressed the attorney general. "Well, it's great to see an Irishman as the state's top attorney, eh, Governor?"

Swainson smiled appreciatively as Kelley beamed. "It was my honor to make the appointment, Mr. President."

"Good move, Governor," the president said.

Kennedy then told the two men that he needed to talk to his agent for a few minutes and make a few calls from his bedroom. A minute later, Bill was alone with the president in the bedroom.

"Simpson," Kennedy began. "I just wanted to take a moment to apologize to you. I've learned that I may have created a ... shall we say diplomatic problem with the agency's hierarchy when you were with us this spring. I'm sorry for my fuck-up."

"Don't worry about it, Mr. President." Bill felt like he was having an out-of-body experience. He could not believe the president was apologizing to him!

"Well, I feel bad about it, but I do want you back on the detail. It may have to be after the '64 election, but I'm going to get it done," the president said as he slipped off his jacket.

"Sir, as much as I want to serve you, you don't have to go out of your way for me. Frankly, it's a bit embarrassing."

"Well, it's not a problem for me," he said. Changing the subject, "You know, a lot of people didn't think I should make this trip. They said Swainson can't beat George Romney. Well, I told them 'Bullshit.' This is a man who fought in the war and lost both of his legs. I'll be goddamned if I won't help a veteran like that. Do you think he has a chance?"

"Well, sir, I've not been following the election too closely—I've been busy with some other cases. But I think he has a chance. Romney will be tough, and Swainson is not as popular as he could be due to his support of a local city income tax bill. Your trip might make the difference."

"Ah, yes, so I've heard," the president said as he picked up his phone and began dialing. Bill realized he was dismissed and quietly left the room.

He was soon in the hall with Peters, Ford, and Carr.

"Well, well, well," Ford said with a smirk. "Look who is having private meetings with the president."

"Cut it out, John," Peters said. "You saw what happened. Bill did nothing to promote himself. I think you are just jealous."

"Jeff," Bill said, "leave it alone. It's not worth getting into. I'm going to check out the lobby." Bill went to the front door to make sure the president's Lincoln Continental was ready for the trip back to the airport. An hour later, Kennedy was on to Flint, where another group of agents were eagerly waiting to handle the details in that blue-collar city. Everyone in the Detroit office breathed a sigh of relief.

Chapter 4
The Hooker

As the weeks went by, the counterfeit investigation dragged on. Bill and Joe continued to follow leads. The process was slow and became routine. In mid-October, Bill got a lead from the Detroit Bank and Trust branch on Jefferson Avenue, on the city's east side. The bank indicated that a woman, a Rita Gray, had passed counterfeit money while making deposits. Bill checked her out with the Detroit police. He was transferred to the vice squad and spoke to an officer who informed him that, while never having been arrested, her name had come up on lists of several high-class hookers in the city.

The weekend before, Joe Kowalski was married. It was a fine, Polish wedding and a great Hamtramck reception. Bill and Anne had fun. They left the kids with Bill's parents, so they drank and danced until the band's last number.

With Joe on his honeymoon and other agents busy on the case, Bill drove by himself to investigate the Gray lead. It was unusual to interview potential suspects without a partner, but he felt he could handle this meeting on his own. He double-checked with Reed Clark, who approved his action.

She lived in Alden Park Apartments, among the more stylish apartments in Detroit, with great views of the Detroit River. Bill had never been there and was looking forward to seeing the inside of one of the apartments.

He entered the building through a sizable lobby. There was a modest security setup, and Bill flashed his ID. The man waved him toward the elevator to the "A" building. He made his way to apartment 720 and knocked.

A moment later the door opened a crack, the chain lock still engaged. A woman's voice said, "Who are you? I'm not expecting anybody."

Bill said, "Miss Gray? My name is William Simpson. I'm with the United States Secret Service and I need to talk to you."

"The Secret Service?" Her laugh was low and husky. "You must be kidding me."

"No ma'am," he said, showing her his identification. "I have a case that, frankly, I don't think has anything to do with you, but you might be able to provide me with some information."

The door closed, the chain loosened. A second later, a well-dressed woman in her early thirties was standing in front of him. "Well, come in," she said, stepping aside. "I have some coffee brewing. Would you like a cup?"

"Yes, ma'am. That would be nice."

"Good. Follow me. And you can cut the 'ma'am' stuff. It makes me feel old. My name is Rita."

Rita was not the stereotypical hooker. Pretty, seemingly intelligent, well-dressed, with a nice figure, her auburn hair was curled up at her shoulders. There were books lining bookshelves around a stylish living room. The apartment was clean and comfortable. In the corner was a fifteen-inch portable TV with the rabbit ears out. Bill suddenly imagined this was a woman Frank Sinatra might sing about, certainly the type of woman who might appear on his album covers.

Sitting down at a small, two-person table in the kitchen, Bill watched Rita pull out a couple of cups and saucers and pour coffee from a percolator on the counter. The table was situated in a little nook with windows that provided a great view of the Detroit River, Belle Isle, and Canada. "Do you take cream or sugar?" she asked over her shoulder.

"Just black."

A moment later, she sat down and looked directly into his eyes. "What's all the mystery about, Mr. Simpson?"

Bill was just a bit disarmed by Rita's confident demeanor. She was not afraid of a cop from the Secret Service, that much was clear.

"Well, Miss Gray, you may or may not know, but one of the crimes that comes under the jurisdiction of the Secret Service is counterfeiting. Your local bank informed us that you have occasionally deposited some counterfeit bills into your account."

Rita started to protest, and Bill put up his hand.

"I'll be through in a minute. We do not suspect you as a perpetrator. You were probably an innocent victim who received some bad money and simply passed it on. Now, while you have a clean record, the Detroit police know that you have modeled, done some work at the auto show and other types of events. Their records indicate that you like being a party girl and might be making a living at it ..."

Again, Rita started to speak, her eyes wide open, and Bill waved her off.

"Now, what you do inside a local jurisdiction is of no interest to us. You've never been charged, your clients are relatively high-class johns, and you have not caused any disturbances in your building. So, I want to confidentially talk to you about any possible clients who may have passed some bad money your way. Our discussion will be confidential, and we have no intention of making any of the information you provide us public."

Bill stopped and took a sip of his coffee. He pulled out his pack of Lucky Strikes, tapped out a cigarette, and started to light it.

Rita seemed nonplussed and even half smiled. "Well, Mr. Simpson, first, what I do in my house is none of your business, but when I'm on my time, I ask you not to smoke. I'm not denying what I do for a living. I live a high life and I do party a lot," she said, sticking with his alternative way to describe her life of prostitution. Meanwhile, Bill returned the pack of cigarettes to his shirt pocket. "If I help you, I need to know that I'm not going to be dragged into any court case, forced to testify, or have my name or photo in the paper. I don't want to look like some cheap hooker."

"You know," he said, "I can't guarantee anything, but if you cooperate, I'll do whatever I can to keep your name out of the case. We don't want to embarrass you with your friends, family, or neighbors. We are just looking for tips that can lead to the arrests of some pretty bad characters."

It was her turn to smile. "So, you don't consider me to be a bad character?"

"No, ma'am."

She let out a belly laugh, "There you go again. It's been a long time since someone called me 'ma'am.' If ever. You make me feel like my mother."

"Well, I don't know your mother ... or your grandmother, but my comment was not intended to denigrate your looks in any way. Now, can we get down to some work?"

"No, not yet. I don't know exactly what you are looking for. What information do you want? I don't want my name to be linked with criminals, and I don't want criminals to know that we are talking."

"Good points. I should have made myself clear. As I said before, we simply want to go over the dates when you passed the bad bills. We hope we can match up the dates with one of your, uh, clients. These might lead to where the bad bills came from. We will confidentially talk to any potential suspects. They will have no idea from whom we received their names. If we get a hit on one of the customers, I mean, clients, we will question them in detail and hope we might be able to find out who is producing the counterfeit bills. So, there is no reason for your name to come out during the investigation. Does this put you more at ease?"

Rita enjoyed making Bill uncomfortable while he tried dancing around her profession. "Okay, I'll give you a chance," she said. "Let's get started."

Bill gave her the dates of when the local bank received deposits of bad bills. Rita began thinking about whom she might have seen during that time. After a few minutes, she said, "You know, I should get my calendar." She got up from the table and went to her bedroom.

She returned with a professional date book.

Rita knew few details about her clients. Some were from the auto industry, some worked for small companies as accountants or lawyers, but many simply lied to her regarding their personal lives. Bill asked her details about each man who had visited her during a span of two or three days prior to a bank visit. Bill also wanted to know if any of the clients had an interest in horse racing or gambling. After three cups of coffee, they began to make a breakthrough, focusing on four men. Bill felt this was enough work for his team for the next phase of the investigation.

He grabbed his coat, and she walked him to the door.

"Well, Mr. Simpson, this has been an interesting day, definitely out of the ordinary."

"I feel the same way," Bill said, his hand on the doorknob. "You've been of great help and, believe me, I'll do everything possible to give you deep cover on this material."

Rita gazed at him, her green eyes emitting a mischievous sparkle. "So, is this the last time I'm going to see you?"

Bill flashed a perfunctory smile. "Probably. Trust me, Miss Gray, the less you see of me, the better."

She looked down at his left hand. "I know you are, no doubt, a happily married man. But if you ever want someone to talk to, don't hesitate to give me a call."

Bill mumbled a goodbye and headed for the elevators.

On the way back to the office, Bill pondered the leads he had gotten from Rita. The names could be the first big break in the case, and she had phone numbers for each man. Then, a pair of green eyes flashed in his mind: Rita was nice, *really* nice. Yes, they had clicked. He thought about her last comments. Were they just a come-on, or an invitation for him to become a client? Probably the latter. He had no desire to cheat on Anne. Still, he whistled a tune under his breath until he got back to the office.

PART II ~ 1963-64
Chapter Five
The Hooker Revisited

On Tuesday morning in late October 1963, Bill drove to Rita Gray's apartment. It had been over a year since their first meeting, and he caught himself pressing the accelerator with a strange eagerness. He realized he was looking forward to once again seeing this captivating woman.

The leads Rita had provided had proved more than useful. One of her regular customers was Sammy "Deadeye" Licavoli, a Windsor resident, with deep connections to the Detroit underworld. Deadeye was an enforcer for an independent thug named Santo "Sam" Perrone, whose territory generally covered Detroit's east side. Perrone was a notorious criminal whose expertise was extortion through intimidation. Perrone had gained fame as a strike breaker, hired by several anti-union, auto-related manufacturers in and around Detroit. Perrone and gang members had links to the assassination attempts on Walter Reuther. Recently, Police Commissioner George Edwards had testified to Congress about how difficult it was for law enforcement officials to bring slippery gangsters like Perrone to justice. Perrone liked his gang members to live across the Detroit River in Canada. Crossing the border was rarely a problem, and Perrone's men were then outside US law enforcement jurisdiction.

Deadeye was not the smartest guy in the world, though. His brother, Louis Licavoli, was Sammy's access to thousands of dollars in counterfeit money. Louie worked directly with the counterfeiting operation in Windsor. He rarely came to the US, but knew Deadeye was a regular visitor, so he opted to give his brother some extra spending money. Deadeye mixed fake money with legitimate bills and spread it around when he thought it was safe. Rita had been a convenient recipient of his bad bills. She was not sophisticated enough to recognize them as counterfeit. And, Deadeye enjoyed her favors at a discounted price.

Dealing with international borders was always a pain in the ass for law enforcement agencies. Bill had to coordinate operations with Ontario. While it was something of a bureaucratic nightmare that added months to the investigation, the Canadian cops were top-notch. They questioned Deadeye at length, and he finally broke and ratted out his brother as part of a counterfeiting ring. Once they got the details, the Canadians held him incommunicado while Bill and his Canadian buddies tracked down and arrested the counterfeiters. Once they were apprehended, there were questions of jurisdiction. While the Canadians wanted a bite out of these guys, the US had stiffer punishment, so Bill had to work through the extradition process.

After nearly seven months, the Canadian legal process ended. The counterfeiting gang was extradited to Michigan, with the understanding that, after a US trial, Canada had the right to bring the men back to their country for a trial, if necessary. Deadeye was granted a deal with the Canadian and US prosecutors. In exchange for his full cooperation, he agreed not to return to the United States for ten years with the understanding that the Canadian government charged him with only with one count of moving illegal tender to another country. Any violation of this arrangement meant immediate prison time. Bill had insisted on the ten-year ban from entering the US as part of the deal to protect Rita Gray.

Bill pulled the big Ford into the Alden Park lot. Unlike his first meeting, he buzzed Rita's apartment before going up. He knocked, then heard the chain rattle as Rita unlatched the door.

"Agent Simpson, come in. Is this a business visit or pleasure? Or both?" she said, smiling and looking extremely sensual in a blue dress with a thick, white belt accenting her figure. His eyes dropped to her small, bare feet: *No nylons.*

"Miss Gray, you know this is business."

"I think it's safe for you to call me Rita. Can I call you Bill, Bill?"

"Ma'am, you can call me anything you want," he said with a smile. He followed her to the kitchen table overlooking the stunningly bright and beautiful Detroit River and beyond.

"I have coffee brewing. Black, right?" He nodded. She brought two cups to the table, where they sat across from each other. The penetrating green eyes made him shift in his chair. "Um, Rita," Bill said, focusing intently on his words, "I think I have good news for you. I assume you have seen some of the articles about the counterfeiting ring in Windsor?"

"Yeah, I saw them. There wasn't much detail, but I figured since Sam had not visited me recently, you must have been successful at something."

"Well, we never want to get into too much detail in the press. The man you call Sam is known to us as Sammy, or Deadeye."

"Deadeye?" Rita laughed. "I never heard that. How the hell do you guys think up these names?"

"We don't, the gangs do. We're probably not creative enough to come up with stuff like that. Well, Deadeye earned his nickname. He works for the gangster Santo Perrone, and we figure he is responsible for at least five killings and numerous beatings on his behalf."

"Oh, shit!" she whistled. The lines on her forehead arched with concern.

"Why did you call him Sam and not Sammy?"

"Well, *Bill*," she began "I've found it makes good sense to call a man by his given name, no nicknames. Men seem to be more respectful that way." Her mischievous look returned. "Who knows? If you come to see me for pleasure next time, I might call you William."

Bill ignored her last comment and said, "You should know that we believe Sammy has no knowledge of how we came to finger him. Funny, he never asked."

Rita ran a red-polished index nail around the rim of her coffee cup. "So, no one knows about my involvement except you?"

"Pretty much," Bill replied, thinking that he had not discussed her with anyone in the office except for Joe. He doubted anyone could make out his logs, written in the not easily decipherable shorthand he created.

"Pretty much doesn't sound too damn convincing," she replied, shooting him a concerned look.

"Look, Rita, except for my partner, I did not mention you to anyone in my office. Even then, your name was on a list of about one hundred people we interviewed, ninety-eight percent of whom provided us with no substantive information. The only person who might retrace his actions to you is Sammy, and I think we've taken care of that."

"How?"

"To get Sammy to talk, we cut a deal with him. He is likely to do some time in Canada, but more importantly he will not be allowed back in the US for ten years. If he violates that clause, he will go to prison for a minimum of fifteen years."

Rita seemed relieved but added, "Well, okay. I hope you're right."

With the most earnest and honest expression he could muster, Bill said, "I can't think of a better way I could have protected you."

She poured him a second cup of coffee. "Bill, while I like giving you shit, in all seriousness, thank you. I don't expect cops at any level to give a girl like me a break. You have, and I appreciate it."

"It's my job." After a pause, he added, "And that is why these are business meetings."

That lifted any tension that might have been in the room. As he finished his coffee, they talked about growing up, school and so forth. It turned out she grew up in the posh Detroit suburb of Birmingham, about fifteen miles north of Detroit. Her father had been a mid-level auto executive. During her junior year of high school, she got pregnant. She was sent away to have the baby, which she gave up for adoption. With her relationship with her family strained, she was on her own at seventeen. With her good looks, she found modeling jobs. Detroit had a lot of ad agencies always in need of models. The annual September auto show and other events provided jobs for smart and attractive women. Then, she learned that she could add significantly to her income by providing extra services. By the time she was twenty-five, she was earning most of her money from the side work.

After hearing her story, Bill empathized. "Rita, I can't believe I'm saying this, but, through a lot of adversity, you seem to have maintained yourself in a very rough and tumble world."

"Thanks," was her cool response.

"Still, before I go, I just want to say one thing. Not from a moralistic, but rather a practical perspective: save as much money as you can and figure out a way to break free. You can't live forever doing this."

"Yeah, I know. I'm keeping a nest egg for when it's time to move on."

They talked a bit more about her future, investing her funds, and staying safe. Rita walked him to the door. This time, she opened it for him.

"Goodbye, Agent Simpson. I hope you come my way someday."

Then he was on his way to an assignment that would change his life.

Chapter Six
Chicago

The next morning, Halloween, Bill was at his desk working on routine investigations when Reed Clark stuck his head into the glass-walled office. "Bill, I need to see you ASAP."

Bill followed Clark into the conference room next to his boss's office. In the room were three other senior agents. Reed began: "Boys, I was just contacted by Bob Montague, chief of the Chicago office. They need our help. President Kennedy is scheduled to attend the Army-Air Force game on Saturday at Soldier Field. It turns out that yesterday a source tipped off the Chicago FBI of a possible assassination attempt. They suspect it might occur along one of the overpasses on the Northwest Expressway, between O'Hare and the Loop. The FBI tipster ID'd himself as Lee."

Clark paused and let the information sink in for a few moments.

"Okay, does anyone here know Montague?"

The other men exchanged glances. Agent Joe Bishop raised his hand, "Yeah, I worked with Bob in Cincinnati. He's a good guy."

"Good," Clark said. "Anyone else?"

No one reacted.

Clark shifted in his chair and went on. "Okay, Montague told me that the Chicago office is understaffed and that they need help. They have at least one agent coming in from Minneapolis. I expect other nearby offices will also pitch in. I told him he could count on us. I want Joe and Bill Simpson to help. Understood?"

Bill and Joe nodded in unison as Clark rose from his seat and went to the door. "Maggie!" he shouted. Bill and Joe exchanged uneasy glances. Reed Clark was generally a soft-spoken man. He rarely raised his voice.

Maggie Vega, Reed's secretary, stepped into the room. "Yes, sir?" she said.

"I need you to drop everything immediately and find the earliest flight that Bishop and Simpson can take to Chicago. If need be, talk to airline management and get them to hold the flight for these two guys. Tell the airlines this is a matter of national security. Got it?"

"Yes sir!" she responded, already heading back to her desk.

Looking back at his agents, Clark said, "Guys, see Maggie and let her know how quickly you can get to Metro."

The two agents went to the secretary's desk. Along the way, Bishop reminded Bill that he lived in Grosse Pointe Woods and could easily pick him up on the way to Metro Airport. As they got to Maggie's desk, she was already working the phone. Bill and Bishop waited, their body language indicating their impatience.

Maggie, talking on the phone, said, "Oh, that's great. And you will hold the flight? Thanks." She hung up. "Okay, boys, you have a two-fifteen flight with United. They will hold the flight for fifteen minutes, if necessary. The plane will land at two-thirty, Chicago time. Call me when you're at the airport, and I will have hotel reservations for you at the Drake, if possible.

Walking back to his office to collect his things, Bill thought, *No wonder Maggie works for the chief. She is one efficient woman.*

When he arrived home, Anne was cleaning house, and the kids were taking naps. Bill had called her just before he left the office but had no time to explain anything.

He sailed through the living room on his way to the bedroom to pack. "I have an hour to get to the airport. Joe will be here in a few minutes to pick me up. All I can tell you is I have to leave for Chicago."

"What's going on? What's the rush?" Anne asked, setting aside her dust cloth and trailing him down the hallway.

"There's not much I can say," Bill said as he grabbed a small, pre-packed suitcase from the bedroom closet. He opened and scanned the contents and added a few other items.

"Jesus, Bill! That's not much to go on."

"Sorry, honey. That's all I can say except there's a major project going on, and the Chicago office needs help. I have to be there before the close of business."

Their bedroom window looked out onto the street. Bill saw Bishop pull into the driveway. "Sorry, babe. Got to go." He gave her a peck on the cheek and ran out the door.

"But tonight is Halloween!" she protested from the front door.

Bill felt a surge of annoyance as he jumped into Bishop's car. *Christ! He remembered, he was supposed to take Debbie trick-or-treating to-*

night. He felt bad, but Debbie is three and Johnny is one. They won't know the difference.

***

Bill and Bishop arrived at the Chicago Secret Service office at four-twenty, and it was obvious that this was not business as usual. People were either on the phone or in meetings. No one was sitting at their desks. Faces looked stressed. Bishop contacted the receptionist, and, within a few minutes, Bob Montague greeted the Detroit agents and motioned them to follow him to his office. They left their luggage with the receptionist and followed their new boss.

The gray-haired, middle-aged Montague looked harried as he motioned toward two wooden chairs. The agents sat down. "Guys, I apologize for these optics. Normally, things in this office are very controlled. Since we learned about the assassination threat, our people have been working their asses off following leads and checking out every source we have in the area."

The Detroit men acknowledged the situation. Bill added that the president had been in Detroit just three weeks ago, and things were chaotic then, but there had been no threats of violence.

"I appreciate that," Montague said. "We have been working with the Chicago police. The FBI wants nothing to do with this investigation. I guess they feel that protecting the president here is our jurisdiction, and they don't want to get in our way."

The chief was interrupted by a black man who stuck his head in the door and spoke in a soft voice. Bill strained to hear him but couldn't make out what he said.

Montague nodded and replied, "Yes, have Harris follow them. Tell him not to lose them, especially if they move. If they move, tell me. I want to be in the radio room giving commands."

"Larry, before you go, I want you to meet our agents from Detroit. Larry McRae, meet Joe Bishop and Bill Simpson. I'll be assigning them to check out some of our leads. Guys, if you need some help, ask anyone, but Larry knows it all and can help you if you have any questions."

The men shook hands, and McRae excused himself.

Montague continued. "Okay, we will be working late tonight. If you haven't checked into your hotel, get that done and report back here. Joe, I'm going to assign you to Larry McRae, so check with him when you return. He and others are working on tracking down the four major suspects, two two-man teams armed with weapons and ammunition. The

FBI tells us these four guys are right-wing, para-military fanatics, and that an assassination could be attempted from one of the Northwest Freeway overpasses as the president comes in from the airport. We also know that the men's landlady has seen four rifles with telescopic sites in one of the rooms and a newspaper diagram of the president's route. As you heard, we have an agent tailing two of the men and could make an arrest at any time. Larry will provide you with details and will have a specific assignment for you.

"Simpson, we have a secondary lead on a man named Thomas Arthur Vallee." Handing Bill a sheet of paper, Montague continued, "Here is what we have on him—it's not much. When you get back, check him out and see what else you can find on him. Earlier today, a couple of our agents checked out Vallee's apartment. They found a carbine rifle, an M-1, and twenty-five hundred rounds of ammunition. We are working with the Chicago Police on this lead. Call Officer Daniel Kranz—I wrote his number down—when you get back. Clear?"

Bill nodded. "Yes, sir. I've got it."

"Good, now you guys get out of here. Check into your hotel, splash some water on your faces, and get back here pronto. We all have a lot of work to do."

Forty-five minutes later, the men were back at the office. Bishop found McRae and became engrossed on that element of the job. Bill found a phone and dialed Kranz's phone number. A secretary at his precinct answered, said Kranz was out and that she would give him a message to call back as soon as he returned. Bill pressed her to radio Kranz, if possible.

Then, Bill focused on the fact sheet Montague provided. It really could not be called a fact sheet. It had Vallee's name, age—thirty—his address, and his job as an apprentice at the IPP Litho-plate company at 625 West Jackson. Bill looked up at a large Chicago map on the wall. The building was a block off the route that President Kennedy's motorcade was going to be traveling on Saturday morning. Bill felt a rush of adrenaline surge through his body.

The next challenge was how to get more information on Vallee. Bill contacted the Washington Secret Service headquarters. He wanted to talk to the Service's research section. He was told the appropriate staff would call back. *Shit! It's pushing seven-thirty in Detroit and on the east coast. These people have gone home for the night.* He left a message for the staff to call him ASAP. *Now what?* He needed a source who could see if another government agency had any detailed information on this guy.

Then, it hit him … Fred Fry, an FBI agent with the Detroit office. They had worked together on a couple of cases and, most importantly, Bill had Fry's home phone number. Without hesitation, Bill dialed, and after four long rings a woman answered.

"Hello. Mrs. Fry?"

There was a brief hesitation. *"Yes? Can I help you?"*

"Hi, my name is Bill Simpson, with the Detroit office of the Secret Service. Fred and I have worked together before. Is he available?"

"Yes, Mr. Simpson, of course. I'll get Fred right away." *He had passed the test.*

About twenty seconds later, Bill could hear the phone being picked up. "Hello? Bill, buddy, are you there?"

"Hey, Fred, how you doing?" Bill didn't wait for an answer. "Listen, I don't know how much I'm supposed to be telling you, so can we keep this call confidential?"

"Sure, Bill, I don't see why not. What's up?"

"This afternoon I was called to Chicago. All I can tell you is that there's been a death threat on the president, and they are taking it pretty seriously around here."

"Christ," Fry said.

"Yeah, I know. Listen, I need some information on a possible suspect. Our people in DC seem to have headed home for the night. Is there a chance you could contact your DC office and get any potential info for me ASAP?"

There was a pause, then, in a professional voice, Fry said, "Yep, I think I can make that happen. What do you need?"

Bill shared the information he had on Vallee and said he was looking to develop a more detailed profile on him.

"Yeah, I have access to a twenty-four-hour number with the bureau. I can see what they have. Should I have them send you the information or do you want it to come through me?"

"I want it as quickly as possible, but I don't want to raise any eyebrows either. And I don't want to get you into any trouble. The best is if you or the DC office could teletype it to our Chicago office, in care of me. Is that possible?"

"I think I can handle that. I know most of the guys in our research office. I should be able to get something to you pretty quickly. I'll simply say the truth, that we are helping a sister agency with some background regarding a prospective felony—with no other details. Do you have a teletype code for me?"

Breathing a sigh of relief, Bill asked Fred to hold on while he went to the receptionist's desk to get the Chicago office's number. "Fred," he said when he returned to the phone, "remember, not a word to anyone regarding the plot. I'm pretty damned sure that the White House wants a tight lid on this."

"Got it. Don't worry," Fry said as he hung up.

Bill paced around the office. He was waiting for two contacts now, the call back from Kranz and the information from the Washington FBI research department. He did not see Bishop anywhere, but his eyes fell on Larry McRae, who was sitting in a small, paneled office, drumming his fingers on the desktop.

Bill stuck his head in the doorway. "So, are you like me, waiting for information?"

McRae looked up, coming out of his trance. "Oh, yeah. Simpson, right?"

Bill nodded.

"Yep, I have four phone calls I'm waiting on, and each one can take me to a different part of the city."

"So, what do you have Joe doing?"

Smiling, McRae said, "Oh, he's on the street with one of our other agents, trying to track down two of the four renegades. Having two under surveillance is good, but we sure as hell don't want two guys floating around the Loop heavily armed and possibly after our president."

The comment jogged Bill's memory. "Say, Larry, last year I was rotated to the presidential detail. I heard the year before a Chicago agent had been out there. Was that you?"

McRae laughed heartily. "You mean you heard a Chicago *colored* agent had been assigned to the detail, right? Yeah, that was me."

Bill smiled sheepishly. "Yep, that was pretty much how you were described."

"Overall, I had a good experience—"

Before McRae could finish, the receptionist called out, "Simpson, Bill Simpson! Phone call on line four."

Bill ran to his desk. He punched the blinking button on the phone and was greeted by a booming voice with a hint of a European accent: "Bill Simpson? This is Officer Kranz."

"Thanks for getting back with me, Officer. I think you may know that I've been assigned to work with you on this Vallee lead."

"Yeah, I heard. From Detroit, right?"

"That's right."

"We've been trying to keep our eyes on him, from a distance. I have two uniforms stationed inconspicuously outside of his boarding house. If he moves, we will follow. Have you been able to learn anything on Vallee?"

"I'm working on it. One of my buddies from the FBI is trying to get their DC research office to find out what they can. He anticipates I will hear something soon."

"Good. We don't know how seriously to take this guy."

"Yeah, but Christ, he works right along the motorcade's route."

"I know."

"By the way, I'm Bill; you're Dan, right?"

"Yeah, good … Bill. Listen, I think the best thing is for you to get that information from the Feds. As soon as you get it, call me." Kranz gave him several numbers, including a direct office number and his home number.

"Will do. You can reach me here or at the Drake."

"Good. Ah, Bill, I don't know if you've been briefed on this, but we have a special security coordination group that meets at least once a day to provide briefings and assignments. We're meeting tomorrow at seven-thirty sharp in the auditorium at police headquarters at Eleventh and State. Can you be there?"

"Yeah, count on me. I'll double-check with Montague to make sure I'm not screwing up any procedures on this side."

"Good idea. Call me if there's a problem."

"Got it. It will be good to sit down and go over what we have."

Kranz snorted into the phone. "Well, we're sure as hell not going to be sitting around. As soon as the meeting is over, we'll find Vallee. I really want to find a way to arrest this guy and get him off the streets."

"Good, let's get the bastard."

Kranz laughed. "No shit."

Bill looked around the office. Things were still busy, but not nearly as hectic as when they had first arrived. There were not quite as many people scattered throughout the open office area. It looked like some of the secretarial office may have left. It was Halloween and many of the women probably had family responsibilities. There were some clerical staff still around. Joe Bishop had not returned, so that meant he was busy tracking his leads. Bill pulled a notebook, his log, and began updating his activities.

A few minutes later, the receptionist brought him his teletype from the FBI.

Bill began poring over the contents.

Thomas Arthur Vallee was born and raised in Chicago. He joined the Marines late in the Korean War. After the war, he was assigned to an American intelligence unit at an Army base in Japan. Without mentioning the name of the base, the term "Joint Technical Advisory Group" was written following "Army base." Bill thought this had CIA written all over it. He was identified as a schizophrenic paranoid loner, and he collected guns. He was honorably discharged.

Vallee was recruited in the late 1950s and early 1960s to train members of a fiercely anti-Castro guerrilla group whose objective was to assassinate Cuban leader Fidel Castro. Their training facility was near Levittown, Long Island.

Also, Vallee had ties to the John Birch Society. The information also had a quote attributed to Vallee after President Kennedy had withheld air support for the CIA-funded Bay of Pigs invasion in Cuba: "We lost a lot of good men down there." He had been arrested on four occasions in different local jurisdictions—over personal control issues.

That was it. A Marine Corps vet who possibly worked at an American intelligence base in Japan—possibly under the CIA. Vallee apparently opposed President Kennedy's decision to hold off air support of the Cuban guerrillas. To top it off, the guy had mental issues. And, in two days, Kennedy was going to be in a motorcade going right by Vallee's place of employment.

When Bill phoned Kranz, the Chicago cop's reaction was the same as Bill's. "Jesus Christ, we have to get this motherfucker off the streets. We still have some time. I'd like to do it legally but, one way or another, we're going to bring this guy in."

Bill decided it was time to brief Montague. He found him in the agency's radio room, crowded with several other agents. Montague motioned him toward an empty chair. Bill took a seat and listened in.

A moment later, Bill heard the static of an open mic then a report. *"Chief, I'm following the two suspects. They are on Clark, near Division. Over."*

"Alright, Harris," Montague replied. "Stay within sight, but don't blow your cover. Over."

"Yes, sir. Suspects are turning into an alley. We are very close to their rooming house. I'm following. Over."

There was a pause that took just a couple of seconds, but seemed like minutes.

Then, the static again. *"Oh shit, the alley must be a dead end. Suspects have turned around, coming my way. Jesus."*

Montague, in a calm but tense voice said, "Okay, don't panic. Give them space. Act like you're searching for an address. Over."

"Oh shit, sir. The alley's too narrow. They're on to us. They've heard everything you just said."

"How the hell could they do that?" Montague exploded.

"My window was down. I guess so was their window."

Montague was standing now. Before he pressed the mic's button down, he said, "Son of a bitch! We didn't get any goddamned evidence." Quickly composing himself, he pressed down the button and said, "Okay, Harris. Turn around and get those guys. Looks like we don't have evidence, but we have to make the arrest. Don't let the bastards get away. OVER!"

After about ten minutes, the static came over the speaker: *"Harris here. We've made the arrest. Over."*

"Good. Now get those guys down here for interrogation. Be as discrete as possible. The less anyone knows about this the better. Over." Montague, pacing the room, said more to himself than anyone else, "What a colossal-fuck up! Son of a bitch!"

The other men in the room started cracking jokes at Harris's expense. "What an amateur," one guy said. "How could anyone blow a cover like this?" another agent asked. Montague told them to knock it off and prepare two rooms for interrogation. Then, he motioned to Bill to follow him to his office.

A moment later, with his office door closed, Montague said, "What have you got, Simpson?"

Bill told him he contacted Kranz and said the policeman wanted him to come to Friday morning's special security coordination team's meeting. Montague nodded his approval.

Bill then went over the information on Vallee. Montague seemed impressed. "Good. You say you got this info from the FBI? They were cooperative?"

"Yes, sir. My contact in Detroit is as good as they get. Now sir, I've shared this information with Kranz. He's of the opinion, and I agree, that we have to get Vallee off the streets. The issue is evidence. Our plan is to let him go to work tomorrow and then search his rooming house. Is there a way we can get a search warrant?"

"Not from a federal judge. Local cops have to get it. Remember, it's not a federal crime to kill or attempt to kill the president—it's all local jurisdiction. Rely on Kranz on this matter. If you can, at tomorrow's meeting, talk to Captain Linsky. He can give you good advice."

"Okay, thanks."

"Stick around for our interrogation of these guys," he said.

It took forever for Harris and his team to bring the two suspects to the office. The men appeared to be of Latin American background—someone suggested they were Cubans. They were wearing light jackets, unkempt hair, baggy pants, and about a day's growth of beard. The two men were separated and put into two interrogation rooms on opposite sides of the Secret Service offices.

Harris went to the room near the front of the offices and an agent named Morse took the other to the rear. After a couple of hours of interrogation, no solid information was picked up from either man. It turned out that no weapons were found in their possession, their vehicle, or the rooming house.

Bill was surprised how much some of the senior agents teased and harassed Harris over his error in the alley. Anytime he came out of the interrogation room, the agents took every opportunity to throw an insult or a dig. Harris glared at them in indignation.

As the night progressed, it was clear that the agents were not going to get anything out of these men. Around one o'clock, Bill asked Montague if he could be excused to get some sleep. Montague seemed surprised that Bill was still hanging around and told him to get going and to call in the morning if anything of interest turned up.

Chapter Seven
Cat and Mouse Game

Bill put his head down on his bed at the Drake. The next thing he knew, the phone rang. A woman's cheerful voice said, "Good morning, it's six o'clock." Feeling the tug of sleep deprivation, Bill began to slide back into a sleeping position, then suddenly realized he had to get moving to make his seven-thirty meeting. He jumped out of bed and headed to the bathroom.

Bill grabbed a cab and headed to police headquarters, making it about ten minutes before the meeting time. About fifty people were milling around the auditorium, waiting for the meeting to convene. He walked up to a uniformed officer and asked if he knew Officer Dan Kranz. The officer looked around and said he did not see him. Bill asked if Captain Linsky was there. The officer pointed to a medium-height, uniformed man with a significant belly standing on the stage with other officers.

Bill walked down the aisle to the stage, where Linsky was in animated conversation. He moved close to Linsky, who looked over at him.

"What can I do for you? You're not press, are you?" Linsky inquired in a brisk but not unfriendly voice.

"I'm Secret Service agent Bill Simpson. I'm here to meet Officer Kranz, but my chief, Bob Montague, asked me to try to catch up with you. You know that we are following a lead on a suspect—"

"Yeah, I know all about that."

"Good. Montague is concerned about getting a local judge to authorize a search warrant in Vallee's rooming house."

"Yeah, that's a really good point," Linsky replied. Then, looking around the room, he said, "You haven't met Kranz yet?"

"No, we talked last night a couple of times."

"Good. Dan Kranz is an up-and-comer. Aggressive and a good cop." Then Linsky's eyes locked on someone, and he called, "Dan, Dan Kranz!" and with his left hand waved a man in civilian clothes over. A moment later, Bill was introduced to a guy who looked like he could have been an offensive lineman for the Chicago Bears.

Linsky moved the men to the far-left corner of the stage and looked at Kranz. "Alright, Dan, listen. We are just over twenty-four hours before the president is in town. I want to get that son of a bitch Vallee off the streets faster than my new goddamned Cadillac needs a tank of gas. I don't want you wasting time here. We have to deal with the security at Soldier Field, the Conrad Hilton, and the motorcade routes to and from the Loop. Go to Judge Hoffman's chambers and tell him I need a search warrant ASAP. If he is not in, tell his staff to find him. Just get it done."

"Yes sir," Kranz said.

"Look," Linsky went on, "I want any searches done by us to be legal." Bill thought the Chicago cop might be referencing the Secret Service's illegal search of the rooming house. Continuing, Linsky said, "I want this guy off the streets, but I want it done legally, at least for today. If we don't have him by nine tomorrow morning, we pull him off the streets, period. Got it?"

"Yes, sir," he replied.

Linsky walked back to the center of the stage and called the meeting to order. After they listened to several reports, Kranz looked at Bill: "Simpson, let's get out of here." They went to Judge Hoffman's office and waited until he arrived. By nine-thirty, they had their search warrant, and fifteen minutes later, they were headed to Vallee's rooming house in an unmarked black Chevy. Along the way, Kranz checked with the officers tailing Vallee to confirm he was at work. Kranz informed the officers they were going to search the rooming house and then probably relieve the officers, who had been shadowing Vallee since six o'clock the previous evening.

The two men arrived at the shabby rooming house and found the landlord, who told them he didn't want any trouble as he provided access to the room. Kranz told him there would be no trouble if the man kept his mouth shut.

The bare room was tidy. The bed was made, clothes were hung up, a coffee pot, canned soup, and some snacks were on a small table. The men began going through the chest of drawers, closets, and any other place where something might be hidden.

"Holy shit! Look at this!" Kranz said as he removed five boxes of ammunition from underneath some neatly folded shirts.

A moment later, Bill reached inside the front corner of the closet. "Dan, check this out." He pulled out a handkerchief from his front pants pocket and wrapped it around a freshly oiled M-1 rifle, followed by a carbine rifle.

"Looky here," Kranz quipped as he waved Bill to come and look at a .38 pistol he found in the chest of drawers.

After a little more searching, Kranz said, "Okay, Bill, we have what we need. We'll leave this stuff for now and hope we can catch him red-handed when we make an arrest. My boys need to be relieved."

Thirty minutes later, the men relieved the other officers, who pointed out Vallee's car, a two-door, green and white '58 Plymouth. Kranz parked where both the front entrance and the Plymouth were visible. After a couple of hours, they debated going into the warehouse and picking him up, but decided they didn't want to provoke more attention than necessary.

"Remember, Linsky said to make a clean arrest, if possible," Kranz said.

"I know, but we can't let him get away," Bill responded.

"We won't. Listen, I'm going to get some lunch. What do you want?"

Bill gave him an order and Kranz headed to a small deli down the street. When he returned, they wolfed down sandwiches as they kept their eyes trained on their targets.

Finally, at three-twenty, Bill saw their man exit the warehouse through a side door. "I think that's our guy."

He and Kranz watched the thin, lanky man walk directly to the Plymouth.

They followed Vallee as he worked his way back to the rooming house. Along the way, he stopped at a deli, apparently picking up his dinner. He returned to his room and the men remained outside the building. At seven, they were relieved by the night shift.Kranz told the new guys, "Boys, we'll be back at 7:00 a.m.—if this son of a bitch does anything out of the ordinary, I want to know, got it?"

Kranz took Bill back to the Secret Service office, commenting that, as long as Vallee was stationary, all was good. He told Bill to be at the front door of the Drake at six-thirty the next morning, Saturday, the day of President Kennedy's arrival.

Bill walked into the office after Kranz dropped him off. The pace was slower than the night before, but it was still busy. He spotted Montague. Bill had kept the Chicago chief up to date throughout his day. Montague had seemed vaguely interested—Bill could tell the man's focus was elsewhere.

Joe Bishop was in a corner office, talking with other agents. From a respectful distance, Bill caught Joe's eye. He signaled with a finger to

Bill that he'd be there in a minute. Loose paper, disposable coffee cups, and full ashtrays littered almost all the desks. Bill went back to the desk he had used the previous night and called Anne.

His wife seemed mildly interested in his activities. Bill couldn't provide much detail, telling her he had been working hard with little sleep. "If all goes well," he added, "I'll be home tomorrow, Sunday by the latest."

"That'll be nice, honey. The kids miss you," she replied.

"I miss them, too … and you." Bill looked up: Joe had appeared and was standing next to the desk. "Maybe on Sunday, if it's a nice day, we can drive out to the cider mill."

"That would be nice. Isn't there a Lions game?"

"Yeah, but I can catch the second half," Bill said.

Joe leaned down and whispered: "It's at San Francisco."

"Joe here says they are playing the 49ers, so it won't start until four. Listen, honey, I need to run. I'll call you when I can. Bye." He hung up and turned to Joe. "Are you guys winding down? Do you have time for dinner?"

"Yeah, I think we're just about done for the night. Give me another half hour or so, and we can head back to the hotel."

"Good. That will give me some time to work on my log."

Joe, heading back to the smoke-filled corner office, said, "Okay, as soon as we're done we'll get out of here and compare notes."

An hour later, they got to the hotel, washed up, and located a good steak place. It turned out that the full focus of the Chicago office's effort was finding the other two Cuban suspects. Joe said he and his Chicago partners had traveled the city, tracing leads, but nothing turned up. They were going to gather at six on Saturday morning and re-examine the motorcade route to and from Soldier Field.

Bill felt like he and Kranz were part of a secondary effort. He told himself that any suspect could be a killer and to stay focused. That said, Joe Bishop made clear that his team was the primary effort of the Chicago office. Bill decided that was fine.

Chapter Eight
The Letdown

"Good morning, it's five-forty-five," the operator said when Bill, startled from deep sleep, answered his wake-up call.

As he grabbed a quick shave in the bathroom, he thought about the day ahead. Saturday, the day the president was coming. He hoped he and his colleagues would bring any and all perpetrators involved with a presidential assassination attempt to justice, hopefully with little or no publicity.

Just past six-thirty, Dan Kranz pulled up to the Drake's main entrance. "Morning," Dan said, handing him a cup of coffee and pointing to a bag on the seat. "Donuts in there; help yourself."

Bill reached for the paper bag and removed a cruller. "Any news from the stakeout?"

"All is quiet. We'll watch him and make an arrest the first chance we get."

"Good," Bill replied. "My boss agrees with Linsky. We want the son of a bitch off the street no later than nine. The president is scheduled to arrive by ten-thirty."

"Right."

A few minutes later, the men relieved the other officers on Wilson Street, in front of Vallee's building. The officers informed them that the Plymouth was parked six parking spots down the street from their present location. Dan and Bill waited. It was a cloudy, chilly autumn morning. The car engine remained off until the men needed a warm-up. About seven-thirty, Vallee emerged and casually walked to his car. When he drove off, Bill and Dan were discreetly on his tail. Traffic was light that early Saturday morning.

Vallee made a left turn without signaling. "We've got him now," Dan said. He rolled down his window and placed a cherry light on the roof. A moment later, the Chicago cop flicked the flasher on and sped up. He was nearly touching the Plymouth's rear bumper. Vallee braked, then appeared to hesitate for a moment before he pulled over to the side of the road in a no-standing area.

Bill started to get out of the car, but Dan reached out and touched his shoulder. "Stay here and cover me. I think we should make this stop as routine as possible."

"Okay," Bill said as he pulled out his revolver.

Dan stepped out of the car and walked up to the Plymouth. Vallee had already rolled down his window. He started to talk, upset that he had been stopped. Dan's wave told him to stay quiet. Bill watched as the officer looked inside the car. Soon he ordered Vallee to step out. A moment later, Dan held up a sheathed hunting knife. That was all he needed, a violation of Chicago traffic code, carrying a dangerous weapon in the front seat. Vallee was arrested on the spot.

Bill and Dan searched the Plymouth. There were no other weapons. They left the car parked at the side of the road and drove to the nearest police station. Two Chicago detectives were waiting to interrogate the suspect. Once those officers and Vallee were in the interrogation room, Dan and Bill stood outside, watching through a one-way mirror and listening through a tinny sounding speaker.

The detectives got Vallee talking. He said the John Birch Society was right, that America was in deep trouble unless Barry Goldwater defeated Kennedy in the upcoming election. Then, Vallee added that Mayor Richard Daley's corrupt political machine could not steal the election a second time.

Even though the detectives knew about the weapons in the boarding house, they asked and then pressed, Vallee to accompany them to the boarding house for a search. Vallee said no. One of the detectives slammed his fist into the table and told Vallee that if he didn't cooperate, he was going to take him to a back room. Vallee complied.

The two detectives, with Dan and Bill following, took Vallee to his rooming house. The weapons were in the same spots Bill and Dan had left them the day before.

Dan said, "Kid, you're in a lot of fucking trouble."

"That's what you say," Vallee snapped cockily.

The detectives drove him to their home precinct, Chicago's twentieth, to be held until after the president's visit was over. It was twenty past ten. Bill called Montague, but could not reach him. Dan took him to the downtown Secret Service office. They said goodbye, not knowing if they would see each other again.

Bill walked into the office. The place was like a morgue compared to earlier. "Oh, man, what a fucking mess," Joe Bishop whispered to him. "Kennedy has canceled; his office is saying that he has a cold and that there's a mess going on in Vietnam. But the real reason is the DC office said it's too dangerous to let the president come to Chicago with potential assassins roaming the streets."

"So, you guys never found them, eh?"

"No, how about your guy?"

"We arrested him. He was interrogated, admitted nothing. He's a real right-wing nutcase. And, of course, we found all the weapons in his place. He's held tight over at the twentieth."

"Good," Bishop said.

With Kennedy not coming, there was a great sense of emptiness. Mayor Daley and thousands of citizens already lined up to see the president were deeply disappointed. And the police and Secret Service agents who had worked so hard had no way of knowing if there was an actual assassination attempt planned. Still, they had done their job and done it well; the president was safe.

The two Detroit agents hung around the office until Montague thanked them for their assistance and hard work, and told them to head home. He also said he wanted a full report of their activities in Chicago by early next week.

***

Bill was home by seven that night. He was exhausted, both physically and emotionally, but he was happy to see Anne and the kids. Anne didn't say much. She knew that whatever Bill had been up to in Chicago could not be divulged. Over a wonderful dinner that she'd prepared, she said the plan was to see her parents after church on Sunday, then take a drive to the cider mill.

Bill watched the end of The Jackie Gleason Show after dinner and fell asleep on the couch. He woke up three hours later and went to bed. As much as he felt let down by Kennedy's cancellation, he realized that they had been successful in keeping the president safe, his major employment objective.

The next morning while still in a deep sleep, his three-year-old daughter jumped on him with a big kiss.

About twenty miles north of their house, the Yates Cider Mill was always a great experience. With the sun out and the temperature in the low fifties, it was a good day to get donuts and cider. The mill was across from Bloomer State Park, so they crossed the street and let Debbie run around, eat donuts, and drink cider as much as she wanted. Anne finally had to cut her off. Heading home, the kids were asleep almost as soon as Bill shifted the car into drive.

Anne looked over at him. "Boy, you were exhausted last night. I don't think I've ever seen you sleep so hard. You must have been working your ass off. Did you see much of Chicago?"

"Yeah, we worked hard," Bill replied as he maneuvered onto the highway. "We didn't see too much of the city, except the ugly side. Joe and I had a good dinner at a steak place on Friday night. That was about it."

"So, what were you doing?"

Always a sore topic, Bill said, "Well, you know I can't say much, but we were chasing leads to a potential major crime. Nothing panned out."

"Really? All that time and energy for nothing?"

Bill began to get irritated. He had worked his ass off trying to break a case that could have involved the assassination of a US president. That was not, as Anne said, "nothing." "Damn it, hon, you know I can't talk about it. But it was not about nothing. If we are successful, no one knows. If we fail, its front-page news."

"Jesus, I was just trying to find out a little bit about what you were doing."

"I know, and I'm sorry. There's not much more to be said."

They remained silent for rest of the ride. When they got home, Bill fell asleep watching the Lions game. Later, he went to his desk in the basement and worked on his report.

Chapter Nine
Questions from Headquarters

Monday morning, Bill drove into the office, feeling surprisingly good. He had done good work in Chicago, and both he and Bishop had helped their fellow agents. What could have been a national disaster hadn't happened. Once in the office, Bill and Bishop were pulled into Reed Clark's conference room for a debriefing. After forty-five minutes, their boss said, "Good work, boys. I think you did the Detroit office and the Service proud. I suspect, after I talk with Montague, you will have some nice commendations for your personnel files. Now let's get back to work." The men returned to their desks to dig through overflowing in-baskets.

Reed came out of his office mid-morning with Bishop behind him. He said to Bill in a low voice, "Follow me. The three of us have to talk."

Something is up.

Reed shut the door to the conference room and motioned for the men to sit down. "Joe, Bill, about half an hour ago I got a call from Washington. They were short on information but strong on orders. They said in no uncertain terms that no one is to ever talk about the Chicago assignment, *ever.*"

Both Joe and Bill started to talk, but Reed waved them off.

"It gets worse. I need to collect your logs, notes, and any other written or physical material you might have from the Chicago assignment."

"Now wait a second, Reed," Bishop protested. "They can't do that. You know these records are to protect agents as well as the Service. And, by the way, what about receipts? We have cab fare, meals, and the hotel bill to be dealt with. We need to be reimbursed."

"I know, I know," Reed responded, clearly just as frustrated as his agents. "Regarding any costs that we owe, just add it all, and I'll deal with it. Regarding the orders, there is nothing I can do. This comes from the top. After the DC call, I checked with Montague. He's just as frustrated ... no, he is just pissed off. He knows the work that you and his agents did. He doesn't get it, either, but he has to follow orders." Reed paused. "And so do we. Now go back to your desks and pull everything you've got on this, and bring it here in ten minutes. Clear?"

"Alright," muttered a pissed-off Joe Bishop.

"Yep, got it," Bill said as got out of his seat.

All his material was in his briefcase. The previous night, he had begun putting a report together, but didn't like it. He had laid it aside in a drawer in his beat-up desk in his basement. He intended to start a new draft today.

Bill sat at his desk and looked out at Michigan Avenue, originally the old road to Chicago. He should go home and get the draft. While not in final form, it chronicled all he had done while in Chicago. *No. Fuck 'em.* He was going to keep that draft and put it in a very safe place. *Fuck 'em.*

Five minutes later, he walked into Reed's office with the material. Reed could tell how dejected Bill was. "Bill, look, this is plain wrong, and I feel terrible for you guys. Listen, you've worked hard. Why don't you just blow off the rest of the day. Go home, fool around with your wife, see a movie, or just drive around, but get the hell out of here. I'm telling Bishop the same thing when he gets here. Now go, that's an order."

Bill headed home. Anne was surprised to see him, and he simply said that Reed had told him to take some comp time. Later that day, he drove to his parents' modest, two-story house located in a working-class neighborhood of bungalows and some larger homes. His dad was working, his mom was out, probably running errands. This suited his purpose.

He let himself in and went up to his old bedroom, carrying an eight-by-ten envelope. The room had been cleaned up from his high school days, but there were still a few drawers of his old stuff in the dresser. He pulled out a drawer and emptied it. He opened a false bottom he had made some twenty years earlier. Some of the dirty photos he had from his high school days were still there, a sign that this was still a good place to store private stuff. With a smile, he grabbed the pictures to throw them out later. He took the envelope with the draft report from the previous night and placed it into the secret hiding place for safe keeping.

***

The next two weeks were routine for Bill until Tuesday afternoon, November 19. At his desk, Bill was putting his strategy together for another counterfeiting case. This time bad bills were coming from Michigan's Upper Peninsula. Kelly, the receptionist, buzzed him and told him Fred Fry was on the line. Bill felt badly that he had not called Fred to thank him again for his help in Chicago, but according to orders he was not to discuss the case with anybody.

"Bill, listen old buddy, I need to talk to you," Fred said. "Do you have any time to meet tomorrow?"

"Yeah, sure, Fred. Breakfast would be best, but I can do anytime for you."

"No, no, breakfast is fine. Name the time and place."

Fred lived in the fast-growing suburb of Warren, so Bill suggested Cupids at Conner and Warren at seven-thirty. Bill arrived at the art-deco designed restaurant—originally a drive-in that had become a family restaurant—the next morning, walked back to the dining room area and spotted Fred at a corner table. As he walked over to Fred, much to his surprise, he saw his dad at another table, having breakfast with several men. Bill walked over to greet Jimmy, holding a hand up to Fred.

Jimmy greeted his son with a handshake and a one-armed hug. After Bill explained he was meeting with a guy before work, Jimmy said, "So am I." He introduced Bill to the other people at the table, all of whom, except for Jimmy, were wearing business suits. The men were all higher-ups in the United Auto Workers union.

"Bill, I want you to meet Emil Mazey, Ken Morris, and Ken Bannon." Bill shook hands with the men, who also rose to meet the son of one of their members. "Emil, I think you know, is the UAW's secretary-treasurer. Ken Morris is the regional director for this area. And Ken Bannon is the director of the UAW's Ford Department. Now, don't you dare tell your mother yet, but I'm talking to these guys about running for president of Local 400." With a smile, he added, "They are all telling me I'm nuts to run. But you know each of these guys ran in elections that they were never supposed to win, and look at them. They all won!"

The other men chuckled, then sat down to finish their breakfasts. Bill headed across the room to meet his fellow agent.

Fred was dressed in sweater and slacks. *No suit?* Highly unusual for an FBI man. Fred was tall, with a full head of blond hair. He had put on some weight since the last time Bill had seen him. After the waitress took their orders, Bill asked Fred what was going on.

"You're looking kind of relaxed for a workday," he said.

"Yeah, well, you've come right to the point of the meeting. I've had some disciplinary action taken against me. I've been demoted a pay grade and I have to take a week, this week, off without pay."

"Holy shit! Is this my fault?" Bill was stunned. This was the last thing he had expected.

"Oh, man," Fred replied, his face furrowed with emotion. "Only in a way, Bill. Yes, you called and yes, I found a way to help you. But I don't hold you at fault. I was doing what anyone in law enforcement would do for a colleague. No, something is wrong with our agency. I don't know if it was interagency rivalry or not, but something's wrong. By the way, did the info help?"

"Oh, yeah. The information was critical to understanding who this guy was. He hated the president and was a complete right-wing stooge. A John Bircher all the way."

"I'm glad it helped," Fred said. "You know, I really didn't need to drag you into this mess. I just felt you should know."

"Oh no, I'm glad you told me."

"Well, don't worry about me. I'll be okay. I have a lot of support in the Detroit office. My boss is terrific and just as upset as I am. In time, I'll be back. Don't worry."

Chapter Ten
We Lost Him

The office was quiet. Two days after meeting Fred, Bill made some phone calls and set up meetings for leads on his counterfeiting case. At lunch time, he grabbed the sandwich he'd brought from home and got a Coke from the machine down the hall. He ate at his desk, reading the *Detroit Free Press* sports section, taking special interest in the preview of Sunday's Lions game against the Vikings.

About one, Joe Bishop broke the quiet when he rushed out of his office and shouted "Who's got a radio? The president's been shot!"

Instantly, the office came to life. Joe Kowalski turned on his new transistor radio, turning the dial to 760 WJR.

"...Shots were fired. It appears President Kennedy was shot during his motorcade in downtown Dallas..."

Everyone gathered around the radio. A few minutes later, Reed Clark came in, listened a couple of minutes, then discretely exited. Bill assumed he was going to check in with Washington headquarters. Initially, the radio broadcasters said the president had been shot, but it was not clear how serious the wounds were to the leader of the free world. As the broadcast continued, the seriousness of the shooting became clear. Just before two, the radio switched to a reporter at Parkland Hospital in Dallas. The reporter said he and other members of the press were waiting for an announcement. His tone was grim. At two-thirty, a reporter said a White House staffer just announced that President Kennedy had died at one o'clock, Central Standard Time, two o'clock in Detroit.

The room fell silent. Some wept. Bill thought about the person he knew and so admired. He was a man's man, always detached from others, yet with almost an unfailing empathy. A tough boss, but a person who seemed to make the people around him better. Bill had felt Kennedy's special spirit from the moment he met him, nearly two years earlier. He never thought John F. Kennedy would be gone, at least not like this.

"People," Reed Clark said in a commanding voice. He had been in and out of his office without saying much. "I can only imagine the feelings you all must have right now. We all are shocked by what has happened. I expect that we will know more about the shooting from the radio and directly from headquarters. Take a few minutes to gather yourselves, say a prayer, call your wives or other family members. I don't know exactly what assignments we will have, but plan to stay late tonight and don't leave without getting permission from me. Agents, I want you in the conference room at three-fifteen sharp."

Bill returned to his office. He called home. Anne did not answer. He tried his mother-in-law's house. She answered, and she put Anne on immediately.

"Oh Bill, oh God! I'm so sorry."

"We've lost him," he said, feeling himself start to choke up.

"God, it's so scary. When are you going to be home?"

"I don't know. It's going to be late. Reed's called a meeting in just a few minutes. I expect he will give out some assignments. I'll let you know as soon as I know something."

Bill sat at his desk and composed himself. He had to put on his professional face. He could let his guard down at home, not now.

Just after three, the agents assembled in the conference room. The radio had been taken out of the room and placed at the receptionist's desk. Reed entered and shut the door.

"Alright, fellas, I've been on the phone with DC a couple of times since we broke up. Air Force One is going to bring the president … er, I mean President Kennedy and President Johnson back to Washington. There are only two injuries that we know of. Of course, President Kennedy and then Governor John Connolly, who is seriously wounded, but should live. We also have word that the Dallas police are hunting down a suspect, but I don't have any details on that.

"We need people to go to the Ambassador Bridge, the tunnel, and up to the Blue Water Bridge. Joe Bishop, Link Farrall, and Jake Stone, you guys split up the border crossings and head over there as soon as possible. Talk to whoever is in charge. Tell them to be on the alert for any suspicious travelers—especially men travelling by themselves or in small groups. Tell them they should be on high alert through Monday. Remember, if these guys are escaping Dallas by car, there are four Michigan crossings to Canada—that's a lot of opportunities for assassins. We will provide any updates if we get any more details. Also, ask your contacts at the crossings to reach out to their Canadian counterparts with the same instructions. Joe Kowalski!"

Joe jumped when his name was called.

"I want you to see Maggie. Get two hundred dollars from petty cash." At that point, Maggie walked in with what appeared to be a teletype in her hand and gave it to Reed. He quickly read the document and continued, "Kowalski, I want you to get two hundred dollars and go out and buy a goddamned TV. This is the best way to keep up with what the hell is going on."

Kowalski's face fell. What he thought would be a big assignment turned out to be the job of an errand boy.

Rereading the teletype, Reed said, "Okay, boys, it appears a suspect has been arrested. A man named Lee Harvey Oswald has been picked up, apparently at a Dallas movie theater. That's all I have at this point.

"Bill Simpson, you probably have the best contacts with the Canadians. Call them, ask them to share the information that Bishop, Farrall, and Stone are delivering at the border crossings. Also, see if they can coordinate the Sault Ste. Marie crossing. Let's try to get everyone in Canada on the same page. Oh, and call the US customs at the Sault border crossing and give them the same message that we are giving to all the other crossings."

"No problem, Chief," Bill said. "Should I also see if they might have any information on this guy, Oswald?"

"Yep, good idea."

"This could take a lot of phone calls and we don't have much time left in the day. Joe K. knows a number of these people; can he be assigned to me?"

"Of course. Joe, after you get back, check in with Bill," Reed said. Bill glanced over at Joe, whose disappointment morphed into satisfaction.

Reed dished out a few more tasks, then said, "Okay, I think everyone has assignments. I'm asking the secretaries to man the phones twenty-four hours a day until further notice. After today's assignments, it might prove to be difficult to get information during the weekend. If you get any information that you think needs to be followed up on, do it. I don't care what time or where it is. Just get it done. All agents will receive a schedule to ensure that there is an agent here at all hours of the day and night. I want your phone numbers wherever you are. I want each and every one of you to be available at all times. If you're not at home, I want your relatives' numbers, or in some cases, your girlfriends' numbers. Got it?"

***

Bill rolled into his driveway around nine-thirty Friday night. During the previous six hours, he and Joe were able to contact several Canadian counterparts. It was late in the day, and no one had any information regarding Oswald. Those with appropriate responsibility had indicated that security would be increased at the border crossings, not only at Michigan border crossings, but at all US and Canadian borders.

By six o'clock, there was really nothing to do. They kept track of activities by watching Chet Huntley and David Brinkley on Detroit's Channel 4. The newly purchased television turned out to be handy. They saw Air Force One land at Andrews Air Force base. They watched in silence as Jackie and Robert Kennedy escorted President Kennedy's coffin off the plane's rear cargo hatch. They did comment on a couple of the president's detail awkwardly trying to negotiate the coffin off the plane and into the awaiting ambulance.

Bill wondered if any of them had been drinking. Then they heard President Johnson address the country. Nearly everyone in the office was mesmerized. A few people, like Maggie, were focused on specific chores, but for everyone else, they just wanted to be together and watch the news ... any news.

The teletype provided little information. Reed Clark guessed there was so much going on in DC that there was little focus on the field offices around the country. By eight, there was little to do. Bill waited until around nine, got his assignments confirmed for Saturday evening and Sunday midnight, and went home.

When he walked in the front door, Anne, clearly shaken, rushed over and hugged him tightly for an unusually long moment.

"Do you think the Russians did it?" she asked after Bill sat down. She pulled a warm plate from the oven and sat it in front of him.

"It's too early to know. Oswald was in the Soviet Union and has a Russian wife, but I think if there were any direct links, we would have heard something."

"Daddy thinks Johnson did it."

Bill nearly choked on his chicken. "Jesus Christ!" he stammered, knowing her father's political views and that he was a Goldwater supporter. "He doesn't know what he's talking about."

"I know, he's just Daddy. No one knows anything."

"Oswald was probably just a nut job and looking for some fame. Listen, I have to cover the office between six and midnight on Saturday and then the midnight shift on Sunday. I'd like to be with the kids. Maybe tomorrow morning I can take them around Belle Isle?"

"Good," Anne replied. "It will be good for you and good for them."

They watched TV the rest of the night. Bill's dad called, and they talked for some time. Jimmy invited the family over for a late breakfast or lunch after church on Sunday.

When Bill went to bed, he couldn't sleep. He lay there, his mind racing. He thought of the Chicago assignment, just a few weeks ago. He thought of Vallee, a lone man, a former Marine, a potential suspect in an assassination attempt. He thought of the presidential detail assignment and of the president, his wife, and the two children … and then, for some reason, he thought about Rita Gray and wondered what she might be thinking about now. Bill rolled over, put his arm over Anne's sleeping body, and pulled her close.

On Saturday, Bill took the kids for a drive around Belle Isle, a park on an island in the middle of the Detroit River. He had spent many enjoyable days there while growing up. Returning to his house in a roundabout way, he drove down Lake Shore drive and along the Grosse Pointe coastline of Lake St. Clair. It was always a drive that Debbie enjoyed, especially looking at the spectacular mansions along the lakefront. After dropping the kids off at home, he did his shift downtown. It was dead quiet. He and one of the secretaries, Mary Robinson, talked and watched the news.

And there was *so much* news. Since the assassination, ABC, NBC, and CBS ran nonstop coverage. No commercials. Bill took special interest in what was known about Oswald. He was just twenty-four, a former Marine who had defected to the Soviet Union. *A big red flag.* He had left Russia with a young wife and lived in the Dallas area. Bill expected more news on Oswald as interrogations should last for weeks.

For his birthday the previous September, Bill's mother-in-law had given him the book, *Seven Days in May*, a book about a military coup to replace the president of the United States. Bill enjoyed reading, but never seemed to carve out enough time to read many books, so he brought it from home thinking there might enough dead time to open it up. After the first couple of hours, Reed Clark called to check in. With not much to do and no interest in looking at his in-basket, Bill began reading the political thriller.

On Sunday morning, Bill and the family drove over to his parents' place. When Bill entered the house, Jimmy gave his son a bear hug in sympathy for the fallen president. His mom did the same thing. They all headed downstairs to the finished basement, where his mom and Anne later brought down an egg casserole and other food. The TV was on, as it likely was in most houses in America.

Jimmy said, "They are moving Oswald to the Dallas County jail soon. I want to watch it."

Jimmy, Bill, and the two kids remained in the basement, watching TV while the women cleaned up the dishes. Three-year-old Debbie loved climbing on her grandfather's lap when he was in his easy chair. The mood was somber, even with the children babbling.

A little after noon, the TV stations turned their coverage to the basement of the Dallas police station. The TV camera was focused on a hallway in the apparent direction of the building's elevators. Around twelve-fifteen, there seemed to be more activity in the hallway as the TV announcer said Oswald was on his way. A few minutes later, Oswald came into view, escorted by two Dallas police officers, both clutching one of his arms. Oswald was walking toward the camera. Suddenly, a man walked quickly up to Oswald, a handgun flashing in his right hand, then the muffled sound of a gunshot echoing through the hallway was heard by millions of television viewers. Oswald grimaced in pain and doubled over. Pandemonium broke out.

Jimmy reacted first. "Jesus Christ! Did you see that?"

"I saw it, but I don't believe it." Bill had never seen anything like this before in his life. A murder on live television. The announcers, likewise, could not believe what they had witnessed. After a few minutes of shocked silence, Bill excused himself to call the office on the upstairs phone. Maggie answered.

"Did you see it?" he asked.

"Yes," she said, sounding out of breath. "I can't believe it. Do you want to talk to Joe?"

"Bishop or Kowalski?"

"Bishop."

"Put him on."

Bishop was as dumbfounded as everyone else. After they both reviewed what they saw, Joe said, "Bill, you know we just lost the most important witness to the biggest murder since Lincoln."

"Yeah, I know."

"Right before you called, it occurred to me that our office has been absolutely dead this weekend. We are just sitting around. The networks keep playing Oswald talking to the press over and over. I was thinking it might make sense to try and transcribe everything he's saying publicly to see if it gives us any clues to responsibility. What do you think?"

"Joe, it's a great idea. I'd double-check it with Reed. But now, more than ever, we need to know what Oswald has been saying. I'm sure they will be replaying the tape of Oswald's comments."

"Good. I'll give Clark a call right now. When do you come in?"

"Midnight."

"I'll leave a copy for you. Do you mind keeping an eye on the tube and seeing if you can add to or clean up anything in my draft?"

"No problem," Bill replied. By the time Bill got to the office just before midnight, Oswald had been dead for hours. Bill reviewed the product Joe and Maggie had created as he kept an eye on the television. It seemed, about every couple of hours, the networks returned to the Oswald shooting and then replayed Oswald's comments from the time he arrived at the police station. Bill and Ethel Polk, the secretary assigned to his shift, continued to review and improve the transcript.

Bill and Ethel developed a routine. Both sat around the TV, listening for Oswald's tapes or any other news of interest. When something of value came on, she and Bill each tried to transcribe it the best that they could. Even with that, Bill had plenty of time to listen to additional news analysis, now focusing more on Monday's funeral than the Oswald killing. Bill had time to read and finish his book, *Seven Days in May,* by the time his shift ended.

Chapter Eleven
The Aftermath

Reed Clark convened a staff meeting Monday morning. Sitting at the head of the conference table, he said, "Let me begin by saying we are still not getting much in the way of communication from Washington. Again, I think they've been pretty damned busy with all that's been going on there and in Dallas. My understanding is that there are a hell of a lot of dignitaries in DC for the funeral. I'm sure there are all kinds of security issues being addressed. Nonetheless, I've been forwarding our activities to headquarters. They are particularly pleased with our efforts to alert border crossing officials to any unusual activity—good work to all of you who participated in this effort.

"Now I don't have to tell you that this has been one of the most unusual weekends we've ever been through. Part of what made it unique was the fact that a prime suspect had so much conversation with reporters. In the end, this availability may have cost Oswald his life and, since there will be no trial, we may never know what happened on Friday."

Reed went on to thank Joe and Maggie for transcribing everything Oswald said.

"This was a great idea and great work that I know several of you helped with. I've sent this memo to headquarters this morning."

Then Reed opened a folder and passed out copies of the memo to the agents. "Take a moment to read this."

Bill read the memo. It was from Joe Bishop to Reed Clark. The subject line said: "Words of Lee Harvey Oswald November 22-24."

Friday, November 22, 1963

3:54 p.m. (CST): NBC newsman Bill Ryan reported that "Lee Oswald seems to be the prime suspect in the assassination of John F. Kennedy."

6:30 p.m.: Oswald being moved from a lineup of witnesses. He yelled to reporters present in a Dallas police station hallway, "I want to get in touch with a lawyer, Mr. Abt, in New York City. I never killed anybody."

7:50 p.m.: Oswald says, "I'd like to get legal representation. Police officers have not allowed me to have any. In fact, I don't know what this is all about."

Reporter yells: "Did you kill the president?"

Oswald: "I work in that building."

Reporter: "Were you in the building at the time?"

Oswald: "Well, naturally, if I work in the building, yes sir. They've taken me in because I visited in the Soviet Union. I'm just a patsy."

11:20 p.m.: The police allowed Oswald to participate in a press conference. These are his quotes:

"A cop hit me," when asked about his black eye. When discussing his arraignment, Oswald said, "Well, I was questioned by Judge Johnston. However, I protested at that time that I was not allowed legal representation during that very short and sweet hearing. I really don't know what the situation is about. Nobody has told me anything except that I am accused of murdering a policeman. I know nothing more than that. And I do request someone to come forward to give me legal assistance."

Oswald was asked if he killed the president. "No. I have not been charged with that. In fact, nobody has said that to me yet. The first thing I heard about it was when the newspaper reporters in the hall asked me that question. I did not do it. I did not do it. I did not shoot anyone."

Oswald was kept away from reporters on Saturday, November 23, and most of Sunday morning on November 24, until 11:15 a.m., when he was escorted to the basement of the police station. Reporters, as well as Jack Ruby, were waiting for him, but Oswald made no comments before he was shot.

Lee Harvey Oswald statistics:

Age: 24

Height: 5'9"Weight: 140

Military Service: enlisted October 24, 1956, at age 17. He became a radar operator and was granted security clearance. On July 9, 1957, was assigned to Marine Air Squadron 1 at the Naval Air Facility at Atsugi, Japan. He was demoted from Private First Class to Private after shooting himself. On September 11, 1959, he received a hardship discharge from active service.

Russia: Traveled to the Soviet Union in October 1959. On October 31, he went to the American Embassy and renounced his US citizenship. He was sent to Minsk. On May 24, 1962, he went to the American Embassy wanting to return to the US with his new wife and infant daughter. On June 1, 1962, the American Embassy gave Oswald and family permission to return to the United States.

"Well, this is a hell of a summary." Reed said. "Great job. I sure would like to know what he said in the interrogation sessions. I doubt that he confessed. If he had, I suspect we would have heard about it by now."

Reed concluded the meeting, saying that the TV would be set up in the interrogation room.

"Feel free to watch the funeral. Anything related to the assassination is a top priority. If something breaks, let me know. Other than that, return to your regular assignments," he said. "We will be back to work as normal tomorrow morning."

That night, Bill lay in bed, wide awake. Around two a.m. he finally dozed until a thought flashed across his mind: *Vallee and Oswald, the similarities are incredible. Is it coincidence?*

With his heart pounding, Bill quietly got out of bed and moved to the living room, where he could pace and think. Both Vallee and Oswald enlisted in the Marines and served at US air bases in Japan during the fifties. Both were slight men, well under six feet. Both had black hair. Both worked in warehouses and were apparent drifters. Vallee had an interest in Castro's Cuba, although appearing to serve different perspectives. Oswald had an interest in the Soviets. Vallee might have been a pawn for the four men identified as planning the Chicago JFK hit. Oswald said to reporters that he was a patsy. Both were in the city where JFK was to be assassinated: in Chicago, the plot failed; in Dallas an assassination succeeded.

Bill sat in his favorite chair. His breathing relaxed as he identified what had been nagging him all day since he read the Oswald transcripts. He knew these were probable coincidences, but what if they weren't? What if it was a plan, a plan by dangerous forces?

He needed to talk with Reed Clark. Not tomorrow, but maybe on Wednesday or Friday. The office was closed on Thursday for Thanksgiving. A couple of days to get his thoughts in order and, perhaps, he could glean more information from newspapers or around the office. Feeling more comfortable, he returned to the bedroom and fell into a deep sleep.

Chapter Twelve
Questions

Bill and his family spent Thanksgiving Day with his parents. Like most Americans, this Thanksgiving was a time of mourning their lost president. Still, normal life was beginning to return. Bill was pleased to learn that his dad had accepted a job as a UAW international representative for Ken Morris, the man he had met at Cupids. This was a big deal in Jimmy's career, and Bill was happy for him.

On Friday morning just after ten, Bill stuck his head into Reed Clark's office. "Reed, have you got a few minutes?"

His boss looked up from reading what looked like a report. "Sure, Bill, you know Fridays after Thanksgiving are as slow as it gets." Clark motioned him to a small, two-chair conference table in the corner of his office. Apparently sensing this might be a confidential conversation, Clark closed his office door before he joined Bill at the table. "So, what's up?"

Bill had a manila folder that contained a draft memorandum and a few notes, along with the transcript of Oswald's public statements from the Bishop memo. He explained the coincidences between Dallas and Chicago that had bothered him. Clark listened intently.

When Bill finished, Clark said, "Yep, this is worth a couple of minutes. Bill, you know, we have no idea what Oswald said while the Dallas police interrogated him. There might have been a local FBI agent there, but I don't know if anyone was there from our agency."

"Is there a way to find out?"

"Yeah, maybe. I've worked with the Dallas Secret Service chief a couple of times. I will try to reach him and see what he knows."

Bill raised an eyebrow. "Aren't you going out of protocol?"

"Perhaps. But for right now, I'd like to keep this informal. I don't know what apple carts we might be overturning."

"Yeah, I know."

"Okay, then," Clark said. "Don't know if I'll make contact today, but I'll let you know when I hear something."

On Monday, December 2, Clark walked into Bill's office. "I made contact with Dallas today. I was pretty much told to keep my nose out of

Dallas. Regarding the interrogations, I did learn they had no idea what had gone on, but a Dallas FBI agent attended some, if not most, of the interrogations. Of course, had Oswald lived, all the information from the interrogations would have been available in a courtroom. Still, I'm going to send the info to DC. They should evaluate it."

The next morning, Bill was at his desk when the phone rang. The receptionist said the caller did not want to give his name. This was common, as many tipsters and informants did not want to leave their names. The call was buzzed through, and Bill answered.

"Yep, hi Bill. It's Fred Fry."

"Fred, how're you doing?"

"I'm fine. Things are kind of back to normal. But, hey, are you open for lunch?"

"Sure, where do you want to go?"

"I'll meet you at Lafayette Coney Island at twelve-thirty."

"No problem, I'll see you then."

The restaurant was a cramped little diner with a counter and about ten tables scattered about. Fred was already at a corner table when Bill arrived. This was a public place, so it could not be much of a confidential meeting. Bill shook Fred's hand and sat down opposite him. They talked about the assassination for a time before they were interrupted by a Greek waiter. A moment later, the waiter yelled in heavily accented English, "Four Coneys, one fry, two Cokes!" and walked away.

Fred spoke softly, "Listen, Bill, I've got some information I think you guys ought to have. When we leave, I will slip you a copy of a short memo that we wrote up for Hoover—you know, he sees everything."

"Fred, are you sure you want to do this?" Why on earth would Fred want to slip him what might be overly sensitive information in such a public place?

"Bill, you bet I want to share this. It could be a lead and, if so, it's important to get it to the right people."

"Okay, but why here? There are no secrets in this place," Bill said, looking around.

Fred smiled. "Yeah, I know. Such a public place, it's my cover. After all, who would be stupid enough to talk about, let alone give someone sensitive information, in a place like this?" They both laughed.

Speaking in a low voice, Fred said, "Last week, our office received a call from a Windsor attorney. He said he has it from an unconfirmed source that Lee Oswald had, in the not-too-distant past, been to Montreal and Quebec and that he engaged in "Ban the Bomb" protests. He could not give us exact dates, nor any names other than Oswald. Still, I know someone is piecing together information on the movements of this guy, and I wanted your office to know what was going on."

Before Bill could respond, the waiter brought their orders.

"This sounds interesting," Bill said after the waiter had left. "You're right, we have been doing some of our own research on Oswald. This could come in handy."

The men spoke in whispers as they ate in the small dining area with the noise of other conversations filling the room. When they finished, they walked out together and Fred unobtrusively handed an envelope to Bill, who casually slipped it into the inside pocket of his suit jacket.

Back at the office, Joe Kowalski, almost out of breath, stopped by Bill's office. "Bill, our Ontario contact got back to us. He is telecopying some information about Oswald being in Canada."

Bill blinked. "What's he sending?"

"I don't know exactly—he didn't want to go over details on the phone."

"Okay, bring it to me as soon as you get it."

Joe left the room, and Bill pulled out the envelope Fry had given him. In it was a clean white page that had been teletyped to FBI Director J. Edgar Hoover from the Detroit office, dated November 27, 1963. The subject was, "Assassination of President Kennedy, Dallas, Texas, November Twenty Two." It read:

> Today, Roger L. Williams, Attorney, Windsor, Ontario, telephonically advised field agent Fred Fry that he had heard a rumor from unconfirmed source that Lee H. Oswald had at some unspecified date been in Montreal, Quebec, engaged in "Ban-the-Bomb" protests. He advised he could not recall the original sources and had no further information in his possession regarding this nor did he have further information concerning captioned matter.

About ten minutes later, Joe returned with some paper. Bill quickly scanned it. One page was a bad copy of a newspaper clipping from *The Montreal Star*. The article was titled, "Oswald Connection?" The article said that Lee Oswald had been in Montreal and participated in a "Ban-the-Bomb" demonstration the previous summer and that some of these demonstrations were in front of the United States Consulate.

The second document was a single-page memorandum from the American Consul in Montreal to the State Department. It referenced the newspaper clipping and provided information that a US Customs official had been contacted by several people stating that Oswald had been in Montreal the previous summer, passing out "Fair Play for Cuba" pamphlets. Several people, including US government officials, identified Oswald along with a short, homely, heavy woman and two other men about Oswald's age and size.

Bill put the documents on his desk. He looked up at Joe. The young man's face was full of excitement. Bill quickly decided to protect his young colleague.

Joe, beginning to show some doubt in his face, said, "Aren't we going to take it to the chief?"

"I'll do that a little later," Bill said, in essence dismissing him.

Clearly upset, Joe walked out of the office. He wanted to be with Bill when he shared it with Clark, but Bill knew it was possible this research on Oswald could blow up in their faces. He thought the fewer involved the better. Why risk too many careers?

Bill waited fifteen minutes, then reread the documents. The coincidence was stunning. This information didn't have anything to do with his theory, but it did demonstrate that Oswald apparently had the money and time to travel from Texas to Montreal for one or two demonstrations. He got up and went to Clark's office.

When Reed finished going over Bill's report, Reed emitted a low whistle. "Wow, there seems to be more and more to this case. A lone assassin? I'm not so sure anymore. You know, with the president creating a commission to look at the assassination, these people are going to need all the information they can get. I'm going to write up your concerns of Oswald's Canadian travel into a memorandum to headquarters. I suspect they already have assumed or learned of this information, but I don't want it to fall through the cracks. Macalister is smart. He'll figure this stuff out."

"Sounds good," Bill said. "Also, sir, Joe Kowalski is pretty pissed off at me. He has done some good work getting this information." He nodded toward the documents on Clark's desk. "He wanted to be here when I briefed you. I don't know, Reed, but I just thought the fewer involved the better. I don't know where this thing is headed."

"Yeah, I get your point. Kowalski is young. He'll learn. I'll talk to him."

"Thanks."

PART III ~ 1964
Chapter Thirteen
The Set-up

Talk of the assassination and Oswald gradually declined. Bill and Anne prepared for Christmas. Debbie was so excited about Santa Claus she could hardly contain herself. Johnny was too young to appreciate all the anticipation, but he seemed to know something different was happening. At lunch hour, Bill bought gifts at Hudson's department store. The day after Christmas, Reed Clark buzzed him and asked him to come to his office. "What's up, Reed? Did you have a good Christmas?"

Reed dismissed his question with a frown. "Close the door," he said abruptly before motioning Bill to the conference table.

As they sat down, Reed reached into his shirt pocket for a cigarette and offered one to Bill, which he accepted. After both lit up, Reed said, "I just got off the telephone with Macallister. As of the first of the year, I've been reassigned to run the Albuquerque, New Mexico, office."

"What?" Bill responded, "I didn't know we had an office in Albuquerque."

"Yeah, it's a two-man, one-secretary office."

"Jesus Christ, what the hell is this about?"

"The memos I sent in November. They're not happy. They didn't have a problem with what we did with Canada. In fact, they complimented our initiative there. The problem was the Oswald/Vallee memo. They were upset that I put anything in writing referencing Chicago and a potential assassination attempt. Mac made it clear that absolutely no mention of the Chicago incident was ever to be made. I knew that, but I thought that after November 22, all bets were off regarding Chicago."

"Did they say anything about me, Bishop, or anyone else?"

"No, but I don't know that that means anything. Joe might be on the short list to replace me, so that's good news," Reed said, taking a drag on his Lucky Strike. "Mac mentioned him, but said they might bring in someone from outside, so that's a loose end that needs to be figured out."

"What about the wife and kids?"

"Well, I haven't talked to Sharon yet. I think this will be a difficult move. She may want to stay here to finish out the school year. I don't know; we'll see."

"Reed, this is really shitty. You're doing your job and doing it well."

"Thanks Bill. You're a good agent but keep your nose down. I didn't use your name, but headquarters will probably figure it out, if they want. Or maybe I'm just some type of scapegoat. I don't know. Maybe after a few years of purgatory, I'll be able to redeem my career." Clark put his cigarette out in the ashtray.

"Reed, you're a great boss. If there's anything Anne or I can do, just let us know."

The shaken man looked Bill in the eyes. "Thanks Bill, I appreciate that."

Bill walked back to his office feeling like someone had slugged him in the stomach with a baseball bat. He had really come to know, like, and respect Reed Clark. He had never been through an office shake-up, so this was new. Plus, he felt guilty. If he had not raised the Oswald/Vallee links, Reed might never have been transferred and, for all practical purposes, demoted. Still, Reed seemed to have successfully kept Bill's name out of the issue.

***

Joe Bishop was appointed acting chief of the Detroit Office toward the end of the first week in January. He was a bit younger than a typical chief, but he was well liked, a professional, and Bill had come to appreciate him during their Chicago assignment.

On January 23, a Thursday, Bishop buzzed Bill and asked him to come by his office. Outside of normal business meetings and Bill congratulating him on his promotion, there had not been much communication between the two. Bill was hoping the meeting might lead to another assignment, as he was wrapping up the frigid Upper Peninsula counterfeiting case without having to make a trip to the UP. Joe had rearranged his office since Clark had been transferred. Instead of meeting at the small conference table, Joe had a couple of chairs opposite his desk. He indicated Bill should take one of the seats. Joe took an extra minute to finish reading a report before he looked up at Bill with a frown. "Bill, this is awkward as hell, but I have an unpleasant chore to do. Effective immediately, you are suspended, with pay, from duties," he said.

Bill felt every muscle in his body tense as beads of sweat began to break out on his temple and forehead. He started to speak, but Joe motioned him to hold his thoughts.

"Let me finish. On Monday, investigators are going to be here for a series of interviews. I don't know what they have, but it relates to the Windsor counterfeiting case from '62 and '63."

Bill thought that was a clear-cut case. He instantly knew he had done nothing wrong. "Joe, I don't know what the hell this is about, but I ran that case by the book."

"Bill, I don't know the details, but I know this is serious shit. I probably shouldn't be saying this, but if I were you, I'd get a good lawyer—a criminal lawyer."

"Jesus Christ, this can't be happening!"

"Bill, spend tomorrow and the weekend going through everything you can on the case. You can't take anything home, but search your memory on everything. I don't want to embarrass you, but I need your key to the office, your gun, and badge. I'm going to have Maggie walk with you back to your office and escort you out as quietly as possible. You can take only your personal belongings, no files or anything that belongs here in the office. Let's not make a big deal out of this."

"Not a big deal?" Bill repeated.

"Well, I only meant getting you out of the office without any unnecessary embarrassment."

"Oh," Bill said, only half listening, then adding, "Can I bring my attorney Monday?"

"No, no attorney at the internal hearing. I just think you need to get someone if this case goes to trial. Now, get out of here and let's hope this thing blows over."

Bill left the lobby elevator wondering what he was going to do. He did not want to go home so early in the day. Spying the bank of pay phones he had walked by for years and never used, he reached in his pocket and felt for a dime. A moment later, he was put through to his father, who was in the third week of his new job at the UAW's Solidarity House headquarters.

"Dad," Bill said, his voice starting to break, "I'm in trouble."

"Son, Jesus Christ, whatever it is, I'm here," Jimmy replied, instantly recognizing the tension in his son's voice.

"Dad, I can't believe it—you won't believe it—but I've been suspended from the Service, and I have a hearing on Monday. I was advised to get a lawyer, but the only criminal lawyers I know aren't the kind of men I'd ever associate with."

"Alright, Bill, let me think. You're at your office, right?"

"Yeah, in the lobby."

"Okay, jump in your car and come down here. When you get inside, you'll see a desk on the upstairs landing. Just ask for me."

"Are you sure? I can wait until after work."

"No, get over here now. There might be some people here who can give us advice."

Twenty minutes later, Bill was standing in the lobby of the UAW international headquarters. His dad emerged from a side door and the two of them embraced. "I don't know what's going on," Jimmy said, "but you know I'll do my damnedest to help. I know you'd never do anything wrong."

"Thanks, Dad, but this could be a problem we can't talk our way out of." Jimmy escorted his son through a hallway of small, partitioned offices.

"This is my office," Jimmy said, motioning him inside the small room.

There was enough room for a desk and a couple of chairs for visitors—certainly not plush, but very functional. Bill told his father the reason he was suspended.

"Listen, Bill," Jimmy said, "I'm not sure exactly where to go with this thing. My boss, Ken Morris, is in his office. He's worked with lawyers his entire career. He was once beaten up, almost to death, by some of the toughest customers in Detroit. I thought he might be a good sounding board for you. Is this okay?"

"Dad, I'm still in shock—"

"I know," Jimmy cut in, "but you did say you probably needed a lawyer, and there is a meeting on Monday. I think time is of the essence. It sure as hell looks to me like you're being railroaded."

"Yeah, I know. Okay, let's go see Mr. Morris."

The two walked down the hall, passing similar, cramped offices. At the end of the hall, they entered a small office with three secretaries working at desks. Jimmy said, "Marge, is Ken available? He's expecting me."

The woman with the flaming red hair responded in a raspy voice: "Go right in. He's waiting for you."

They walked into a corner office, with windows on two sides of the room offering views of the Detroit River and Belle Isle. The smaller, balding, middle-aged man in his shirtsleeves was behind a large desk, talking on the phone. With a welcoming hand, he motioned the two men toward a couch.

Bill gazed around the room, taking in the photos of politicians and labor leaders, all smiling and shaking hands. A few framed family photos were arranged on a credenza behind the desk. Piles of papers, manila files, and other paper indicated that Morris was a busy person who could never quite get caught up. Minutes later, Morris ended the call with a polite goodbye.

He walked over and shook Bill's hand. "I remember you. We met a couple of months ago at Cupids, right?"

"Yes, that's right," Bill responded as Morris pulled up a chair.

"Bill, Jimmy told me that you have problems, but he didn't have much information. I don't know if I can help or not, but why don't you tell me what you can."

"Thanks, Mr. Morris."

Morris raised a hand and stopped him. In a soft, friendly voice, he said, "Bill, I'm Ken."

With Jimmy smiling broadly, Bill began his story. He reviewed the Deadeye case and explained everything he could in about fifteen minutes, with the other men occasionally asking a question. Morris gave Bill his full attention.

When he concluded, Morris said, "Well, this is one hell of a story, and it's way out of my league." Bill deflated, but the labor leader continued, "Your dad said you don't have an attorney, and it sounds like you may need one."

"Maybe not immediately, but I will need someone soon."

"Okay, I work with the Roth Law firm. They generally handle labor issues, but they do broader stuff, too. If they don't do criminal law, they might be able to recommend someone. I'd like to call them if it's okay with you."

Bill blanched when he heard the reference to criminal law, but found himself saying, "That's fine."

Morris went to the door and called out: "Get me Charlie Martin!"

By the time he returned to his desk, a buzzer went off on his phone. He picked it up. Morris was soon speaking to a man like intimate old friends, and it did not take much time for them to get down to business. "Okay," Morris said, "why don't we do Cupids at three-thirty? There won't be many people there, so we can talk. Okay, hold on a moment." Morris looked at Jimmy and Bill and said, "Can you guys make a 3:30 at Cupids?" The Simpson men nodded. Walking them to the office door, Morris said, "Okay, Charlie Martin, who's one of the top attorneys in Detroit, is going to meet with us. He's not sure he can help directly, but he wants to hear your story and, one way or another, he will recommend someone you can trust."

As they passed through the outer office, Morris said, "Marge, call Pat and tell him I need to cancel my four o'clock meeting with the Local 212 guys. See if they can meet me at Cupids tomorrow morning at seven-thirty."

Bill was surprised by what he heard. This busy man, whom he really didn't know, was cancelling a meeting just for him.

Bill hung out with his father the rest of the afternoon. He tried calling Anne several times but there was no answer. She was probably at her mother's house. He didn't want to call her there. This was too personal and too sudden.

Jimmy and Bill waited in the car at the Cupids parking lot until Ken showed up. Jimmy did not want to walk in until Ken was there to introduce them to the lawyer. Ken showed up about ten minutes late, driving his tan, 1962 Chrysler New Yorker. The three walked into Cupids and headed into the dining room. Right away, Ken waved to Charlie Martin, who was seated in the back corner.

Martin, a tall man in his late forties with a winning grin, was wearing a bow tie and a pompadour haircut. The waitress brought coffee as another man appeared. He seemed animated and full of energy as he greeted Ken. The labor leader introduced Danny Masouris, owner of the restaurant. The short, friendly man seemed to know this was a business meeting and immediately excused himself. Bill had the feeling Cupids was like a second office for Morris.

Bill took about twenty minutes explaining the case, the potential charges and the internal discipline process. Bill told Charlie about Monday's meeting with investigators and that he could be charged and go to trial.

Charlie had not said much up to this point. "So," he said, "do you think you need an attorney by Monday?"

"I'm very sure that attorneys are not allowed in this session," Bill replied.

"But you're not positive?"

"No, but I could find out."

Charlie thought on that. "No, that's okay." His dark blue eyes veered to Ken. "Ken, do you know Bernie Levine?"

"No, I don't think so."

"Well, you'd remember him if you met him. He's a short fellow, with long hair, horn-rimmed glasses, clothes that look like they haven't been to the cleaners in a year, and possibly that was the last time he saw a bath." Charlie laughed at his own observation. "But, he's one hell of a criminal lawyer, especially public corruption. He's had clients from both sides of the street. I thought of him because I know he has defended, and defended successfully, Detroit cops. And, twenty-five or thirty years ago, he was a US attorney—during the Roosevelt years. He's got an office in the Michigan Theater Building."

Ken turned to Bill: "What do you think?"

"Well, to be honest, I'm not sure what to think. My head's still spinning. How much will this cost?"

Charlie stepped up. "Well, we charge thirty-five dollars an hour, but we have a lot of overhead. Bernie doesn't have any of what we have—you'll know what I mean when you walk into his office."

Ken looked at Charlie, and with a smile, said, "Sounds like I should go to Bernie instead of you guys. I didn't realize how expensive you guys are."

Charlie ignored Ken's friendly jab and kept his focus on Bill. "All I can say is that many of Bernie's clients come from your income bracket. Whatever the costs, I think he'll work with you."

Charlie asked Bill a few more questions before asking, "Do you want me to give Bernie a call? He might have time tomorrow. If nothing else, he can give you some pointers regarding your Monday meeting."

Bill looked over at his dad, who nodded. "Yeah, that would be great if you could make contact."

Charlie went over to the pay phones near the restrooms and made a call. When he returned, he asked Bill, "What are you doing around ten tomorrow morning?"

"I think I'm meeting with Bernie Levine."

Charlie smiled, then turned serious. "Let me ask you something, Bill. If you, in fact, didn't do anything wrong in this case, could it be something else? Is this another way to get at you? Are you being set up?

Bill thought of Reed's memo and transfer. "It's possible."

"Well," Charlie said, "make sure you raise the issue with Bernie."

When they adjourned, Ken picked up the tab, and Bill thanked both Ken and Charlie.

As he drove the short distance home, Bill felt slightly better since Bishop had delivered the stunning blow. He prepared himself for the oncoming, difficult discussion with Anne. He never knew what to expect from her; there were times she was supportive of him and his career, then there were days when the mere mention of work started an argument, usually about the hours he spent away from home.

When he walked into the house, he was met with general bedlam from the kids playing. Bill gave each child a big hug and kiss. He gave his wife a short hug and kiss. She asked him to watch the kids while she finished getting dinner ready. When dinner was long over and the kids were in bed, the TV played softly in the background. *Rawhide* was just starting. The time had come to open up to his wife.

"Hon, something really bad happened at work today. We have to talk."

After the kids were put down, it was usually Anne's time to relax. Tonight, she was looking at the *Detroit Free Press*. She put the paper down and said, "Bad news? You aren't being transferred, are you?"

"No, I don't think that will be the issue."

She studied him. "Well, if we don't have to move, it can't be that terrible."

"It is. I was called into Joe Bishop's office today. Apparently, they think that I did something wrong regarding the Windsor counterfeiting case from a year or so ago."

She looked at him with a blank stare. "Bill, I don't know anything about a Windsor case. You never tell me anything about work."

"Well, they suspended me from work today. In fact, I spent most of the day with Dad and Ken Morris. Mr. Morris met with us, set up a meeting with his lawyer, and his lawyer recommended a criminal lawyer that I'm going to see tomorrow."

Anne's face flushed. "A criminal lawyer? Jesus, Bill what have you done?"

"I've done nothing, not a goddamned thing, except do my job."

"You said 'suspended,' not 'fired.' What does that mean?"

"I'm not sure. I am suspended, with pay, for now. There is a hearing on Monday morning where I will learn more about what this is all about.

It's possible I could be fired, perhaps demoted. Shit, I don't know, maybe transferred, like they did to Reed. Or they could charge me with something. I just don't know."

"And you don't know what you did? You must have done something?"

Bill was growing irritated at her barrage of questions. "Anne, I don't think I've done anything wrong. I've worked on these types of cases throughout my career. I've never had any questions from my bosses or anyone else about what I've done. Almost all my cases have led to convictions. I don't have a goddamned thing to hide. Believe me, I'm as bewildered and scared as you."

They talked back and forth until ten. She went to bed with a disgusted look, and he stared at the black-and-white TV. He flipped the station to Channel 4 and stared blankly at *The Edie Adams Show* as he began backtracking his actions on the Windsor case. In his mind, he followed every major step and had taken appropriate action. There was nothing wrong. Sure, there were things he might have done differently, with 20/20 hindsight. But, overall, he thought it was one of his best cases. At eleven-thirty he watched Johnny Carson's monologue before heading to bed. Anne was on her side, her back to him, sleeping near the edge of the bed.

Chapter Fourteen
The Lawyer

Bill parked in the underground garage at Grand Circus Park in downtown Detroit the next morning and walked the two blocks to the Michigan Theater. The forty-year-old building had an ornate movie theater and a separate thirteen-story office building. Its best days had come and gone. A glassed-framed menu on a wall listed the lawyers, dentists, and other professionals in the office building. He located the "Bernie Levine Law Office" on the fifth floor. Bill could feel his heart beating as he approached Levine's office door.

He entered a small reception office. The secretary, an attractive, middle-aged woman with black hair, looked up from her work. "I bet you are Mr. Simpson," she said with a smile.

Bill was surprised and comforted by her demeanor and smiled back. "You guessed it."

Bill sat down on a wooden business chair while the women went to get the lawyer. The room was not what he expected—yes, it was a bit disheveled but looked as if people were just too busy to take care of the finer details of maintaining office space. Soon, the rear door opened, and a short man in his sixties appeared. He was, as Martin indicated, sporting shirtsleeves, his shirt was half sticking out of his trousers, suspenders, and a loosened tie. His secretary was right behind him.

"Bill Simpson! I'm Bernie Levine. Good to meet you. And, like I tell all my potential clients, call me Bernie."

Bill, surprised by the informality, rose and shook the man's hand. "Good to meet you Mr.—eh, Bernie."

"Good. Come on in." Bernie turned to his secretary. "Shirley, bring in a few cookies."

They walked into the Bernie's spacious office. Tables and chairs were randomly stationed around the room, many of them piled with stacks of documents and newspapers. The lawyer noticed Bill looking around. "Bill," he said, "I'm not your typical attorney, as you'll see. By way of example, Shirley makes great chocolate chip cookies. To control my impulses and my waistline, whenever a potential new client comes in for a visit, we use that as an excuse to have some cookies, so thanks for coming in."

As if on cue, the door opened, and Shirley placed a tray with five cookies on a coffee table in front of a couch, then brought in a pot of coffee and cups. "Let me know if you boys need anything," she said as she walked out and closed the door.

"Bill, sit down on the sofa. I'll just pull up a chair, here," Bernie said as he dragged a chair to the coffee table. He caught Bill again examining the office. "You know, some first-timers come into the office here and think we are a disorganized operation. In fact, it's not so. Each pile of material you see on these tables represents ongoing cases. Rather than close things up, I keep my files out and, shall we say, in a vertical file. When we close the case, we file the case material in an appropriate place.

"Before we get to your case, tell me about your family, where you live, how long you've been with the Secret Service and then, what the hell happened to you."

Bill liked the man. He reviewed his situation as Bernie started on the cookies. Forty-five minutes later, the cookie plate was empty.

"Interesting story," Bernie concluded as he brushed crumbs off his shirt. "Sounds to me like you're being set up. Someone is out to get you, either from your office or from somewhere else. This could be bad, but it sounds like you have an excellent record."

Bill nodded."Look, I know I'm the first attorney you've talked to," Bernie added. "You should go visit some others. It won't hurt my feelings. I'll tell you up front, I don't charge as much as some of the big boys around town. They are good, but they are more expensive. I know I'm as good as anyone in the city, but I operate from a different paradigm. I'm not out to make a lot of money or have a lot of attorneys work for me. My wife and I have lived in a house for twenty-five years in northwest Detroit. I've been here, in this office, for about fifteen years, and it's just Shirley and me, plus some occasional help—expert witnesses, detective work, and so on. Overall, my overhead costs aren't high. I charge twenty-two dollars an hour. You will be billed every other week and, if you have any trouble making payments, let me know—we will work something out."

Bernie rose, and Bill followed the lawyer's lead.

"Bernie, I don't need to talk to other lawyers, I'm comfortable with you," Bill said.

There was a slight moment of satisfaction on Bernie's face before he replied, "Good. I'll have Shirley put some papers together, and let's sit down and talk some strategy."

They talked for another twenty minutes before Bernie said, "This meeting on Monday, I think I should be there."

"I don't think that's a good idea. They won't let you attend the meeting. It's supposed to be me and the investigators."

"Well, I'll tell you what, what if I just showed up? If they don't let me in, they don't let me in. On the other hand, they just might. If not, then we can meet right afterward."

"No," Bill said, "To be frank, I have some friends, or at least I think I have some friends, in that office. I really don't want to piss them off."

Bernie thought about that for a second. "You know, you are probably right. I just hate like hell to see you go into a meeting not being represented."

"That's okay. I think I can handle myself."

"Alright," said the attorney. "I'm going to have to review every single detail after the meeting. In time, there will be discovery and I'll see all their documents, assuming they take something to court. But I want to know every single one of your strengths and weaknesses as we move forward. No lies, no half-truths. Got it?"

"Yep, I'll be straight with you."

"Good, go home and begin writing down everything you know about this case. We can make changes after Monday morning's meeting. When you get over here, we will have a better chance of knowing what the hell is going on."

"Bernie, this sounds great, thank you so much." Looking around the office, Bill considered that the files on the small tables represented other people's lives, and now his life was about to become a new pile. When he emerged into the waiting area, another anxious client was waiting.

***

Bill walked into his old office on Monday morning just before nine. There were a couple of awkward acknowledgments, but no one came over to say hello or chat. Obviously, word had spread that he was now persona non grata.

He entered the conference room. Joe Bishop was at the table with two men he did not know and a female court reporter. Joe gave Bill a neutral look as he rose from the conference table. "Bill, good to see you.

Let me introduce you to agents Williams and Jolly. Taking the minutes is Mrs. Helen Stone."

"I will let you guys get down to work," Joe said. "If you need anything, let me or Maggie know." He walked out, closing the door softly behind him.

The men sat, Williams and Jolly on one side of the conference table, Bill on the other.

Williams began. "Agent Simpson, we are convening this hearing after reports have been received regarding several irregularities that occurred during the 1962-63 counterfeiting case number A482491. While this is an official hearing, we will try to be as informal as possible. If it's alright with you, why don't you give us a summary of the case and review your activities regarding it?"

Bill, feeling his heart pounding, said, "Yes, that's fine. I kind of expected you might ask something like this, so I made some notes over the weekend. Is it okay if I refer to them?"

Williams nodded.

Bill reached down to his thin portfolio and fumbled for his yellow pad. God, he was nervous. Maybe it was because someone was transcribing the meeting, which only served to emphasize that this official record might well determine his future. Within the first few minutes, all three men pulled out packs of cigarettes, and smoke soon filled the room.

Bill began telling a longer version of what he had told Bernie and others the previous week. Forty-five minutes later, Bill completed his review.

"Okay, why don't we take a five-minute break," Williams said before turning to Agent Jolly and saying, "Mike, let's see if we can get some coffee in here, maybe some water."

As the door opened, the agents and court recorder left, and the heavy smoke in the room began to dissipate. Bill did not want to leave the room, so he just stood up and paced around. About ten minutes later, the meeting reconvened.

"We appreciate your testimony," Williams said after they'd all been seated again. "The only problem are the missing gaps." Bill looked puzzled, but Williams's face signaled not to interrupt. "We have a number of questions that we need answers to.

"First, can you explain why the records of the investigation indicate that $33,485 in counterfeit bills were confiscated during the investigation, yet now we find $11,500 of that amount is missing? You, Agent

Simpson, were one of the few people who had access to the evidence. What is your explanation?"

Bill was dumbfounded. "Agent Williams, I have no knowledge of any missing bills. You're looking at the wrong man. I did not take anything from the evidence cage."

"Alright, Simpson, if that's the position you are taking, it's only going to be tougher on you. Please, simply tell the truth."

"Sir, I've told the truth. There is nothing to confess."

"In late September of 1962, did you take a vacation to western states, including Colorado, Wyoming, and South Dakota?"

"Yes, my family and I took about two weeks off."

"In the middle of an investigation?"

"Sir, there is always an investigation. This case was winding down, and it was really a good time. I had leave time, and I felt it was important that my wife and I, and the kids, spend time together. We all needed a break from my routine."

Williams cast a skeptical look. "Well, I'm sure you and your wife had a swell time. Then, can you explain the counterfeit bills found in stores, restaurants, and motels in Grand Lake, Colorado, in and around Yellowstone National Park, and Rapid City, South Dakota, during this period?

Bill screwed up his face in consternation. "That's not from me. It's not possible."

"That's all you're going to say? Come on, tell us the truth. It will be easier on you."

"There's nothing to say; it's not true."

"Are you saying that no counterfeit money was found in these locations?"

"No, I'm saying I had nothing to do with it."

Williams's head shook in disgust. "Okay, that's your story. Mike, go ahead."

"Alright, Agent Simpson," Jolly started, "let me ask you, is it Secret Service policy to travel in teams, with your partner, during interviews with leads and witnesses?"

Bill's response was swift: "No, I mean yes, we should always be in teams unless there is a good reason not to."

"Okay, so can you explain why you went by yourself to question a known prostitute, a Rita Gray, who was passing around counterfeit bills?"

Bill could feel beads of sweat sprouting on his temples. "Yes, my partner, Joe Kowalski, was out—he was on his honeymoon—and I didn't want to slow the investigation down. We had a lot of work to do on this case, it was labor intensive, and we were short on bodies. I really didn't think this lead would be significant, so I made a judgment call not to pull anyone off their jobs, and I made this and several other calls on my own."

"There was no one who could go with you?"

"Like I said, we were shorthanded, I did not want to take anyone off their duties. There were a series of routine leads that needed to be followed up. I did ask the office director, Reed Clark, if it was okay and he said 'go ahead.'"

"So, this was a routine lead?"

"Well, we thought it was. As it turned out, Miss Gray's interview was the major lead that broke the case."

"So, this was not routine. Tell me, how many times did you visit this woman?"

"Once … no, twice. I had the initial meeting with her, where she provided key leads that, as I've said, broke the case wide open. Then, nearly a year later, after the investigation closed, I visited her to provide an update on the case. She was a private person and was worried her identity might become known to the mob."

"So, you say you did not want to invade the privacy of a prostitute?" Jolly asked.

"No, she had been a cooperative witness, and I wanted to respect her wishes as best as I could."

"You say you only visited her twice, both times alone?"

"Yes, just twice. The last time was a short visit on my way to work last October. I thought she should know what was happening with the case."

"So, that's all you did on these visits? Don't tell us you just talked."

"Yes. Well," as he paused, the agents leaned in to hear the next words, "and she made coffee, so we drank some coffee in her kitchen." The two men returned to the normal posture, each letting out a breath.

"That's it? And we want the truth," Jolly said.

"That's all. What are you insinuating?"

"Come on, Simpson. Isn't it true you visited her on at least five occasions? On each of these visits, didn't you engage in sexual relations with this woman?"

"No, no! Absolutely not."

"That's your story? Come on, man, do you think we're that stupid?" Williams said.

"It's the truth."

The two agents looked at each other. The atmosphere in the room was so tense, the cigarette smoke only served to enhance the feeling. "Agent Simpson, do you have anything else to say?" Williams asked.

Bill thought, his head spinning with the allegations. "No, I've told you the truth."

"Understand," Williams continued, "if you cooperate, admit to your mistakes, we can't save your job, but we can keep this case from going to trial, where you are sure to be convicted and serve time in a federal penitentiary."

"I have nothing more to add except to repeat I am innocent, and I think I'm being set up."

"With that," Williams said, "this hearing is closed. You will be hearing from the Department soon. We will give you a week to rethink this testimony and get back to us."

Bill did not shake hands or acknowledge the men. He walked out of the office and walked down to Washington Boulevard, breathing in the crisp, cold air of a January day and exhaling clouds of vapor.

He immediately went to Bernie's office and summarized the meeting for the lawyer. Bernie looked out the window for a moment, then swiveled his chair around, looking straight at Bill.

"Those sons of bitches; they are getting ready to indict you. I'm sure they're working with an existing grand jury."

"How can you be so sure?" Bill asked.

"Simple. They feel they have you on at least three counts: stealing eleven and a half thousand counterfeit dollars, disbursing counterfeit money, abusing the public trust, and possibly more. If this is it, we are dealing with circumstantial evidence."

"So, you think we can refute the charges?"

"Oh, we'll refute them. But remember, you will be facing a jury. The public is rarely sympathetic to any kind of public corruption. This hooker issue really scares the hell out of me."

Chapter Fifteen
The Blowup

The telephone rang, waking Bill from a deep sleep at six-fifteen in the morning three days after his meeting with Williams and Jolly. Bill staggered out of bed and answered.

"Bill, did you see the *Free Press* yet?" his father asked when Bill picked up.

"No, I just got out of bed."

"Put the phone down, and see if it's there."

Bill looked on the porch, then came back to the phone. "We don't have it yet. Dad, what is it?"

"Son, this is bad news. There is a front-page story. Here's the headline: 'Federal Agent in Love Nest with Prostitute' and sub-headline, 'Secret Service agent accused of stealing counterfeit money and in hooker's arms.'"

"Oh, Christ, Dad! This is all bullshit," Bill said as he glanced down the hall toward the bedroom, knowing Anne would be getting up soon. "Okay, Dad, let me throw some clothes on and get a paper. I'll call back in fifteen minutes." He hung up, not waiting for a response.

He went into the bedroom and began changing clothes.

"What's wrong?" Anne asked.

"That was Dad. The *Free Press* has a front-page story on me. It's not good. I'm going to the corner store to get the paper. I guess we will have to see what the *News* says this afternoon."

"Jesus Christ, Bill, what have you done to us?"

He did not respond as he walked quickly down the hall to the side door.

Ten minutes later, he pulled back into his driveway with copies of the *Free Press*. He walked through the side door into the kitchen. The *Free Press* must have arrived during his absence as Anne was reading the paper at the kitchen table. She looked at him, her face crunched up in cold fury. "You goddamned piece of shit!" She got up, snatched the paper, and walked toward their bedroom just as the phone rang.

Bill picked up. "Dad, it's a bad time—"

"This is Bernie. You've seen the paper? Those fucking bastards."

"Yeah, tell that to my wife," Bill responded.

"I will. Do you want me to come over?"

"Yeah, that might be a good idea. When can you get here?"

"In about forty-five minutes."

"Good, I hope she will still be here."

He walked down the hall toward their bedroom, his mind in a swirl of thoughts and emotions. He had never been the subject of a story before. He knew a few reporters around town, but did not know the reporter who wrote this story. Now, he had to focus on Anne. Hopefully, he could get her to calm down before the kids woke up. The door was shut. He opened it slowly and walked in as she was re-reading the article.

"Anne, this story is total bullshit. The Secret Service set me up. Jesus, I should have known something like this might happen."

"I don't understand you," she said, her voice on the edge of cracking as she tried to control her own emotions. "Why would you do this to me? To our kids, your parents, our friends? God, what are people going to say about us? How can I show my face? God, we will have to move to another city. It's the only way."

"Anne, get a grip. Listen to me. I did not do any of the stuff that's in the paper. None of it is true. Bernie's on his way over. He wants to talk to you."

"What, you invited a stranger over to our house now? What is it? Seven? Jesus Christ, what's wrong with you? I can't think now. Get out of my way, I have to get cleaned up and get the kids up. Goddamn it, get in the kitchen and make some goddamned coffee." She pushed him out of the way as she stormed into the bathroom. Bill didn't know if Bernie would help or exacerbate the situation.

To Bill, it seemed to take forever, but before long, Bernie pulled into the driveway in a 1962 blue Pontiac Bonneville. A few minutes later, he was in their kitchen, sipping a cup of black coffee and talking about the article.

"Look," Bernie said, "I can literally feel the tension in the house. Maybe the best thing I can do is talk to Mrs. Simpson."

Bill sighed. "Yeah. Maybe. Excuse me, I'll see if she will come out."

He knocked lightly on the bedroom door. "Anne, hon, are you ready? Bernie would like to talk to you." Not hearing an answer, he walked in. Anne was straightening her skirt and looking into the mirror over their dresser. "Listen, honey. Bernie thinks he can help you understand what's going on with the newspapers and the case."

She eyed him coolly. "I'm going to listen to this man, but don't you ever invite a stranger to our house without telling me first."

"Okay," Bill said, marveling that, with all the shit going on, her biggest issue now seemed to be Bernie coming over unannounced. *Jesus, what screwed-up thinking.*

They walked into the kitchen. Anne forced a smile, saying, "Mr. Levine, I'm sorry that I don't have anything for you to eat. Bill didn't give me much warning."

Bernie put up his hands. "No, no, no. Think nothing of it. I'm the one barging in, and please, just call me Bernie."

Bill's lawyer proceeded to woo his wife with words of reassurance.

"Look, Mrs. Simpson, this newspaper story is full of innuendo and gossip. It's one of the worst things I've ever seen a government agency do, and I am a former US attorney here in Detroit. For reasons totally unknown, the Secret Service is out to get Bill. Based on everything I can determine, there is no significant substance to their case, so they jazzed it up by providing a sensational news story that they know newspapers love to print."

He and Anne talked for the next thirty minutes; Bill listened. Bernie tried to get Anne to show some interest in Bill's case. "Look, Mrs. Simpson," he said finally, "one key element in this case is going to be your demeanor in the courtroom."

Anne sat back in shock. "Who said I'm going to be in a courtroom and be a part of this newspaper circus?"

Bernie was flabbergasted. "I've never heard a client's spouse indicate so little support for their partner. Ma'am, your support for Bill is crucial. Look, I think I can blow this case out of the water. They have no real evidence, but if you're not there, supporting your husband with firm conviction, that's really going to hurt."

"Well, Bill and I have a lot of talking to do. Regardless, his career is over with the government. I don't know what we're going to do."

"Please, Mrs. Simpson, what I've learned through many years of dealing with difficult situations is that it is important to address issues one step at a time. Otherwise, we all get overwhelmed."

"But what will we have to live on? How will we pay you?"

"Ma'am, I've already told Bill that, one way or another, we will work out my fees. I'm not a wealthy man, but I know I can work out payments over time."

A few minutes later, Bernie commented that he had overstayed his welcome and it was time to leave. Anne went to check on the kids. The doorbell rang.

"Hi. Mr. Simpson?" a young man asked when Bill opened the door. "I'm Mark Lindsey from *The Detroit News*."

Bernie gently pushed Bill aside. "Listen, young man, I'm Mr. Simpson's attorney. We have no comment except to say that Bill Simpson is innocent. The *Free Press* got its facts wrong. Do you want to do the same?"

The reporter stepped back, rethinking his approach. Bernie had hit his mark. The *News* and the *Free Press* were bitter rivals. If the morning paper had made a mistake, Lindsey did not want to make the same mistake in his afternoon paper. Just then, a station wagon pulled up with a "Channel 7" logo on its side. Bill swallowed. This *was* going to be a media circus.

Chapter Sixteen
The Trial

Bill was indicted by a federal grand jury at the request of the South-east Michigan US Attorney in March. He was released after posting bond. The trial was set to begin on June 22, 1964. Bernie was not a happy man leading up to the trial. They had drawn Federal Judge Herbert Wilson, a 1931 appointee of President Herbert Hoover. Wilson was seventy-one and not known for being friendly to defendants.

Bill was now living with his parents. His pay and employment had ended in early April, and times were difficult. After the indictment, Anne told Bill she did not want to see him any more than was necessary. Bill was still paying the mortgage on the house and other expenses—which was taking a real bite out of his bank account. Anne had reluctantly agreed to go to the trial.

On the morning of the trial, Bill and his parents stopped by to get Anne, who was curt—almost rude—to her in-laws, to say nothing of her attitude toward Bill. Bill's mom stayed at Anne's with the children.

Bill, his dad, and Anne met Bernie at a café across from the federal building. After reviewing some last-minute details, they headed to the courthouse. The courtroom was half full of people, primarily print and television reporters. Judge Wilson entered the chambers and the clerk called the trial to order.

The first day was spent mostly on selecting the seven men and five women for the jury, who were lectured by the judge about the do's and don'ts of their responsibilities. He said he wanted to get this trial completed by the end of the week.

The assistant US attorney rose to make a motion. The government prosecutor said, "Your honor, the government would like to move to close this hearing to the public."

"On what grounds?"

"Well, your honor, this case is unique. The government has sensitive material that is likely to be part of testimony or evidence. There's the fact that some highly classified issues may be discussed that should not be aired in public. Finally, sir, we will have at least one witness whose identity has remained out of the public eye. We do not feel this witness deserves to be part of a media circus and have their name and reputation smeared in the newspapers and on TV."

"What do you mean, 'highly classified issues?'"

"Well, your honor, we would like to discuss these sensitive issues in chambers, out of the public eye, which I'm sure you understand."

"Defense, Mr. Levine, what say you to this motion?"

Bernie rose, looking confident. "Your honor, like you, I am surprised and do not understand all the issues the government is referring to. But on its face, the defense is opposed to this motion. I've received no discovery information indicating sensitive material. We are not some communist country that prevents the public from knowing what is going on during trials and other government activities. The public has a right to see government work, especially its legal system. If it's a matter of a single witness, I'm sure we can work something out. Further, I have asked to bring Reed Clark, the previous Detroit office director of the Secret Service, in to testify. You have refused his testimony, and we need an answer to such decisions."

Bernie sat down, and the judge called the attorneys to his chamber for further discussion. Half an hour later, the judge and attorneys re-entered the courtroom. Judge Wilson said, "The court rules in favor of the government on closing court testimony and excusing Mr. Reed Clark from testimony. We will adjourn for the day. Tomorrow the doors will be closed to visitors. Witnesses will be held in a conference room adjoining the court. The trial will begin promptly at nine. This court is now adjourned."

The courtroom buzzed with activity. Reporters were shouting questions at the attorneys. The assistant US attorney, James McHale, seemed eager to answer all questions. Bill could overhear him mentioning corruption in every sentence he uttered. Finally, after Bernie had finished with reporters, he took Bill into the hall and found a quiet spot where they could talk.

"Bill," Bernie whispered hoarsely, "this is a stacked deck. Wilson is a tool for the goddamned government. Let me ask you, why on earth would the government argue that top secret information they referred to had something to do with the Kennedy assassination?"

"The Kennedy assassination?" Bill repeated. Then he smiled. *So this is it; this is the reason they came after me.* "Bernie, remember I told you about Reed Clark being transferred to New Mexico last Christmas?"

The attorney nodded. "Well, we, he and I, were asking questions about some things that didn't make sense regarding the Kennedy assassination. There are other issues as well, some of which the Secret Service has deemed cannot be discussed by agents."

"You are aware of these activities?"

"Yes, I was in the middle of some of this, but I'm handcuffed by these restrictions, even though I am no longer employed by the Secret Service."

"This explains why the government is getting their way with the judge. Bill, this is not good news, but we are going to fight these bastards." Then, Bernie shifted gears. "I did get the judge to allow your wife and parents to attend."

***

The trial was over in twelve days. Bernie made himself a pest with motion after motion, all of which Judge Wilson denied. Bernie was hoping that, by raising questions about procedure, they might get a hung jury.

While the government's case was not substantively strong, a surprise witness, Rita Gray, was called to testify. Bernie objected, he said the defense did not see Miss Gray's name on the list of witnesses to be called. The judge overruled his objection. Rita Gray's testimony was devastating. She lied through her teeth about her and Bill's relationship. Bill studied her carefully during the testimony. She continued to dress well, like a career woman, but when he just focused on her face and eyes, she looked terrified. She was not the confident person he remembered. Something had shaken her. Was it the government, the underworld, or something else? Whatever it was, she was tentative and extremely nervous.

She said they had sexual relations at least five times, then named the dates. She said Bill gave her counterfeit bills to pay her for services rendered. She concluded by saying that, even though she was not a perfect person, she believed in government. She believed in those people who chose public service as a career. Then she met Bill Simpson. A scumbag if ever there was one. She could never trust government again after this experience.

Bernie aggressively cross-examined her, perhaps too aggressively. He reviewed each date she had supposedly met Bill. He pressed her on the types of men who were part of her client base. Some, she said, were government officials. Bernie asked why these public officials were respectable and Bill Simpson was not. She replied that these men were gentlemen, Bill was cheating everyone—his wife, his employer, the government, and he was a crook, too. As Bernie was finishing, he provided the court with documentary evidence that Bill was, on at least two occasions, at other verified locations.

"So, you lied to the court on at least two of these occasions, why should we believe you on the other three so-called dates?" Bernie asked.

She looked Bernie in the eye and said, "Because I know what I did and to whom I did it with," she said. "Perhaps I mixed up a date or two, but I know what I did."

"Your honor, I'm through questioning this witness, but I am asking you to charge Miss Gray with committing perjury to this court."

"Duly noted," the judge responded.

That afternoon, Bill and Jimmy drove home, with Anne in the back seat of Jimmy's Ford. There was little conversation. When they got to Bill and Anne's house, Bill walked her to the door.

On the doorstep, he said, "I'm sorry, hon. This was a tough day."

"Yes, it was … and Bill, I'm not going down to that courtroom again. You are unfit to be a husband, a father, or a son." She opened the door just as Bill's mother was coming out.

The next day, Joe Bishop testified that Bill Simpson was a decent, but not exceptional agent for the Secret Service. He noted several times where he thought Bill's work had not been competent. Upon cross-examination, Bernie hit him hard on their Chicago trip.

"Agent Bishop, was Bill Simpson professional on his trip to Chicago?"

Bishop paused too long, and Bernie said, "I can read from the depositions provided by Chicago agents and members of the Chicago police department."

"Let me simply say I am not permitted to talk about the Chicago assignment, but also that I never saw Bill Simpson do anything wrong. I thought he could have been a better, more competent agent."

Joe Kowalski testified that Bill was always trying to take shortcuts and that Bill taught him how to skim part of the counterfeit money they came across. He also said Bill had a relationship with the Windsor counterfeiters and was on the take. Then, to a direct question, he said that Bill was usually on the make with women, and that was why he probably waited for when he was on his honeymoon to visit Rita Gray.

Bill did not believe what he was hearing. He kept whispering to Bernie that each statement was a lie, then another lie. Bernie rose to question the young agent.

"Mr. Kowalski, you know that no one, except for an acknowledged prostitute, has made such outlandish statements against Bill Simpson. We have statement after statement vouching for his integrity and professionalism. Do you still stand by your statement?"

Without a moment's hesitation, Joe said, "Yes, I do. He taught me to be a lazy and unprofessional agent. Because of him, I have had to fight inside the agency to get my integrity back."

"Your honor!" Bernie looked at the judge, shaking his head. "This is another example of perjury and I hope you will take action against this man. Further, I request that you declare this a mistrial."

The judge seemed surprised by the second request. "Mr. Levine, I will not declare a mistrial. You, sir, are going to continue to argue this case, and we are going to complete this trial in a timely fashion. Frankly, we have taken too much time as it is."

The jury deliberated for two days. Only one juror had to agree to Bill's innocence for Bill to get off.

On July 10, 1964, the jury convicted him in a unanimous decision.

Chapter Seventeen
Precious Days

Between the verdict and sentencing, Bill had fourteen days of freedom. He was ordered to stay in the state, but other than that, he was free to visit friends, family, and spend time with his kids. He took the kids to the beaches at Belle Isle and Metropolitan Beach on Lake St. Clair. These were precious times for Bill, yet he figured his kids would forget these experiences. Still, he wanted to be with Debbie and Johnny as much as possible. Anne did not go with them on any of these excursions.

Five days before his sentencing hearing, Bill was at his parents's house reading the Sunday newspapers when the phone rang.

"Hello, is this Bill Simpson?"

The voice was familiar, but he could not place it. "Yes, it is."

"Bill, this is Larry McRae from the Chicago field office."

"Ah, yes, yes. Of course, I remember you. How are you, Larry?"

"Well, sir, I'm perhaps a bit better off than you, but not by much."

"What do you mean, Larry?"

"Well, I've been suspended, and I'm afraid a grand jury is going to indict me."

"Shit! God, Larry, I had no idea. You know about me?"

"Yes, I can't believe it," Larry said. "Listen, I really don't want to talk about this over the phone. Do you think we might be able to meet somewhere between Chicago and Detroit?"

"Yeah, but it would have to be in Michigan."

They settled on a late-morning meeting at a Howard Johnson's restaurant and motel just west of Battle Creek in a couple of days.

What the hell is going on? Is there a witch-hunt in the Secret Service?

That Wednesday, as Bill drove along Interstate 94 toward Battle Creek, he made some modest detours onto local roads to see if he was being followed. It did not appear anyone was tailing him. As he drove off the ramp at the Capital Avenue interchange in Battle Creek, the only development in sight was a gas station and the familiar, orange-roofed buildings of the Howard Johnson's restaurant and motor lodge.

Bill spotted Larry McRae in the far corner of the restaurant's dining room. No one was at any of the adjacent booths or tables. Larry, dressed in a suit and tie, already had a cup of coffee on the table. They ordered breakfast and, after it was served, Larry got down to business.

"Bill, I know this is a special time for you, getting things in order and such, so I really appreciate you taking the time to drive here so we could talk."

"Are you kidding?" Bill responded. "As soon as I heard you say you were being investigated, I had to learn more. Nothing was going to stop me from getting to this meeting. Were you tailed?"

"Na, well, yes, actually. There was a car following me, but I lost them on the south side of Chicago. Whoever it was, they don't know our city streets very well."

For the next two and a half hours, the men consumed their breakfasts, an abnormal amount of coffee and many cigarettes.

Bill briefed McRae on his trial. He talked about his family, and how he felt his whole life was falling apart. He added that he had no idea how he was going to face prison time and was scared to death.

McRae's reaction was stark. "Jesus Christ, those bastards are doing to me the same as they did to you. They're taking a case I was working on and have changed the evidence to make it look like I was in cahoots with counterfeiters." He gave Bill all the details.

"I know Bob Montague had nothing but respect for you," Bill said.

"Yeah, but Montague was reassigned."

"Boy, that really fits. The same thing happened to our director, Reed Clark. Christ, it looks like they are using the same tactics against you that they used on me. But why? What the hell did you do?"

"Well, you know, after the assassination I reminded people about how sloppy some of the detail was in protecting President Kennedy. I know you must have seen it."

"Yeah, I know exactly what you mean. I did not accept the attitudes of the good ol' boys, and I got written up over it."

McRae raised an eyebrow. "Well, in May, after the assassination, I was in DC for a conference, and I decided to contact the Warren Commission regarding my low regard for the president's detail. Like you, I saw the drinking. Not only that, but I heard that the night before the assassination, the detail was drinking and partying until four in the morning at a bar in Fort Worth. They had to be hung over as hell the next day. Their reflexes were probably much slower than they should have been. What if those guys were more alert, would President Kennedy be alive today?"

"I didn't know that," Bill said.

"Yeah, I felt the Warren Commission investigators needed to know that the president was exposed to an assassin while his sworn protectors were not necessarily at their top mental or physical states. I also wanted to see if anyone was aware of the Chicago incident you and I investigated. So, on a break during the conference, I called the Warren Commission staff. I did not get through and left my name and number. I think their staff reported me to headquarters. Headquarters, not wanting bad publicity, took immediate action against me."

"That fits, too," Bill marveled. "Now I understand why they came after me."

A few minutes later, Bill changed the subject. "You know, there's a couple of things that have been bothering me."

"What's that?" McRae asked.

"Well, look at Oswald. The guy serves in a top-secret base in Japan. He decides he's through with the United States. He renounces our country and goes to the Soviet Union for a couple of years. Then he decides to come back. We let the bastard come back, with a wife and baby. We don't charge the guy with treason, we just let him walk right in. It makes no sense to me. Then after the assassination, he simply says he's a patsy."

"Makes no sense … unless he was a CIA plant. What else?"

"Then back to Chicago. Vallee said he was innocent. Still, he's caught with weapons and a ton of ammunition. I checked with Officer Kranz, and he said Vallee was simply let go after the weekend. And those two gunmen brought into your headquarters were released, too. No charges. How does that happen?"

"Beats the shit out of me, unless there was somebody with a lot of power on the inside."

By one o'clock, the two men had talked enough. They did not arrive at any action to take except to continue to tell the truth. Bill learned that McRae's judge was also an older man and, based on what he had seen, Larry felt the judge was biased against him—not because he was black, but because he was challenging a government institution, the Secret Service.

Two weeks after his trial ended, Judge Wilson sentenced Bill to ten to twenty years in the federal penitentiary system.

PART IV ~ 1964-1967
Chapter 17
Prison

Bill Simpson lay in his bunk in the federal prison in Milan, Michigan. He had already been incarcerated for more than six months, but sleep still came in spurts. Usually, he woke in a dream, a recurring dream where he was walking through a doorway, and a heavy door slammed shut behind him, with metallic sounds echoing throughout. He relived his first day in prison again and again.

The day Bill was inducted into the prison system at Milan, about fifteen miles south of Ann Arbor, he was filled with anxiety. He had no idea what to expect. When he got there, the prison guards were cold, and he saw very few inmates. He received a haircut, was deloused, and dressed in prison clothes.

Those first few days were the worst. He stayed there three days before being transferred to the maximum-security prison at Terre Haute, Indiana, where he stayed six months before being transferred back to Milan.

The prospect of going to Terre Haute had terrified him even more than going to Milan. Once identified as a former Secret Service agent, a cop, he figured he'd be a sitting duck for being roughed up. Gratefully, that didn't happen. Instead, he was put to work in one of the prison's manufacturing facilities, making office furniture. He began meeting people, and since Bill was a good judge of character, he became close to four men who were each in prison for different reasons. These men stressed that Bill could survive in the prison system if he kept his nose clean and stayed out of trouble. Bill followed their advice and mostly stayed to himself. He began reading books from the prison library—all kinds of books. He read Charles Dickens, Victor Hugo, Alexandre Dumas, and then moved on to political and historical biographies.

Without any notification, he was transferred back to Milan, a small, medium security facility, about 1,200-1,400 inmates at any given time. There was a lot of good farmland around the prison, and many prisoners were assigned farm work. As spring approached, Bill became a farmer, or more accurately, a farm worker. He enjoyed the work. It kept him busy, and he was out in the sunshine. The Michigan growing season was short compared to some other parts of the country, and the harvests were completed by late September or early October. Then, he was assigned to indoor work.

In the wee hours, Bill lay in his upper bunk, thinking. All he could do at night was read, sleep, or think. His thoughts tended to revolve around four areas: his family, the trial, Rita Gray, and the others who testified against him.

Life with Anne had not been good for many years. He was aware that much of the problem was his own lack of interest in their marriage. Still, he felt his wife never really tried. A month after he began serving his time, Anne filed for divorce. Bill asked Bernie Levine for help and, as always, the man was there for him. Bernie told him that no judge in the world would prevent the divorce.

The real issue, he said, was the property and the children. Bill told Bernie that his wife could have all his property, except a few personal items. For the sake of the children, Anne tried to stay on good terms with Bill's mother and father, so he instructed Bernie to have his parents work with Anne regarding disposal of his private possessions. Bill told Bernie he could work out the best situation possible regarding visitation, especially with his parents. He did not expect the children to visit him in prison and knew Anne would receive full custody. His mother informed him Anne had returned to work as a receptionist at the law firm where she had previously worked. Jenny and Anne's mother alternated caring for the children while Anne was at work. As the months passed, he thought less and less about Anne. He *did* think about the kids and his parents.

The trial haunted him. Bernie had been right. Even with the circumstantial evidence, the testimonies of Rita Gray and Joe Kowalski killed him. As a public servant linked to corruption and a sex scandal, he never had a chance. Still, he reran the trial in his head constantly. When he had questions or questioned strategy, he wrote Bernie.

He never questioned Bernie's intent, but just like being a Monday morning quarterback, he wondered if things might have been different with alternative approaches. Bernie always wrote back, sometimes suggesting that he might have been wrong on a direction he took, but always concluded that this was a fix. Bernie always suspected that Judge Wilson felt pressure from the Secret Service and the US attorney. Always at the end of Bernie's letter was a handwritten note from Shirley, with a sentence or two of encouragement.

Bill wondered about Bernie and Shirley. He was sure they were having an affair. While it was none of his business, he was entertained thinking about a possible relationship between the two.

Bernie never pressed about payment. Before Bill turned himself in to begin his sentence, Bernie, Bill, and his dad talked. Bill indicated that money was tight, and he was not sure how he could pay Bernie in full. His dad said that he would pay Bernie a small sum each week. Bill told his dad not to do it, but Jimmy said, "Son, simply consider this a loan and that you will pay me back when you get out. Once you're out and start working, you'll pick up the payments. Fair?" All Bill could do was nod his head and feel like he was a twelve-year-old kid in trouble with the school principal. His dad had come to bail him out; he always had.

Bill often wondered how he could have been so wrong about Rita Gray. Regardless of her profession, he thought she was a woman of character. He did not think of her as a hooker, but as a woman who made her own independent decision to take advantage of her beauty and apparent uninhibited nature to earn a living. He often went back and forth on such thoughts. Was it because he liked her as a person that caused these feelings? Perhaps. Still, thinking about her body language at the trial, he was convinced that someone had gotten to her—perhaps the Secret Service, perhaps the mob—he wasn't sure.

Then there was Joe Kowalski, who surprised him the most. He had worked with the young man and tried to give him the benefit of everything he knew. He made sure that, after the Kennedy assassination, Joe had been included in the investigation activities, instead of simply running errands for Reed Clark. As a young man, just married, perhaps he did not want to get on the wrong side of his superiors in the office. He didn't know or understand Kowalski's testimony against him. Outright lies, one after another. It destroyed him, perhaps more than Rita's testimony.

***

Bill quickly learned the routine of prison life. Once he settled in at Milan in January 1965, he had time to focus on himself. He remembered one guy he had met at Terre Haute, a black guy named Fred Harris who had befriended him in the furniture shop. Fred was a slim guy, about six feet tall. Bill never saw him exercise, but he had the body of an athlete. During his stint at Terre Haute, the men became close, and Fred offered him many tips on survival. One of them was "stay healthy."

One day in the furniture shop, while they waited for some parts to arrive, Fred said to him, "Why in the hell do you smoke them cigarettes?

That smoke is no damned good for you. Man, if you want to live to see your kids grow up, you need to stop."

Up until then, Bill hadn't given his smoking much thought. He wasn't a heavy smoker. He had started in high school, smoked heavily while serving in Korea, and kept it up when he came back. He never smoked as much as his father, who smoked three packs a day. Anne had never said a word about his smoking, although she never smoked.

One day during a recreation period, Fred said to him, "Look at you, man. You are getting fat. Look around you. The guys who have a purpose in life exercise and stay fit."

"I never see you work out," Bill responded.

"Well, you're right about that. But, shit, I'm an old man."

"You're not that old."

"Bullshit! I'm sixty-eight years old!"

Bill looked at the man in disbelief. "Like hell you are! You look like you could run a four-minute mile."

Fred grinned. "Shit, man. You know, fifty years ago, I broke almost every track record in Flint, but you know what?"

Bill shook his head.

"Them crackers who ran the Flint recreation league didn't recognize my records because I was a black boy. Shit."

Bill looked at him. "So, why don't you work out?"

"Oh man, I don't need to. I'll tell you what, anytime you want, I'll beat you in a half-mile run. You know my age, and I'm telling you I will beat your white fanny."

Nothing came of that challenge, but Bill committed himself to stop smoking, start running, lift weights. He was a good athlete in high school, and at thirty-three, he was confident he could get back into shape. Even though it was winter, Bill started running outside during recreation time. He started lifting weights. Through it all, he was hampered by short breath. He cut cigarettes out of his life. At first he struggled, but in time he conquered his nicotine addiction.

By the spring of 1965, Bill had lost eighteen pounds, his body was toned with a sculpted shape he had not known since basic training. No cigarettes and lots of exercise made the difference. Working out, along with voracious reading, helped to make the time pass.

The months dragged on. He worked hard and played hard at everything he could get involved with inside the prison. He worked on the farm and, as spring turned into summer, he developed a tan, ran on the track as much as time allowed, lifted weights, played on one of the prison's baseball teams, and played pickup basketball. As a natural athlete, he found true relaxation in team competition. He was a favored teammate. During baseball games, inmates bet cigarettes on whether Bill would get on base and bet again on whether he'd make it to third base or score before the inning was over. He was popular, but never got too close with many inmates. The other inmates seemed to understand. They all knew he had worked for law enforcement, but most did not hold it against him. If anything, they tended to respect him and gave him his space.

Bill managed to do better than most in the prison system. For many others, it was just another part of a terrible life. He saw racism and other abuses of prisoners. Bill seemed to be one of the few prisoners who crossed racial divides inside the system. In time, he gained the trust of several of the prison's black athletes. They discussed many subjects, but the most animated topics were on race and the rise of the Black Muslims. One of the inmates slipped him a copy of *The Autobiography of Malcom X*, which had been published that January. It was an intimate portrait of the man and had a powerful effect on Bill, who came to view Malcom X's assassination as a great loss to society.

He would have been a lot worse off at a high-security facility. Still, prison was prison. He did not see his kids and rarely saw his parents. His confinement was just that, and he grew to hate it. He sometimes wondered why he worked so hard. After all, who gave a damn? Still, he always came back to Fred Harris and his advice. He didn't want to let his friend down. He'd keep fit and hope one day his kids saw him as a strong man and not just an ex-con.

Chapter Nineteen
Lung Cancer

Bill counted on seeing his parents at three- to six-month intervals. These visits were pleasant breaks, but always included a tinge of sadness. Jimmy and Jenny could not accept that their boy was in prison, and it was a weight that affected both in different ways. In late November 1966, Bill walked into the visitor center and instantly knew something was wrong. He sat down at his assigned cubical, his parents on the other side of the glass partition. There was a small vent in the window so they could hear one another.

Bill looked at his father. "What's wrong, Dad?"

Jimmy, who never deceived Bill, said, "Son, I've had some bad coughing spells the last couple of months, sometimes spitting up blood, shortness of breath, and other things. So I went to the doctor two weeks ago. They had me X-rayed and did a bunch of tests. It looks like I've got cancer, lung cancer." Jimmy's voice began to crack as Bill's mother held back tears. "Next week," his dad went on, "I'm going over to St. John Hospital. They're going to open me up and cut out the cancer—it's my only chance."

Bill spent the next week thinking about his father. He had always been an anchor to his life, dependable and consistent. What would he do without him? How would his mother survive? Losing Jimmy would be a disaster for her, and Bill was stuck in a federal prison. He was heartbroken.

The surgery was difficult. Bill's mother wrote letters almost daily, and he called her whenever he could. After a week, Jimmy was still not allowed home. Bill and his mom were worried. Bill asked to talk to Warden O'Neil about seeing his father. As they sat in his office, the man was sympathetic but explained that, if he accepted Bill's request, everyone else in the facility would expect the same treatment.

Bill put his face in his hands. The warden remained silent for a minute or so. Finally, he said, "Simpson, you have a spotless record here. I'll tell you what. I don't know if your father will live or die, but I will give you a choice. You can see him now or, if he dies, you can go to his funeral. Your choice—you can't do both. Further, you or your family will have to pay the expense of the guards who will accompany you on the trip."

Bill thought about it and the choice was simple: he'd rather see his dad alive than in a coffin. Two days later, he was on the expressway, in a prison-owned Chevrolet, heading to see his father, with one armed guard driving and another in the passenger seat. Bill was in the secured back seat wearing civilian clothes and in handcuffs. The cuffs were tight, but not unbearable.

Being on the outside provided no relief for Bill. The drive to Detroit's east side was quick, taking just over an hour. They exited the expressway and were soon in front of the massive hospital at the foot of Chandler Park Drive. This was close to Bill's old neighborhood, but that thought brought him no joy. A few minutes later, they walked out of an elevator and down a long hall to Jimmy's room. His mother was sitting next to the bed, his father seemingly immobile.

The guards looked around the room briefly before uncuffing Bill.

"We'll be right outside," one of them said before closing the door. Bill hugged his mother. Jimmy lay in the hospital bed, propped up, eyes closed, tubes seemingly coming from everywhere. It was all Bill could do not to collapse. His father slowly opened his eyes. "Bill ... Bill, is that you?" His voice was weak and raspy.

"Dad," Bill said, "you knew I'd get here." He released his mother and moved over to the bed, slowly lowering himself to the edge of the mattress, trying to avoid the IV tube running from his father's forearm. He took his father's hand, giving it a gentle squeeze. Jimmy mustered a weak grip in return.

Bill spoke quietly to his father, offering encouraging words. A minute later, his mother said she wanted to get some coffee.

"You go ahead, Mom. Dad and I will be fine."

After she was gone, Jimmy said, "Billy, oh my Billy boy. I don't want to lose you."

"Dad, don't worry. Everything's going to be okay."

"Son, I don't think I'm going to make it."

"Dad, don't—"

"No, it's okay. I've thought about this a lot," his voice straining at the length of the sentence.

"Dad, don't. You're too tired."

"No, I need to say some things while your mother is out of the room."

"Dad, it's okay."

Ignoring him, Jimmy said, "Don't worry about your mom, she will be okay. I have insurance. The UAW will help. They have a great pension." Jimmy coughed and motioned for a glass of water. Bill poured a glass from a carafe on a nearby tray and lifted it to his father's lips. Jimmy took two or three small sips before he went on. "Bill, I don't know when you are going to get out, but when you do, go see Ken Morris. We've had several talks." Jimmy coughed again, but not as badly. "He'll help with a job. It may not be much, but it can be your start. Help you get on your feet sort of."

Bill's eyes welled and he squeezed his father's hand once more. Then, he leaned in and embraced the man who continued to be his rock, even in his weakened last days. "Dad, you're the best," he whispered.

"My boy," he softly whispered as he drifted off.

Bill sat there, holding his father's hand. About a half hour later, Jenny came back. She hugged Bill and grabbed his hand as if she would never let go.

Another half hour passed before one of the guards came in and politely said, "Bill, we have to think about hitting the road."

Before he could respond, Jenny said, "Oh no, officer. Please, just another hour more, please."

The guard smiled. "Bill, you've got a half hour."

That 30 minutes went by too quickly for Bill. When it was time to go, he hugged his mother tightly. "You know, Mom, Dad's a tough son of a bitch."

"Bill, this is not the place to use that kind of language."

Bill smiled through his tears. "Mom, that's exactly what he would say." He leaned over and kissed his father goodbye for the last time. The guards did not cuff him until they were back in the vehicle, heading back to the prison.

Jimmy died eight days later.

Chapter Twenty
The Hooker's Redemption

On a cool March day in 1967, Jenny Simpson heard the doorbell ring. When she opened the door, a pretty, auburn-haired woman, maybe in her thirties, was standing on her porch.

"Can I help you?" she said, thinking this woman might be a door-to-door cosmetics salesgirl.

"Mrs. Simpson, my name is Rita Gray. Do you have a moment? I'd like to talk to you." Jenny hesitated. The woman added, "It's about Bill."

Jenny felt her heart skip a beat. She stepped aside and invited the woman to sit down in the living room.

"First, I want to say I was so sorry when I read of your husband's death," Rita said. "I know these past few months must have been terrible for you."

"Well, thank you, Miss Gray. But what is it you want? How can I help?"

"You don't remember me, do you?"

"No, I'm afraid I don't."

"It's been a couple of years, but you may recall I testified at Bill's trial."

Jenny gasped at the memory. She was not in court that day, but there was only one woman who testified at Bill's trial, the prostitute. She felt a sudden surge of anger, but checked herself as her nails dug into the fabric of the couch. Her words were measured and cold. "You don't remember, I wasn't in court that day; I was babysitting Bill's kids. What do you want with me?"

"Ma'am, I ... I haven't been able to live with myself since I testified. When I read your husband's obituary in the paper, I knew I had to set things straight ... or at least try."

Jenny shook her head, confused. "What are you trying to say?"

"Please bear with me," Rita answered. She took a deep breath and nervously scratched her right forearm before continuing. "Before the trial, I was visited by some government people. They knew that I desperately wanted to keep my privacy. I did not want the way I earned my living to be public. They knew I was scared. These men said that if I wanted to protect my reputation, I needed to cooperate." She paused, "Mrs. Simpson, I'm sorry, but may I have a glass of water?"

"Of course," Jenny replied, returning from the kitchen a few seconds later with a glass.

"Thank you," Rita said. She took a drink and set the glass down on a coaster with an image of Mackinac Island. "For a promise of my cooperation, the men said they'd keep my name out of the press. If I didn't cooperate, they said I'd be charged as a co-conspirator with Bill and likely face five or more years in jail. After a lot of back and forth, I caved and gave them what they wanted."

Jenny sat back. "You mean you li—"

Rita put up her hand, "Wait. Please let me finish ... please. First, I never had any kind of inappropriate relationship with your son. The two times we talked, he could not have been more of a gentleman. Second, Bill never gave me any counterfeit money. He was a consummate professional, focused only on the case. We did have some good conversations over a couple of cups of coffee, but nothing more. Finally, I never thought Bill was anything but a good government agent going after bad guys. I respected him for that."

Rita paused as Jenny struggled to choose her words carefully. She had never believed this woman's testimony. Her Bill would never have consorted with a prostitute. "Miss Gray," she began, "thank you for having the courage to come here. You know, of course, that your testimony, your *lying* testimony, is the main reason my son is in prison. What do you expect me to do with what you've just told me?"

Rita's lower lip quivered, and she swallowed hard. "Ma'am, I don't want to go to jail. I'd like to spare my family any public humiliation. But I also think that now, more than ever, I need to set the record straight."

Jenny resisted the urge to slap the woman. "So, you think just coming to my home and confessing exonerates you for what you did to my boy?"

"No, ma'am. I don't. I have changed my life for the better, though. I have Bill to partly thank for that. I don't see men anymore. I've found an entry level job at a public relations agency in Birmingham. I'm trying to avoid having my reputation tarnished. I could find myself on the street in no time."

"What about Bill's reputation? Did it ever occur to you that you ruined *his* reputation? Not to mention you destroyed his family, made it so his children are growing up without a father."

Rita looked away, blinking back a tear.

Jenny eyed Rita for a several seconds, trying to gauge her sincerity. "You don't have a family?" she asked finally.

"Not really. My father and I never saw eye to eye. After the trial, even though no publicity was directed at me, my parents washed their hands of me."

Jenny was thinking fast, searching for next steps. *What would Jimmy do?*

"Miss Gray, I don't want you to go to prison, either. There's been too much of that. Let me think about this for a day or so. Can you leave me your phone number?

Rita faced her once more and let out a sigh ... one Jenny sensed was one of relief. "Of course," she replied as she reached for her purse.

Chapter Twenty-One
Jenny Takes Action

Two days later, Jimmy's old boss, Ken Morris, and one of his closest friends and staff members, Pat Caruso, visited Jenny. Morris, who had started his labor activism as a union committeeman for the Auto Workers in 1938, had a reputation for resolving workers's problems, whether they were work related or personal issues. He always tried to be there for his people. In time, that hard work had propelled him to the presidency of his local union, then a spot on the UAW International Executive Board, the governing body of the second largest union in the country.

Ken listened to Jenny's story with great intensity, occasionally asking questions.

"Ken," she said finally, "what do I do?"

Ken reflexively reached for the non-existent cigarette pack in his shirt pocket, but stopped mid-way. He had quit a year earlier. "Jenny, I don't know for sure. I need to think about this. I never believed Bill was guilty, and this sheds new light on an ugly situation. Is she willing to talk to me and perhaps some attorneys?"

Jenny thought for a moment. "I think so. She doesn't want any publicity, and she doesn't want to go to jail."

Ken slightly grinned. "Of course. No one wants bad publicity or to go to jail. But we have to start somewhere. I'd only have her talk with trusted people, some of the same people Bill talked to when he first got into this jam. Or, perhaps, Bernie Levine. But, you know, that might be a conflict of interest. No, we'll leave Bernie out of this for now."

***

Morris and Caruso met with Rita Gray to hear her story and size her up. They believed her. Then he had her repeat the story to his attorney and friend, Charlie Martin.

After Rita left, Martin said, "Jesus Christ, Ken, that's quite a story. Assuming she is telling the truth, if she goes to law enforcement, she's likely to be tried for perjury. That's public, and she could do jail time. And Kenny, she could be putting her life in danger. If the Secret Service went to that kind of trouble getting her to testify, someone might want to make sure she never testifies in a public courtroom."

Ken digested this. He knew this was an issue beyond his expertise. He set up a meeting with the top two men in the UAW, Walter Reuther and Emil Mazey. He preferred a five o'clock meeting after normal working hours, so they were not likely to be limited on time. On March 21, the three men met in Reuther's conference room on the second floor of the UAW headquarters, or Solidarity House, at 8000 E. Jefferson in Detroit.

Ken maintained close relationships with both Reuther and Mazey. When the UAW was formed in the 1930s, it consisted of many factions, including a strong far-left communist party, socialists, conservative Catholic forces, and, in the middle, were the Reuther/Mazey forces. Both men grew up as socialists. They were firmly anti-communist, but as the years passed, they shifted more to the political middle of UAW politics.

Ken totally respected the breadth and power of Reuther. He was the greatest man he had ever known, a man who talked with presidents and world leaders. He was nationally quoted, even in popular films. By the 1950s, Ken was elected to the position of regional director, which made him the head of one of the UAW's regional territories. In this role, he was also included on the UAW's top governing body, the International Executive Board. Both Reuther and Mazey knew enough to respect Ken and his geographic region on Detroit's east side.

Reuther said in a friendly, but business-like manner, "Alright, Kenny, what's the big deal? How come no one would tell me what the hell this meeting is about? Emil, did Kenny inform you?"

"No, Ken didn't tell me a damn thing."

Ken began, "Walter, Emil, sorry for all the mystery. Frankly, I did not want the purpose of this meeting on any calendar—it's possible it could prove embarrassing." Turning to Emil, Ken said, "Do you remember meeting Bill Simpson, Jimmy's son? We were at Cupids."

Emil, looking through black framed glasses, said, "Yeah, he's the one who went to prison on a counterfeiting rap."

"That's right," and then turning to Walter, Ken said, "Walter, Bill Simpson is the son of Jimmy Simpson, who passed—"

"Yeah, yeah," Reuther broke in, "I know Bill Simpson. We met at the White House when he was briefly assigned to the presidential detail. In fact, I was pretty pissed off that no one told me the son of a UAW man was working at the White House, but it was one of those things that I never followed up on."

"Well, good, so you both know him." Ken briefed the two men on Bill's career and the trial, adding that Bill had served nearly three years of his sentence. Then, he told them of Jenny Simpson's call and her meeting with Rita Gray, along with the meeting with Gray and Charlie Martin.

"You believe a hooker?" Emil responded. "Jesus Christ, Ken! I didn't think you were that gullible."

Walter and Emil quizzed Ken with many questions, then Reuther took control of the meeting. "Alright, let's just suppose the woman's story is accurate." Looking at Emil, he said, "Of all unions, we should know that such actions are not above any law enforcement organization. If she is telling the truth, what can we do? Christ, Kenny, I don't know, but we should do something."

"Well, Walter, you know that I have a habit of passing the buck. Looks like I'm doing it again." Ken smiled.

"Ken, there are many things you do, but passing the buck is not one of them."

Walter looked at his watch. "Okay, we have a son of a union brother, who as far as we know, has been a patriot who served his country in Korea and did an outstanding job with the Secret Service. Then, suddenly the Secret Service charges him with counterfeit corruption. If we believe the woman's story, it's entirely possible that this boy was set up. Emil, do you still have contacts with any private detectives?"

Mazey looked at the others knowingly. Nearly twenty years earlier, Reuther had been the target of an attempted assassination. A shotgun blast through his kitchen window nearly killed him. As the number two man in the union, Emil replaced Walter during his long convalescence. Then, about a year after the shooting, Walter's brother, Victor Reuther, was shot while reading in his living room late one night. Victor survived the shooting but lost an eye. The entire UAW leadership felt the Detroit Police Department only paid lip service when it came to finding the people behind the assaults. Emil took over the investigations for the union, hiring private detectives to find leads. In time, these investigators felt they had found the people responsible, the gang of Detroit hoodlum Santo Perrone, but no one was arrested. Still, Emil was the go-to guy on such issues.

"Yeah, I have contacts."

"Good. Can you get some guys to do a background check on the woman?" Emil nodded. "And, see if they can discretely look into the Secret Service and determine if this kind of corrupt activity is considered possible."

Mazey eyed the redheaded labor leader. "What's your timeline?"

"See if you can have it done by the end of the month. I'm hoping to meet with the president in early April."

Reuther had met with every US President since Franklin Roosevelt, but Ken had never heard him refer to these meetings in such a casual manner. Then, in a flash, it became clear. Reuther had been no fan of Lyndon Johnson and in fact, had fought against Jack Kennedy's selection of him as vice president at the 1960 Democratic Convention. After Kennedy's assassination, President Johnson needed Reuther's help to solidify his base in the liberal wing of the Democratic Party. Ken also knew that his friend, and Reuther's other brother, Roy, had been sent to the South in 1964 to organize voter registration efforts of previously disenfranchised black voters. President Johnson considered it a great favor, as Roy Reuther was a born political organizer. *Johnson owes Walter*, Ken thought.

The meeting broke up. Reuther walked Ken out of the room and thanked him for bringing the issue to his attention. "I don't know," Reuther said. "With some luck we might make a difference in this young man's life. It's the least we can do for Jimmy."

Ken felt a deep sense of satisfaction as he and Emil walked out of the room.

Chapter Twenty-Two
The White House (Again)

In the late afternoon of April 6, Walter Reuther walked down the same corridor in the White House where he and Bill Simpson had their brief conversation nearly five years earlier. He was ushered into the Oval Office, and LBJ motioned him to the couch in the middle of the room. The president pulled a padded chair close to where Walter was seated, so he was looking slightly down at the labor leader. They talked about several issues, with special focus on the president's War on Poverty programs.

When the right moment came, Reuther said, "Mr. President, I have a piece of personal union business I would like to bring up. I may need a favor or simply direction from your spectacular knowledge of how this government works."

The president waved off the flattery, and Reuther quickly told the story of Bill Simpson. When he finished, he asked, "Is there anything that can be done?"

The president sighed. "Oh, Walter, I know now why you asked for a private meeting. This is juicy shit, a real humdinger. I'm going to have to get some research done on this. So, your information tells you the Secret Service has some problems—drinking, womanizing, and so forth. You know," he said, reaching for a telephone, "anything we do here is very sensitive and has to be secret." Pressing a button on the phone, he spoke into the handset, "Get Josh Diggs up here, pronto."

"Now, Walter," LBJ said as he hung up, "I want you to understand I'm going to do my damnedest to help this young man. But there is one little favor I'd ask you to think about. You know, you've got that Mazey fella on your board and some others who are kicking my ass on Vietnam. I want you to tell them I'm no goddamned fascist. I can't negotiate the Vietnam War until the other side wants to sit down and negotiate. It's just like your negotiations. You can't negotiate until Ford or GM is ready to deal, right?"

"Sure, Mr. President."

Diggs entered the room, and the president quickly brought him up to speed. Diggs was a young man, with dark hair and black horn-rimmed glasses. He had a reputation as being LBJ's go-to man on tough issues.

"Ah, Josh, now, you listen to me. I want you to check out this story. I want to know about this man, Simpson, and I want to know about the court case. I don't think I can use a pardon here, so we must be goddamned creative. And, I don't want the Secret Service, or the FBI, or the CIA to have any goddamned idea we are looking into this. You understand, boy?" Johnson did not give Diggs a chance to respond. "You know, a Secret Service man probably saved my life in Dallas. I don't want those people pissed off with me. You get to work, and you call Walter if you have questions."

Once in the corridor, Diggs said, "Walter, let me think about this and make a few inquiries. Do you have any files I can look at?"

Reuther opened a thin briefcase and pulled out a manila folder."Here is the report compiled by a detective agency we occasionally use."

"This is great. I will get on this issue tonight. I'll be back to you, hopefully within two weeks."

***

Ken Morris was in a meeting on April 19 in his office regarding safety issues at the Jefferson Avenue Chrysler plant. His secretary stuck her head in the doorway. "Ken, Walter's office just called. They want you and Emil to be there at ten-thirty."

Ken looked at his watch. *Five after ten.* "Okay. Is Emil coming?"

"I'll let you know if he has a problem."

"Tell Emil I will stop by his office and get him."

Ken picked up Emil, whose suite of offices was across the hall from Reuther's.

Irv Bluestone, Reuther's top administrative assistant and most trusted aide, was with Reuther when Ken and Emil entered. Reuther motioned the men to sit down on two green, upholstered hardwood chairs across from his desk. Bluestone stood off to the side of Reuther's desk.

"Gentlemen, it looks like we have a deal for Bill Simpson," Reuther said. "At nine-thirty, the president called. He said he would not grant a pardon or commutation. Instead, Josh Diggs has worked out an arrangement and will be calling in about in fifteen minutes. I wanted you here. I want you three to know what we might be agreeing to, and if any of you are uncomfortable with anything that is being said, give me a high sign. Got it?"

The men nodded. At 10:47, the buzzer on Reuther's phone sounded. He picked up and there was an exchange with secretaries connecting the principles.

"Josh, it's good to hear your voice. Yes, yes, the president called, and he seemed extremely pleased with your work," Reuther said. "Before you start, I would like to put you on the speaker phone. There are some men here who need to know exactly what is said, so that I don't misinterpret anything."

After some conversation from the other end, Reuther said, "Josh, I trust these men with my life. I would trust them with my family. More significantly, I trust them with our union membership."

A moment later, Reuther pressed the button for the speaker system.

Reuther explained to Diggs the significance of each man in the room and added, "Emil supervised the UAW's investigations in the late forties during the violence directed at top UAW leadership. He hired private investigators to check out the bastards that shot me, and then my brother, Victor. About the same time, Ken, here, was nearly beaten to death by hoodlums. We are convinced all this violence was linked—all in an effort to weaken our union."

"Well, Walter," Diggs replied, "I didn't know that history. I look forward to meeting Emil and Ken soon."

"Also, of the people in this room, Ken is the closest to Bill Simpson and his mother, Jenny. It was Jenny Simpson who reached out to Ken regarding the story that has brought us all together today."

"I see."

"Josh, just tell us what you've come up with as if you were talking to me only. If the guys here have any questions or comments, I'll let you know."

"There's a lot to cover here, and I will be as brief as I can," Diggs started. "It's one thing for a president to pardon or commute a federal prison sentence, which as we know is not an option here. It is almost unheard of for a president to try to alter a sentence. That being said, we took the approach that we were not going to change a sentence or even advocate for a lesser sentence. The president called the trial judge, Judge Wilson. Of course, Wilson's been on the bench forever and is a crusty old bastard. But what I learned about him is that he believes in government institutions. So much so that when the US attorney and the Secret Service approached him before the Simpson trial, he did something he's not supposed to do. He had privileged conversations on a case without including the defendant's attorney. He did this because he believed in the Secret Service mission and believed that if these men were trying to address sensitive issues, he could understand that and would help them."

Changing the tone of his voice, Diggs said, "You know, I hate conducting meetings like this. I should have grabbed a plane to Detroit for this discussion, so we could do it face to face. Am I making sense to you all?"

"Josh, we are fine here. Just go on," Reuther responded.

"Okay. Well, when the boss talked to the judge, Wilson didn't show any inclination to give Simpson a break. Now, all the president said to the judge was that I'd be calling him with some more details about the case, that he, the president, had accidentally learned some scandalous information about one of our federal agencies regarding the Simpson trial and that he wanted me to talk to Judge Wilson about it. There was some push-back from Wilson, but you know what? Not too many people can push back against Lyndon Johnson, and after two or three minutes of the president using his power of persuasion, Judge Wilson agreed to talk to me. So, yesterday, I flew into Detroit to talk to Judge Wilson. Walter, I'm sorry I didn't try to get by to see you, but I was in and out, and, more importantly, I didn't want anyone to know I was there."

"No problem," Reuther said. "Go on."

"So, I told the judge about the threats made by the Secret Service to obtain Miss Gray's testimony. I showed him court transcripts of each instance where Miss Gray lied about Bill Simpson and his activities. After about a forty-five-minute discussion, Wilson was furious. Then, the issue of what to do about this mess came up. I asked him how we could right the wrong that had been done to Bill Simpson. The judge said President Johnson should pardon him. I told him that wasn't going to happen. I said that the president felt he, Judge Wilson, should take the lead on this issue. The judge thought about this for a minute and said, 'You're damned right I should! I'm so pissed with the Secret Service and the goddamned US attorney's office I can hardly contain myself.'

"The judge said he'd take care of everything in the next few days. He did not, however, tell me what he was going to do regarding Simpson. He said that by the end of the week, he was going to call in the US attorney, the Secret Service, and Simpson's attorney, ah,"—there was the sound of pages being flipped— "a guy named Levine. So, my question to you is, what kind of guy is Levine, and will he be able to handle himself discretely with the judge, the US attorney, and the Secret Service?"

Reuther looked at Ken. "Josh, I'm going to let Ken Morris handle that."

Ken spoke up. "Josh, it was my attorney, Charlie Martin, who recommended Levine to us. Charlie is one of the best labor attorneys in the country, and he encouraged Simpson to call Bernie Levine. I can tell you that Bernie Levine is a tough criminal attorney. I think he was a US attorney during the Roosevelt years. He's defended cops and criminals. He's not shy."

"That sounds good," Diggs said. "We will let Judge Wilson have his meeting, and if he gets pushed around by the US attorney or the Secret Service, we will figure something else out. But I'll tell you, based on my conversation with the judge, I think the Secret Service and the US attorney aren't going to know what hit them."

Chapter Twenty-Three
An Infuriated Judge

That same afternoon, Bernie Levine was in a meeting with a client when Shirley stuck her head in and said, "Bernie, Judge Wilson, from federal court, is on the phone. He wants to talk to you now."

"Judge Wilson wants to talk to me? Okay." Excusing himself, he told his client, "I've learned never to leave a judge waiting," and picked up the phone.

"Levine?" Wilson asked over the phone.

"Yes, sir. What can I do for you?"

"Levine, I want you in my chambers Friday morning at ten. This is about your client, William Simpson. Also in attendance will be the US attorney and representatives of the Secret Service. Can you make it?"

"Friday? Yes, sir. I can move a few things around." Bernie actually had nothing on his calendar for that day.

"Good. Don't be late." The old man hung up, and Bernie wondered what just hit him. Bernie did not dare call Anne Simpson for any clues on this matter, but Shirley suggested he call Bill's mother, who gave him a fairly good idea what was going on.

After the call, he walked around his desk and grabbed his long-time secretary, pulling her close. After a long and passionate kiss, he declared, "Sweetheart, I'm not sure how it happened, but I think Friday is going to be a great day!"

***

Friday morning, Bernie entered Judge Herbert Wilson's office in the federal building. He dutifully took a seat by the receptionist's desk. A few minutes later, in walked the US attorney, along with Joe Bishop from the Secret Service. They nodded at each other. Bernie instantly sensed that none of his old adversaries had any idea what this meeting was about. Just before ten, the receptionist ushered the three into the judge's conference room, and they waited.

Shortly after ten, Wilson, in shirtsleeves, walked in. All the people in the room stood up. Wilson nodded at the group and sat down, with the others following suit.

"This should be a brief meeting," Wilson began. He looked straight at the US attorney: "You, sir, and the Secret Service, have betrayed my trust, and frankly, that is unacceptable. You asked for my help and support during the Simpson case, and I gave you my support. Then, just a few days ago, and from the highest and most unimpeachable source, I learned that you put at least one witness on the stand who committed total and complete perjury due to your coercion. If you didn't know about this, the Secret Service did. This is totally unacceptable, not in my courtroom."

The US attorney opened his mouth to speak. "Silence!" said the judge. "You have no authority in my chambers. You will listen, and you will hope that I don't bring disbarment proceedings against you and the trial attorney in this case."

Bernie masked a laugh with an abrupt cough.

The judge continued. "As a result of the perjury that the government knew had been committed during the trial of William Simpson, I am, as of Monday next, reducing his sentence to time served."

Again, the US attorney tried to protest, and again Wilson raised his hand. "I don't want to hear another word from you unless I ask for it." Wilson turned to Bernie. "Now, Mr. Levine, there are some conditions for this reduction of sentence. I do not want to see any countersuits on this or any other related charges. His conviction will stand. He can work anywhere he likes, so long as it's not government related. I do, however, want to know where he is working after his release. Is that clear?"

"Yes, sir."

"Again, I do not want Simpson trying to regain his employment with the Secret Service or any other federal government agency. All benefits, including lost pay and retirement, are waived. Clear?"

"Yes sir, but—"

"Mr. Levine, there are no buts. You either accept my proposal or the original sentence stands. Do you have any questions?" Bernie didn't utter a word. The judge looked once more at the US attorney. "Enclosed in this envelope is my order. See that it is immediately enforced. Work with Mr. Levine regarding release details. Am I clear?"

"Yes," replied the deflated, top federal attorney in southeast Michigan.

Then, the judge turned to Joe Bishop. "Mr. Bishop, you sir, should be ashamed of yourself. You are damned lucky I am not retaliating against you, your job, and your agency. Pressuring witnesses to commit perjury in my courtroom, or for that matter, in any United States courtroom, is totally unacceptable and of course, a crime. On top of that, I accepted your goddamned argument not to bring in that supervisor to testify. You are damned lucky I am not substituting you in Simpson's prison cell. Higher forces prevent me from doing what I want. You, sir, are damned lucky."

Joe Bishop, sweat running down his forehead, did not respond.

"Levine? If you have any trouble with these, these poor excuses of government servants, so-called officers of the court, you contact me immediately."

"Yes, sir."

When the door closed behind the judge as he exited the room, there was a collective exhale.

Bernie passed his business card to the US attorney. "Please call me with the details of Bill Simpson's release. I guess, with this being Friday morning, you will get back to me later today."

"Well, we'll see about that. We'll see if anyone is going to get released," the US attorney said, with a bravado that no one in the room believed.

"Well, sonny," Bernie said, standing up in a suit that looked like it had not been dry cleaned since Simpson's trial, "I've been around a long time. I don't think I'd fuck around with this judge. He will destroy you."

The following Monday, Bernie was outside the Milan prison gate when Bill came walking out in his civilian clothes, confused, but incredibly happy. Ninety minutes later, Bill was in the home he grew up in, hugging his sobbing mother.

PART V ~ 1967-1969
Chapter 23
Freedom

Bill woke up with a start and looked at the wind-up alarm clock's luminous hands. It was four in the morning, and he was wide awake in his boyhood bedroom. Sleep was not going to come—it was a good time to think.

The giddiness of freedom was starting to move to the reality of freedom. The first three days post-release had been a wonderful blur of activities, but it was time to begin considering his future. Later that day, Bill was scheduled to see his children for the first time since his release. He could not wait, and with these fresh thoughts he rolled over and fell back asleep.

At two that afternoon, Jenny drove Bill to Anne's mother's home to see the kids. Earlier, they had bought the children some gifts. Bill could not believe how excited— and nervous—he was as they drove to the house.

Anne's mother, Sharon, opened the door and greeted Bill with a cool handshake. Bill and Jenny entered, and the kids ran to their grandmother with hugs.

Debbie stepped back from Jenny and looked at Bill. After a moment, she said, "Daddy?"

Bill smiled and held out his hands. "Yes, sweetheart."

The little girl took a moment and surveyed the man she vaguely remembered. Not knowing quite what to do, she grabbed his hand, then smiled and reached for a hug. Bill held back some tears and squeezed her tightly.

Four-year-old Johnny watched his sister hug the strange man.

Jenny softly said, "Debbie, why don't you introduce your father to your brother? Remember, he was too young to remember him before he went away."

Debbie turned to her brother and said, "Johnny, come here. You need to meet Daddy." The boy hesitated. "Johnny, Daddy is wonderful, and look, he brought us presents!"

Bill said, "Johnny, come here. Let's shake hands and let's look at some toys we bought for you and Debbie." With that, the ice was broken. The kids played with the toys, sometimes including Bill. At times, Johnny came close to giving his father a hug. Soon, the boy was laughing with and hugging his father.

Anne walked in around five-thirty. Bill was astonished. She had lost weight and was dressed in a professional business suit. Bill could see that working at the law firm had been good for her. She had moved up from a receptionist to one of the office managers and was making decent money. Except for a brief clasp of their hands, she did not let him touch her.

"So, you got out. I'm happy for you," she said in a tone that lacked feeling.

"Yes, I'm out. Thanks for letting me see the kids. They are great."

"Yeah, of course, you know you have no right to see them. You said you didn't want to see them, so I'm really surprised." Anne's voice dripped with sarcasm. "I suppose we have to talk to our attorneys and work out some sort of new arrangement."

"You knew that was while I was in prison. Look Anne, believe me, I've had more than ample time to think about us, our children and the mistakes I made during our marriage. I can't change the past, nor do I want to debate it. I hope we can have a shared future with the most important part of our lives, our children."

"Anne, dear," her mother said, "let's not spoil Bill's time with Debbie and Johnny."

Anne's eyes narrowed as she kept her eyes on Bill but addressed her mother. "Okay, but you know, I've talked to some of the attorneys in the firm, and they can't figure out how Bill got out."

"Well, let's not worry about that now," Bill's former mother-in-law said.

Anne looked at Bill and their children, "Mom, you're right. It won't be easy for me, but I will do my best to make sure this situation works."

***

The next night, lying in his narrow bed, Bill knew that his living arrangements needed to change. He was thirty-six. He loved his mother and was so incredibly appreciative of her actions to get him freed, but her house was not going to be a permanent home for him.

The next day, he updated his driver's license and checked the classified section of the paper for used cars. Ken Morris had called his mother during the week to make sure Bill was out, and his transition was going smoothly. He suggested Bill meet him on Friday morning at Cupids to talk about some job opportunities. Jenny said he would be there.

Bill arrived at Cupids fifteen minutes early. Not much later, Ken Morris walked in, dressed in his characteristic business suit. Bill felt a bit awkward in his casual clothes—he had not had a chance to update his wardrobe. His physical fitness program in prison had changed his body, and his old clothes did not fit very well.

Morris greeted Bill like an old friend. Jenny had told her son about Rita Gray's visit and of the role that Morris and his union had played in his release. She had no idea of the remarkable details that made it all happen.

"Bill," Morris said, "I can only imagine the terrible experiences you've had in prison. No one will be able to erase all of that, but we can help you with a new start in life."

"Jesus, Ken, you have been so good to me—from the moment I called my dad the day I was suspended, to now. Thank you so much."

"Bill, your father was a good union man and he saw his son in an unjust situation. Helping is part of what we do. Before he died, Jimmy asked if I could help get you back on your feet."

"I know. I saw Dad right before he died. He told me about his conversation with you."

"You are a talented person, probably too talented for what I have to offer. I can help you get a job in the plant, a Ford shop. It is clearly something you are overqualified for, but it can be a base for getting you some independence. Working in the plant can be what you want it to be. You will make a decent wage, with excellent benefits. If you want more, you can go to college at night. Perhaps move up inside the company or something else. You could even get involved in union activity. It's all up to you."

Bill nodded. "Which factory are you thinking of?"

"Well, like I said, we are thinking of Ford. They have a progressive policy of hiring people who have paid their debt to society after being convicted of a crime."

Bill cringed.

"The plant we are thinking of is in Birmingham."

"Birmingham? That's where the executives live."

"Yeah, but on the far east side of the city is an industrial zone. There is a Ford Tractor warehouse where the company provides parts to its dealers around the country. It's a good place to work, the hours are eight to four-thirty. There is rarely any overtime. The best I could do was get you a base wage at about three-fifty an hour—that's about seven thousand a year. Does that work for you?"

"Yep. I can make that work. I'm not sure what the cut on alimony and child support will be, plus I have to continue to pay my lawyer, but I can make that work."

"If it helps, we go into contract negotiations with Ford later this year. I'm sure there will be a wage increase."

Bill smiled. "When do I start?"

"I have to confirm it with the plant manager, but how about a week from Monday?"

The two men shook hands.

Chapter Twenty-Five
A New Job; A New Life

Bill's mom offered to give him fifteen-hundred dollars to buy a car, clothes, and other necessities to get ready for work in the factory. He told her it was a loan.

He checked out the Sunday *Free Press* classifieds for a good used car. He settled on a 1964 Ford Mustang for eight-fifty.

A week later, he drove his new car down Eight Mile Road to Woodward Avenue. From there, he drove seven miles to Maple Road and turned right. A mile later he was at the Ford Tractor facility, in the personnel office with fifteen minutes to spare. He was sent to a nearby medical clinic for a physical.

Upon returning, Bill was escorted into the large warehouse with row after row of packed bins full of tractor parts. The personnel guy walked with him to the far end of the warehouse and introduced him to his foreman, Lou Delvero, a short, wiry, fifty-year-old.

"Bill Simpson," he said, shaking Bill's hand. "I thought you'd be here earlier this morning."

"I was, but they sent me out for a physical."

"Well, everything is normal—no one told me," Delvero said, looking back toward the management offices with some disgust. "Well, okay. Listen, you have pretty much of a cake job. You will be a picker, packer, checker. Look around you. You see a huge warehouse, but think of it as a giant supermarket. Every morning, you will get a shopping list from Henry over there of parts needed for repairs by a dealer somewhere. You take one of those oversized carts over there and pick the pieces on your list that are located by the row and bin number. Once you complete the dealer's order, you come back here, find a work spot by the conveyor belt, and box up the order. Then you double-check the order and send it down the conveyor belt to the guy who weighs it for shipping. So, you pick the parts, pack the parts, and then double check your work—thus you are a picker, packer, checker. Get it?"

Bill nodded. "Yeah, I think I've got it."

"Now, did they tell you up front that you are a probationary employee for ninety days? That means you have no union protection, and we can fire you for any reason."

"Yeah, we went over that."

"Good." Delvero said. "I'm going to assign you to one of the guys for the rest of the day. He'll show you what to do, and what not to do. Listen, if you put in a full day's work and keep your nose clean, you'll have no problems with me."

"Lou, you don't know me, but all I can say is that if I cause an issue for you in any way, you let me know. The last thing I want is a problem working with you."

"Good," Delvero replied. He called out to a short, stocky man who looked to be in his late forties. "Adolph, come over here, will you?"

Soon, Adolph, in his eastern European accent, was showing Bill the ropes. It was easy stuff, much easier than working on an assembly line. By the end of the week, Bill felt like a veteran. The only real problem with the job was the monotony. Still, he got the work done, he kept to himself, and didn't get too friendly with anyone. Bill believed keeping his privacy was a good thing, and outside of Adolph, he didn't go out of his way to talk to anyone. He liked Adolph because he didn't ask questions.

After a month on the job, he had some money left after paying Anne child support and alimony. He made so little money that, by the time he calculated all the deductions, he was only saving about four hundred a month. With this, he had to put money aside to pay back his mother and Bernie. He was lucky that his dad had paid Bernie a hundred dollars a month. His mother continued the payment, but at fifty dollars per month. He still owed Bernie sixteen hundred dollars. He decided to set aside a hundred a month for the debt.

He found an upstairs flat between his mother's house and work in the older Detroit suburb of Royal Oak, for a hundred a month. He was a block north of Eleven Mile Road and two blocks west of Main Street, less than a five-minute walk from the once prosperous downtown area. Unlike downtown Birmingham, Royal Oak did not have chic retail stores. Instead, it seemed to have been a town that never recovered from the Depression. Still, there was something Bill liked about it. There was a sense of a town in the middle of suburban Detroit. He could walk to three old movie theaters that ran second-run films for a dollar. A half-dozen restaurants and bars were within walking distance. Nearly everything Bill might need was nearby. And, he was only about a fifteen-minute drive from work.

The flat was owned by an older retiree, Angelo, who lived a few blocks to the north. Angelo was a bit of a character who owned a couple of houses as a way of supplementing his meager pension and Social Security payments. Bill's flat had a small kitchen, a large living room looking out onto his street, a good-sized bedroom, and an updated bathroom. Angelo introduced him to the young couple on the ground floor.

His mother understood and supported Bill's move. She helped him with extra kitchen goods, some furniture from her basement, and an old black-and-white portable GE television. He bought a double bed from a local retailer who agreed to deliver it the following week. He was able to coordinate phone installation with the mattress delivery and asked his mother if she could be there when the service men arrived. He was not comfortable taking time off work during his probationary period. Not only did she comply, but after the delivery and the phone installation, she went to JCPenney and bought curtains for his new place.

By the end of June, he had a set routine. He worked eight and a half almost always uneventful hours, was home by five or five-thirty, and sometimes cooked dinner for himself, though he often walked to a nearby restaurant or bar for a meal. He went to his mother's house at least once a week for dinner. He usually saw one or two movies a week at the Main, Washington, or Royal Oak theaters. A few times a week, he worked out at the nearby Dondero High School track, usually running about two or three miles and then doing some calisthenics. When he entered prison, he weighed about 210. He made sure not to eat too much since he had been out and was pleased that, at 175 pounds, he looked and felt strong.

Bill also filled some of his time reading. At work, he usually read at lunch and sometimes on breaks. If he dined out alone, he almost always had a magazine or newspaper with him. Most of the books he read came from the Royal Oak library and, as time passed, he spent more time there.

He got to know his new neighbors, Mike and Kathy Paxton. Mike was a student at Wayne State University Law School, and Kathy taught elementary school in the neighboring suburb of Berkley. Mike was a tall, thin guy with long hair, and Kathy was a pretty brunette.

The couple often invited Bill to stop by for a beer or to share a bottle of wine. They were nice people. They enjoyed music and had a lot of records, mostly rock and roll. Most people Bill had known played their records on a large console record player. Mike had a stereo system made up of components that included a turntable, speakers, and amplifier.

One weekend night in late June, Mike wanted Bill to come down for dinner and listen to the new Beatles album, "Sgt. Pepper's Lonely Hearts

Club Band." Bill grimaced. "Why do I want to listen to them? I think I'm a little old for those guys."

"No, no," said Mike enthusiastically. "Bill, man, these are not the same guys you heard on Ed Sullivan."

Bill had never watched Ed Sullivan when the Beatles came to the US. Bill looked at his younger friends; they seemed so fresh and naïve. Dressed in what he considered hippie clothes. Mike, so slim and focused on school and music. Kathy, so pretty, with long, flowing brown hair. They were so in love with each other.

They listened to the album while the charcoal in Mike's grill was heating up. They ate their burgers and listened to the album again. Mike was excited to have the record in his hands. Bill was not impressed.

Mike glanced at Kathy and then looked back at Bill. "Do you want to try some pot?"

Bill looked at his new friends as a flurry of thoughts flew through his mind. He knew guys at Milan smoked, but he was not close to them. Of course, it was illegal, and that bothered him. Then, he was concerned about the notion that it might lead to harder drugs. Still, it was common; many of the anti-war students smoked pot, and no one seemed to care.

He finally said, "You know, I've never smoked that stuff."

Kathy laughed. "Oh, we know."

Mike said, "Look, when it's done in the right environment, it's great to get high. It might take a couple of times, but give it a try. I give you my word it won't hurt you." And then, as if reading Bill's mind, he added, "And don't worry, it doesn't lead to harder stuff. It's more like getting a buzz from too many drinks, but you don't have a hangover. You probably won't get high the first time or two. And, when you do get high, music will simply sound awesome. You will hear each and every instrument during a song. You will know when it happens."

Mike went into the bedroom and returned with a cigar box and was soon rolling a joint. Kathy quietly got up and locked the doors, closed the windows, and pulled the blinds. Bill smoked the stuff, but nothing much happened—he did sleep well that night.

About five days later, he and Mike smoked a joint. Kathy was not around. Something different happened. He never forgot was how great the "Sgt. Pepper" album sounded.

***

In early July, Bill and his mom chatted after dinner in her living room.

"Bill, I think you should contact Rita Gray," Jenny said. "The only reason you are here is because of her. You owe her a big debt of gratitude."

Bill looked at her in surprise. "You know, Mom, I've thought of her several times since you told me the story. Bernie also told me what he knew of how the whole thing went down. He said that between all the lies that Rita and Kowalski told in court, the US attorney and Secret Service could not tell who cracked and squealed to the judge. And they were too afraid of Judge Wilson to pursue the issue."

"I know. Bernie told me that, too."

"You know, I have no idea how to reach her. I suppose I could go to her apartment on Jefferson and see if she's still there."

His mother stood up from her chair and walked over to her tiny telephone table. "You don't have to do that. I have her number right here."

Three nights later, on a Sunday night, Bill dialed the number. He felt nervous and wondered what he was going to say. After three rings, Rita answered.

"Hello?"

"Hi, um, Rita?"

"Yes?"

"This is Bill Simpson." There was a long pause—it was only seconds, but to Bill it seemed like minutes. Finally, she said, "Well, Mr. Simpson, it must be that you finally got out of prison."

"Yes, I did, and as soon as my mother gave me your phone number, I wanted to call and thank you. It took a lot of courage to do what you did."

"I'm glad I did it. It cleared my conscious from all my lies. How long have you been out?"

"A few months ago. I'm working and live in Royal Oak."

"Okay, that's enough. I'm happy for you, but I really don't want to talk any more. I know I'm being short with you, but I have to go. I hope you have a great life now that you're free. I, too, have a new life and I'm hoping that I can get beyond you and my past. So, good bye, Mr. Simpson."

Before Bill could respond, she hung up. He hadn't known what to expect, but he never expected such a cold conversation. He couldn't understand what he had done wrong. She was the one who had stepped forward. She had ruined and then restored his life. He was puzzled by her reaction, but as the weeks passed, the uncomfortable conversation faded from his mind.

Chapter Twenty-Six
The Summer of 1967

One of the bars Bill frequented made particularly good cheeseburgers. Sitting at the bar one night, he noticed a black guy, several years younger than he, sitting a few stools down. The guy was flirting with a waitress, joking, and obviously checking out her figure. Bill could never do that with a woman.

After the woman left to wait on a table, Bill caught his eye and nodded. "So, does this approach work well?" he asked.

The guy laughed. "Well, it works about three out of ten times. That's not too bad!" His laugh was infectious.

The two men introduced themselves and spent the next hour talking. Bill ran into Sam Starr a couple of more times. Sam noted that Bill was in good shape and asked if he played tennis.

"Not really," Bill replied.

But Bill bought a tennis racket, and the two began playing on weekends and occasionally on weeknights. Eaton Park in Birmingham had an ice rink that doubled in the summer as tennis courts. It had lights that allowed the men to play well into the evening. It didn't hurt that a lot of women played there. Bill was not nearly as good a tennis player as Sam, but he was a better athlete. In time, he was sure he could compete with the young stud.

Sam had an outgoing personality and, for him, making friendships, especially with women, was a breeze. He was a master of conversation, especially the small talk that Bill didn't have in his repertoire. One time, Bill asked him why he lived in the apartments nearby, rather than Detroit or some other cooler place. Sam said, "This area is great for meeting women. As one of the few black guys around, I'm kind of a curiosity, and you know," he said laughing, "women just *love* curiosities." Bill watched Sam perform his magic with amazement. Sam had the smile, wit, and looks to be a ladies' man, but Bill knew that lifestyle was not for him.

In late July, something ugly happened in Detroit. The day leading up to it—a Saturday—had started out great for Bill: he got in a good game of tennis with Sam, after which he enjoyed a nice dinner at Mike and

Kathy's. After they ate, they got high and listened to a couple of albums, including one from the Lovin' Spoonful. Bill especially liked the song, "Summer in the City." Sometime before midnight, he went upstairs to bed.

Around nine on Sunday morning, the phone rang. "Bill, are you alright?" his mother asked when he answered groggily.

"Mom, I'm fine. What's wrong?"

"You haven't heard? There are some kind of riots going on. It started on Twelfth Street, on the west side."

"Are you alright? Do you want me to come over?"

"No, I think I'm okay. Everything is quiet around here. You know my neighbors, they keep an eye out for me."

After he was sure his mom was okay, Bill turned on the TV. There was a bulletin during a commercial break saying Channel 7 would televise an extended news program on the civil disturbances at noon. Bill kept the television on as he searched the radio for news. Information was sketchy, but the disturbance seemed to be spreading across the city. People had been killed. Detroit Mayor Jerome Cavanagh was trying to manage the chaos. Bill stayed in most of Sunday trying to stay on top of what was going on. He kept in touch with his mom and went downstairs to discuss the latest with Mike and Kathy. He also called Sam to make sure he was safe.

"Do you want to come over?" Bill asked.

"No, I'm good. I want to be around my place in case my family might need me," Sam replied.

Bill watched the news on Sunday night, flipping between Channels 2, 4, and 7. Businesses were going to be shut down for the duration of the disturbance, but Bill was not clear if the factories in the suburbs were closing.

He got up on Monday morning and drove to the plant. When he arrived, there were few cars in the parking lot. He entered the building. Mr. Gregory, head of personnel, informed him and a few other guys from the plant that work was suspended until at least Wednesday. He said they might be down longer, depending on what happened with curfews and marshal law.

Bill bought a *Detroit Free Press*, went to a diner, and read the paper over breakfast. He had a sick feeling in his stomach as he read. People thought Detroit was a progressive city. No one could have imagined that the spark that started the disturbance was a police raid on an illegal after-hours club on Detroit's west side at four o'clock Sunday morning. Now, hundreds of buildings had been burned and looted. People had been killed. The Detroit police were out of their depth in handling the huge crowds of protesters, looters, and bottle throwers. A photo in the paper showed an exhausted Mayor Cavanagh and Governor George Romney meeting.

The rumor was Cavanagh and Romney were going to ask President Johnson to send in federal troops. Bill thought this made sense—the Detroit police were not able to handle the crowds, and he didn't think Michigan's National Guard was competent enough to handle a civil disturbance. The Guard was largely populated by men simply trying to avoid service in Vietnam. Federal troops were the best way to restore order.

On his way to his mother's house, Detroit police stopped him at a road block. They were not going to let him cross Eight Mile Road, the border between Detroit and many northern suburbs. They seemed more focused on his hair, which he had let grow long, than his concern for his mother. Bill finally persuaded the nervous officers that he was not a problem, and they let him pass. When he arrived at his mom's, all appeared calm. The neighbors were on the sidewalk or sitting on their porches, talking to one another. Jenny was fine. She wanted to feed Bill, but he refused. She told him she had checked with Anne, and that she and the kids were staying at her sister's house in Southfield, a northern Detroit suburb.

As he was leaving, she said, "So, Bill, why don't you use this time off to get a haircut? You're looking like one of those hippies."

Bill smiled. "Aw, Mom, you know I would, but all the barbershops are closed today."

"Don't get smart with me, young man. Ford can still fire you."

"Don't worry, Mom. I do my job better than just about anyone else. I'm fine."

Bill jumped into his Mustang and worked his way home. He was thinking that he had, in fact, become one of the most efficient workers in the plant. He was the go-to guy when they needed a rush order. Then, he looked at himself in the rearview mirror. His long hair was blowing in the wind as he drove down Eight Mile Road. He wasn't sure why he was growing his hair—maybe it was because he had been forced to keep it short in prison, and this was his form of rebellion. All he knew was it made him feel good. The biggest problem was his long hair was streaked with gray. Still, he liked it.

Bill felt the world was operating in two separate universes. One, inside Detroit, where police, firefighters, and the National Guard were fighting to control an angry, largely unarmed group of black people. Yet, here Bill was, driving on Eight Mile, with the windows open and heading back to the white suburbs. He and his neighbors lived totally unaware of what too many Detroit black residents faced every day.

He learned that almost all facilities like movie theaters or other gathering places were closed, but smaller businesses outside Detroit were open. Tennis courts were, of course, open. As soon as he got home, he called Sam. Besides hoping to play tennis, he wanted to make sure his friend was alright. They spent two and a half hours on the courts before he and Sam spent the rest of the day between his flat and Mike and Kathy's.

President Johnson and Governor Romney agreed to send federal troops on Monday night. At midday Tuesday, the troops entered Detroit. Many of these men had been to Vietnam—now they were in Detroit, protecting people and property from other Americans. The key result was the reduction of killings. The Detroit police were guilty of abusing black—and some white—residents. Seven thousand people were arrested, fifteen hundred buildings were burned down, and forty-three people were killed. By Wednesday, Bill was back to work, and by Friday, all seemed normal—at least in the Detroit suburbs. Life was never the same in the city.

Chapter Twenty-Seven
The Strike

By September, life was back to normal, or so Bill thought. On September 6, the UAW called a strike against the Ford Motor Co. because Ford refused to negotiate with the UAW on pay, cost-of-living adjustments, and a host of other issues. The company demanded a greater increase in worker pension contributions, a lower cost-of-living formula, and a few other items. Bill joined his co-workers in picketing the plant. They worked in shifts of four hours each and received fifty dollars a week in strike benefits. Bill was able to survive on these benefits, but he suspended his payments to Bernie until the strike was settled. To his surprise, Anne was agreeable to suspending his alimony and child support until the strike was over, but she demanded Bill work out a schedule to repay all the missed payments.

It didn't take long to figure out this strike wouldn't be a short one.

Workers with large families or high mortgage payments struggled. Even though Bill had few worries, the strike affected him, too. He, like his co-workers, was eager to get back to work.

In October, negotiators got down to business, and by the second week of the month, a tentative agreement was reached. Workers around the country met to debate and hopefully ratify the agreement. Even though the tractor parts plant was a tiny group of workers, they too had to meet and vote for or against ratification. Bill's local union met at a nearby local union. As was often the case, there were people who opposed the agreement and said the national UAW did not look out for their specific interests. They said the UAW sold them out. There was significant debate among the various factions. At one point, Bill raised his hand and asked to be recognized.

The president of the plant's local recognized him, and Bill rose from his seat. He had seen his dad and other labor leaders address groups like this, and he felt comfortable as he took a moment and surveyed the group of about 65 people. In a strong voice, he said, "I recognize that most of you don't know me very well. Frankly, I think I have the lowest seniority in the group—I just started last May and got my ninety days in on September fourth. I will receive the fewest benefits of anyone in this room, and I rise to support the new contract."

There was some murmuring in the crowd. Bill heard a couple of remarks about his long hair and the word "hippie." He continued, "This agreement is not about our shop. Frankly, all of us know that we have a safe and decent workplace as compared to our counterparts in factories around the country. But we do have workers who are raising families, paying bills, and saving for college for their kids. I say this is a good contract. It addresses our everyday issues and improves our benefits. It's time to go back to work, so let's ratify the agreement."

Bill sat down to a round of applause. A couple of guys sitting next to him patted his back in approval. The local president recognized someone in the audience. The man rose and said, "On that note, I move the question to close debate." The motion was seconded, and the question called. The motion won overwhelmingly. The workers then voted by secret ballot on the contract. They were back to work on October 23, working ten hours a day and the next Saturday catching up on the backlog of orders.

***

By the first week in November, things were back to a normal routine. Despite Bill's comments, he continued to keep to himself. Some of the guys on the floor thought he was arrogant and aloof. They knew he was well educated, but they could not get him into any conversations, whether it was about politics, race, sports, or anything else. Bill tried to be friendly, but he did not want to answer any questions about his past, and the best way to do that was not to engage. Some of the guys ribbed him over his hair, which was long and at times unruly. To keep it in place, he wore a Tigers baseball cap.

With the cooler weather, Bill and Sam did not play tennis. They usually met once or twice a week at their regular bar for dinner and a couple of beers. They joined the local YMCA, which was only a half mile from Bill's place. Bill enjoyed running on their inside track and lifting weights. There were times he felt like he was in prison, except that when his workouts were over, he walked outside into the crisp air and went home. He and Sam also enjoyed pickup basketball games. Bill was in great shape. His stomach was hard as a rock.

With Mike's help, Bill bought a modest stereo system. Besides borrowing Mike's records, he was beginning to build a collection for himself. Life in prison had opened his mind to different music genres, from rock and roll to blues to jazz. He enjoyed listening to Johnny Cash, Marvin Gaye, and the Temptations. He also bought every Bob Dylan album. Bill continued to spend time with Kathy and Mike.

The news was full of the war, the protests, civil rights, and hippies. They had lively discussions over dinner, with the evening news playing in the background. Bill was quite naive on the war protests and so-called hippie movement. His friends, while not overly active, had attended local protests.

He noticed Mike's hair was getting longer, and there were times when he thought Kathy dressed like she was from San Francisco, with her flowing dresses. After dinner, and to stop talking about the war, they often smoked a joint and listened to music. Mike picked up a new album by the Moody Blues, *Days of Future Passed*. They loved it, especially the artwork on the album cover.

Chapter Twenty-Eight
The Encounter

After work on a Friday in early November, Bill stopped by the supermarket just a short distance from the plant. The store was busy, so Bill focused on getting in and out as quickly as possible. While examining some apples, he looked up and saw a woman watching him. She was embarrassed when she realized she had been caught staring.

"Bill? Bill Simpson is that you?"

With a smile of recognition, Bill said, "Rita, you look great." He was not exaggerating, Rita Gray was in a bright business suit, wearing high heels that accented her legs. There were a few more lines in her face, especially around the eyes. Still, she was a very good looking woman.

The two briefly clasped hands.

"Wow, you look different than the last time I saw you. Look at you, long hair, jeans, not the Bill Simpson I remember. And, you look like you've lost weight, too."

"Well, I'm in a different line of work now. I work in the parts warehouse across the street at the Tractor Plant."

"Oh, okay," Rita said, somewhat surprised. "Listen, I owe you an apology."

"Why? You don't owe me anything."

"No, I do. When you called me last summer, I had just switched to a new job with an advertising agency, and I didn't want any reminders of my past. You called at the wrong time."

"Don't worry about it," Bill said, taking a step and trying to move on.

"No, it's bothered me for months. I'm glad I saw you."

"Alright, you've moved up in the world and I've kind of moved on, too, but in a different way. No matter, that's life, and because of you, I'm able to enjoy it. And I'm so glad you are doing well. You look terrific."

Rita blushed. "Listen," she said, "tomorrow night a girlfriend, her husband, and I are going to The Chess Mate. Joni Mitchell and her husband, Chuck, are performing. Would you like to join us?"

A coffeehouse? Folk singers? Bill was more into Jimi Hendrix, Bob Dylan, and The Mamas and Papas. But yes, just spending time with Rita sounded great. It wasn't like he had a heavy social calendar.

"That sounds terrific," he said with a warm smile.

"They live in Royal Oak."

"So do I," Bill offered.

"They are on Vinsetta Street. Why don't I come and pick you up, and then we'll go over to Jim and Linda's house and go with them? I'll pick you up around five-thirty. We'll probably get a drink and a bite to eat on the way. The show starts at nine-thirty, but we have to be in line by at least eight if we expect to find a table."

Rita threw so much at him he could barely react. She was asking him out. She was picking him up. That was all fine. She gave him a full smile with twinkling eyes and turned around to continue her shopping. Then she stopped. "Damnit, I forgot to get your address and phone number."

Bill realized he had no pen or paper, a problem she quickly resolved by reaching into her purse. He wrote down the information and she walked off.

One never knows.

***

Bill was nervous all day Saturday. He bought a new sweater and some pants. After his release, he almost exclusively wore jeans, sweaters, shorts, or tennis shirts, depending on the season. The new clothes made him feel good. Then, he went and did something he hadn't done in a long time—he got a haircut. He gave strict orders for a trim, telling the barber he wanted his hair's length to be about the same, but to trim it and shape it up. The barber complied, cutting and combing Bill's hair a little bit differently than he was used to. It was now straight back on his head and hung neatly over his ears and collar. Bill liked it, but knew it would never be short enough to satisfy his mother.

Just after five-thirty, Rita pulled up in a red 1966 GTO. *A hot car, to be sure.* Bill did not want her to see his spartan apartment, so he ran down the steps and jumped in her car.

"Look at you," she said with a smile. "You cleaned up."

"Yeah," Bill said sheepishly. "When you work in a factory five days a week, it's easy to let your appearance slip." He looked at Rita, dressed in a nice sweater and slacks with a leather jacket—she looked great.

As they drove, Rita talked about her two friends, Linda and Jim. "Both are successful, in their mid-thirties. I worked with Linda in my previous job—she's a natural PR person. Jim's in land development. His father ran a landscaping business and died when Jim was just sixteen. He quit high school and ran the company. He's been expanding the company. He's developed apartments and office buildings throughout the area. They have two kids."

"Sounds good."

"Oh, and another thing, Bill. I hope this isn't too awkward. Since I knew you, my life has changed by almost 180 degrees. You know I've moved into the professional world, and the transition has been hard as hell. To help complete my change, I now go by my middle name, Liz, for Elizabeth. No one except my family and a few friends still think of me as Rita."

"Well, that will take some time getting used to. Liz, Liz, Liz," Bill repeated, and the two were laughing as they turned onto Vinsetta Street and pulled into Jim and Linda's driveway. Beyond was a nice, two-story house.

As they got out of the car, Bill said, "Speaking of our histories together, I don't tell anyone about my life before the trial, especially working for the Secret Service. And I never mention my time served."

Rita eyed him with a curious look, took his arm, and squeezed it. "Jesus Christ!" she exclaimed. "You have muscles on top of muscles. Where did those come from?"

Bill looked around and whispered, "Prison, baby." They both laughed.

The four drove to Six Mile Road and Livernois Avenue, across from the University of Detroit campus. They had dinner at a bar and went around the corner to the Chess Mate.

The coffee house was abuzz with conversation. The four secured a table with a decent view of the stage. The place was smaller than Bill expected, very intimate. The atmosphere was electric. Bill looked around; his everyday work clothes would have fit in fine. Almost everyone was in jeans and sweaters. Rita's friends seemed to be fun people. Bill expressed surprise when he learned the club often played music until six in the morning.

"Yeah," Linda remarked. "They don't serve booze, so they don't have a liquor license, so they can stay open all night long—but Bill, we don't stay that late!"

"Good!" Bill replied as they all laughed.

At one point, they started talking about Vietnam.

Jim, who seemed like a classic conservative businessman, looked around the room and observed, "Well, I've got a feeling if there were a poll taken about Vietnam, I'd be one of the few here who support drawing a line in the sand in support of stopping the communists and fighting them now, versus fighting them in Japan, Korea, or California. Most importantly, instead of denigrating our troops, we need to support them. And, I'm sick and tired of these hippies protesting the war and not serving our country."

Rita said, "Oh boy, here we go again."

Linda looked at Bill, "I suppose Liz didn't warn you, but my Jim is very conservative. He's a hawk on the war and is only here tonight because he knows the best way to score tonight will be to make me happy." She laughed and smiled at her husband.

Rita said, "Bill, both Linda and I believe the boys should come home, and LBJ can go fight in the jungles of Southeast Asia. What do you think?"

Bill squirmed. All eyes were on him. "Well, I kind of see things from a different perspective. I'm not sure of all the political arguments. But it does bother me that we send black and uneducated white kids to fight this war. The draft used to be fair, and young people from all classes got called up. I knew I'd be drafted after high school, so I joined up and did my time in Korea. It was tough. In today's world, I'd probably have gotten a deferment and some poor kid would be fighting in my place. It doesn't seem fair to me."

Linda said, "That's interesting, man. I've never really thought about that."

"That's because your kids aren't seventeen," Bill said.

Jim said, "Good point, but what do you think about the war—should we be in or out?"

Bill thought for a moment. "You know, I was initially supportive of what we were doing. I don't know. But too many people are dying and being maimed—I'm not sure it's worth it. The French couldn't win; I'm not sure we can. And, I'm probably one of the few in this place that's actually fought in combat and seen fellow soldiers get blown apart. But, I probably agree with Jim that the white privileged kids at Michigan and the Ivy League schools are out there protesting, and they kind of piss me off. I wonder if they protest because they truly oppose the war or if they don't want their cozy lives interrupted by serving their country. It's complicated, I don't know …"

"You're damn right," Jim said. "What about those damned draft dodgers burning the American flag?"

Bill looked him in the eye and said, "Well, Jim, I'm probably going to disappoint you on that issue. As much as it pisses me off when I see our flag being burnt or disrespected, I have to go with the constitution. Under the Bill of Rights, we give people the right to peacefully protest."

Rita, who had been studying Bill, changed the subject. "Jeez, Bill, that's the most you've said all night long. Now, tell me, can the Tigers win the Series in '68?"

Around ten, the stage darkened, and there was a hush in the crowd as Joni and Chuck Mitchell were introduced. They received a warm round of applause. Bill listened, captivated. They performed many songs together, but they went solo, too. There was one song that affected Bill to his core. Joni introduced the song as a work in progress entitled: *Both Sides, Now.* It was mesmerizing, and when Joni finished, the audience went wild.

The Mitchells finished their show just before midnight. The women looked at each other, indicating it was time to go. The guys offered no argument.

By the time they got to Jim's and Linda's, it was almost one. Linda asked if they wanted to come in, but Rita begged off.

Rita gave Bill her keys to drive back to his house. He held the passenger door open for her and then jumped in the driver's seat.

Bill pulled into his driveway directly behind the Mustang and turned off the ignition. He started to say thank you for a wonderful evening, but he never got the chance. Rita moved toward him, and a second later they were kissing. He hadn't kissed in a car like this since before Debbie was born. He was just as eager as she, but the car's console between the bucket seats was a major deterrent.

"Bill, let's go upstairs," Rita whispered.

"Oh God, yes."

On the way into the house, an anxious Bill whispered, "I wasn't, you know, expecting company." He had little in the way of creature comforts. He had been with two women since prison, one a fix-up by Sam, the other he had met at the library. Neither had Rita's resume.

He opened the door and flicked on the overhead light. Rita surveyed the apartment. "Yeah, I see what you mean about 'spartan,' but don't worry, darling. This night is all for you."

They fell into each other's arms and headed for the bedroom as clothes were shed from the front door to bedside. Wanton passion ensued. Some hours later, as they lay in bed, Rita, her head on Bill's shoulder, voice quivering, pleaded with Bill for forgiveness for her testimony at the trial.

"You're forgiven; don't worry," he whispered, stroking her cheek with the back of his finger. He covered her in kisses.

In the early morning hours, Bill asked if Rita had any interest in a joint, and she responded, "Oh, yeah, that would be great." Then, laughing softly, she added, "God, when you were in my apartment in the old days, I could not imagine you getting high. But one look in the grocery store and I knew you got high."

He got up, put on the album *Time Out* by Dave Brubeck, with the volume just loud enough to be heard but not disturb his neighbors. They smoked the marijuana and resumed their manic, magic lovemaking until they fell asleep as the sun was coming up.

Bill woke with Rita's naked body spooning him. He rolled over and she looked at him with her fathomless, green eyes, her hair a soft storm around her head. "I wondered if you were going to wake up," she half-whispered. "I thought I might have killed you. I hope you can take me to breakfast."

After a little more fooling around, Rita hopped out of bed. "How about that breakfast? Do you have an old sweater or jersey?"

Bill jumped up, reached in his closet, and offered her a couple of choices. Rita grabbed a V-neck sweater and went into the bathroom. Bill walked into the kitchen and put on a pot of coffee. He looked at the kitchen clock. *Ten-thirty! Jesus Christ! What a night!* He walked into the living room and pulled out some records.

She came out of the bathroom, her hair combed casually, his blue sweater clinging to her curves. Bill took a quick shower.

They had a great breakfast at a local grill. As they walked back to his place arm-in-arm, Rita was pensive.

"Bill," she said finally, "there is something you have to understand."

"What's that?"

"Last night and this morning couldn't have been any better"—she paused on the sidewalk and looked at him—but my life, it's so different now. I don't want anyone from my past to be part of it. I have to move on."

Bill frowned. "Has anyone from the past contacted you?"

"Not really—only one man, a former client. He actually helped me get my first job in the marketing business. If there are others, they don't have the courage to come up to me."

"Good," he said, holding her loosely by the waist.

"Bill, as much as I know I am drawn to you, I can't see you. I just can't do anything to take me back to the past. Can you understand? This is not easy for me." She began to tear up.

Bill had just spent one of the happiest nights of his life with this woman, but what could he do? The rejection hurt like hell, but he tried to hide his emotions as best he could. He struggled for words.

"It's hard for you, well, it's just as hard for me," he said at last. "Shit, I don't want to lose you! I feel like I just found you!"

"I know, baby," Rita said as they started walking again. "You know, without your visits to my apartment years ago, I don't know that I had honestly thought about my future. Just like the man who helped me with my job, with just a few words, you helped save my life."

Bill squeezed her hand. They said nothing else until they got back to his apartment. They went upstairs and Rita grabbed her things. Bill walked her downstairs to her car.

She smiled as she climbed into the driver's seat.

"You know," he reminded her, "you're wearing my sweater."

"I know, and I'm never giving it back."

Rita pulled away without looking back.

Bill turned around and walked back inside, his heart aching. Just then Mike came out of his flat, a cheesy grin on his face. "So, I guess you had a pretty good time last night?"

"You heard?" Bill said, feeling the blood rush to his cheeks.

"Oh, yeah, we heard—all night long."

"She was an old friend," Bill said, and added, "She won't be back. God, I have to lie down." He walked upstairs and put the Lions pregame on WJR radio. He listened to Van Patrick doing the announcing while he drifted in and out of sleep. His team lost to the Chicago Bears, but his mind kept replaying scenes of the previous night with Rita Gray. It had been wonderful … every second of it.

Chapter Twenty-Nine
1968

Bill spent New Year's Eve and New Year's Day at his mother's house. They had the kids, which made ringing in the New Year great fun. At seven and five, Debbie and Johnny were still a source of great joy. They loved Bill's Christmas gifts and played into the night. Both insisted they were going to make it until midnight to ring in the New Year. They never came close, and Bill carried them from the basement and put them in a makeshift "tent" Jenny had put together in the living room.

As he went to sleep that night, Bill thought about his children. He was spending less and less time with them. If he could have nights like this, a sleepover here and there, their relationship with him might grow stronger. Anne simply refused to consider such options. The only reason he had them for New Year's was because Anne was dating again. He didn't know the guy, but he was genuinely happy for his ex-wife. She worked hard to be a professional at the law firm, and she worked equally hard on her looks. Things were looking up for her. Maybe this change in her life would create more opportunities for him to be with the kids.

Bill returned the kids to their mother around noon on New Year's Day. He drove home and watched the Rose Bowl game between USC and Indiana with Mike and Kathy. O.J. Simpson had a great game, scoring two touchdowns in an easy USC win.

Mike had just graduated from law school and talked about his future. He was clerking for a liberal law firm in Detroit and studying for the bar exam. Bill was happy for him.

The next day, Tuesday, Bill was back to work. As he processed orders for tractor parts and handled small emergencies for his boss, he sensed a changing mood on the shop floor. The white guys were talking more about Vietnam, anti-war protests, hippies, and race—often with a tinge of anger or frustration in their voices. Things were changing, and change was difficult to accept for many.

In February, the North Vietnamese managed a massive attack on US and South Vietnamese soldiers. It had happened during Tet, the Vietnamese New Year. Bill nearly became sick to his stomach on more than one occasion during evening newscasts as he watched American troops wounded and dying. He became more convinced that his country was making a terrible mistake by not getting out of Southeast Asia.

March 12 was the New Hampshire presidential primary. President Johnson had not officially announced as a candidate, but expected to do extremely well as a write-in candidate. The only other candidate was an upstart, a self-proclaimed peace candidate, US Senator Eugene McCarthy. In what stunned the American electorate, McCarthy lost by only seven percent against the powerful incumbent president. Four days later, Bobby Kennedy jumped into the race. Bill and many others were cynical of Kennedy's presidential ambitions. Most assumed he hadn't originally run because he did not want to take on a powerful sitting president. Now, after McCarthy exposed Johnson's vulnerability, Kennedy had the gall to jump into the race. Though Bill's White House experience had left a bad taste in his mouth, when it came to Bobby Kennedy, he had to admit that the man represented his views on the war and on domestic issues better than any other candidate.

On a Sunday night, March 31, Bill sat down to watch *The Smothers Brothers Comedy Hour*. He enjoyed the irreverent political jabs and the musical guests. All at once the show was interrupted by a special bulletin: President Johnson was about to address the nation.

The president spoke about the efforts of the South Vietnamese to add more troops, and said he was adding more American troops to the current 525,000 already deployed in Vietnam. He focused on the US government's interest in negotiating a cessation of the bombing of North Vietnam, while being frustrated by a lack of attention from Hanoi. Johnson said there had been success in strengthening the South Vietnamese military and government.

Johnson looked weary and ashen. He was sporting new glasses that altered his appearance. Bill wondered who had written the speech, the military or the CIA. Suddenly, the president seemed to refocus his thoughts.

Johnson said he planned to devote the remaining year of his term to negotiate peace in Vietnam. Then...

> "I have concluded that I should not permit the presidency to become involved in the partisan divisions that are developing in this political year. With America's sons in the fields far away, with America's future under challenge right here at home, with our hopes and the world's hopes for each in the balance every day, I do not believe

that I should devote an hour or a day of my time to any personal partisan causes or to any duties other than the awesome duties of this office—the presidency of your country. Accordingly, I shall not seek, and I will not accept, the nomination of my party for another term as your president."

Bill stared at the television in disbelief. Had he heard Johnson correctly? As the president concluded and CBS switched back to the TV newsmen, they confirmed Johnson's statement and their own astonishment. They scrambled to put the president's statement into perspective, not doing a particularly good job. The press was as stunned as the nation.

On Thursday, Bill was walking into his apartment, returning from a workout at the Y with Sam, when Mike poked his head out of his door: "Have you heard?" he said.

"Heard what?"

"Martin Luther King was shot in Memphis. He's dead."

"What? Jesus Christ!" Bill exclaimed as Mike opened the door wider and motioned for him to come in. Kathy was glued to the television and barely acknowledged Bill's entry. Bill sat down as Mike handed him a Coke.

As he listened to frantic broadcasters, Bill reflected on King's decade of prominence. The charismatic pastor had been knocked off the pinnacle of his success after his "I Have a Dream" speech in 1963. As his fight for civil rights efforts moved to the northern states, whites took strong exception to his actions. In Chicago, some white nationalists and others protested his efforts for more open housing. He came out against the war, much to Johnson's displeasure. Bill shook his head as he sipped his Coke. It was a senseless loss, and it had come on the heels of several others: President Kennedy, Malcolm X, and Medgar Evers among them. Sleep eluded him that night as his mind replayed the scene on the Memphis motel balcony over and over.

***

Sports often proved to be a cathartic experience for communities, and this was true in Detroit and Michigan, in 1968. The Detroit Tigers became the best baseball team in the country, starting off the season with a nine and one record and never looking back, winning 103 games. Different players came through in the eighth or ninth innings to win games. An ex-convict from Ohio named Gates Brown won three games with pinch-hit home runs. The Tiger season was special as it captured the imagination of the entire state. Many said, and Bill agreed, that considering the violent rage of 1967, the 1968 Detroit Tigers brought a greater sense of unity to the city than anyone could have imagined.

As the weather warmed, Sam and Bill hit the tennis courts. The two were striking figures as they charged the net. Bill had a great backhand and could cover almost every shot on the court. His silver-streaked brown hair, often pulled into a ponytail, flowed with his entire body when he chased down a ball. It was not uncommon for people to stop and watch their rallies, where the volleys could add up to over twenty back-and-forth shots.

On the morning of Wednesday, June 5, Bill walked into his bathroom to get ready for work. He flipped on the overhead light and hit the dial on his transistor radio, expecting to wake up to his favorite top forty hits from the Canadian station, CKLW. Instead, he heard the nasal drone of a news director reading a bulletin from a wire service. The man's words hit Bill like a gut-punch: Robert Kennedy was near death after an assassin had shot the senator shortly after he had declared victory over McCarthy in the California primary.

Bill hurried to the living room and flipped on the TV. It was too early for Hugh Downs and the *Today Show*, but NBC news was recapping the events. Bobby Kennedy was in the hospital, fighting for his life after a man had shot him and five others in the kitchen of the Beverly Hills Ambassador Hotel. Bill was in shock—first Jack Kennedy, then Martin Luther King, and now Robert Kennedy. Bill felt that Bobby had become a better man, less rude and abrupt, after his brother's assassination. *What a terrible loss for the country*. He hustled to get to work on time. His co-workers appeared equally shaken by the news.

The following Saturday, Bill watched the televised funeral. Senator Ted Kennedy's eulogy was extremely moving. Bill spent the day watching the train ride from New York to Washington, followed by the procession to Arlington Cemetery. He was riveted. At times, Mike or Kathy came up and watched with him. Other times, he moved down to their place and watched. On Sunday, Bill spent the day with his mother, Debbie, and Johnny.

Chapter Thirty
Romance

During the third week of August, Sam and Bill were in a first-set battle at the Eaton Park tennis courts in Birmingham. Their rallies were long, with many baseline shots, each player looking for an opportunity to charge the net. Two attractive women in their late twenties or early thirties were watching as they waited for an open court. Bill found himself playing a bit more aggressively.

But Sam finished off the set with an overhead smash that caught Bill watching the ball flash by out of reach. Bill laughed and said, "You bastard!" He walked to the net to congratulate Sam.

Sam, always on the make, said, "Thanks, Billy. Hey, man, do you want to ask those girls if they want to play some doubles?"

Bill, always shy around women, said, "Sure. You head over, and I'll hold the court."

Sam went over and engaged in his typical banter, and about three minutes later the three of them walked over to their court.

"Bill, this is Sue and Cindy." Bill nodded and shook their hands. "Cindy says Sue is the better player, and between the two of us, we know who is best," he said with a big grin. "So, Cindy and I will take on you and Sue. Make sense?"

"All sounds good to me. Sue, as you probably saw, I'm going to need all the help I can get." The five-foot, three-inch woman had short blond hair and blue eyes. She smiled and said, "We were watching you guys, and I've got to tell you boys that we're *not* in your class!" She emitted a lively laugh.

Bill said, "Well, we'll see. Most of all, let's have some fun."

The two women were strong players. Sue was a real athlete, with a great instinct for the game. *She probably had lessons*, Bill thought as he watched her move gracefully to take shots with a powerful follow-through. In one rally, the two had control of the net, and Sam tried to lob the ball over Sue's head. She stepped back and smashed the ball at Sam's feet. He had no time to react as he fumbled his return shot into the net. Sam was incredibly competitive, and Bill noticed he shot her a look of scorn. Bill stifled a laugh.

Bill was smitten. He liked the way Sue glided on the court. She had a way of moving her body, especially her hips, as she moved to her position to set up for the start of a rally. She had an athlete's body, with firm muscle tone. Her smile was real. Her chatting during the game was fun. And, without trying to be obvious, he just liked the way her body looked in her tennis blouse and shorts. He wanted to get to know her.

After their set was over, Sam suggested they go to a bar for a drink. He selected a nearby place, "a casual place that doesn't mind people with sweaty bodies," he commented.

Shortly after ordering beers and appetizers, the conversation broke off into two discussions: Sam and Cindy, and Bill and Sue.

Sue was a social studies teacher at Birmingham Seaholm High School. She was going into her third year and lived in an apartment house off Woodward Avenue, just north of downtown Birmingham.

"So, Billy, what about you?" she asked, nudging him with her shoulder. "Where do you work?

"Well," he said, almost defensively, "I work at the Ford Tractor facility on Maple Road."

"Really? I've never known anyone who worked there. What do you do, design tractors?"

"No, I work in their parts warehouse." He grinned as he added, "I'm a picker, packer, checker."

Rather than question what the hell a picker, packer, checker was, Sue said, "You know, you have a great smile. Jesus Christ, you should smile more often."

Sam overheard the comment. "Yeah, you need to get that boy to smile more. He's *way* too serious." They all laughed.

After they had a couple of beers and the appetizers, Sam said, "Ah, Bill, I'm going to drive Cindy home. Do you mind if Sue takes you home?"

Sue shot Cindy a critical look and answered for Bill, "Sam, I don't know you that well, but really it's my decision as to whether I take Bill anywhere."

"Excuse me," Sam said sarcastically. "Sue, would you mind dropping off my favorite tennis partner back at his place in Royal Oak? I can promise you one thing—he's no wolf!"

"You know," Sue said, now giving Bill a critical up and down look, "I don't mind giving this boy a ride home."

They all laughed. Minutes later, Bill was riding in Sue's blue 1967 Barracuda. It was a sharp car, with a black racing stripe down the middle. Bill offered his compliments.

"You know," Sue said, ignoring his praise of her car, "Cindy is one of my best friends, but she sometimes really pisses me off. What if I didn't like you? What the hell was I supposed to do then? It could have been pretty damned awkward."

Wow! She likes me!

Sue shrugged before finally acknowledging Bill's admiration for her car. "Well, it's really a pretty basic car. This was all I could afford last year," she said as she patted the automatic floor gear shift between the bucket seats. "In Birmingham, it seems like everyone's a GM person, but my dad works at Chrysler and that makes me a Chrysler girl."

When they arrived at Bill's place, he considered asking her up, but remembered that he hadn't done much cleaning of late—the place was a mess.

"Ah, I don't want to be too forward," Bill said, "but can I get your number? Maybe next week we can do dinner and a movie?"

Sue eyed him with a mischievous grin. "If it means I'll see your smile more often, yeah, you can have my number." Reaching in the backseat for her purse, she took out a pen and a loose piece of paper and scribbled down her name and phone. "Call me," she said as Bill got out of the car. "I think my best night will be Thursday, if that works for you." As she pulled out of the driveway, she said loudly, "Sam's right! You are no wolf!"

***

The next week moved slowly. The National Democratic Convention was taking place in Chicago. In early August, the Republicans had nominated Richard Nixon and some guy named Spiro Agnew as their presidential and vice presidential nominees. What were the Democrats going to do? Since Bobby Kennedy's death, it looked like it was Vice President Hubert Humphrey's nomination to lose. Eugene McCarthy was the anti-war candidate, but he was no Bobby Kennedy. Then, South Dakota senator and Bobby Kennedy's friend George McGovern offered himself as Kennedy's replacement. McGovern was a decent senator, but to Bill he had no magnetism. He did not see him beating Humphrey. Bill had always liked Humphrey, especially on civil rights. He hoped to see an anti-war policy from him, but instinctively knew Humphrey could not break with President Johnson.

On Monday night, August 26, Bill flipped on the television. Perhaps he'd hear some speeches and see what Chet Huntley and David Brinkley, the NBC newscasters, might have to say. He stayed glued to the set as he watched confrontations between Chicago police and thousands of anti-war protesters. The brutality was something he had not seen since the dark days of the civil rights movement in the south. During a commercial break, he ran downstairs to make sure Mike and Kathy were watching. They were watching ABC's coverage.

The violence escalated as the days went on. The protesters were made up of many who called themselves "yippies," members of the Youth International Party, and the Students for a Democratic Society. They were at the convention to voice their opposition to Vietnam. Hordes of angry youths crowded Grant Park, Michigan Avenue, and other locations. There was no question that some of the protesters were out of line. Bill thought lowering an American flag and replacing it with a North Vietnamese flag was wrong; however, he didn't think Mayor Daley should be directing police to beat, gas, and arrest the young people. He, along with the rest of the country, were deeply bothered by what they witnessed.

On Wednesday night, he was watching the events in Mike and Kathy's flat. ABC had two commentators joining the veteran news commentator, Howard K. Smith. One was liberal writer Gore Vidal, and the other was conservative commentator William F. Buckley, *two equally arrogant intellectuals,* Bill thought, based on their tone and mannerisms. Their commentary was lively and exposed the deep schism between those pro-war and anti-war Americans.

During a lull in convention action, the screen shifted to Buckley and Vidal, sitting in chairs with a small table in between. Mike had picked up a pizza and the three of them were washing it down with a few beers. Howard K. Smith referenced the protesters in Grant Park replacing the US flag with a Vietcong flag and asked if it wasn't akin to hanging a Nazi flag during World War II.

Vidal's response was that many people in the United States, and especially in Europe, strongly opposed US involvement in the war. He pointed out that in the American democracy, people could express whatever views they liked. Before Vidal could finish, Buckley interrupted him, implying that some of the protesters were Nazis.

"Shut up a minute!" Vidal said angrily.

Buckley said, "No, I won't. Some people were pro-Nazi and, and the answer is they were well treated by the people who ostracized them. And, I'm for ostracizing people who egg on other people to shoot American Marines and American soldiers. I know you don't care—"

Vidal interrupted Buckley, "As far as I'm concerned, the only pro- or crypto-Nazi I can think of is yourself. Failing that—"

"Let's not call names," Smith said, intervening.

Vidal ignored the mild-mannered TV anchor. "Failing that, I can only say that—"

Buckley leaned over his armrest, getting into Vidal's face, "Now listen, you queer, stop calling me a crypto-Nazi or I'll sock you in your goddamn face, and you'll stay plastered."

The camera cut to Smith, who had lost control of his program. Much of the audience in the United States was stunned by the exchange. Sadly, it had captured the emotion splitting the country regarding Vietnam, as well as the great cultural divide.

Mike was the first to speak. "Did I just hear what I thought I heard?"

Kathy, laughing nervously, said, "Jesus Christ! He called Gore Vidal a queer on television!"

"I know," Bill said, laughing. "I can't believe this … holy fuck."

Thirty minutes later, Bill was up in his place, dialing Sue's phone number to confirm their date for the next evening.

"Sue, it's Bill," he said when she answered. "Are we still on for tomorrow?"

"Oh, Bill, yes, of course, but I wonder if we could make a change in plans," she said. "I don't know about you, but I've been watching this convention all week. Man, I don't want to miss any of it, these goddamned police, *fucking* Mayor Daley and the *fucking* Democrats! What the hell is wrong with the world? Anyway, why don't you come over? We'll have a very informal dinner and watch the convention and see who gets bashed."

Bill, amused at all she had said, replied, "So, do you use 'fuck' a lot when you're teaching?"

"Fuck no!" she said, laughing. "I don't, really I don't. Jesus, I don't really know you, but I feel I do. Anyhow, I have to watch my potty mouth. It's just these people, they make me so goddamned mad."

***

The modern construction of Sue's apartment complex appealed to Bill. *Nice, something that a young professional might have.* There were several buildings, two stories each. Sue was on the top floor of Building B. When she opened her door, Bill feasted his eyes on the young woman dressed in white shorts, a blue blouse, and wearing that captivating smile.

"Very nice," he said, handing her a bottle of wine.

"Thank you," she replied, taking him by the arm and ushering him inside. She looked at the bottle and frowned. "This is definitely better wine than I'm used to drinking."

"Well, I doubt that," he said with a smile. He had promised himself that he was going to smile more tonight.

"Well, listen, I'm not much of a cook. I'm just going to throw on some steaks. I have baked potatoes and some veggies already cooking. Is that alright?"

"Sounds great. Better than what I'm used to."

They sat down to eat with the television droning in the background. Bill asked her about teaching, which she loved. She said school started in one week, the Thursday after Labor Day, but teachers started two days earlier.

"So, how did you become such a good tennis player?"

Sue shook her head and wiped her mouth with a paper napkin. "Shit, you saw me—I'm not that good."

"Don't undersell yourself, you are good. You took lessons?"

Sue shrugged. "Yeah, my father's a member out at the Birmingham Country Club. He always wanted a son, but was stuck with me and my sister. I was the tomboy, so I learned tennis and golf."

"Golf, too? Very good."

"You play?"

"Not really," Bill replied. "I haven't touched a club in years, but maybe we can get out and try a round."

Sue nodded and sat back in her chair. "So, mister strong and silent man, enough about me, what about you?

"Well, I grew up on Detroit's east side. My dad worked in a Ford plant and then became involved in the UAW. He died a few years ago. Cancer."

"I'm sorry."

"It's okay. I miss him, but the cigarettes got him."

Sue sighed. "Yeah, I hate fucking cigarettes." They looked at each other and started laughing. "I know, my mouth," she said. "I will work on it. Somehow, I never swear in class and rarely in the building. Never around my parents. I guess I picked it up at Michigan State. You know, the dorm life. Hey, you changed the subject. What about you? Goddamn it, do you realize how hard it is to get you to talk about yourself?"

"You wanted me to smile more, and I'm trying. Let's work on one thing at a time."

"Okay. You played sports in school?"

Bill took a sip of wine. "Yep. Football, basketball, a little baseball. I was pretty good in football. I played receiver but was a better defensive back.

"Were you in the Army?"

"Korea, but that's a long story. Let's just say this business of war being about heroes and medals is bullshit." Pointing to the TV, Bill said, "You know, it looks like things are getting started. Why don't you sit down on the couch, and I'll clean up."

"No, absolutely not. I can do the dishes and clean up later."

"No, ma'am. I take pleasure in doing dishes, especially after a great dinner."

"Great, my ass. All I did was throw some meat and potatoes in the oven."

Bill casually grabbed her arm and led her from the table to the couch. He stepped over to the color TV and turned up the volume. Her protesting body relaxed, and she settled in on the couch and watched. Fifteen minutes later, the dishes were washed and drying in the dish rack, and he was wiping the table. "Wine, beer, or something else?" Bill asked.

Sue turned around and looked at him. "Hey, that's my job. I don't know that I know you well enough for you to be snooping through my cabinets." He acquiesced and sat while she got up and brought some beers over to the small coffee table.

The convention convened. Hubert Humphrey had easily been nominated late the night before. Tonight, Humphrey and his vice presidential running mate, Edmund Muskie, a stoic liberal senator from Maine, were to give their acceptance speeches.

At one point during the coverage, a camera caught Humphrey looking out of his hotel room at the protesters on the street below. He had a sick look on his face. "Hubert is looking at his election going down the drain," Bill commented dryly.

Sue looked at him. "You sound like you know him?"

"No, I don't know him, but I saw him a couple of times."

"Really, how?"

Bill had become so comfortable with this woman that he had slipped back to those months in Washington some six years earlier, when he had seen Humphrey coming and going from the White House. "Oh," he said casually, "for a while I had a job in Washington."

The television shifted to some police action at Grant Park. Later, Muskie gave his acceptance speech. While the man was somewhat stiff, he was younger than the typical candidate for a national ticket, and the convention delegates liked him. He gave a good speech seeking unity, protecting the environment, and bringing an end to the war.

Bill looked at his watch. Tomorrow was a workday. "Listen, I've got to get going. I've got to get up early tomorrow. Are you around this weekend?"

"Yeah, I should be pretty clear. We could play tennis, maybe with Sam and Cindy?"

"Well, how about this? Let's see if we can do tennis on Saturday, during the day, and maybe you and I can do a movie on Saturday night."

"Yeah, that's good," Sue said.

Saturday was a perfect day for the traditional end of summer, and for tennis. The courts were not too busy. Bill and Sue took on Sam and Cindy. After ninety minutes, they split their match by winning one set each. Afterward, Sue announced that her dad had given her four box seats to the Tigers game on Sunday. All three jumped at the chance to see the Tigers take on Baltimore. Denny McLain, who was having a season for the ages, was pitching.

Bill and Sue decided that they'd go see a special showing of *The Graduate* at the Radio City Theatre in Ferndale, then have dinner at Pasquale's.

After the movie, on the way to the restaurant, Sue said, "Jesus Christ, I've never seen a movie like that."

Bill laughed. "Me neither. I think it's for a different generation. I don't know about you, but when I graduated from college, my first objective was getting a job." He glanced over at Sue and smiled. "But," he added, "I don't know. I think meeting someone like Mrs. Robinson might have been good for me."

"Fuck you!" Sue said, turning her head and looking out the passenger window in mock anger. "But there were some very funny scenes."

Pasquale's was mobbed. Bill and Sue put their names on the wait list and squeezed into a small space at the bar. Bill ordered a beer and Sue ordered a Bloody Mary. They were called to their table just as their drinks needed replenishing. The server brought fresh drinks, and they ordered a large pizza.

During dinner, they talked more about the movie. Sue said, "You know, I come from a pretty comfortable background, like those people in the movie. Man, I don't know anyone like the people portrayed in the film. My dad worked hard, made good money, and my mom made sure my sister and I were active in school activities and got good grades."

Bill pulled a string of mozzarella off his slice and ate it. "My life was very different from yours. No country clubs, no great schools. There were months when my dad didn't know if he'd be able to make his mortgage payment. I don't know that I could have gone to college without the GI Bill."

Sue frowned. "Jesus, don't get defensive on me. I was just comparing my life with Dustin Hoffman and Katherine Ross."

"I'm not defensive. I'm just pointing out that I come from a very different background than you. Still, except for some of the funny scenes, I really didn't identify with those people. Like you, but for different reasons. It must be a good movie if it's causing discussions like this all around the country."

Sue looked at him and smirked. "You know, I did identify with Elaine with something."

"What was that?"

"There was this guy. We were supposed to get married, but I just couldn't do it."

Bill immediately perked up. "Whoa, who's this guy? What did he do to you?"

"No, he didn't do anything to me, or at least nothing that I didn't agree to," Sue said with a smile … a smile that, for Bill, sparked a twinge of jealousy.

"He reminds me a little of the guy who played Elaine's boyfriend in the movie," Sue said. "Anyhow, James, my guy, my family knew his family. We both have cottages on Lake Charlevoix up north. Perhaps we'll go there sometime," she added with a grin. "Anyhow, we knew each other growing up. He went to Michigan; I went to Michigan State. He's a year older. He graduated with a business degree and started in a GM management program. I eventually got my education degree and started teaching in Birmingham, first at Derby Junior High, then over at Seaholm." She paused and took a drink, looking around. "So, Bill, darling, about a year or so ago, we started seeing each other or, as he said, taking our friendship to the next level. It was serious. Last Christmas he proposed to me, and I accepted."

Bill listened intently. Sue continued between bites of pizza. "Our families were delighted. My mom wanted the perfect wedding. But somehow, as spring approached, I got nervous. Something wasn't right. He treated me well, but I just began to feel like I was an ornament, a decoration for his arm. I just knew I didn't love him and would never be happy, that I was just doing something I was supposed to do—you know? In May, I broke it off. It's been a bitch of a summer. My folks were mad, friends were mad. Just about everyone but Cindy decided to ignore me."

"Good for you" Bill said. "You were stronger than Elaine in the movie. The last thing you want to do is get married if you're not comfortable. Jesus, people have a tough enough time making a good marriage. Now more than ever."

Sue laughed. "Billy boy, I really like you, a lot. I don't have a goddamned clue as to why I like you. You don't tell me anything. For all I know you're some goddamned rapist with a criminal record." Bill flinched, hoping she didn't notice. "Bill, I'm still not over James. Don't worry, he's not going to be a problem. He's at Harvard getting a master's in business administration. I'm just afraid. I don't know that I'm ready for something serious yet. Goddamn it, I hope you will just give me some time."

"Damn," he said. "I can't believe we're having this discussion here, of all places."

She laughed. "I know, it must be the damned movie."

"Well, I'll tell you what … let's get our bill and I'll take you home. We'll go up, have a nightcap, and I promise I'll talk about myself—and I'll go home. You know, there is something about you, I don't know what the hell it is, but I don't think I could ever hurt you."

She smiled and grabbed his hand under the table. The electricity between them felt real.

He paid the bill and they walked out into the warm, late summer evening. Bill opened the passenger door of his Mustang. Sue started to sit down, but he impulsively pulled her to him and kissed her. Their mouths melded together as one, their tongues intertwining. After a minute, they broke apart, took some deep breaths, and Bill drove her home, their hands clasped between his shifting gears.

A light rain started to fall as he drove. He explored Sue's thighs with his right hand, and they kissed at every stoplight. Soon, they were in her apartment. She kept him at arm's length as she poured some red wine, and they moved to the couch. After a few sips, Sue looked into his eyes and said, "Now, it's your turn."

"Okay, I'm going to tell you some things—some of these things no one knows, except for my mother, my lawyer, and my ex. Not even Sam. This is between you and me, right?"

She nodded, smiling, her blue eyes twinkling with anticipation.

"First, you should know I used to be a Secret Service agent."

"Damn it, I was right!" she said.

"What?" Bill looked at her, puzzled.

"Bill, I don't have any problems where you work, but I knew you were educated. I knew you were more than a guy working in the shop."

"Okay," he said, setting down his wine and putting his hands on her shoulders. "This is going to be tough enough. I want to get through this, so give me some space, okay?"

Sue shook her head. "Yeah, I'm sorry. You know me, sometimes I can't control myself."

Bill rolled his eyes. *"Oh really?"* he said. He told her about Korea, his Secret Service job, the experience on President Kennedy's detail, his prime job of dealing with counterfeiters, the charges brought against him, his trial, his time in jail, his divorce, his surprisingly early release, and then the help the UAW gave him in finding a decent job. He had never poured out his soul like he did then.

Sue was flabbergasted. "Jesus Christ! You worked with Kennedy? Do you know how lucky you are?"

"It's the highlight of my life," he said, finishing his wine. He poured himself another glass and topped off hers.

"You knew Bobby?"

"Well, I didn't know him. We were, at times, in the same room together or I saw him in the White House meeting the president. Frankly, I didn't like him in those days. Later, after he was a senator and began running for president, I realized he was someone special. I came to admire him."

"Okay, tell me about your wife."

Bill wasn't expecting that request. He expected questions on prison life and being a felon.

"Anne was and is a fine person. I probably was not fair to her. I worked a lot. I couldn't tell her much about my work, which made things tough. During my White House assignment, she was pregnant and essentially on her own. We were probably too young to get married. I know she thought I cheated on her. I never did. But, when the accusation came up, she believed it. You have to understand that it came out on the front page of the newspapers. She was humiliated—we all were—my family, me. It wasn't true, but there was nothing we could do. Still, by that time we had already drifted apart. Now, we have two lives that neither one of us would have expected when Johnny was born."

"The kids?"

"I love my kids, but Anne's new life will make it difficult for me to have any type of decent relationship with them. I'm a felon and I really I have no standing in the court. If she were a bad mother, that might be one thing, but she's not."

Sue leaned over, took his wine, and put it on the coffee table. Then she wrapped her arms around him, and they kissed. After several minutes of mashing on the sofa, Bill gently pushed her away. "I have to go."

"Yeah, I know… but I don't want you to go."

Bill started to protest, and she stopped him.

"Look, can I trust you? You bastard, I'm falling for you."

He chuckled. "You think you're falling for me? Jesus, I fell for you the first moment I saw you."

"Bullshit. Now, I'm serious, can I trust you? I want you to stay. I'm not ready for sex, but God, I just want to sleep with you, hold you and, yes, goddammit, I want to kiss you. So, can I trust you?"

Bill sighed. "You know, I was hoping we were going to be together the moment I met you. I can't wait to make love with you, but it's not going to be tonight."

It took some time, but they finally made it to the bedroom. They helped each other undress, Bill to his underwear, Sue to pajamas. Soon they were under the covers, kissing, hugging, touching, and holding one another. In time, she fell asleep in his arms. Bill, lying on his back with his arm around her, enjoyed the feeling of being happy and contented. God, her body was so soft and felt so good coiled up next to his.

On Sunday, they saw the Tigers whip Baltimore, seven to three. McLain won the game and moved his record to an amazing 27-5. Sue had impressed everyone with the box seats along the first-base line. They teased her over having a father with such pull.

"Buy a Chrysler," she said with a grin.

Chapter Thirty-One
The Detroit Tigers

Detroit was a special place to be during the fall of 1968. The Tigers continued their great season. The pitching was fantastic. McLain and Mickey Lolich were the Tigers' aces and claimed forty-eight out of the team's 103 wins, McLain with thirty-one of them. Having won the American League pennant by a whopping 12 games over the Baltimore Orioles, the Tigers went on to play the St. Louis Cardinals with superstar pitcher Bob Gibson in October's World Series. Only Detroit fans gave the Tigers a chance of taking the series.

During the first week of the series, Sam called Bill, saying that his boss had given him a couple of tickets to game five in Detroit. Bill had plenty of leave time available, but his boss was being a bit finicky and wanted to know the reason for his request. When Bill told him it was a World Series game, Delvero smiled and said, "Hell yes, you can have the day off. Just bring home a winner."

Monday was cool and overcast, in the fifties, but no rain. The game was a sellout, but Bill was not sure the stadium would fill up. The Tigers had lost two straight and were down in the best-of-seven series, three games to one. Jose Feliciano sang the National Anthem. Most fans were excited to hear the popular singer, but his version of the anthem was different than most were used to, a slower, Latin jazz performance. Many fans booed, thinking this was another counterculture protest of the Vietnam War. Sam looked at Bill and said, "Cool."

One of the big plays in the game came in the top of the fifth with the Tigers down, 3-2.

Cardinals speedster Lou Brock was on second base, when Julian Javier cracked a single to left field. Tigers left fielder Willie Horton, normally an average fielder, charged the ball, picked it up, and made a perfect, one-bounce throw to Bill Freehan at the plate. Brock, running to home like lightning, did not slide as would be the usual strategy. Instead, he tried to stick his foot around the stocky Freehan to get to the plate. The umpire called Brock out, raising his right hand. The fans, Bill and Sam included, went wild.

The Tigers scored three times in the bottom of the seventh to win, and headed back to St. Louis down, three games to two.

Sam and Bill were ecstatic. They walked down Michigan Avenue as the fans were celebrating and went to Lafayette Coney Island. The place was jammed, but they managed to get a couple of beers and Coneys. Then they headed to the Lindell AC bar, the top sports bar in Detroit, another place that was jammed. Sam and Bill were excited to see two Detroit Lions football legends, Alex Karras and Joe Schmidt, holding court. Karras was a defensive lineman, and Schmidt, who had created the role of middle linebacker in the NFL, was now the team's head coach.

Almost as soon as Sam dropped Bill off, Bill was on the phone with Sue making plans for later in the week.

The remainder of the week was probably one of the lowest productivity weeks the city had ever known. Radios popped up everywhere. Someone could walk down the hall of an office building and track the World Series action. The Tigers won game six on Wednesday in St. Louis, tying the series at three games each.

Sue told Bill that trying to teach high school students with all the mayhem was impossible. Not only were the Tigers playing in the World Series, but her high school was preparing for a day-long event on Friday called Field Day, a series of fun competitions between classes with races, tugs of war, and other activities. Sue would assist the junior class competitors that day.

Bill listened to the games on his transistor radio during work on Wednesday and Thursday. In Thursday's deciding game, Lolich picked off both Brock and Curt Flood in the fifth, and the Tiger offense finally got to Gibson as Detroit won, 4-1. Detroit fans went into a wild celebration.

Bill had previously agreed to meet Sue for a late dinner on Thursday night.

He arrived early at the restaurant on Woodward in Birmingham, anticipating that getting a table would be tough. Sue was running late, so he sat at the bar, watching TV coverage of the game and the wild fans in downtown Detroit afterward. Suddenly, Sue was standing next to him, and they embraced with a long kiss.

She bit his ear lightly and said, "Jesus, what a day. The Tigers are world champs, and my eleventh-graders are in the best shape possible to take on our seniors tomorrow. Jesus Christ, what a fucking day. Sorry, I'm late, I walked over."

Bill released her. "God, you feel great."

After waiting for a half an hour, they decided to eat at the bar. The hum, excess drinking, and excited patrons created an energy in his hometown that Bill had never seen.

Service was slow, but they had a fun evening despite that.

Bill drove Sue back to her place, and as he stopped the car, Sue said, "Come up. I don't want to be alone tonight."

In Sue's apartment, they grabbed drinks from the kitchen and hit the sofa, laughing and kissing. Before long, Bill's hands had wandered underneath Sue's blouse.

"Bill, sweetheart," she cooed. "Let's move to the bedroom."

"Are you sure?"

"I've never been so sure in my entire fucking life."

***

Sue's clock radio alarm sounded at six the next morning, with a Detroit DJ's booming voice rousing Bill from deep, content slumber. *"Good morning, Detroit! I know no one wants to get up today, so don't. Just stay in bed all day listening to WXYZ radio, the home of the best Detroit Tiger fans and the world champions!"*

Sue rubbed her eyes. "Jesus, I have to get going. I have to be at school by seven."

Bill pulled her firm, naked body next to his. Their night of lovemaking was more than he could have imagined. He could not remember a time he was so happy, except perhaps when his daughter was born. He reached for her hips as he felt her body giving in to his.

"God damn, Bill, I have to go," Sue said, giggling.

Twenty minutes, later she rolled over. "Okay, big boy, that's enough. I've got to get my sorry ass in gear."

Bill grinned. "There's nothing sorry about your sweet ass. Yeah," he said, "I have to get out of here. I've got to get home, change, and shower."

"You know," she said with a smile, "this better not be a one-night stand. I think you need to keep a change of clothes here, because I am sure of one thing: I want more nights like last night."

Chapter Thirty-Two
A Change of Direction

For the first time in a long time, Bill looked to a bright future. His mother adored Sue and encouraged the romance. By the end of the year, Bill had yet to introduce his kids to his girlfriend, but that was just a question of the right time. The good news was that Anne's romance was strong, and the guy had proposed to her. They were planning a wedding that summer. The marriage would take a lot of financial pressure off of Bill. He wondered if Anne could find her way to welcome Sue into his life, as he had been supportive of her new relationship.

Sue's father was a bit of a problem. Paul was protective of his daughter and did not fancy her dating some Ford factory working stiff. He kept telling Sue that it didn't seem like a good match, that she would tire of him. "Daddy," Sue told him on the phone one night at her place as Bill eavesdropped, "you don't know what you're talking about. And you're damned lucky that Mom's within earshot, because otherwise I'd give you more salty language than you've heard in a year."

***

On a Saturday in early January 1969, Bill met Bernie Levine for lunch at Lou's Deli on Six Mile Road, on Detroit's west side. Bill had been paying Bernie promptly each month. Today he was making his final payment. It was a big deal, but Bill had some other things on his mind, as well.

Bill spied his former attorney sitting in a booth. As he walked over, he realized it had been nearly five years since he had first met the eccentric but savvy barrister. *God, it seems like twenty years.*

Bernie folded up the newspaper he was reading, and the two men greeted each other warmly. After a few moments of catching up, Bill handed Bernie his final check—his financial debt had finally been paid. The aging attorney was touched, his eyes welling with tears.

As they ate their sandwiches, Bill raised another subject. "Bernie, you know I love my job. I will always be thankful to you and the UAW guys for setting me up there."

"But—" the old man began.

"But nothing. In many ways, I could stay there forever, except for one thing. I've met a girl, and if things keep going as well as they have been, I think I'm going to ask her to marry me. She's a teacher, well educated, from a family with money. Her father thinks I'm kind of a bum. That I don't have ambition, you know?"

"Does she, ah, does she know your history?" Bernie asked.

"She does, but I'm not sure she appreciates how much I might be limited in the future. We have to talk more about that. She hasn't told her father anything about my record."

"It seems to me," Bernie said with a sly smile, "you've told me you're the best picker, packer, checker that Ford ever had."

"Yeah, that goes without saying. You know that Mr. Morris found me a place that is essentially the country club of factory work."

"Yeah, I know. But I think you're trying to tell me something more," Bernie said.

"Yep. The good thing about my job is there is rarely any overtime, my hours are very stable. I'm done working every day at four-thirty."

"So, I guess you're saying you work banker's hours and have time on your hands."

"Not quite. I'm saying that I might be able to go back to school. I was thinking that night school could work very well for me, and, frankly, I wanted to ask you that, considering my record, could I go to law school?"

"Shit, law school, that's a hell of a jump." Before Bill could protest, Bernie raised his hand. "But, you know, you certainly can go to law school. There might be a felon and prison time issue, but you've had a great record since getting out, and any law school should be happy to take you."

"Yeah, except for those two little problems," Bill said.

"But I think we might be able to handle those issues. Have you thought about where you want to go to school?"

"No. It has to be a place where I could work my regular shift. I just kind of figured my two best options might be Wayne State or Detroit College of Law."

"Your conclusions are correct. I used to teach at the College of Law. It's a particularly good school, I know people in the administration there who might be able to help."

"Wow, that's great." Bill paused. "Maybe, if I'm going back to school, I should say 'groovy.'"

Bernie looked at him, his bushy eyebrows arched like stunned centipedes. "Jesus Christ, don't tell me you're into that kind of talk!"

Bill laughed. "No. Just wanted to get a rise out of you. Seriously, though, if I get through law school, could I become a lawyer?"

Bernie looked thoughtful. "Well, that's where things can get tricky. To practice law, you must pass the state bar exam and meet their other requirements. One of those requirements is you can't be a felon. *But*, the felon rule is not rock solid. If memory serves me correctly, people with felonies have, on occasion, been granted reprieves."

"Okay, so what happens if I don't get a reprieve?"

"It's not the end of the world, Bill. A lot of people get a law degree and never practice law. Sometimes they can't pass the state bar exam. Sometimes their heart is not into lawyering. If you have a law degree, you can still have a very good career. It can help you to attain certain jobs—research positions, management at Ford or other places—hell, you could even become a private investigator, you know, like those guys in *77 Sunset Strip*."

Bill laughed at the reference to the old TV show.

"Seriously, Bill, with your background at Secret Service, the work you did on counterfeiting and other investigations, you could easily set up some type of investigative or security agency. You might make fairly good money and it might be fun."

PART VI ~ 1970
Chapter 32
The Funeral

Bill opened a can of Coca-Cola, tossed the tab in a nearby wastebasket, and sat down for a few minutes. The March days remained breezy and brisk. He looked out his front window at the brown grass and leafless trees on this Saturday afternoon, winter debris blowing down the street. The landscape looked like a black-and-white photo. He loved the seasons of Michigan, but November and March were ugly, dismal months as the seasons changed. Bill reflected on the last year and a half and how his life had changed. He hoped his gamble proved worthwhile.

Bernie had gone to work on his behalf right after their lunch meeting back in January 1969, contacting friends at the Detroit College of Law. To be considered for enrollment in September, Bill had to do two things. He had to be interviewed by the school's admittance office staff, and he needed to get a decent score on the national Law School Admission Test the next month.

Bernie agreed to coach him for the LSAT two nights a week. On those nights, Bill was at Bernie's office by five-thirty. Shirley picked up a carry-out dinner around six-thirty and the two men finished their work around eight-thirty. The test involved a lot of logic and problem-solving questions. Some of these questions were mathematical, which proved a struggle for Bill. Still, with a lot of hard work and Bernie's tutoring, he managed a decent score, good enough to be admitted.

Bill was beyond excited, and he and Sue took Bernie and Shirley out to dinner at the Caucus Club in Detroit's financial district. It was a wonderful evening, although the maître d' was not sure what to do when he spotted Bill's shoulder length hair, pulled back in a ponytail. "It's okay, I'm a rock musician," Bill reassured him, bringing laughs from all.

On the way home after dinner, Sue said, "Yep, they are definitely an item."

Sue fully supported him in his law school endeavor, but Bill did not fully appreciate how much it meant. Sue still had not told her dad about Bill's prison record, but his entrance into law school helped to heal the rift between father and daughter.

Mike and Kathy had their first child, a boy, and had moved to their first house, still in Royal Oak. Mike helped Bill as much as he could to prepare for classes. His help was invaluable and made Bill's first semester a success.

During the second semester, Bill joined a study group with four other students. To his surprise, Sue showed some jealousy when she discovered one of the members of the group was a woman who worked full-time for Detroit Mayor Roman Gribbs. Bill listened with amusement to Sue's probing questions one evening at her place before reassuring her that she had nothing to worry about. "Besides," he commented, "Valerie is too young for me."

"How old is she?" Sue asked.

"About twenty-eight."

"You goddamned bastard," she said in a low, warning tone. "I was that age when we started dating."

"Sweetheart," he said, pulling her into his arms and down onto the sofa. "Yes, now you are thirty and finally old enough for this old fart." He gave her a deep kiss, and she pushed him away.

"So now I'm old, am I?"

Bill couldn't win, so he had just squeezed her tightly.

Pulling himself back to reality from watching dried leaves and musing, Bill tossed the Coke can into the waste basket and went back to studying.

***

April was in full bloom as Bill continued his second semester. He did well on his quizzes and in oral discussions, but preparing for final exams was tough. Sometimes, to ease the pressure, he went to the YMCA with Sam; they always found some guys for a pick-up game of basketball. Then, instead of enjoying a couple of beers with his friend, he went back to study, usually closing his books between eleven and midnight. Sue often spent the night during these weeks, which meant a lot to him. He knew her apartment was far more comfortable than his walk-up. She would bring a change of clothes and some lesson plans to work on as Bill moved from book to book and to his notes, struggling to understand legal concepts that he was not positive he could explain in a few pages of an exam.

The exams were tough, but he was confident he passed. His grades came and he enjoyed a combination of A's and B's. Bill had proven to himself that he could compete with smarter, better educated students than he. The upcoming summer break would be a time to rest and recharge.

One Sunday in early May, Sue and Bill lay in bed at her apartment. They were enjoying the beautiful spring weekends: tennis one day, golf the next. Today, Sue was going to take him golfing at a local course. Her father was planning to take the two of them golfing at the Birmingham Country Club in June, and Bill didn't want to embarrass Sue.

Lying in bed, Bill massaged her body, indicating that lovemaking was in the cards before they got up. They were interrupted by the telephone on the nightstand. She picked it up.

After a few words, she handed the handset to Bill. "It's your mother."

Bill grabbed the phone. "Hi, Mom. Is everything alright?"

"Bill, I'm sorry I'm bothering you at Sue's house. I'm so glad you gave me her number."

"Okay, Mom, so what's up? God, it's only eight-fifteen."

"Yes, I know. I take it you haven't heard the news. Walter Reuther died last night in a plane crash up north."

"Oh, God, no!" Bill said, sitting up in bed. "Do you have more details?"

"No, it's all very sketchy. I turned on WJR this morning and heard the news. He and his wife were going to Black Lake to inspect the UAW's new education center. I know there will be more information coming out during the day."

When they finished speaking, Bill handed the receiver back to Sue and stared into space. She replaced the receiver in the cradle. "Are you okay?" she asked.

"You know," he said, "I only met him once, but I know he changed my life for the better. Without him, I'm pretty sure I'd still be in prison."

Sue rested her chin on his shoulder. "Where did you meet him?"

"I thought I told you—maybe not." Bill told her the time he talked to Reuther at the White House. "In some ways, it got me in trouble with some higher-ups, but I was glad I did it."

He added that Reuther probably had something to do with getting his prison sentence commuted. "Mom told a UAW official, who I think told Walter, and within weeks I was released. I know it wasn't that simple. Still, it's pretty incredible."

Sue sat up and sighed. "You know, you told me some of this, but not in so much detail."

"Well, that's about all I know."

Bill reached over and turned on the radio to hear the reports on Reuther's crash.

By that evening, Bill had learned that Reuther; his wife, May; the Black Lake Education Center's nationally acclaimed architect, Oskar Stonorov; and Bill Wolfman, Reuther's bodyguard; were in the small jet, along with the pilot and co-pilot. The sixty-two-year-old Reuther, his wife, and Stonorov were making the final inspection of the new UAW education facility, about 220 miles north of Detroit, before its grand opening in June. The Lear jet apparently overshot the small, Pellston airport's runway and hit some trees in the wooded hills around the airport. All were burned beyond recognition. It had been an exciting time for the Reuthers recently, and for their lives to end in such a horrific fashion was a great tragedy. The couple left behind two daughters in their twenties.

A viewing for the public to pay their respects was to be held the following Wednesday and Thursday, with the funeral on Friday. Bill, Sue, and his mother decided to go on Wednesday.

They picked Jenny up at her house and headed down to the Veterans Memorial Building, located at the foot of Woodward Avenue on the Detroit River. There was already a long line coming out of the building, so Bill dropped off the ladies and parked the car.

There was profound sadness, as one might expect following such a sudden end to the life of one of America's great leaders. There were also laughs from people as they shared stories about Reuther, especially stories about the early UAW days. People talked about the challenge of listening to him during his long-winded speeches. All the comments, regardless of the level of seriousness, were made with love and respect for the late couple, who meant so much to the working people of Detroit, as well as the country.

After about an hour, Bill, his mom and Sue could see the closed caskets in the lobby, sitting side by side, with a UAW flag draped over Walter's. People were quiet as they approached, many praying silently.

As he passed the coffins, Bill thought of his father. Jimmy would have been devastated. Bill took a deep breath, looked at Sue, and said, "I think it's appropriate to find a bar and get a drink and some dinner."

As they were exiting the lobby, Bill noticed Ken Morris, the labor leader who had helped him regain his freedom and arranged his job at Ford. He wondered if Morris would remember him. He led Sue and Jenny toward Morris, who was accompanied by a woman and a young man.

"Mr. Morris, Ken, I don't know if you remember."

Morris paused and after a moment a look of recognition washed over his face. "Of course, Bill, how are you? And, Jenny, it's a terrible time, but so good to see the both of you."

Morris introduced his wife and son. Mrs. Morris seemed kind and asked polite questions. When she learned that Sue was a teacher at Seaholm, she commented that her children had attended the school. The boy had graduated from Seaholm the previous year but had not been in any of Sue's classes. As they talked, Bill and Ken quietly stepped aside.

"Bill, tell me, how are things going?" Ken asked as his eyes took in Bill's ponytail.

"Life is good. The job, as you originally told me, isn't demanding, but the people from top management down to the guys on the floor are good people. You took good care of me."

"I just opened a door, you did the rest. Don't forget that." Ken nodded toward Sue. "And, it looks like your social life is going well."

"Yep, Sue is great and has changed my life in many ways. You should also know that I'm just finishing my first year at the Detroit College of Law."

"Really? That's wonderful news. You know, the UAW is often looking for good, young lawyers, and I have connections with some good firms. Stay in touch, and when you're through, let me know. I know several people who have worked in the plant by day and went to law school at night. You, my friend, are traveling a path that a good number of UAW activists have followed. Good for you."

Bill hesitated, hoping his next words were not inappropriate. "Ken, I know it's probably impossible, but I wonder if it might be possible to attend Friday's memorial service?"

Ken thought a moment. "There might be a possibility, I'll have to see." He reached into the inside pocket of his suit jacket and pulled out a pen and his week-at-a-glance book. "Give me a number I can reach you at tonight."

Bill gave him both his and Sue's phone numbers. "I'll be at one of these locations."

Ken nodded. "Let me do some checking—perhaps you can be an usher."

Fifteen minutes later, Bill was treating the two most important women in his life to an expensive dinner at the Top of the Pontch, on the top floor of the Pontchartrain Hotel.

Just after ten that night, Sue's phone rang. It was Ken Morris.

"Bill," Ken said, "I think things are going to work out well for Friday. We do need ushers, and you should plan to attend. A guy from my staff, Bill Lawrence, is going to contact Ford's labor relations office in Dearborn tomorrow. Unless you hear otherwise, you will be on administrative leave this Friday. Let your foreman or labor relations officer know that they will be getting a call from Dearborn requesting your release. Report to the Ford Auditorium lobby at eight a.m. Friday morning."

Bill hung up and turned to Sue. "I'm going to go to Walter's funeral. I'm going to be an usher or something. And I'm going to be on administrative leave, so I don't have to take a day off."

Bill got to the Ford Auditorium lobby early that Friday. Things were still getting organized. An older man noticed him hanging about the lobby and asked what he was doing there. Bill told him that Ken Morris had sent him down to usher. The man said, "Stick with me. I'll let the people coordinating our ushers know that you are now with me."

The man soon returned and introduced himself as Greg Lent, the assistant director of the UAW's public relations office. Greg had Bill assist in setting the stage to a specific layout. The coffins were already on the stage, but Bill, Greg, and others moved the coffins to fit the union's floor plan. After that job was complete, Greg pointed toward where the press, particularly the camera and film people, were going to be located. Lent told him to marshal the area and only let in people who had specific credentials. He was to turn away anyone without credentials and send them to the public affairs table in the lobby.

A UAW technical guy was also assigned to the group to assist camera and film people with various technical feeds and other issues. By nine, Bill was checking in national and international camera crews, photographers, and reporters in the roped-off area. People started drifting into the auditorium, and by fifteen minutes before the service, the auditorium was filled to its 3,000-person capacity.

Dignitaries and pallbearers came onto the stage. Among the officials filing in were Emil Mazey and Ken Morris, in their roles as pallbearers. At ten, everyone rose for a moment of silence. This group joined autoworkers throughout the country as assembly lines and other work stopped for three minutes of silence in respect for their fallen leader. At that point, the program began. Bill and was impressed by the diversity of the eleven speakers.

The first was an old UAW activist and retiree, Dave Miller, who represented the UAW workers. He told several old stories of Reuther in the organizing days of the union back in the 1930s. A younger man named Sam Brown, who had coordinated the massive and peaceful 1969 national demonstration against the Vietnam War, acknowledged Reuther's guidance and support through that effort.

More personal remembrances followed, including comments by Michigan Senator Philip Hart; Whitney Young, director of the National Urban League; and John Gardner of the National Urban Coalition.

Next up was a woman Bill had only read about in history books: Marian Anderson, a black opera singer, who broke many racial barriers and was known throughout the world. In 1939, she was prohibited from singing at an event held in a building owned by the Daughters of the American Revolution. To protest the insult, Eleanor Roosevelt and other social justice leaders had organized an open-air concert at the Lincoln Memorial, attended by 75,000 people. Anderson opened that performance with an historic rendition of *America* (*My Country, 'Tis of Thee*) that resonated throughout the country as people, listening on the radio, were mesmerized by her powerful voice.

On this day of Reuther's funeral, Anderson came out of retirement to commemorate his life, singing *He's Got the Whole World in His Hands*. Coretta Scott King, widow of Dr. Martin Luther King Jr., spoke of the warm relationship Reuther had with her husband and his never-ending support of the American civil rights movement. It was a powerful moment. She was followed by several other speakers, with Irving Bluestone, Reuther's friend and assistant, giving a final warm and personal perspective of both Reuthers, Walter and May.

As Bluestone walked back to his seat, a rich, full voice from behind the stage started singing. It was the old union anthem, *Joe Hill.* All 3,000 people stood, some singing quietly along, as the song captured the spirit of Walter Reuther more than any other words spoken in the previous ninety minutes.

Bill was deeply moved, grateful he could be part of the final memorial to a man who had made a difference in the world—and his own life.

Chapter Thirty-Four
A Proposal

Back at work Monday, it did not take long for Bill's co-workers to learn he was at the Reuther funeral. Many were surprised as Bill was not an active UAW member. Most people, including Delvero, were genuinely curious about his experience.

Bill became interested in how the UAW planned to pick a new president and followed the selection process in Detroit's two major daily newspapers. UAW Vice President Leonard Woodcock was elected by the UAW's executive board to fill out the remaining term as president. Bill knew nothing about Woodcock and wondered how Mazey and Morris might have voted.

The following weekend it was tennis with Sam on Saturday, and golf with Sue on Sunday. Bill was still uncomfortable with his skills as he prepared for the big golf match with Sue and her father in a few weeks.

On June 3, a Wednesday, the secretary for the personnel office came on the floor and handed Bill a note. Ken Morris had given Bill his office and home phone numbers and asked Bill to call him after six o'clock that night. Bill folded the note and tucked it into his jeans.

That night, Bill called Morris' home number. The phone rang a couple of times and a woman answered. Bill reintroduced himself to Mrs. Morris, who said her husband was not home yet, adding in mock disgust, "I never quite know when to have dinner ready for him."

About eight-thirty, Morris returned the call, saying he and Emil Mazey wanted to meet with Bill sometime in the next couple of days. Morris provided no further details. They settled on meeting the next night at six at the Gaslight restaurant at Bagley and Grand River in downtown Detroit, across the street from Bernie's office.

The next evening after work, Bill changed into some casual clothes. He knew Morris and Mazey wore suits, but he was not going to get that dressed up. He was the first to arrive at the Gaslight, his first time there, and scanned around the large, dimly lit, wood-paneled room with lots of seating. He asked for a booth with a view of the door. The restaurant had been around for years; the booths were slightly worn. Soon, Morris walked in, followed shortly by Mazey and another man.

Morris introduced the fourth man, Roy Frescura, as an aide to Mazey. They ordered drinks, and Morris started the meeting.

"As we've discussed, Walter's death has shaken the UAW to its core," he said. "During the last few weeks, no one has played a greater role in creating stability for our union than Emil. He made the difference. He took himself out of the president's race and managed what turned out to be a remarkably close election between Leonard Woodcock and Doug Fraser. We are meeting with you because Emil has accepted a new charge, and after talking about it, we think you can be a big help."

Mazey took over. "Bill, we are thinking of putting together some kind of commission to look into the plane crash. There are many in our union, and elsewhere, who feel the crash might not have been an accident."

Bill tried not to show his shock as Mazey continued.

"We look at the histories of people who have tried to assassinate, kidnap, or otherwise do physical harm to Walter in the past thirty-five years. We look at the past seven years and see the assassinations of Jack Kennedy, Martin Luther King, and Bobby Kennedy. We look at the fact that Walter was a key supporter and idea man for each of these men. Since Walter died, I can't tell you how many people have come up to me or to Ken, Leonard Woodcock, and others, saying with all sincerity that Walter was a victim of foul play."

Mazey shifted in his seat and took a sip of wine. "Now," leaning forward toward Bill, he continued, "setting up a commission is one thing. But as we were discussing this matter earlier in the week, Ken reminded me that we have a member of our union, you, who has had professional experience in investigating criminal activities. So, if you are agreeable, we are thinking of pulling you out of the plant for a few weeks, or months, or whatever it takes, to do an independent investigation. Depending on what the commission discovers, we may add your findings, or we may keep them separate, again depending on any number of circumstances." Mazey paused, and Bill knew it was time for him to say something.

"First, Mr. Mazey—"

"Emil, please."

"Alright, Emil, you should know I'm a bit rusty in this game, but more importantly, why do a separate or dual investigation? Don't you trust your own commission members?"

"Of course, we will trust them. But frankly, they simply might not be as cynical as a seasoned investigator might be. Plus, we are still not positive about the commission idea. When there was an attempt to assassinate Walter back in 1948, I hired a couple of private investigators to look at the whole thing. It took time, but they found the guys who did it—the same bastards who nearly beat Ken here to death. We think it makes sense for you to do your own work. We'll compare it with any potential commission report and see if there is agreement between their conclusions and yours. And your work won't be part of a committee where a consensus might water down a conclusion. You can say what you believe is true. You can go out on a limb, if you choose, and there won't be any repercussions. Does this make sense?"

Bill nodded. "Yeah, it makes sense. I don't know if you know it, but I'm currently in law school. We're on summer break now, but I will need to be done with this work by September."

"Ken told me you had started going to the Detroit College of Law. That's where my brother, Bill, went while he still worked in the plant. Ken, you should talk to him— his firm might be able to hire a smart attorney out of the plant."

The men hoped to get Bill out of the plant by the following Monday. Mazey said he didn't expect to have any problems. He would ask Leonard Woodcock to call Henry Ford to request Bill's leave of absence. Bill was to receive the same pay as a UAW international representative, a significant increase. Morris agreed to provide Bill workspace in his regional offices at Solidarity House, plus a secretary. Mazey and Morris also said there were people who might have some insight on a potential assassination plot, and they would share those names when Bill started work. Morris said he would let him know soon when the assignment would begin.

As they were getting ready to leave, Mazey said, as diplomatically as he could, "Bill, you know, there is no greater foe of the goddamn Vietnam War than me. I sympathize with the war protesters. I have no problems with guys who let their hair grow. But you're going to be interacting with people who have far more conservative views on this kind of stuff than I do. You might want to consider a haircut."

Bill was not surprised by the comment. It wasn't the first time he'd heard it. He was nonetheless impressed to learn of Mazey's position on the war. He said, "Emil, I tell you what, if I think the length of my hair causes any problems with me completing this assignment, I will get it cut—no problem."

Mazey grinned and extended his hand. "Deal."

Bill went straight to Sue's apartment and filled her in. She was almost as excited as he was. The difference was, her excitement was about his opportunity, whereas Bill was excited over investigating Walter Reuther's death.

Chapter Thirty-Five
Solidarity House

"So, you do have a lot of pull. Looks like you're getting pulled out of the plant, eh?" Delvero asked Bill at work on Monday.

Bill hesitated, not wanting to say more than he should and a bit irritated that he had not heard from Morris. "Yeah, they contacted me last week and indicated I might be able to help them on a project."

Delvero's eyes twinkled. "My guess is that it has something to do with Reuther's death."

"I'm not sure what it's all going to involve."

"Bill, I've done some research on you. I know about some of your troubles. The court case and so forth."

Bill was stunned. He had no idea that Delvero knew, and he had kept the information to himself. "Lou—"

Delvero cut him off. "Don't worry, I'm not poking my nose in where it doesn't belong. I've watched you since you've been here. You're unlike any employee I've ever had. You have secrets, secrets I don't want to know, and somehow you ended up on my crew. Just be careful out there, and we all hope you come back." He looked at Bill thoughtfully and added, "When you get back, I'm going to do whatever I can to move you up in the Ford organization. You're one of the best employees I've ever had, and you're being wasted here."

"Thanks, Lou. I'll be back in about four or five weeks."

"Good."

***

On Wednesday, Bill reported to Solidarity House for his new gig. The security guard at the gate checked his list and allowed him to pass. He entered Region 1B's area on the first floor of the five-story building and headed to Ken Morris's office, a place he had visited six years earlier with his father—under entirely different circumstances. Morris' secretary, Marge, greeted him and let her boss know that Bill was waiting.

"Bill, I've got to tell you that space is very tight here," Morris said after leading Bill into his office. "Things will be better next year when we move out to a new office building. If you don't mind, I'm going to put you in an office with Paul Silver. Paul is a crusty character whom I think you will come to enjoy. Paul knows just about everything there is to know about the UAW—he could be a good resource. He knows that everything you do is confidential. There are several filing cabinets that have locks in the office, so your work will be protected.

"Also, I'm assigning you one of our best secretaries, Sophie Blair. Sophie works for some other staff guys, as well, including Paul. She understands your work is a priority and confidential. *And*, she doesn't gossip."

While this was not exactly what Bill expected, he said, "I'm sure we can make this work."

"Good," Morris replied with a look of satisfaction. "Now, let me go through a list of people Emil and I think you should contact for potential background information."

Bill pulled out a spiral notebook.

"First is Joe Rauh. He heads the ADA." Morris noted a quizzical look on Bill's face. "Americans for Democratic Action. Joe, Walter, Hubert Humphrey, and others started the ADA in the late forties to advocate for civil rights for all. The ADA was also active in fighting McCarthyism in the fifties. Joe's a great guy who understands the way Washington works, and he might be able to give you background and perhaps several key leads. I'm also going to ask him to set up a meeting with Senator Phil Hart.

"Then there's Paul Schrade. You may recall that when Bobby Kennedy was shot, several other people were shot with him. Paul was shot in the forehead. He used to work on Walter's staff. He became a regional director about eight years ago, the same job I have, but his region covers California and other western states. Paul's a good guy but he really hasn't recovered emotionally from his shooting. Who would? Still, his insights could be powerful.

"You should also talk to Victor Reuther, Walter's brother. Victor was the closest person in Walter's life. He's still grieving, but we hope he'll be back to work soon."

Morris and Bill spent the rest of the hour going through other names and possible approaches Bill could take to start the investigation. Morris took Bill down to his new office, where he met Silver and Blair. Bill immediately recognized Silver as a unique character with a good soul. Blair was in her late twenties and seemed like a no-nonsense individual. Bill wanted to do some research on key political assassinations, and asked Morris if Sue could volunteer to help after school broke for the summer the following week. Morris had no problem with that.

Chapter Thirty-Six
Washington

The commercial jet rumbled down the runway and lifted off, heading west. Bill was on his way from Washington's Dulles Airport to Los Angeles. As the Boeing 707 leveled off, Bill looked down from his window seat at the United States drifting by from 33,000 feet. He flipped his tray down, unbuckled his seat belt, and began reviewing paperwork. It had been three weeks since he started his work for the UAW. He needed to complete notes on his recent DC meetings and continue reading the information Sue had included.

After the school year ended, Sue began preliminary research on political assassinations in the US. She spent a solid week in various libraries around Detroit and Ann Arbor, digging up some impressive work on President Kennedy's assassination, a subject that brought back old memories for Bill. Some of her research revealed questions on the Martin Luther King and Robert Kennedy shootings, as well. She also found some underground newspaper articles critical of the CIA and FBI—some of which, to Bill, rang true.

During the Washington trip, Bill had followed Morris's advice and met with the ADA's Joe Rauh in his office on K Street. Rauh was a Harvard man who had played center on the basketball team. In his sixties, with gray taking over his black wavy hair. Rauh's intimidating stature made Bill think he must still be athletic. Bill warmed to the man's outgoing charm and openness. Rauh, still stunned by Reuther's death, said there was not much he could add to what the newspapers said about the plane crash. He had not thought seriously about a conspiracy, but upon reflection, he could see why Mazey and other UAW leaders thought it possible.

"You know, few people will ever realize what Walter and the UAW contributed to this country, both in terms of economic strength for blue collar workers and the fight for social justice," Rauh said. "I honestly think that Martin Luther King's success was due in a large part to Walter's and the UAW's financial support. The same can be said about Cesar Chavez."

"So, there might be a motive for some people to eliminate Walter?" Bill said.

"Yeah, hell yes. The more I think about it, the scarier the possibility seems. King, the Kennedys, yeah, there are some bad actors out there. The right-wing, some members of the FBI, the CIA. Yep, some real bad guys." Then Rauh shifted gears: "I followed up on Ken's request and set up your meeting with Phil Hart."

"I appreciate your help on that."

"Phil's a great guy. He's so nice that some people just don't appreciate his deep understanding of government. He's worked in the federal government, was a US attorney, legal advisor to Governor 'Soapy' Williams, and then Soapy picked him to be his lieutenant governor. He knows where a lot of bodies are buried. Don't let his modesty fool you. Press him."

Hart was short in stature and the mild mannered man in his fifties that Rauh had described, with a reputation as being the conscience of the Senate. Hart's first reaction was, "Any friend of Emil Mazey and Ken Morris is a friend of mine. These guys have only one interest, and that's helping working people achieve a decent wage and the dignity they deserve. I'm lucky to know them."

They talked for some time, but without getting to any details. Bill finally reminded Hart that he had been assigned to investigate Reuther's death.

Hart took a moment before he responded, "You know, one of my war buddies is pretty high up in the FBI—a guy named Elliot Glenn—he might be worth your time."

Thinking about the damage he may have done to Fred Fry in Detroit's FBI office during his time in Chicago, Bill said, "He might be a good lead. I'd like to meet him, but I think it should be somewhere private and off the record."

"Let me see what I can do," Hart said.

Later, Bill phoned the FBI's Detroit office, and asked for Fry. *"Bill, is that you? My God, where have you been, buddy?"*

It had been almost seven years since the two had spoken. Fry was a friend, but Bill had been uncomfortable contacting anyone from his past. Not reaching out to Fry was a mistake, and he felt guilty about it. Bill spent about three or four minutes updating the FBI agent on his activities.

After he finished, Fry said, *"We have to get together and catch up. Law school, that's cool."*

"Absolutely. I'm in DC right now, but when I get back, we will. How're you doing?"

"Great. Our little episode set my career back for a while, but I'm now one of the assistant directors of the office. I work a lot with our US attorney's office. How can I help you?"

"I'm wondering if you know a guy named Elliot Glenn?"

"Oh, yeah, I know Elliot. A Northeast establishment type. He's top shelf, a good guy."

"Where is he inside the organization?"

"He's in the criminal division. I've worked with him on a few cases, including the Joe Yablonski killing."

Bill immediately recognized the name. Yablonski was with the United Mine Workers and was the reform candidate who ran for president of the union in 1969 against the incumbent UMW president, the disgraceful Tony Boyle. Yablonski lost in what was believed to be a crooked election. On the last day of 1969, Yablonski, his wife, and daughter were murdered in their sleep in their home.

"I thought Yablonski was murdered in Pennsylvania. That's a little out of your jurisdiction, isn't it?" Bill asked.

"Oh, hell, yes. I was a small potato in the case. They needed some work in Detroit, and I drew the short straw."

"So, you think I can trust this guy?"

"Absolutely."

Bill spent the remainder of the day going over the material Sue had packed for him, and he checked in with Sophie. He wanted to schedule a meeting with Victor Reuther, who lived in DC, but he could not reach him. Around seven, he was relaxing at his hotel when the phone rang.

"Bill Simpson?" a man's voice inquired.

"Yep, that's me."

"This is Elliot Glenn. Phil Hart asked me to get in touch with you." And then, almost as an afterthought, he added, "I'm on a pay phone, so you don't need to worry about any taps."

Bill was impressed.

"Look, I don't know what Senator Hart said," Bill said, "but I think we need to meet in a private place, outside the public eye. I've had some run-ins with the FBI, and I don't want to put you in any jeopardy."

"Why don't you come over to my place—I'm out past the zoo."

Fifteen minutes later, Bill was in a cab headed to Glenn's home in Chevy Chase, an upper-middle class area in Maryland, just north of DC. A man in his fifties, trim, about 6-foot-2, met him at the door. Glenn surveyed Bill's hair but made no comment. Bill briefly met Mrs. Glenn, who seemed not at all surprised by a last-minute meeting between her husband and some character from Detroit.

The men moved into a comfortable study whose walls were filled with items such as a Yale undergraduate degree, a Princeton law degree. photos, awards, and other collectable items that a successful FBI agent might have on his walls. The older man motioned Bill to a seat and offered him a drink. Bill asked what Glenn liked to drink and, in a moment, they settled on imported scotch. Glenn sat across from Bill, with drinks, cheese, and crackers on a table between them.

"Elliot, let me start by saying you have a fan inside the bureau."

"That's interesting, I didn't know I had any support from my colleagues," the man with the salt-and-pepper crew cut responded.

"Yeah, Fred Fry, out of Detroit, has enjoyed working with you."

"Ah, Fred, a good man." Glenn smiled. "The director is not a big fan of his, but Fred's career inside the Bureau will come. I hope he sticks it out because he'll make office director or more."

That opening allowed Bill to indicate that Bill might be the reason for Hoover's low opinion of Fry. Bill reviewed the mess that had started with the Chicago investigation. Glenn seemed mildly interested in the story, but then abruptly changed topics.

"So, what's the story of your prison record?"

Bill tried not to show his surprise because he knew a good FBI man could easily check his background. He explained the incident, that he thought he'd been framed, and that he believed that, at best, the Secret Service's sloppy protection of President Kennedy might have put the president in harm's way, and at worst, they might have been complicit in a cover-up of some kind.

"Well, then," Glenn replied matter-of-factly, "now that we have that off the table, tell me what brings you to Washington, and why does Senator Hart call me with an urgent request to meet with you?"

Bill shifted in his chair. "Well, it didn't have to be an urgent request. Senator Hart said you and he were old war buddies and that he thought you might be able to find some time for me."

"Any time a senator asks for a favor, especially a friend of mine, it's an urgent request," Glenn replied. "And when he tells me the meeting needs to be off the books, it's even more urgent. We weren't really war buddies. We met while recovering from war injuries at the Fort Custer hospital in Battle Creek. So, tell me, what's the story?"

Bill reviewed the details of the Reuther plane crash and the nagging concern that it might be more than an accident. "While these labor leaders had concerns, they weren't sure what to do about them."

"So, they came to you. Why?"

"I've been working in a Ford factory since I was released from prison. I'm currently working days and going to law school at night." Glenn's eyebrows raised slightly. "Only a very few people at work and in the union know of my Secret Service background. So, after the Reuthers's deaths, a couple of UAW leaders thought I might be able to help them."

"Again, why?"

"They knew I had a background in criminal investigation, and that they could easily get me out of the plant for a while to do the work."

"So, what have you found out?"

Bill sighed. "To be honest, not much. Everything is circumstantial. We know Reuther's business jet was a rental and unguarded while it sat in the executive section of the Detroit Metropolitan Airport. Someone might have had an opportunity to tamper with the plane. We know that Reuther was a huge supporter of Jack and Bobby Kennedy, and he was a significant friend and financial backer of King. The Kennedys and King were assassinated, and there is at minimum, some question about who the true assailants were."

Glenn raised a hand. "Whoa, are you saying people in the government are responsible for all these deaths? Do you really want to bark up that tree?"

Bill shook his head. "I'm not barking up any tree .... not yet. It's possible the military or other agencies are involved. It could be the private sector—you know Reuther was once called the most dangerous man in Detroit by George Romney? Then there's the mob."

"So, you really don't know where you are going with this."

"Not yet. That's one reason I'm talking to some select people in DC."

Glenn leaned forward in his chair. "Do you really think I would give you any sensitive information about any of these targets? Based on what you've told me, there's no way I'd tell you anything." After a pause, he added, "At least not yet."

At least there's an opening.

But how could he take advantage of this opportunity? His mind raced. How could he get some information out of this man? He sipped his drink to buy time. "You know, Elliot, you're right. If I were in your place, I wouldn't say anything to some guy who just walked into your house one night asking uncomfortable questions. But I need direction. I want to know which tree I can bark up."

"Well, I'm not saying anything to you. I'm a twenty-two-year man in the service of my country, and I hope to be here for another decade or so."

"But if something stinks, shouldn't it be dealt with?"

Glenn paused. "The only reason this conversation is happening is because of Phil Hart—"

"I know," Bill stopped him. "How about if I don't ask you to say anything?"

"What do you mean?"

"Let me just ask some very general questions. Basic questions."

"I told you, I'm not saying a thing."

"I know. I don't want you to," Bill replied. "Here's my proposal. I'm going to ask you a few questions. You don't respond, but instead you give me a thumbs up or thumbs down. Then, after I do some more work, you give me a chance to come back and tell you what I know."

Glenn looked Bill in the eye for a moment. "Okay, thumbs up or thumbs down. I can do that."

Glenn refilled each man's glass with ice and scotch before Bill asked, "Okay, did Lee Harvey Oswald act alone?"

Glenn looked at him. He didn't say anything but held his hand out in a fist and pointed his thumb horizontally.

"You're telling me you don't know, but it's possible?"

Glenn nodded.

"Were there people in the government, particularly in the CIA and military, who wanted President Kennedy killed?" Glenn once again pointed horizontally.

"Was the FBI aware of a possible assassination plot before November twenty-second?" The thumb pointed horizontally.

"Were people in the FBI aware of a possible assassination plot after November twenty-second?" Glenn's thumb pointed upward.

"Did Sirhan Sirhan act alone in killing Bobby Kennedy?" The thumb pointed horizontally.

"Were there people in the FBI who were happy with the assassination of Martin Luther King?" Glenn contemplated for a bit before he gave a thumbs-up.

"Was the FBI aware of an assassination plot against King?" There was a long pause this time before the thumb stuck out horizontally.

"Would members of the intelligence branches have reasons to support or be sympathetic to the elimination of Walter Reuther?" Again, the thumb was horizontal.

Twenty minutes later, a taxi was outside the Glenn household. Bill thanked Glenn, who said that if Bill dug up some real evidence, they should meet again.

On the cab ride back to the hotel, Bill was disappointed in himself. His questions were terrible. He should have been better prepared. Still, he learned a lot. He expected Glenn to reject any notion that the government was involved or aware of assassinations of government or private citizens. The man did not agree that there was actual involvement by governmental agencies, but they may have known and did nothing to stop the killings or may have known after the fact. He had a lot of work to do and was already looking forward to another meeting with Glenn.

Chapter Thirty-Seven
Los Angeles

After landing at LAX, Bill rented a car and drove to a motel in Hollywood along Sunset Boulevard near Vine Street. Once there, he called Paul Schrade's office. He didn't understand why they didn't meet in Detroit, but Schrade had let Emil Mazey know he preferred to meet on his home turf. Bill was not sure what to expect at this meeting, but Mazey felt the trip might be productive and instructive. Schrade's secretary said her boss had been delayed in Washington state, but was expected back the next day. She suggested a restaurant in Hollywood that Schrade liked and said she would make reservations for the two of them for dinner tomorrow.

With nothing else to do for the time being, Bill took a late afternoon walk down the Sunset Strip and then over to Hollywood Avenue, a touristy area made for movie nuts, of which he was one. He enjoyed walking around the front of Sid Grauman's Chinese Theatre, looking at the feet and hand imprints of famous stars in cement, sometimes accented with cheeky quotes. He picked up a postcard with the Grauman Theatre on it and wrote a quick note to Sue. He bought a five-cent stamp and dropped the card into a nearby mailbox.

The next day, Bill drove downtown to the Los Angeles Public Library's Central Branch. He found a lot of information on Robert Kennedy's assassination, including many articles not in Detroit library systems. One article mentioned that after Kennedy's victory speech, the senator had turned and asked for Schrade to join him as they walked off the podium and followed staff through the Ambassador Hotel's kitchen. Bobby wanted to return to the Kennedy suite of rooms to celebrate among friends. While walking through the kitchen, Kennedy shook the hands of several hotel workers before the shots were fired. Schrade was the first one hit, a .22 caliber shot in the forehead. There was a photo of Schrade in the hospital, recovering from his wounds and talking with reporters. His head, from the ears up, was completely covered by white bandage wrappings.

After a couple of hours at the library, he headed back to his hotel room, for which he'd been granted a late check-out time. After the

Schrade dinner meeting, he planned to catch a redeye flight back to Detroit. At the restaurant and already seated at a table, he saw a man, roughly forty-five, tall, with a head of thick, wavy black hair, and black rimmed glasses heading through the restaurant in his direction.

Bill could tell Paul Schrade was sizing him up, even before they shook hands as Bill's long hair and casual dress were not typical of UAW officials. But Schrade seemed pleasantly surprised. Bill also noticed that, upon closer inspection, Schrade's hair had a lot of gray specks in it. The pinkish scar from the bullet hole in his forehead was obvious.

"Thanks for coming out this way," Schrade said. "You know, Woodcock and I are not on good terms. He's going to run someone against me in '72. He thinks I'm not a team player, so I stay out of Detroit as much as I can."

"No problem," Bill replied. "I've never met Leonard. But almost all the UAW leadership seems to be comfortable with him."

"They are, but, like everywhere, people have agendas and that is where the problems come from. I suppose Leonard thinks I'm someone with an agenda separate from UAW leadership."

The conversation moved on to the UAW. Schrade had started at the GM plant in LA. He got involved in the union and became a staffer to Walter Reuther. He'd originally been part of Reuther's opposition. But Reuther noticed that Schade was a smart guy, and Reuther did what Reuther often did—he brought the opposition into his camp. Schrade didn't know Bill's dad. He said he knew Ken Morris, but not well. He knew, and thought very highly of, Emil Mazey. He appreciated Mazey's strong stance against the Vietnam War.

After ordering drinks and dinner, the more serious conversation took place.

"So, you want to talk about the Reuther killing, eh?" Schrade asked.

"Yep, both Emil and Ken wanted me to talk to you—they thought you might have insights into a possible conspiracy involving the plane crash."

Schrade raised his eyebrows.

Bill decided to go into his own background in the Secret Service, and the rest of the story of how he came to be seated there with Schrade.

Schrade, who had a certain intensity about him, said, "So, what do you think so far?"

"Nothing. No proof of anything. Of course, the FAA is still conducting its investigation. I've talked to the lead investigator. He thinks it might be a faulty altimeter but won't confirm anything until the report comes out sometime later in the year. The jet was at the executive terminal at Metro Airport. After landing, the pilots left the plane to relax in the terminal. There is no security at the executive terminal—anyone could have tampered with it."

Bill paused as dinner was served. "While there was some opposition to Reuther inside the union, I don't see anything serious enough to merit an assassination through a conspiracy—after all, his retirement was in four years."

"I agree with you there. And I don't think the industry would come after him. This is not 1948," he said, referring to the year of the Reuther assassination attempt.

"There is always the possibility of an underworld hit," Bill said. "Walter ran a clean union that left few opportunities for the mob. There is always the issue of gambling in the plants. Reuther, Mazey, and the leadership has, as far as I know, worked well with the industry to try to eliminate gambling in the plants. So, I'd rate the possibility of mob activity, on a scale of one to ten, at a solid three. It's possible, but not likely."

"So, where does that lead you?" Schrade asked.

"Again, no proof, just conjecture. In the 1960s, there were four, high-level political hits: Malcolm X, Martin Luther King, Robert Kennedy and the biggest of them all, President Kennedy. The Malcolm X shooting appears to be an internal hit by Black Muslims, but I'm not positive on that one." Bill took a sip of beer.

"Malcolm X," Schrade said, with a nod of his head. "Most people wouldn't have placed him in the same category as the Kennedys and King."

"I don't know if it makes sense or not," Bill said defensively. "It's just that so many people, especially whites, didn't appreciate the pull and persuasion he had in the black community. If you haven't, you should pick up a copy of *The Autobiography of Malcom X*."

"No, no," Schrade raised his hand, "I've read it and I agree. The whole Black Panther movement out here is a direct result of Malcolm's speeches and teaching."

"Next is Martin Luther King," Bill went on. "Was it a hit? It's possible, maybe probable. Remember, King moved left in the mid-sixties. He opposed Johnson on Vietnam and was moving aggressively beyond LBJ's War on Poverty. He was making enemies. Ironically, King's influence was declining as he took his war against racism and poverty north.

I don't know who might have fronted the assassination. James Earl Ray was a bad guy, no question. A racist, for sure. Ray traveled extensively, so he seemed to have money and access to fake passports. He had resources that a petty crook doesn't have. Maybe he was employed by a right-wing group, or maybe it was a mob hit? I don't know.

"Still, King was killed, and another of Walter's allies died. I know you know that Walter cared for and provided a great deal of UAW financial support to King's causes. If President Kennedy's shooting was a planned hit, it's possible that King's interest in taking his cause north, or his anti-Vietnam position, attracted the attention of the same people. Would these same people want Reuther, a visionary who funded and advised King and the Kennedys, to find a future civil rights or political leader? Maybe not. Whether King was killed by the underworld or some other group, then the idea that King was assassinated by the mob or other nefarious groups is at a six in ten level."

Schrade shrugged. "The guy who knows more about Walter's activities than anyone else is Irv Bluestone, Walter's long-time AA. Of course, now he's been elevated to vice president. If you haven't, talk to him."

"He's been so busy with his new post I haven't had a chance to meet him yet. I will get on that when I return."

"Okay," Bill said after the two had finished eating, "we have the Kennedys. First there's the president's death. Again, I have no proof or resources to investigate, but I feel there is something so odd about the shooting. Not just his killing, but Oswald's, too. And Jack Ruby is about as shady as you can get, and he died so quickly—they said it was cancer. Then there's the Chicago incident—"

"What Chicago incident?" Schrade asked with interest.

Bill explained his experience in Chicago, with special emphasis on the fact a man named Lee tipped off the FBI about a potential assassination. He added that they had arrested a man who fit the description of a loner and worked in a warehouse along the route that Kennedy's motorcade was to take. Bill also mentioned several Cubans were discovered with a stash of weapons, and that all suspects were inexplicably released.

"I had no idea of any of this," Schrade said, shaking his head.

"Well, it gets worse; and this is confidential. Without getting into too many details, immediately after the Chicago event, all our notes and any other material from the Chicago assignment were confiscated by our headquarters in DC. Orders were given that Secret Service agents were not ever to speak of this—it was like Chicago never happened. After the assassination, an agent in Chicago named McRae and I, without any coordination with one another, raised some concerns about the shooting. Our office was hit by a series of transfers, and that's when I was framed by the Service and sent to prison. McRae was, too."

"Jesus Christ. Just fucking amazing," Schrade said.

"Yeah, so I know there's something dirty about the JFK killing," Bill responded. "It is possible, but I don't think likely, that the Secret Service went after Reuther. I also think they were just sloppy regarding President Kennedy's death. But who did it? The mob, Cuba, the Soviets, or could it have been a hit by other subversive entities? Don't forget the other US governmental agencies–the FBI, CIA, the military... I rate a conspiracy at a seven out of ten.

"So that leaves us with Bobby," Schrade said.

"Yeah, you're the expert on him."

Schrade took a sip of his drink. "You know, I first met Jack and Bobby at the 1956 Democratic Convention. That's when Jack tried to gain the vice-presidential nomination. The Kennedys impressed us in the UAW. No one focused on specific objectives and goals like those two brothers did, especially Bobby. After that '56 convention, we knew we liked Jack and thought there was a future for him, and we wanted to be part of that future. First, we told him he had to improve his record on labor issues. Up until that time, Jack had not been a strong advocate of organized labor."

"I guess I didn't know that."

Schrade nodded. "Yeah, and Jack understood the problem, and so did Bobby. Bobby pursued the job of chief attorney on the McClellan labor rackets committee, which could have been a labor witch hunt, but instead went after labor's bad guys. Jack served on that committee. While they certainly went after some bad customers, like the Teamsters's Dave Beck and Jimmy Hoffa, Senator Goldwater insisted they investigate Reuther, and they did. They found nothing of any substance." Schrade laughed. "Walter was so clean that Goldwater insisted on stopping the Reuther investigation because he knew they were not going to come up with any dirt.

"In the early sixties, I returned to California and eventually became the UAW's West Coast director. This allowed me to be my own man. I was far away from Walter and Detroit—I had nothing against Walter; I just wanted my own independence within the goals and objectives of my union. Besides our rank-and-file activities, I helped lead the fight out here for working people. It started with civil rights, then the Farm Workers and Caesar Chavez, and finally the anti-war movement. I was fine with Walter on civil rights and the Farm Workers, but he was not happy with me on my anti-war activities. He opposed the war, but he did not want to get on the wrong side of Johnson. I didn't have that concern. Meanwhile, Bobby and I maintained close contact, especially after the 1960 election. I pushed him on civil rights. I know I introduced him and Walter to the Farm Workers fight."

"Isn't Emil a big supporter of Chavez?" Bill asked.

"Oh, yeah, Emil was always there, just as he was always against the war. You know, it took a while for Bobby to come out against the war. Jack, as president, was ahead of him on that issue. Bobby was too hawkish. Finally, after the assassination, Bobby saw the massive build-up, and he knew it was not what his brother would have done. He came to realize the war was unwinnable and immoral. We were supporting a corrupt South Vietnamese regime. By 1967, Bobby was making public statements on 'Face the Nation' and elsewhere. He did not want to pick a fight with LBJ, but he had to take a position."

Bill glanced at his watch. He was running short on time to catch his flight. "So, you were Bobby's guy on the West Coast. You knew everyone."

"Yeah, that's true, but Bob and I never disagreed on anything. On issues, or political strategy. You know, after his brother's assassination, he grew so much as a person. He had a broader view of people. He really thought he could bring the country together."

"So, what do you remember of Bobby's assassination?"

"Well, I remember winning, of course. Bob's speech was wonderful, especially the 'On to Chicago' comment. I remember the walk into the kitchen. There were people everywhere, just total confusion, with some pushing and pulling to get near Bob. Then, I guess, the shots rang out. I don't remember them or anything after that. I was hit by one of the early shots, maybe the first or second bullet."

"So, what do you think happened? Did Sirhan act alone?"

Schrade took a deep breath and slowly exhaled. "Well, here's what I think. Again, I am not accusing anyone of anything. Obviously, I think about this a lot. I've talked to just about everyone I know who was in the kitchen, and I will continue to talk with more witnesses. I think the LA police did a shitty job of investigating what happened."

Schrade hesitated a moment.

"Now, I'm going to tell you a story. Again, I'm not accusing anyone. I'm just going to follow the evidence of what we know today. So, Sirhan's pistol had eight shots, a .22 caliber. The first or second shot hit me. By the time the second shot was fired, Sirhan was surrounded and being apprehended by Rosie Grier, George Plimpton, Rafer Johnson, and others. He was wildly firing the remaining shots in the pistol. So, while Sirhan fired all eight shots, only two shots were aimed at anyone, and one of those shots hit me.

"Now, Kennedy was facing Sirhan, and witnesses have told me that Sirhan never got closer than two feet from him. Yet, the coroner said that one bullet struck Kennedy in the back of the head, just under his right ear—the shot that killed him. Another shot hit him in his spine. A third shot hit him near the right armpit and a fourth missed, tearing his jacket's right shoulder. All the bullets were fired at point-blank range. The bullets that went into his body left powder burns. Sirhan's weapon never got that close."

Bill frowned. "You're not saying Sirhan's an innocent victim?"

"No, I'm not saying that at all. I'm just saying that his pistol did not kill Bob Kennedy."

"If there are two shooters, there's a conspiracy."

"I'm not saying that, you are. But I don't disagree."

"Assuming a conspiracy is possible, who might be involved, especially as it might relate to Reuther's death?"

Schrade put up his hands. "I'm not in the speculation game."

"Come on, Paul. You can't tell me that you have not thought about this stuff. I've got nothing of substance here. You're much closer to this than I am, your thoughts might be incredibly important to my findings."

Schrade paused again. "Okay," he conceded, "yes, there are some remarkably interesting possibilities. Look at Jack Kennedy. He goes through the Bay of Pigs fiasco and believes the military and CIA set him up. In the Cuban Missile Crisis, he proposes a peaceful solution. The military and intelligent services want to invade or blow Cuba out of the water; the president says no. But the military still fights Kennedy, even though his embargo saved the day. Then, there's Vietnam. More information will come out, but I think Jack Kennedy wanted to get out of 'Nam, and the military and CIA wanted to fight. Finally, Kennedy did the 1963 nuclear disarmament treaty with the Soviets, which the military and CIA strongly opposed."

Bill knew it made sense, just from his time with President Kennedy. He put his newly UAW-issued credit card down on the bill as Schrade continued.

"Then Kennedy's assassinated. Did the military and the CIA hatch a plot? There's a decent chance they did.

Then, there's Bob Kennedy. He was a son of a bitch to deal with during his brother's administration. He pushed the CIA and the military around. We are just beginning to learn about the inside workings of the Kennedy White House, and it probably won't be very pretty when it all comes to light. But Bob becomes a US Senator and opposes the war, he effectively wages a campaign on behalf of poor southern kids and starts his presidential bid. By this time, Johnson will soon be out of the race. Could he have become a target? A target of the military? Of the intelligence community? You bet."

"Yeah," Bill agreed, "but what about the mob and Hoffa?"

"Good points. That's one reason I want to keep my powder dry and not get into the 'who done it' game. I just stick to the evidence."

"You don't exclude them, though?"

"Of course not. It's possible some elements of the underworld might have worked with the CIA on this and other issues."

Bill looked at his watch. "Okay, I've got to get to LAX," he said as he quickly signed the bill.

"I hope you feel this has been productive," Schrade said, handing Bill a business card with his home number scrawled on the back.

"Absolutely, in many ways. I'll have a lot to think about on the flight back."

Chapter Thirty-Eight
Real Proof?

It was Bill's first red-eye flight, and especially considering the length of it, he hoped it would be his last.

As he had been doing for years, he pulled out his journal and started writing. He entered a general summary of the Schrade meeting before sitting back and wondering where all this was leading. He had no concrete recommendations, just probabilities and possibilities.

As thoughts rambled into his head, he wrote them down. His objective: to determine if the Reuther death was a hit. There was no proof … he jotted that down. Then he wrote, "CIA, intelligence, military." He looked at those words. If any of these elements were involved in the Kennedy or King assassinations, did they lead to Reuther? He wrote "no solid connections" linking government agencies. Then he jotted, "What about me? I was loyal employee, yet framed by SS." He wrote, "Who knows how to prove?" and circled those last two phrases. Fatigue finally hit him, and he closed the notebook and drifted into a deep sleep.

Two hours later, he woke up thinking of Sue. He could not wait to see her, to hold her.

Sue was waiting at the gate when Bill landed. They came together with a long embrace and several kisses. Walking to the lower level to collect his suitcase, they brought each other up to date on various activities. Sue said that Ken Morris wanted to buy them breakfast at Cupids, so they stopped there before heading to Solidarity House.

Morris was joined at his table by Mazey and Roy Frescura. Though a bit surprised at the larger-than-expected gathering, Bill took it in stride. He said he did not have all his thoughts together yet and still had work to do, but summarized the key parts of his trip.

Mazey was especially interested in the Elliot Glenn meeting. "Are you sure you can trust him? Jesus! The FBI, Hoover, Christ!" he exclaimed.

"All I can say," Bill replied, "is that Phil Hart strongly recommended him. They met at the Fort Custer hospital recovering from war wounds. He and Hart, and I think some other current senators, recovered there. I thought he was a straight shooter."

That seemed to satisfy Mazey. Bill said he planned to have a second meeting with the National Transportation Safety Board next week. He also indicated Schrade encouraged him to meet with Irv Bluestone.

"If you have trouble setting it up with Irv, let me know," Mazey said. Back at his office at Solidarity House, Bill reviewed some of his fifteen or so messages. The only one of interest was from John Phillips of the NTSB. Bill called him, and Phillips asked if they could meet. They set a time the following Wednesday at Phillips's Detroit office.

Bill and Sue went through the material in his in-basket. Included was a four-volume set of books entitled *Forgive My Grief* by Penn Jones Jr. He looked at the cover and saw that Jones was a long-time owner of the small-town newspaper, *Midlothian Mirror.*

"Where the hell is the *Midlothian Mirror*?" Bill asked with a mix of sarcasm and frustration.

Sue smiled. "I knew that would be your reaction. Midlothian is a small town in Texas, about twenty miles from Dallas."

"Hmm, looks good, but I don't know how the hell I'm going to get through all of this."

"Don't worry," she said, "I can give you a cheat sheet. I think there's good stuff in there."

Bill was starting to get drowsy. "Let's take all this stuff home," he said. "I need a nap. We can go over it later."

Sue's eyes lit up at the suggestion of a nap. They left the office arm-in-arm.

***

The next day, Bill read the material from Sue and began putting an outline together for his report. He also began reading *Forgive My Grief.* It was an interesting story, much like Mark Lane's *Rush to Judgment.* The author focused on the large number of witnesses to President Kennedy's assassination who had died in the months and years after the shooting.

He and Sue took his mother out to dinner that evening. Bill was pleased that Jenny and Sue got along so well—even if sometimes he felt like the odd man out.

Sunday was a gorgeous Michigan summer day; it was mostly sunny and about eighty degrees by noon. Bill, Sue, and her father, Paul, had a twelve-thirty tee time at the Birmingham Country Club. The three had played in mid-June, and Bill had lost to the older and more experienced player by six strokes, but felt good about his game. Bill was looking forward to narrowing the gap this time.

Sue and Bill walked and were assigned caddies; Paul took a cart. Bill got off to a rough start, but settled down and was within three strokes of Paul at the turn. Bill kept his good play going as they started the back nine and managed to pull even with Paul after the 15th hole. Both men parred the next two holes, so they were tied going into the 18th and final hole.

"Looks like this one's for drinks," Paul said to Bill.

Bill knew the older man was dead serious and really wanted to win the match. Following their tee shots, Paul sped ahead in his cart, while Bill and Sue walked down the fairway. Sue murmured, "Don't worry. It's just Dad."

Paul bogied the 18th, which should have given Bill an opening for the win. But Bill hit an easy nine-iron into the creek in front of the green for a penalty and ended with a double-bogey, losing to Paul by a single stroke, 84-85.

After the final putt, all shook hands with smiles and compliments on a round well-played. Walking away, Paul said, "Gee, I guess I won the match. How about that?" He jumped into his cart and drove off to the clubhouse.

"You chunked that approach shot, didn't you?" Sue asked Bill.

"No shit I chunked it; my worst shot of the day," Bill replied.

"Yeah, but you did it so Dad would win. You gave him the round."

"Well, I wouldn't say that. I actually choked, no question about that."

"You know, I'm a schoolteacher and I can spot a bullshitter a mile away."

Bill waved her off. "Ah, don't make a big deal about it. We've got plenty more good rounds of golf in our future. Jesus, I not only have to watch out for your dad, but look at you, Miss 96—your handicap is coming down."

They both laughed.

***

Bill found that while he was in his office, people stopped by wanting to talk. Initially, they were looking for Paul Silver. Of late, more visitors wanted to talk to Bill, though. Some were top UAW leaders, some staffers. Many had conspiracy theories so far out in left field that Bill questioned their common sense. Others had some sophisticated ideas, including concerns about a bad altimeter. Most were convinced that Reuther's death was a conspiracy, plotted by various enemies.

Bill noted that when not attending meetings, Silver was often writing and proofing documents for Ken Morris. The man was a walking encyclopedia on internal UAW issues and policy issues affecting members at the state and local level of governments.

Mid-afternoon on Monday, there was a knock on the office's open door. Silver had just hung up his phone. Reaching to make another call, he looked up. "Hi, Victor. How are you?" he said, his gravelly voice filled with empathy. He got up and gave the man a bear hug.

"Oh, Paul, I'm fine. It's been a hell of a time." The man looked familiar to Bill, maybe in his late fifties or early sixties, balding, a beard.

"Victor Reuther, this is Bill Simpson," Silver said, introducing them.

"Emil told me to come down and meet you," Reuther said. "Do you think you might have a little time to spare?" Reuther, along with his deceased brothers, Roy and Walter, were a sibling threesome unmatched just about anywhere. While Walter was always the leader of the group, both Roy, who died in 1968, and Victor provided their own unique leadership qualities to the UAW and social causes. Roy and Victor were always loyal to Walter and Walter to them. If there was royalty in the UAW, it was the Reuther brothers.

"Of course, Mr. Reuther."

"No, I'm Victor."

"Ah, thanks. Of course," Bill said. "I have time now."

"Now is good. I have a flight back to DC tonight. May I?" Reuther said as Bill motioned to a wooden chair. At the same time, Silver quietly got up, shook hands with Reuther, and left the room.

"Victor, I know how difficult this time must be for you," Bill said. "I lost my dad a few years ago, and it was rough. But I knew he was sick and dying—no way could you have been prepared for something like this."

"Thanks, Bill. I appreciate your words. You know, I didn't know your father, but I knew of him. He was a solid UAW man."

"Thanks. Now, how can I help you?"

"I was just visiting with Emil upstairs, and he told me you had been hired and a little about your background. You seem to be the right man for the right job."

Bill smiled. "I hope so. But you know, there's no easy conclusion on this, I'm afraid. There's still more work to do."

"Emil said you were in Washington last week. I wish I'd known—we could easily have talked then. In fact, Emil kind of kicked himself in the ass for not putting us together sooner."

Bill decided not to mention his efforts to reach him during the DC trip and simply said, "Well, better late than never. Emil probably told you what I'm up to. I've talked to the state police, the FBI, NTSB, and Paul Schrade. I'm going back to the NTSB later this week."

"Good. This could be good timing. I have a story to tell you. That's why I came down."

In a measured voice, Reuther talked about the time he and Walter were flying into Washington's Dulles Airport last October. "Walter and I were in a Lear jet provided by Private Jet Services. That's the same company that provided the jet that went down in Pellston." His voice began to crack. "It was about 11:30 at night, and the pilot went on visual when the runway was in sight. The weather was clear, we were at about five or six hundred feet. As soon as the runway was in sight, the pilots realized the jet was too low. They leveled and the jet hit the runway hard.

"There was a loud jolt; the plane hit something. Both Walter and I thought we were going to be dead in the next second or two. The plane whipped from side to side, but the pilots did a masterful job and held it on the runway until it slowed, so they could move off the runway to a grass field. The pilots got everyone off the plane. Apparently, when we hit the ground, we kind of fishtailed and hit some type of steel girder: that piece of steel was sticking out of the fuselage of the plane. I learned later that this steel spear was part of the inner marker antenna. Now, this is just me talking, I think there might have been an altimeter problem and that's why we were lower than the pilots thought." Reuther looked to Bill for his reaction.

Bill was extremely interested, especially in Reuther's last statement. "Victor, this is an amazing story, and your timing couldn't be better with my meeting with John Phillips of the NTSB on Wednesday."

"Well, I'm glad I could get you this information. You know, as we were standing on the grass outside the jet, I can tell you that Walter and I were rattled. It happened so fast."

"Do you have any insights to the reason Walter's jet went down in Pellston?"

"No, I really don't … no," Reuther stumbled. "I just haven't wanted to think about it. Maybe now, now that it's been a couple of months. I don't know. People have been trying to kill Walter for decades … maybe they finally got him." He paused. "A little after our near-crash back then, the airline officials let us go, and we were driven to Washington. Walter said, 'I guess this wasn't intended to be our time.' I've thought about that quite bit since Pellston."

"This is really good information. How did you find out about the antenna?"

"I have a copy of the NTSB's preliminary report."

"Can you send it to me?"

Reuther said that he would, and Bill wondered if this could be the break he needed.

Chapter Thirty-Nine
Progress

Late Tuesday afternoon, Bill walked upstairs to see Irv Bluestone, a meeting that had been scheduled by his secretary the previous day. Bill recalled Bluestone's strong voice at Walter Reuther's funeral and that he seemed to be universally respected by people inside and outside the UAW. He had been Reuther's top aide for years, and was known for his brilliant, yet down-to-earth mind. The new UAW president, Leonard Woodcock, had been vice president of the union, overseeing all relations with General Motors for many years, a huge job inside the UAW. With Woodcock's election to replace Reuther, Bluestone was promoted to vice president, with GM in his portfolio. Bill was looking forward to talking to him.

Bluestone's office featured a wonderful view of the Detroit River, with Belle Isle in the background. There were only a few photos on the wall and a family photo on the credenza behind the desk. Otherwise the office looked bare, a sign he had just moved in.

Bluestone greeted Bill with an outstretched hand. He was in his mid-fifties, his graying black hair combed straight back, wearing a suit and a bow tie. He looked like a college professor rather than a labor leader. As Bill took a seat across from the desk, Bluestone said in a warm, baritone voice, "Bill, I'm aware of your assignment, and it's a task that needs to be done. How are you coming?"

Bill gave a quick overview of his activities then added, "Irv, I know you were extremely close to Walter, and I know you two traveled together a lot. Can you give me some perspective of what it was like to travel with him, and perhaps any experiences that might stick out?"

Bluestone digested the question for slightly more than a moment. "Walter was a special man—brilliant, inquisitive, articulate, curious, and a workaholic. Some people felt he lacked a sense of humor. That's not true. Walter could be funny and warm. He is the greatest person I've ever known. On the road, he was quiet, usually retiring after dinner to his room to work, read, or make phone calls. I don't think he really enjoyed traveling, but you know the UAW is an international union, and if one is going to be part of its leadership, then one is going to travel a hell of a lot. He really loved to spend time with his wife, May. That was a great love story. He always felt guilty about not being around his daughters more."

"Were there any hints of violence during these trips?"

"Not really," Irv responded. "Of course, after that assassination attempt in '48, Walter always had a bodyguard. That restricted his life on the road quite a bit and could be one reason he didn't socialize much. But, you know, we did enjoy many pleasant dinners with different people. If we were in Washington, it might be a senator or a key administration official. If we were on the West Coast, it might be dinner with someone like Danny Kaye or Harry Belafonte. Walter knew an incredible cadre of people. As I think about it, you should know that Belafonte, like Walter, helped fund Martin Luther King's work. Harry's funding was more personal than ours—we could help fund Martin's nonprofit entities—but Harry helped him in all sorts of ways, including bailing him out of jail and supplementing his household income."

"But no violence, no scares?"

"No, no scares." Irv paused. "Well, wait a minute, that's not quite true. A few years ago, Walter and I were flying back from somewhere, I think DC. We were in a jet, it was a new plane, maybe a 737, but I'm not sure. So, I was in the window seat as Walter always preferred the aisle seat— more elbow room for him to work. As we flew over Detroit, I realized that we had been circling around Metro Airport. This went on for about a half an hour. The pilot came on the intercom and said they had indicators of an engine problem, but told us not to worry. Well, you can imagine some of the reactions of the passengers. I looked out the window, the runway was sprayed with foam, and they were getting ready for a crash landing. Ambulances and firetrucks were lined up along the runway. Both Walter and I were bracing ourselves for a bumpy ride. Well, it turned out to be a false alarm. The plane landed and we taxied to our gate without any problems. That's about the most excitement I ever had traveling with Walter."

"Do you remember when that was?"

"No, but I can check my calendar. I know LBJ was president then."

They talked a little while longer until Irv paused, looked down at his desk pad thoughtfully and asked, "Bill, has Ken told you the full story of how you were released from prison?"

Bill shook his head. "No details, and I've never pushed him. He essentially said the union was able to get the story of the person who perjured herself to higher-ups in the Johnson Administration, and then some good things started to happen."

"Well, I don't think Ken, or Emil for that matter, would object if I shared a few more details with you." With that, Bluestone told Bill how Walter Reuther took his case to LBJ, how Johnson called Judge Wilson and strongly suggested that the judge find a way to get Bill out of prison. Then the judge agreed once he learned the Secret Service and the US attorney knowingly allowed a witness to commit perjury.

Bill was amazed by these new details of his story.

"Pretty amazing what Walter would do for the son of a UAW member," Bluestone said. "So, within a matter of days, our union righted a major miscarriage of justice. Why? Because it was the right thing to do."

"I knew bits and pieces of the story, but I had no idea about the direct involvement of the White House or the president," Bill said.

"Talk to Ken Morris. Ken doesn't gossip like some of us," Bluestone said with a smile. "But he knows the details far better than I do. He should be able to fill in the missing blanks, especially since Walter's gone, and Johnson is out of the White House."

As Bluestone walked him out of the office, Bill noted an eleven-by-fourteen framed photo taken at the 1963 March on Washington that showed Walter Reuther from behind, standing on the steps of the Lincoln Memorial and speaking to the hundreds of thousands of people encircling the reflecting pool, the crowd reaching to the Washington Monument. It was a powerful and impressive image.

Bluestone, noting Bill's interest, said, "That was a great day. You know, of course, that President Kennedy wanted Walter to help organize the event."

"I think I knew that. You know, I served on the president's Secret Service detail in 1962. I saw Walter at the White House one evening and I introduced myself."

Bluestone nodded as his gaze remained on the photo. "Well, I was standing near the photographer when that photo was snapped, and I'm so glad I was able to get a copy. You know, there were about ten people who spoke that day. Of course, Dr. King's speech was special. But what I most remember is that when Walter was done and leaving the podium, he walked by two young black girls, in their late teens or early twenties, college kids I suspect. They were standing right in front of me. Well, one girl says to the other, 'Who is that man?' Her friend responded, 'Don't you know? That's Walter Reuther, he's the white Martin Luther King.' How about that!" Bluestone chuckled. "Walter so enjoyed that story."

The next morning, when Bill entered his office he found a handwritten note on his chair. It read, *"Bill, I enjoyed our chat yesterday. Walter and I were returning from Washington on February 15, 1968, about 9:00 that evening. If you have any questions, just call. Irv."* Imagine that, Bill thought, this incredibly busy and powerful guy checked his records and hand-delivered the note before the start of work.

***

That afternoon, Bill headed downtown to the federal building to meet with John Phillips, the main NTSB investigator. Their first meeting had not been very productive; Bill hoped this one would go better.

Bill hadn't been inside the federal building in six years and was surprised at some of the emotions swirling through his mind. There were so many memories, too many bad ones. He knew Judge Wilson had died—his mother had seen the obituary in the *Free Press*. He was worried he might run into someone from the Secret Service office, members of which he'd lost all contact since January 1964. He reflected for a moment on how his life had changed since then. It was like he had closed the door on his old life and walked into a brand-new world. His new life was mostly better, except for not being close to his kids; that hurt the most.

At the customs office, a thin man in his forties, with prematurely gray hair, came down a corridor at a brisk pace.

Phillips said, "Sorry for the inconvenience, but the NTSB doesn't have offices here in Michigan."

"Why wouldn't you use the FAA or some transportation agency when you travel?" Bill asked as Phillips led him down a hallway.

"Back in the '20s when we were created, we were put under the Department of Commerce. The feeling was we needed to be an independent agency, so the idea was to remove us from any relationship with transportation agencies. We are a strictly independent agency. When we travel, we ask agencies outside the Department of Transportation if they can host us. In Michigan, we use the customs office." They moved into a small conference room; Phillips's material was laid out at the head of a table. They got some coffee and sat down at the table.

"I'm under some pressure to get my assignment completed," Bill said, "and I'm wondering if you can give me any preliminary information on the crash."

"I don't have anything official. I don't expect a final report until late fall, perhaps as late as December."

"What about a preliminary report?"

"Actually, that was published in June. Here, I have a copy for you." Philips opened a manila folder and pulled out a copy of a report about twelve pages long and pushed it across the table. Bill quickly flipped through it.

"Do you have any conclusions?" Bill asked, setting the report aside.

"Ah, we don't like to make conclusions in preliminary reports. But putting that aside, here is what I think happened. The jet was making a circle as it descended onto the Pellston runway. It was moving under a thousand feet. As it turned to align with the runway, two things happened. The pilot had trouble finding visual cues to orient himself—remember, it was dusk—and the airport's landing strip had lights, but no approach lighting, a real problem at rural airports. So that, combined with the pilot's apparently faulty altimeter, caused the pilot to be much lower than he thought. So much so, he clipped the trees, and the jet went down and exploded."

"So, let me get this straight," Bill said. "You think the altimeter was giving bad readings?"

"Yes, sir. I think the pilot believed he was between 200 and 250 feet higher than he was. That, combined with the fact it was nearly dark and there were no obvious visual clues, the trees proved deadly to him and his passengers."

"Jesus Christ," Bill said, trying to remain calm. "So, you think there was a faulty altimeter involved?

Phillips nodded.

"Are you aware that Reuther was involved in a remarkably similar mishap at Dulles late last year? The same company, a similar jet with landing issues almost identical, and they damned near crashed. They hit hard—I guess it wasn't an actual crash, but clearly a serious incident. The pilot came out of his approach turn too low, perhaps by about 500 feet, but he had enough visibility to adjust. Still the plane hit the ground hard and nearly lost control. They fishtailed and hit an antenna tower, which sliced into the fuselage. Reuther and his brother walked away, but it seems these are very similar circumstances to the Pellston crash. You should check this out."

Phillips wrote furiously in his notebook. He kept writing as Bill reviewed the Irv Bluestone experience. Bill concluded, "Three separate issues in a couple of years—what are the odds of that?"

"Not good. The Metro thing is probably a coincidence, but the same problem with two similar, small jets? We are going to be doing more investigating, that's for damned sure."

Chapter Forty
A Secret Service Visit

Bill walked a couple of blocks to the Lafayette Coney Island for two Coney dogs and a Coke. As he ate, he reflected on his meeting with Phillips. A sense of deep satisfaction swept over him. After several weeks of dead ends, some leads were finally starting to come together. After his meal, he worked his way back to his parked car, a block from the federal building. Just as he inserted the key in the door, a voice came from the shadow of a building next to the lot.

"Simpson, what the hell are you up to?"

Bill looked up to see his old partner, Joe Kowalski, whom he hadn't seen since the day he was betrayed in court. Bill told himself to be cool.

Kowalski offered his hand; Bill didn't take it. Kowalski looked older, more mature. He had put more than a few pounds around his mid-section and his suit was of a better cut than he used to wear. Kowalski, too, was sizing Bill up: "Christ, you look like a hippie."

Ignoring the comment, Bill said, "My goodness, Joe Kowalski. I haven't seen you since you sold your soul and sent me up to the big house."

Kowalski flinched. "Bill, we all have to do what we have to do."

"Well, how fucking trite do you have to be? Jesus."

"Listen, they already had the hooker when they came to me. I knew you were going to prison ..."

"Bullshit! My attorney pretty much destroyed her. Your testimony put the final nails in my coffin. And, by the way, you know she recanted."

"Yeah, we know you had to go pretty high up in government to have the pull to get an early release. We figured you must have picked up some connections when you served on the president's detail."

Wrong, asshole.

Kowalski added, "Judge Wilson was pretty pissed off. We figured it was the woman."

"So, what are you doing? Did you get your law degree or are you still with the service?'

"Naw, I'm with the Service. I'm deputy in the office."

"Really?" Bill said. *Well, I know now how the Service paid him off.*

"Yeah, listen," Kowalski said as he looked around, leaning in, lowering his voice. "We got a tip on you that you are now working as a detective for the UAW. What's up with that?"

"Well, if you have a file on me, you know I work in a Ford factory, and I'm a UAW member. When Reuther's plane went down, the leaders in the union wanted to know if it was an accident or not. They knew I had done some criminal investigative work in the past and asked me to help. It's all pretty simple."

"So, you're running around the country meeting with senators, the FBI, and now, the NTSB. What are you up to? Are you trying to interfere with their report?"

Bill was instantly pissed off with himself. He never thought he was being tailed. Of the people he had met with, he was most worried about them getting to Glenn. He'd have to warn him.

"I'm not trying to interfere with anything," Bill said sharply. "I'm just doing my job. The NTSB is a professional organization. They are not going to let me interfere with their investigations. Jesus, you know better than that."

"Bill," his old partner said, softening his voice, "look, I know you had a raw deal and things did not work out the way you wanted. And I know I'm partly responsible. I'm doing my job, too. Be careful. Watch your back. You might be getting into something you can't handle." As Bill was taking all of this in, Joe added, "Now, I've done my job. Be careful," he repeated before he turned and walked away into the bright, midsummer afternoon.

Bill looked at his watch. It was nearly three. He went to his office at Solidarity House with three objectives before he left for the day: write up notes on his NTSB meeting, try to contact Glenn, and think seriously about his conversation with Kowalski.

He pulled out his journal and wrote about his NTSB meeting, with the main point being the failure of the altimeter. He added something about the near-crash at Dulles. Then he focused on the possibility of a conspiracy, which meant murder. He didn't have any facts, but the circumstantial evidence was building.

He removed Glenn's card from his wallet and dialed the number. He was told Glenn wasn't in. "Will he be in later or tomorrow?" Bill asked the woman who'd answered.

"No sir ... ah, I'm sorry. It sounds like you don't know. Mr. Glenn has been in a terrible automobile accident. He's in the hospital, in a"—

her voice started to crack— "a coma. Is there someone else who can help?"

Bill caught his breath as he began to perspire. "No, I'm so sorry. Is … is it alright if I call in a couple of days to see how he's doing?"

"Of course, sir. May I ask who's calling?"

Bill hung up.

Chapter Forty-One
An Action Plan

Bill paced up and down the hallways at Solidarity House before heading to the lobby. He went outside, circled the parking lot, and followed the grass going toward the river. For the first time, he thought he might be in danger. What had Kowalski said? "Watch your back."

Then, his old partner let slip that he had been tailed in Washington and Detroit. He didn't say anything about LA. In Washington, Glenn was fighting for his life. Was Kowalski told to warn him? People wanted Bill to back off, but why? Had he gotten too close to something bad, something sinister? The altimeter problems? If true, these problems led to conspiracy, but by whom?

Bill didn't carry a weapon. He needed to rethink that. And what about the UAW hierarchy, the people he worked with and people he interviewed? And, with a sudden shiver, *What about Sue? Is she in danger?* Probably not, but he had to start thinking about security for her and others. He also considered his files. He had a lot of information, some of it sensitive. *This could get out of hand, really fast.*

After a thirty-minute walk around the UAW grounds, he had his plan just about put together. He returned to his office and called Sue, but there was no answer. He grabbed his notes and journals and moved down to Sophie's office. She was working late and engrossed in her typing. He asked her to try to get a meeting tomorrow, or not later than Friday, with Ken Morris and Emil Mazey. Then he asked her to take his notes and journals to the copying room. He told her he was going to be working on a draft of his report to Mazey sometime late next week. Next, he asked her to book him an early flight on Monday to DC, with an evening return. Then, as an afterthought, he said, "Can you also see if you can find out about recent traffic accidents in DC and if an Elliot Glenn might have been involved? Also, I'll need to rent a car. And," he added, "some maps of the DC area would be good."

Sophie nodded, replying in her no-nonsense voice, "No problem." She asked for no explanations.

Bill returned to his desk and organized his material, including many of the books and magazine articles Sue had collected on assassination attacks on key leaders in the US. He had not read all of them, something to be corrected by Saturday.

He remembered to call Sue. They agreed to meet at six-thirty at Alban's, a casual restaurant in Birmingham. He had an hour before he needed to leave. He tried to shake the eerie feeling that time was running out.

Bill pulled out of the Solidarity House parking lot in his new, red Barracuda. Normally, he took a left turn onto Jefferson heading toward downtown Detroit before jumping on the Chrysler Expressway and heading north to his house or Sue's apartment. This time, he took a different route, needing to know if he was being followed. He made his normal left onto Jefferson, but then made a fast, hard right onto Grand Boulevard, heading north. He didn't notice anyone following. A few blocks down, he hung a hard left onto Lafayette Street, heading toward the Chrysler Expressway. Again, he saw no cars following. He kept an eye out all the way to Birmingham, but noticed no suspicious traffic.

Alban's was a combination wine, cheese, and other food accessories store with a small, but particularly good cafeteria in the back. Sue was already at a table, sipping a glass of red wine. Bill was relieved to see her warm smile. He kissed her on the lips and sat down next to her.

Sue reached into her purse and fumbled around until she pulled out a postcard. "Something came in the mail yesterday," she said with a smile. In her hand was the Grauman's postcard he had sent the previous week. "I love it," she added, leaning in, giving him another kiss.

A waitress brought his Stroh's draft, then they went through the cafeteria-style line to get roast beef and side dishes. Back in their seats, they shared their days between bites.

Bill told Sue about the productive NTSB meeting, which captured Sue's interest. He talked about the surprise encounter with Kowalski. Sue knew about Bill's past, but not all the details, including people he had worked with during his Secret Service days. He filled in some of those blanks.

Sue set aside her fork. "Should we be scared?" she asked, deadly serious.

"I don't know that we should be scared, but I think we need to take some precautions," Bill replied. "

I've asked Sophie to have copies made of my notes and my journals. I think I want that material at home as well as in the office. As I think about it, let's store it at your place, if that's okay?"

"Yep, I'll make room."

"Also—and you're not going to like this—but I don't think it's a good idea for you to come down to Solidarity House anymore. You can help me at the library or at home."

Sue sat back and frowned. "Whoa, what makes you think you can get away from me that easily? I'm part of this effort."

"Look," Bill began, knowing he had hurt her feelings, "you know I love you, and I want to spend the rest of my life with you." He took her hand, pulled it close to his chest, and looked into her sparkling, blue eyes. "We may have lost an FBI man. I don't want you to be any kind of collateral casualty here. Things could get pretty rough."

"Oh, Bill, you know I want to be there for you—"

"But you are. I'm probably worrying about absolutely nothing. It could be that in a couple of weeks, we'll be laughing at my concerns. But, we will still be together. You will still be doing your research. Dammit, hon, I can't operate at full-strength if I have to worry about your safety."

"Don't patronize me, I can take care of myself," Sue insisted with a testy, yet alluring pout.

"Jesus, I'm not patronizing you. I love you. Sweetheart, I've been trained to deal with these kinds of people. I might be a bit rusty, but I'm fairly sure I can get the job done."

"Are you dumping me?" Her voice quivered, and a tear rolled down her cheek.

Bill leaned over and gave her a full, wet kiss. Some people stopped eating and stared. When he released her, he glanced around the restaurant before he whispered, "No fucking way."

Sue grinned and squeezed his hand. "I want you at my place—*now.*"

Chapter Forty-Two
Protection

That Friday, Morris, Mazey, and Frescura, who always seemed to be with Mazey, met Bill for lunch at Sindbad's, a long-time Detroit establishment whose best feature was its location on the river, minutes from Solidarity House. Bill gave the men a summary of his week, with Mazey or Morris occasionally asking for clarification.

When he finished, Mazey asked, "Bill, do you think you or any of us are in danger?"

"I don't know," he replied. "Clearly, I've been tailed at times. There's no indication anyone followed me on my way home last night or as I came in this morning. I did tell Sue that I still want her to help, but from a distance. I don't want her to come into the office for a while."

"So, you're worried?" Mazey said.

"Yeah, I guess so. At the end of the day, I think we'll be okay, though. We just have to be careful. There are some forces out there I don't fully understand. I am thinking of getting a pistol, something I've not had for many years."

Mazey turned to Frescura. "Roy, after we're done with lunch, take Bill down to see Tony and fit him up with whatever he needs."

"No, problem."

Turning to Bill, Frescura said, "I'll stop by your office around one-thirty. Okay?"

Bill nodded. "My plan is to get an initial draft of my findings to you by the end of next week. Is that reasonable?" he asked Mazey.

Mazey looked at Morris, who nodded and said, "Yeah, that should be fine."

"It might make sense to up the security at Solidarity House, and of people who have been dealing with me," Bill said.

Mazey's response was quick. "I'll take care of that."

Back at his office, Bill told Paul Silver that Frescura was coming down to set him up with a firearm. Bill asked why Roy was the expert on guns.

Silver replied, "Oh, you don't know? Roy is Emil's bodyguard."

Later, Frescura drove Bill to John R Street near Seven Mile Road and pulled up to a small shop in front of a larger structure. "This is Tony's place," Frescura said. "He's a really good guy and cares about the labor movement. We should be able to get what you need. Tony has a range in the warehouse out back, so we can do some shooting now. You can use it whenever you want."

When they entered the shop, they met a short, balding man in his late sixties with a slight eastern European accent.

"Do you know what you're looking for, young man?" Tony asked Bill.

"Yeah, I'm looking for a Smith and Wesson snub nose .38 caliber revolver," Bill said of the .38-caliber handgun he had in mind.

"Ah," Tony said, almost to himself. "Great stopping power. Were you in law enforcement?"

"Yeah, a while back."

"Figures. A cop's gun. I have a three inch barrel."

A few moments later, Tony handed him the weapon. Bill asked for four boxes of bullets. Bill reached into his pocket for his wallet to pay for the gun. Frescura put out his hand. "Emil's going to pick this up." With a smile, he added, "Our international reps don't usually buy weapons." The two men spent an hour or so on the range before heading back to the office. Bill enjoyed getting to know Frescura. It turned out he, along with Morris and Mazey, were all from the same auto plant, the Briggs local, which had turned out a lot of good union men. *It must have been a special place.*

That weekend, Bill caught up on his reading and putting his thoughts into a rough outline for his report. He also reviewed a package Sophie had prepared for his trip. She had much of the information he requested, including newspaper clippings of every traffic incident in the DC area the previous week. He also spent an hour at Tony's gun range. His rust with a pistol showed, but the .38 pistol soon felt good in his hand, and his confidence in the weapon grew. He hoped it served only as a deterrent—he did not want violence.

Chapter Forty-Three
The Hospital

Bill's flight departed at seven Monday morning. He hoped Glenn was conscious and willing to see him, so he could learn if Glenn's crash was a simple traffic accident or something more sinister. Sophie's research had found that he was at Cafritz Memorial Hospital, located in the southeast corner of DC.

He landed at Washington National and picked up the Chrysler 300 from Avis that Sophie reserved. He declined the map offered by the Avis agent—Sophie had exercised her usual efficiency and provided several maps. Bill made a mental note to send her flowers.

Bill drove around aimlessly for a while, making sure he wasn't being followed, then pulled into the hospital's visitor lot. He saw no evidence of a tail.

At the reception desk, he asked for Elliot Glenn's room, saying he was a colleague on his lunch break. The staffer eyed Bill, dressed in a sport jacket, with no tie, and long hair pulled in a ponytail. She pulled up the file on Glenn. "I'm sorry, Mr. Glenn is still very ill and can't accept any visitors."

Not surprised by the rejection, Bill kept an eye out for any information he might be able to get from the sheet the woman used. Reading upside down, he spotted "B-325" by Glenn's name.

"Thank you, ma'am," Bill said and walked away.

Once he was out of her sight, he surveyed the area and spotted the B wing.

Moments later, he was walking down the B wing's third-floor corridor. Just as he passed Room B-308, he heard a woman's shrill voice: "Excuse me! Who are you?" Bill acted like he didn't hear her and continued walking, a bit quicker. He soon felt a firm hand on his upper arm. "Sir, please, what are you doing here?"

He stopped and looked into the face of a no-nonsense nurse in her thirties. He was screwed. He replied, absentmindedly, "Oh, hi. I'm a State Farm insurance agent, and I have a client who was in a car accident, and I wanted to check up on him."

She looked at him, not buying his pitch. "Alright, whom are you here to see?"

"Mr. Glenn. He's in Room 325."

"Nope, that's impossible. Mr. Glenn is still in a coma. There is no way some insurance agent, or whatever you are, is walking into my ward thinking he's going to bother my patient or his family. No way. You come with me."She grabbed him and pushed him to the elevator. Bill felt like his second-grade teacher, Miss Van Ness, was punishing him for talking in class. The elevator doors opened, the nurse dragged him in with her, and pressed the lobby button. When they arrived at the lobby, she waved a hand, motioning him off the elevator. "Okay, buddy. You are out of here, and I don't want to see you again. Got it?"

"You won't have any problems from me," Bill said. The nurse kept an eye on him until he exited the building.

When the nurse returned to her station on the third floor, she picked up a card by the phone and dialed the number on it. A few moments later, she said into the receiver,

"Is Agent Schmidt there?"

***

Bill took a short walk around outside, then returned to the hospital, observing the lobby and surrounding area in more detail, something he should have done earlier. He noticed a corridor that people entered in civilian clothes and, a few minutes later, came out in medical scrubs or lab coats. *Ah, employees only*. Most of the men who entered the hallway were dressed primarily in slacks and open shirts. He returned to his car and dumped his sport jacket.

There wasn't enough foot traffic into and out of the corridor for this to be a shift change. *Probably people returning to work from lunch*. Bill saw three men about to enter the corridor, so he quickly stepped in a few feet behind them. A moment later, he was in a large men's locker room. Small groups of men chatted as they dressed.

Bill worked his way to the back, where the sinks and toilets were. He leaned over a sink and washed his hands and face. No one seemed to pay him any attention. He saw a stack of clean hospital scrubs, picked up a set, and moved to a toilet stall. He slipped the scrubs on over his street clothes. As he left the restroom area, he noticed piles of clean scrub caps and lab coats. He grabbed one of each and put them on, stuffing his hair under the cap. He hoped that "Nurse Ratched"—a name he took from a novel he had read in prison—had other issues on her mind.

He took the elevator to the third floor once again, and no one seemed to pay him any mind. He saw "Nurse Ratched" working at her desk, avoided eye contact and kept walking. He was soon at B-325, where the open door allowed him to peek inside. Glenn's left leg was heavily bandaged and in traction. His right arm also was heavily bandaged, and his upper head was wrapped in gauze. An IV unit was feeding him liquids. Mrs. Glenn sat next to the bed.

Bill, trying to act professional, reached for the patient's chart. As he scanned it, he said, "So how's the patient today?"

"Just the same, doctor, just the same."

"Well, hopefully, things will improve." Bill looked up from the chart. Mrs. Glenn was staring at him.

"I know you," she said, raising a finger. "I know you, but I don't know how I know you."

"Well, I'm sure we met someplace…"

The woman shook her head. "No, not here. It was recent, but somewhere else."

Bill decided to take a chance. He stuck his head out in the hall and looked up and down, then shut the door and moved toward her chair. He kneelt on one knee, so his face was level with her eyes. She stiffened. Bill could tell she was about to call for help. "Mrs. Glenn, please, relax. I have no agenda except to learn what happened to your husband. Please. Yes, you are right. I met you at your house a couple of weeks ago. Elliot asked me to come over for a meeting. You served great cheese and crackers." As he finished his sentence, he lifted his cap to show his long hair.

Her head started to slowly nod. "Yes, I remember. Elliot liked you. But why are you here dressed like this?"

"I tried to get in earlier but was stopped. I'm only here for a short time and was so hoping Elliot was better. I'm so sorry he has not improved. Do you mind if I ask you a couple of questions? Then I'll be out of here, I promise," he said as he tucked his hair back under his cap.

The woman, clearly under tremendous stress because of her husband's injuries, was weighing what she should do. "Mister … ah, I don't remember your name."

"That's okay. I'm Bill."

"Ah, yes, of course, Bill—and it sounds like Bill does not want to give me a last name," she added in a knowing tone.

Bill smiled. "You are very observant. Mrs. Glenn. I'm here because I think I stumbled on to some information that I wanted to discuss with Elliot. Obviously, I can't do that, at least not now. Could you tell me what happened?"

Her face softened. "Well, ah, Bill, I don't know too much. I know it was after work, and Elliot took an unusual and longer route home. He traveled out of the way and was on Suitland Parkway, nearly in Maryland. Then he was in this terrible crash. They think his brakes failed."

"Really? A parkway's speeds are pretty slow and steady, aren't they?" Bill asked.

"Well, yes, but the officers said he was traveling well over sixty."

"That's unusual. Is there any reason to think he was being followed?"

"I really wouldn't know. I thought Elliot was out of that type of action. But you know, he rarely talked to me about his work."

"Did he say anything about me?"

"No, not really. He did say you were a nice person, which was unlike him. You made a good impression. You know, I don't normally snoop around his office, but a couple of nights ago I did look at his desk. I was curious about what he might have been thinking about before the crash."

"And?"

"Well, that's just it—he had a number of articles on the assassinations of Dr. King and the Kennedys."

"Any files?"

"Oh no. He never left things like that out."

A knock sounded, and the door slowly opened. "Mrs. Glenn?"

"Ah, Agent Schmidt," she said, clearly signaling Bill. "What can I do for you?"

"Well, ma'am, we received a call from the hospital. They said some guy was snooping around here on the floor, and we wanted to come by and see if all is okay. Is it? Have you had any disturbances?"

"Ah, no. Steve—it's Steve, right?"

"Yes ma'am, it is."

"No, just Elliot's doctor, Dr. Bill, has been here giving me an update on Elliot."

"Well, Doc, what's the prognosis?" the agent asked.

"No change, and, you know, that might be a good thing," Bill replied.

"Why so?"

Bill, standing as if he was ready to move on to visit with other patients, said, "Well, sir, some comas are a good thing; it means the body is recovering from the trauma of serious injuries." Bill hoped he sounded convincing.

"Well, then, I guess that is a good thing."

"Yep, it is. Mrs. Glenn, I'll say goodbye for now. Good luck."

Bill left the room and nearly collided with another man just outside. They nodded, and Bill quickly moved on, searching for the nearest stairwell. *That guy must have been Schmidt's partner.* Bill spotted an exit sign at the end of the hall. He moved rapidly down the steps and out the door. He wasn't followed. He decided to head out to Suitland Parkway to see if he could find the accident site.

As Bill was leaving the parking lot, inside the hospital, Agent Schmidt and his partner stopped at the nurses's station. Schmidt made an offhand remark regarding Dr. Bill's update on Glenn's condition. "Nurse Ratched" looked at him quizzically and said, "There's no Dr. Bill who works here."

Chapter Forty-Four
The Crash Site

Bill had no idea how Sophie had obtained local newspaper reports about the traffic accidents so quickly, but she had hit another home run. A short *Washington Post* article covered an accident on Suitland Parkway; no names of drivers or occupants were given.

The crash occurred on eastbound Suitland Parkway SE, between Stanton and Alabama streets, an area typical of DC parkway roads: limited access, lined by trees with plenty of parking for hiking or bike riding. He drove the section of parkway a couple of times, but saw nothing suspicious. After his third pass, he parked and walked the area. The road had a significant curve. Bill was trying to imagine what possibly caused Glenn to hit speeds of sixty or better along this stretch. If his brakes failed, he should have been able to let the car coast to the wide shoulder of the road. No, something or someone had caused him to accelerate. Glenn must have hit the gas and then, at the curve, lost control.

Bill saw nothing unusual. While walking to his car, he noticed some skid marks on the roadway. Traffic was light, so he had time to carefully examine them. He certainly was no expert on crash investigations, but it looked like there was more than one set of skid marks on the road. That explained a lot. He wished he could examine Glenn's vehicle. He didn't have time to do a full investigation but decided to send Mrs. Glenn a letter explaining the possibility. He thought he could do it diplomatically and suggest that she hire an expert to examine the vehicle for any possible involvement with another car.

Suddenly, Bill heard the roar of an engine and looked up to see a vehicle moving in his direction at a fast pace. The four-door, beige Chevrolet grew larger with each second. The car veered off the pavement onto the shoulder toward him. Instinctively, Bill moved as fast as he could toward the shrubbery. With one final, desperate dive, he somersaulted into the bushes as the car's rear wheels kicked up rocks, dirt, and debris before the Chevy sped off. Bill came to a rest and made sure he was okay. He stood up and looked around; the car was long gone. He dusted himself off, ran to his car, and took off in the direction of the attacking vehicle. But he found no trace of the beige Chevy.

Shaken, Bill headed back to Washington National. With luck, he might be able to catch an earlier flight back to Detroit. Instead, he had a three-hour wait. Realizing he had not eaten since his meal on the plane, nine hours earlier, he found a restaurant in the airport and mindlessly wolfed down a dinner and a couple of beers. He wrote his thoughts down and did a journal entry. The Kowalski visit, the visit to the hospital, Mrs. Glenn's comments on the crash, the suspicious markings on the Suitland Parkway, and the attacking Chevrolet had to add up ... but to what? Just like everything else in his investigation, plenty of circumstantial evidence and leads, but nothing conclusive—except for the altimeter tampering. Still, no proof as to who might have tampered with the equipment. He was afraid the UAW was wasting its money on him.

Having nothing to do, Bill walked to his gate early and started reading *The Washington Post*. Forty minutes later, a plane from Detroit landed and began unloading. In the crowd, coming out of the gateway, was Senator Hart, by himself. Bill rose from his seat to greet the senator. At first, Hart did not recognize him.

"Sir," Bill said, "we met in your office a couple of weeks ago. Emil Mazey—"

"Oh, of course, Bill. I remember. You know," the Senator said as a form of apology, "I'm up for election this year, and I guess my mind was on the campaign just now."

"Senator, you don't have to apologize. God, you must meet a hundred people every day."

"Still, I have to be more alert. And, yes, Elliot Glenn got back to me. He said the two of you had an interesting conversation. He thought you were going to have a tough time proving any foul play in Walter's death. You know that Elliot was in a terrible accident?"

"Yes, I was just at the hospital." A look of surprise came to Hart's face. "Elliot's still in a coma, but I had a chance to talk to Mrs. Glenn."

"How's Charlotte doing?"

"Actually, pretty well. I also looked at the accident site." Hart nodded. "Sir, like everything else, there is nothing I can prove, but there seemed to be multiple tread markings on the highway, indicating that Elliot did not just lose control, but that another car might have been involved." Bill didn't mention his near hit-and-run experience.

"Really? That's not what the newspapers reported."

"I know. Sir, I wonder if you could do me a favor?"

The senator hesitated. "If I can. What is it?"

"Senator, would you give Mrs. Glenn a call? Please let her know you talked with 'Dr. Bill.'" Again, Hart looked quizzical. "Don't worry, she'll know. Visitors weren't allowed, and I snuck in as a doctor."

"Jesus Christ," Hart said with a laugh. "You're playing a cloak-and-dagger game, eh?"

"I guess so, but she became my partner. An FBI man came into the room during our conversation. I thought I was nailed. But Mrs. Glenn covered for me. Anyway, I was going to drop her a note, but it would be a lot more effective if you could deliver the message."

"What is it?"

"Well, I don't want to create more stress in her life, but I think Elliot's car should be examined by an independent analyst to see whether or not another vehicle was involved. I know this could be too much for her, but if she waits too long, any evidence could be destroyed—if it hasn't been already."

"You think it's that important?"

"It could be."

"Alright. I'll contact her tonight or tomorrow morning. My office will provide any assistance she might need in finding the right investigator." Hart was looking eager to get moving, and Bill knew he had taken too much of his time.

Thirty minutes later, Bill walked aboard the same plane, back to Detroit.

Chapter Forty-Five
Mac

When Bill arrived at his office Tuesday, Sophie told him it had been pretty quiet while he was out, but that Fred Fry had called the previous afternoon.

"He wanted to meet with you. You know him, right?" she asked.

"Oh, yeah. He's with the FBI, the Detroit office. A good guy. Where does he want to meet?"

"At the Pontchartrain Wine Cellars at six-thirty tonight."

"Hmm, the Wine Cellars?" Bill said, thinking the restaurant was a couple of steps up in class from where they normally met. "That seems a bit unusual for Fred, but okay."

"Mr. Fry said he had some information that you might want. And, yeah, he seems like a nice guy."

Bill spent the morning working on his report, noting too many areas that needed greater substance in his next draft. Around noon, Ken Morris came by and asked if he wanted to join him and his newly appointed administrative assistant and long-time friend, Pat Caruso, for lunch downstairs at the union's cafeteria. Bill agreed. At lunch, Bill reviewed his DC trip with Morris, remembering to sing Sophie's praises. Word continued to spread inside the union about Bill's assignment, and as was typical of his days in the office, he had to answer calls from people who either had questions about Reuther's death or ideas about how it happened. Still, he got some real work done. At five, Sophie said goodnight, and Bill told her to expect his draft report by the end of the week.

He phoned Sue, telling her he was meeting Fry and was not sure about dinner plans but that he'd call her around seven-thirty or eight. "I was at the Wayne State library today and found some interesting information we can talk about later," she said.

"Good, hon. That will be just another reason to spend the night." Bill was imagining her face as he said those words.

"It's been too long," Sue replied.

Bill took a circuitous route to the restaurant, across the street from the Pontchartrain Hotel. He didn't detect a tail. He parked three blocks away and added several extra blocks to his walk, looking for any suspicious characters. But no one seemed to be following. The Wine Cellars was a dark, intimate place, one of the more romantic spots in the city. He told the hostess he was meeting a man named Fry, then followed her to a back corner of the room, expecting to see Fred. Instead, confusion and then recognition crossed Bill's face as another man stood to greet him—the former director of the Secret Service, Jim Macalister.

He was completely bald—*probably shaved his head*. The bushy eyebrows still set his face in a permanent scowl. Bill felt the blood drain from his head. He was almost dizzy, but managed to say, "Mac, it's been a long time. Who are you screwing these days?"

The strong greeting caught Macalister off guard. He started to extend his hand but returned it to his side when Bill did not reciprocate. "Well, okay then. Sit down," he said in his gravelly voice, motioning across the table.

"Where's Fred Fry?" Bill began.

"Fred Fry never called your office. My people did a good imitation."

I should have suspected a scam. Fred was not likely to frequent a high-end restaurant for a meeting—at best, he might go there for an anniversary dinner.

"The waitress will be here for drinks in a minute," Macalister said. "Shit, a few years in the slammer changed you. Or was it working in a factory? You're more direct, surer of yourself than eight years ago. I like it. Plus, you've slimmed down. You look a lot stronger." Bill marveled that Mac had been keeping an eye on him, but *how close of an eye was it?*

"You know, I was pretty pissed off when LBJ got your sentence reduced," Macalister said. "In fact, I went to the Oval Office and bitched. When I was done, he looked at me and said, in that southern drawl of his, 'You know, Mac, sometimes you win, sometimes you lose. Look at it this way, the kid would've gotten out in a few years, anyway. No matter what happens, he's fucked. Boy's got no career, his life's been destroyed. You won.' Well, how about that guy? There was nothing I could say after that. Lyndon Johnson is one smart son of a bitch."

Bill was trying to think through the ramifications of Mac's comments. And why was he talking about this now? Why did this nasty man want to meet with him?

"So, I know you're not head of the agency anymore. What the hell do you do?" Bill asked.

Macalister pulled a pack of cigarettes from his shirt pocket. He waved the pack in Bill's direction, and he shook his head in decline. Macalister pulled out a cigarette, lit it, and took a deep drag. "Yeah, I guess you've been out of circulation for a while, eh kid?" Inhaling again, he stretched a bit and relaxed as the smoke escaped his nose. "Well, in theory, I retired from the Service, but in reality, I took a new, top-secret job in the NSA. I have this little office, down a narrow, out-of-the-way corridor. From there, I do all kind of things."

Bill shuddered at the thought of this man in the National Security Agency. *Jesus Christ, what was this evil bastard up to now?*

They ordered. More people had entered the room, but they were still secluded.

Taking a reasonable tone, Macalister said, "Don't worry, kid. We are going to have a private conversation. I've reserved all the tables around us. We will have an intimate little talk." The man leaned in and stared. "Bill, I've learned that you have come out of retirement and are doing some work for the auto workers."

Measuring his words, Bill said, "Yeah, they've asked me to do a little research."

"On the Reuther crash…" a statement not a question.

What does this bastard know?

They talked Secret Service. Macalister said Reed Clark had resurrected his career and was now running the Kansas City office. They talked sports. Mac said he had inside information that Vince Lombardi was dying of lung cancer. *Lung cancer—those damned cigarettes.* Macalister lit up his third.

Dinner came. Macalister ordered his third scotch on ice; Bill declined a third beer. Water was good enough.

"Bill, I'm glad we could get together. You know, I may have been wrong about you."

"How do you mean?"

"When we first met, I was wrong. I let that group of agents bully you. I don't think you did anything inappropriate, I just thought that if you couldn't fit into the group, it could have a bad effect on their efficiency in protecting the president."

"Oh Mac, come on. You know how bad the detail was. I hope it's more professional now. Jesus, the drinking—especially on trips."

Macalister pulled the crystal ashtray closer. "Look, I know that was a concern of yours, and that was one of the reasons we were so pissed at you for going to the Warren Commission. We didn't need that kind of publicity."

"But I didn't go to the Warren Commission. Larry McRae did, and you got him, too."

"Oh shit, that's right, I got you two mixed up."

Returning to Macalister's original point, Bill said, "Yeah, McRae was right then. Who knows? Quicker reaction time might have made the difference."

"No, it wouldn't have. Kennedy was a dead man," Macalister stated emphatically. That caught Bill's attention. Had Macalister let something slip?

"What else?" Bill asked.

"About what?

"About why you may have been wrong about me?"

Macalister took a drag and blew smoke out his wide nostrils. "Well, the truth is, you were a good agent. You'd have gone far in the agency. But that shit you pulled on the assassination was too much. If you had just held your instincts, if you had just worked through proper channels—"

"I did! I did everything by the book. And so did Reed."

"Yeah, but you wouldn't play ball. You talked about Chicago when you both were forbidden to mention the incident. You made waves."

"So, what is all this? You don't want me to forgive you for framing my ass?"

"No, no I don't. I am thinking that I made a mistake about you, and there might be a way to rectify things, to start off with a clean slate."

"What on earth are you talking about?" Bill was getting upset, but he told himself to keep calm. He would first see where Macalister wanted to take this. He had nothing to lose.

"This investigation you're doing for the union is a minor irritant to us. It does, however, demonstrate you might want to get back in the business. Maybe you are ready for some real work?"

Bill rolled his eyes. "How am I a minor irritant to you?"

"You've opened up a can of worms—perhaps unintended, perhaps by design. We don't know."

"What do you mean by a 'can of worms?' What do you mean by 'we?'"

Macalister looked around. "Son, be cool; keep your voice down. Let me tell you, first, 'we' are only a few people in my NSA office. There aren't many, only about five. I'm thinking you might want to join us. We are doing amazing work. Regarding the 'can of worms,' it's simple. Your work on the Reuther plane crash is raising eyebrows. You raised questions to the NTSB on altimeter issues … big mistake. Then, your questions on the Kennedys, especially Bobby, are raising eyebrows."

Bill felt his blood turn cold. What was this man admitting to? How could they know about his activities, especially the conversations with Schrade? *And why is he telling me this?*

Bill looked at the cold man across the table. "So what are you saying? You want me to be part of your underground den of thieves?"

Macalister was talking in a whisper now. "We are preserving our country; we are providing order. Let's face it … your man, Jack Kennedy, was soft. Soft on the Soviets, soft on Cuba, soft on Vietnam. He was leading us down a path to becoming a second-rate power. Imagine, a nuclear test ban with the Soviets, Jesus Christ. Bob Kennedy at least tried to be tough. In some cases, he was tougher than his brother. Then he decided to run against Johnson on a platform of giveaways to minorities and taking us out of Vietnam. It wasn't going to happen."

"So, you decided to take them out?"

"Look, we are a small group of true patriots. We are people who have fought for our country. Like you, we have been tough when others were weak. There is no one to step up; there is only us, and we always come to an understanding before we act. While we are only five, we have the support of key elements in the military, intelligence agencies, and we get whatever support we need when executing a project."

Bill looked around. He couldn't believe this quiet discussion was going on within a few feet of the general public.

"So why did you try to run me down on Monday?"

"We just wanted to give you a little pushback. If we wanted you dead, you wouldn't be here. We don't want questions raised about the plane crash."

"So you guys took out King, Malcolm X, and Reuther?"

"King was relatively harmless when he talked about Negro equality. But coming out against the war was a huge mistake. He was too establishment for that, plus he was starting to be a bad influence on our military's main source of recruits: black, inner-city kids. Malcolm was truly dangerous, but not when he was doing his Black Muslim thing. It was when he started to broaden his coalition with white Americans that he became dangerous. That was when he had to be stopped."

"And Reuther?"

"Look at Reuther. He was behind every one of these guys except Malcolm. He was the power; it was his time. In some ways, it was a payback."

"But I'm not sure it was Oswald. I don't believe Sirhan was a lone gunman. And I think the real danger in Chicago was the four gunmen; two were apprehended and then released. Was Valee just a patsy, too?"

Mac slowly shook his head back and forth. "Well, I'm not going to get into details until you come on board. Just simply think drugs and hypnosis, baby. People can be made to do things and, most importantly, forget things. Then having backups who can get the job done. Wham, bam, thank you ma'am, and you have a dead man and an accused assassin who really doesn't remember shit. The real guys go off into the sunset. Pretty cool, eh?"

"What else are you guys doing?"

"Well, you can find out. Shed your bleeding-heart image, and come with us."

"What if I don't? What if I go to the press with this?"

"First, what makes you think the press will listen? No one in the main media accepts the JFK conspiracy shit. Second, it's not healthy to talk about these things. All you have to do is look around Dallas. Witnesses and Warren Commission doubters have 'accidents.' And, you know, people can lose loved ones—girlfriends, if you know what I mean."

Bill had heard enough. He stood, reached for his wallet, pulled out two twenty-dollar bills and tossed them on the table. "Okay, it's been interesting, but I've heard enough."

"Kid, I don't need your money. I've got this."

"No." Bill said firmly.

"I take it you don't like my offer. Still, before you leave," Macalister handed Bill a business card, "here, take this card. It's a direct line to my office. Think about it. Being a part of our little fraternity could be good for you."

"That'll be the day," Bill said, recalling John Wayne's reply when told "I hope you die!" in the old movie *The Searchers*.

Bill walked out as Macalister shoved the twenties into his pants pocket.

Chapter Forty-Six
The Chase

The day was ending, and shadows were growing longer. After Bill left the restaurant and his unsettling meeting with Macalister, he wanted to make sure he wasn't followed. So he turned in the opposite direction from his car. After half an hour of aimless walking through downtown Detroit, he worked his way back to the car. He thought that, with Macalister's candor—and Bill's refusal of the man's offer—he was probably a dead man.

Once behind the wheel of the Barracuda, Bill worked his way to Jefferson Avenue, which took him underneath the Cobo Hall convention center. He emerged onto the Lodge Expressway. He couldn't tell if he was being tailed.

He stayed with the traffic flow, which was normal for eight-thirty. After a few miles, Bill moved from the right to the center lane. There was no noticeable reaction by vehicles behind him. He thought if someone was following him, they were probably from DC and didn't know Detroit streets. So he decided to make it difficult for them, if there was anyone.

As he approached the Davison Freeway eastbound ramp, he accelerated hard, making it seem as though he'd pass the ramp. But then he tapped the brakes, swerved right, cut off the car next to him and entered the ramp, fishtailing as he fought for control on the curve. He accelerated hard onto the Davison. When he checked the rearview mirror, he saw a car behind him, also fishtailing on the ramp. Bill continued accelerating; he had never driven his car so hard.

He killed his headlights as he sped through an underpass under the Chrysler Expressway, hoping to confuse the driver behind him. His speedometer read ninety; he was passing cars like they were standing still. Bill knew the Davison soon ended, becoming a city street. He was still flying when he got to that point, but he got lucky; the first traffic signal after the road turned to a city street had just turned yellow. He could make the turn before the light changed to red behind him.

He got into the left-turn lane, and his tires squealed as he cut around a driver, then he proceeded north. He accelerated for a moment, then took a hard left heading back to the west. Just after passing back under the Chrysler Expressway, he made another sharp left onto southbound Oakland Street.

No one seemed to be following.

Bill slowed and blended into traffic, his heart pounding and sweat dripping off his face. He made a second casual turn to westbound Manchester Street. He cruised by the old Ford plant, where the Model T's had been built long ago. He passed Woodward, and zigzagged through several side streets. A moment later, he turned left onto westbound Seven Mile Road, convinced he had lost Macalister's goons. In a bit, he headed toward his house and Sue's apartment. *What now?* Going home was not an option, at least for the moment. Sue was out of the question. He was not putting her, or anyone else, in danger. Then, he remembered the motels on Woodward Avenue near his home. Less than ten minutes later, he stepped into the office of a relatively modern but low-end motel. He rented a room for twenty-two dollars and parked his car as far from the street as possible.

The sparsely furnished room had an acrid smell, hardly worth the money. Bill used the bathroom, washed his face, and sat down to think. He didn't call anyone; their phones might be tapped.

Chapter Forty-Seven
The Last Journal Entry

But he felt he needed to at least let Sue know he was okay. Around ten o'clock, he opened the door to his room. Seeing nothing unusual, he walked south on Woodward and found a public phone between two commercial buildings. He looked around again before depositing a dime.

"Bill, where the hell have you been? I've been worried sick," she said.

"Sorry, hon. I got tied up for dinner and didn't have a chance to call. Look, I can't talk now. Some things came up, and I've got to get over to another location. I won't be over tonight. If I don't make contact later, I'll call you in the morning."

"Okay, but are you sure? Can I help?"

"No, no. All is fine—you'll be amazed at my story. Look, I've gotta run. We'll talk later. Remember, I love you to death." He hung up, knowing the call was too short to be traced.

He continued walking toward downtown Royal Oak and his home as Macalister's agents likely were sitting a few houses down from his flat, watching for his car. As he hurried along, he tapped the snub nose pistol underneath his shirt. He thought how stupid he was heading to his house, but he also thought the odds were on his side. He turned onto his street and ducked between two houses, watching.

It was a hot, humid summer night. Several people were walking back to their homes from downtown Royal Oak. About twenty minutes later, Bill saw it: the red glow from a car cigarette lighter followed by someone inhaling smoke as the tip of the cigarette glowed bright. He inched closer. Two men were in the car. His potential assailants had not picked the best position to watch the house. They could see the front of the house fine, but not the side entrance Bill used. This was good news.

Bill slowly made his way between the houses. He worked his way around the block, checking each parked car ... all empty. When he got to the house directly behind his place, he casually walked around it to the cyclone fence in the backyard. He easily jumped the fence and, with his gun out, worked his way to his door.

Very slowly, without making a sound, he unlocked and opened the door slightly. He waited a full minute, listening for anything unusual. Hearing nothing, he opened the door and slowly worked his way upstairs, not only wanting to alert any potential intruders, but also not wanting to disturb his downstairs neighbors. He opened the door to his flat and entered, his gun still out. He scrutinized the surroundings as his eyes adjusted to the ambient light that came through the windows. Ever so cautiously, Bill checked every part of his house for unwanted visitors or signs that someone had been there. Nothing seemed out of place. He put on shorts, a blue T-shirt that said, "Bless You Boys," and tennis shoes. He grabbed some clothes for the next day and looked for the box with the files he had accumulated in the last few weeks. He threw his clothes into a duffel bag, tucked the box under his arm, and retraced his steps out of the house and back to the motel room, where he updated his journal with all the latest. The next morning, he added a note in his journal about suddenly waking up from a deep sleep in the middle of the night. Rather than bad guys, the noise was a couple from the next room coming back from a night of revelry and enjoying a good night of pleasure.

***

Now, in November 2019, Bill Eaton stopped his typing. That's all there was. Eaton had read everything. *So, what the hell happened after that?*

EPILOGUE
2020

Bill Eaton was mesmerized by his grandmother's material. He talked to his mother and father, but neither could shed much light on his grandmother's early life. He researched the details of the information at libraries and historical archives. The work was slow and difficult, as most of these facilities were open only during the work week. He even took vacation days to dig.

Beginning in January 2020, he tried to locate people who were part of Bill Simpson's story. Many were either dead or could not be located. He preferred to visit people when possible, thinking he could get them to reveal more relevant information than over the phone or through an email. Fortunately for Eaton, his parents offered to subsidize travel and other expenses for the project.

One thing Eaton *did* find out was that Simpson disappeared or died shortly after that last journal entry. Sources seemed to disagree on exactly what had happened to him.

***

Jeff Peters had long since retired from the Secret Service. Bill took a four-day weekend in late January to visit Peters at his home on St. Simons Island in Georgia, before driving to Florida to meet Joe Kowalski.

When Bill walked up to the front porch of the two-story house, an elderly man greeted him.

"So, you are Mr. Eaton," the slightly stooped Peters said in a welcoming, southern accent.

"Come on in."

The pair moved through a musty aroma and some unkemptness to a glassed-in porch that overlooked the Atlantic. "Sorry about the mess. My wife died last year and now I appreciate how much she did to keep our house in order. So, you want to talk about Bill Simpson?" Peters asked.

"Yes, sir. Bill kept a lot of records that I only recently discovered. At various times in his life, he kept daily journals. This started with his time in the White House, where he met you. He liked and respected you."

"Well, thank you, son. Let me tell you, I really liked Bill Simpson. He was a good man. While I think we liked each other, we never got a chance to be real friends. He was in and out of the Service too quickly for that."

"I can understand that. Gee, that was almost sixty years ago—what stands out as you think about him?"

"I can tell you he was a good guy," Peters said. "And Kennedy really liked him. For some reason, that really pissed off some of our detail. It was stupid. But you know, it doesn't take much for little jealousies to gum up an organization, and we had some of that during the sixties."

"Can you tell me more about the Kennedy relationship?"

"Just that they got along. I think Simpson's dad was from a union, and Kennedy liked that. I know Kennedy wanted to bring him to the detail full-time, but the Secret Service leadership killed it."

"What do you know about Bill's arrest and time in prison?"

"Not too much. He was accused of working with counterfeiters, which to this very day I have a hard time believing. Ah, you know, I really regret that I never reached out to Bill during or after the trial. I heard he worked in a factory and became a hippie."

"Well, I don't know about the hippie part," Bill replied with a smile. "Yes, he worked in a factory, and he did have long hair, but after a few years he started law school. Then, I'm not sure you remember who he was, but in 1970, the United Auto Workers President Walter Reuther died in a plane crash. Some UAW leaders knew about Bill's experience in the Secret Service and knew he investigated criminal cases, so they pulled him out of the plant to investigate Reuther's death. They wanted to know if there were any discrepancies with the official reports. It looks like Simpson may have been killed four weeks later."

"Wow, I had no idea. I was in DC in 1970. Still part of the detail. You'd think I would've heard something."

"Did you know Jim Macalister?"

Peters paused for just a moment. "Of course, I knew Mac. He was a son of a bitch, but he was also my boss for quite a while."

"Was he clean?"

"Well, he's long gone now … but was he clean? I don't know. He had a knack for getting things done. You didn't want to be on his bad side. If I remember correctly, he was sorry about Simpson's White House experience and thought he'd have made a good agent. He retired from the Service around '67 or '68. By '73, I was moved from the detail to

278

administrative stuff, still in Washington. I lost touch with him. I think he died in the late seventies—lung cancer."

"Was the Secret Service a corrupt organization?"

"Well, eh, Bill, I'm not going to get into that. I'll simply say that we had some problems like any other organization. I think most of those problems were addressed and solved."

Eaton knew that was the most relevant information he was going to get. He also realized he was overstaying his welcome. "You know, one more thing," the old man said at the front door. "After Mac left the White House, I know he was doing some clandestine stuff. I don't know what, but I do know he kept in close contact with some of Nixon's staff, you know, the guys who got tangled up in Watergate."

"Oh yeah? Do you remember names?" Bill asked.

"Well, I know there was Howard Hunt—boy, what a character. Another guy, a real jerk, was G. Gordon Liddy. Those are the names that come to mind. If I think of anymore, I'll shoot you an email."

Watergate? Macalister was involved in a lot of shit.

***

Joe Kowalski had retired some twenty years earlier to Venice, Florida, south of Sarasota on the Gulf Coast. Bill had contacted Kowalski by email and said he was a grad student working on some old Secret Service cases and, since he was going to be in Florida visiting friends, he wondered if he could stop by to chat. Kowalski lived in a quiet retirement community near downtown Venice. In his late seventies, he was deeply tanned, slightly overweight, with a full head of grey hair. He greeted Bill with a friendly smile and escorted him to his large lanai that covered a good chunk of his backyard and included nice patio furniture and a swimming pool.

When Eaton mentioned that he was studying Bill Simpson, Kowalski's face tensed for a fraction of a second. "Why Simpson?" he asked.

"Well, he may have been murdered. His car was found in the Detroit River, but a body was never found."

"Jesus, he was an ex-con. Who knows what he was messing around with? You know, he became a hippie—long hair, alternative lifestyle. Who knows what he was into? Drugs? Anti-establishment stuff?"

"I came across some journals or diaries, he wrote. I think you know the UAW was using him to investigate Walter Reuther's death ... the plane crash?"

Kowalski slowly nodded his head. "Yeah, I kind of remember that. It's been a long time."

"Of course," Bill said in an understanding tone. "One of the last journal entries included a conversation between you and him in downtown Detroit."

Kowalski gave him a look like he had just been caught with his hand in a cookie jar. "Yeah, yeah, I remember now. Christ, I completely forgot that. Yeah, we had heard he was poking around in some sensitive issues, and I took it upon myself to give him a warning."

"Why? Was he in danger?"

"I didn't think so, but he was on parole, you know, and I didn't want him to get into trouble."

Three lies in one sentence.

Bill heard some cabinets opening and closing from the kitchen and heard a woman's voice. "Joe, I'm home."

A moment later, a trim, attractive woman in her mid-sixties or so came out. After being introduced as Kowalski's second wife, Sally, she asked, "Do you mind if I join you?"

"Well, hon, Bill and I are talking about my early years in the Service. I don't know that it would be that interesting, but if it's okay with Bill, it's okay with me."

Bill nodded, stood up, and pulled back a chair from the patio table.

"My, how thoughtful!" Sally gushed. "I don't get that kind of treatment very often. I guess our honeymoon is over," she added with a playful laugh.

Bill nodded before looking back at Kowalski. "You were telling me about your last conversation with Simpson."

"Yeah, I was trying to keep him out of trouble, you know. I was never a big fan of his."

"Well, we'll get into that in a minute," Eaton said. "Weren't you curious about him possibly being murdered? He was a former agent— wouldn't you have been interested in becoming part of the investigation?"

"Nope, it was not our jurisdiction, and he was fired from the Service years earlier. He really was a non-entity, a dirty agent. I certainly didn't want him harmed, but what he was doing when he died was his problem."

"But you said you warned him of danger. Why?"

"You know, I really don't remember. Like I said, it was a long time ago."

"You and Simpson were partners, right? He was your mentor?"

"Well, I wouldn't say that. I was his partner, and I was new, which meant he gave me all the shit work to do." Kowalski took a swig of beer and quietly belched.

"What did his colleagues think of him?"

"Most of us in the office liked him. He was a comer. He was part of Kennedy's detail. If he had kept his nose clean, he could have gone anywhere in the Secret Service."

"So, why did you testify against him at his trial?"

"I testified to the truth. Look, he was a guest at my first wedding," he said, looking at Sally, who seemed deeply interested.

"You testified that Bill Simpson cheated on his wife on a regular basis. Then you testified that he waited until you were on your honeymoon to see a prostitute. But why, if he was a womanizer, would he need to use your honeymoon as an excuse to see a hooker?"

"That's the way I remembered it." Joe said defensively.

"Okay," Bill said, glancing at Sally. "You also testified that Simpson was involved with a counterfeiting scheme in Windsor, that he taught you how to skim counterfeit money, and he taught you to be a bad agent."

"That's right," Joe said.

"If that's correct, why did Simpson have nothing but glowing comments about you? Why was it that he was picked to rotate to the president's detail? Why did Reed Clark pick him to go to Chicago when there was a threat against President Kennedy?"

"Hey, he was a con artist. That's what they do, fool people. And I got him."

"Okay, I'm not trying to be adversarial; I'm just curious. Just one more thing. Bill Simpson kept journals throughout much of his life. These journals were for his own personal use, sometimes with sensitive information. He specifically cited instances where he protected you and tried to get you to be assigned to more serious duties."

"Ha, I don't believe that. Do you have any proof?" Joe said tersely.

"Remember those days after the Kennedy assassination?"

"Yeah, of course."

"Remember when you were assigned the job of going out and buying a TV set for the office?"

Joe nodded.

"Simpson wrote in his diary—again, a document he never shared with anyone, not even at the trial—how disappointed you were with the TV assignment. He expressly asked Reed Clark, your boss, that you be assigned to work with him with Canadian authorities regarding leads. Did you remember that?"

Joe's voice suddenly changed. "Yeah, Yeah, I guess he did that."

"Also, a few days later, you may recall, you helped find important information on Oswald's possible activity in Canada. Right?"

"Yeah, I remember. He took all the credit for that work with Reed Clark."

"That's not exactly right," Eaton said. "In fact, he praised your work with Clark. In a meeting with Clark, Bill asked that you stay one step removed from being involved to keep you out of any reports because the information might have caused problems with Macalister—which it did. Had you been involved, it could have been detrimental to your career."

Minutes later, Bill left a shaken Joe Kowalski.

***

During February, Eaton tried to contact more people mentioned in Simpson's journals. He found that Reed Clark, his supervisor in the Detroit Secret Service office, had died the previous summer in Hot Springs, Arkansas. Joe Bishop did not want to talk.

He hit pay dirt with Larry McRae, the Secret Service's first black agent who lived in Chicago. McRae had published a tell-all book about his Secret Service experiences a decade earlier. It was a powerful story and showed the similarities between McRae and Simpson—their careers, frame-ups, and prison time. Bill contacted McRae through his Facebook page and arrived at McRae's home around noon on a Saturday. They sat down at the kitchen table, where McRae's adult daughter placed a plate of cookies before leaving the room.

Eaton told McRae how he had discovered the journals and about his grandmother's relationship with Simpson.

"The information in his journals supports the material in your book," Eaton said. "It was illuminating and mesmerizing. Once I felt I understood the information and did my own research on those exceedingly difficult years, I decided to reach out and interview people who were part of Simpson's life."

"For what purpose?" McRae asked at a slow, deliberate pace.

"I don't know really. I want to satisfy my own curiosity. Maybe, depending on where it all leads, I'll write a book. We'll see about that. So, can you tell me what you remember regarding Bill Simpson?"

"I'm sorry," the man said, chuckling. "I didn't mean to give you the third degree. I guess it's just in my nature."

"No problem."

McRae collected himself and told Eaton what he knew about Simpson.

"I vaguely remember him during the Chicago assassination case regarding President Kennedy. We talked only a few times, nothing substantive as I recall. I think we started to compare notes on being rotated into the presidential detail, but nothing significant came from that."

"So, until the counterfeiting charges, you saw him only that one time?"

"As far as I can remember, that's it. In fact, I actually spent more time with the other Detroit agent."

"Joe Bishop?" Bill asked.

"Yeah, that's it."

"How did you link up with Simpson after you were charged in the counterfeiting case?"

"It seems to me a friend of mine told me that a Secret Service agent in Detroit was on trial on a counterfeiting charge. I was being charged with the same thing, so I started visiting the library to read copies of the Detroit newspapers to keep up on the trial. After his sentencing, I decided to reach out to him."

"So, you guys met. In Battle Creek, right?"

McRae nodded. He continued with his story that collaborated the Simpson journals. McRae also talked about his prison experiences and efforts by the government to drug him during his time there. Then McRae said, "You know, I always felt bad that I never tried to find Bill after I was released from prison. I guess it took me awhile to get my footing after losing my career and becoming an ex-con."

"I wouldn't worry too much about that," Eaton said. "I'm sure Simpson was going through those same things."

"Yeah, but then I heard he had died. What a shame."

"They never found a body, but it seems most people think he was killed," Eaton said. "Do you think the Secret Service or the federal government could have been involved?"

"Shit, after what they did to me? Anything is possible."

***

The following Saturday, Bill drove to the Detroit suburb of Farmington Hills to meet Sam Starr. His GPS took him to a subdivision of high-end homes, not much different than the house Bill's parents had in Bloomfield Hills. A few moments after he rang the bell, an African-American gentleman in his late-seventies, with a broad smile and mischievous grin, answered the door.

Starr, who seemed to be in great shape and still had a spring in his step, led Eaton into his study. There were a couple of easy chairs in the spacious room. On one wall was a fifty-five-inch TV. *His man cave.*

"So, you want to talk about Bill Simpson," Starr said after the two had settled into the chairs. "Wow, Bill was a great friend. He taught me a lot, and he changed my life. Even though it's been fifty years, I still miss that guy."

Eaton explained what he was doing and about the material he found in his grandmother's attic.

"Whoa, wait a New York minute. Are you telling me you are Sue Monroe's grandson?"

Bill, not accustomed to hearing his grandmother's maiden name, took an extra second to respond, "Yep, she was my grandma."

"Holy Shit! Sue Monroe! My God, son, if Bill Simpson had stayed alive, you might not have been here … ha! Sue and Bill were going to get married, that's for damned sure."

"So, you knew them?"

"*Knew* them? Hell, I introduced them. Once Sue entered Bill's life, that was it. I saw less of him. It's not that I minded. We still played tennis and b-ball together, but not as often. And all for good reason. They were in love, and there's only so many times that happens to people. Then, the other thing happened … Bill went to law school; worked his ass off. He wanted to get out of the plant and make something of himself. He did it for Sue, but he wanted more."

Eaton reached into a portfolio he had brought and pulled out the photo of his grandmother playing tennis. "Sam, do you remember this?" He handed the image to Sam.

Sam studied the photo and broad smile came to his face. "Oh, yeah, that's Sue; that's your grandma. A fine looking woman."

"Check the back out. Is that you?"

Sam flipped the photo over and read aloud, "'Great backhand. Sam.' Yeah, Jesus Christ, that's me. After all these years." Sam shook his head in wonder.

"Did you know about his life with the Secret Service and his prison time?" Eaton asked.

"Not initially. Bill was quiet. He didn't talk about himself. Over the years, certain things slipped. I knew he understood government, especially at the federal level. I thought he had done time, but I didn't learn it from him. After he died, Sue was a wreck. We talked a lot. She told me about these things.

"At first, we didn't know if he was dead or not. We thought he was, but there was a big question mark about what the hell happened. Details we found out later made us pretty sure he was killed. But, you know, his death changed me. I did what he started to do. I went to night school at Wayne State and studied law. I passed the bar and got a job working as an attorney for Oakland County. That's where I met my wife. She was an opposing attorney, trying to defend some characters who wanted to cheat Oakland County government out of a lot of money. I won that case. Ha!"

Sam went on to tell Bill about his children—Sam Jr., who was a starting quarterback for Western Michigan and was now in Atlanta working for Delta Airlines, and his daughter, Micki.

"She was the surprise package that came late in our lives. She was always a great student. She was an outstanding basketball player in high school, but she was a better golfer. I guess she just took after her dad," Sam said with a laugh. "She went to Michigan State on a golf scholarship and is hoping to get her LPGA card in the next year or two. She might be great!"

Just then, Sam's wife, Vicky, and his daughter, Micki, walked in. Vicky was a lovely, white woman probably about ten years or so younger than Sam. Micki appeared to be in her mid-twenties, and Eaton found her stunning. He liked her quick eyes that followed every movement around her. And the smile on her face made Eaton think that she really enjoyed life, just like her father.

"Jesus, Sam, you and Bill need some refills on your drinks," Vicky said. "And you didn't even consider getting this young man something to eat. What kind of host are you? I'll be back in a minute. Micki, come with me."

"Well, sweetheart, I knew you would be coming back soon," Sam said.

"Yeah, right," she said in mock anger.

Minutes later, the women returned with more beverages and a couple of trays of grapes, cheese, and crackers. "There, that's better," Vicky said with a sense of satisfaction.

"Victoria, I just don't know what the hell I would do without you," Sam said before inviting his wife and daughter to stay.

"Well, you just remember that," his wife responded. "Now why on earth do you want us to hear about your ancient days of running around the city chasing women, going to bars, and whatnot?"

"That is not what we were talking about … at least not yet!" Sam said with a laugh. "You remember I told you about Bill Simpson, my best friend during the sixties? Bill Eaton here is the grandson of Sue Monroe. She nearly married Bill Simpson before he was assassinated. You remember Sue; you met her at those Obama fundraisers."

Bill's ears pricked up at the word "assassinated." *So Sam thinks there was a hit on Simpson.*

"Micki, you remember me talking about Bill Simpson, don't you?"

"Oh, Daddy, only about a hundred and one times."

Sam then told her for the 102nd time. "Sweetheart," he said, "you know when someone is a best friend, he is always there. Bill was that for me, and I tried to be for him. Gosh, we played hundreds of hours of tennis and basketball. We went to concerts together, hung out at jazz bars. Oh my, we had fun. Saw a World Series game. We went to anti-war marches. Hell, he, Sue, and I went to the first Earth Day event in Michigan.

"More importantly, though, he got me to think about issues. When he started going to law school, I thought I needed to seriously think about my future. He's the reason I decided to change my life and become an attorney. And, you know, without Bill Simpson, I never would have met your mom."

He stopped for a breath, took a drink of his Arnold Palmer, and looked at his wife with an extra twinkle in his eyes.

"So it sounds like you guys kind of fed off each other," Eaton said.

"I suppose that's true," Sam said. Looking at Bill and then Micki, he added, "You know about the '67 riots, right?"

Both nodded.

"Well, let me tell you something. That was a scary time, especially if you were black. I was living in a Royal Oak apartment—back then everything in Royal Oak was white. Hell, I still don't know how I got the landlord to rent to me—must have been my personality. So, when the riots, or I guess I should be politically correct and say rebellion, started, everything was shut down at night, Detroit and the suburbs.

"Bill and I couldn't go to work, so we played a lot of tennis and drank beer in the backyard of his flat. I was so paranoid that if I didn't have Bill as a friend, I probably never would have left my apartment. Bill made sure I was included and made doubly sure no one messed with me. We talked about the riot and its causes, but Bill was convinced it wasn't about race so much as about economics. He said if people don't have a job at a decent wage, how can they have a decent place to live, with decent schools, and safe neighborhoods? That guy was ahead of his time."

"So, Daddy, he was just a good guy, eh?" Micki asked.

"Yes, sweetheart, that's exactly what he was. He treated me like I was a man, not a black man, but just a man. I didn't fully appreciate what I had until he was gone."

As the conversation was dying down, Vicky invited Eaton to join the family for dinner. He tried to beg off, but she responded, "Is there somewhere you've got to be? Do you have a date?"

He shook his head.

"Then, young man, you are going to join us for dinner." Looking at her husband, she said, "Now Sam, we are going to have steaks, so I want you to get the grill going. I know it's cold, but I don't want any back-talk." Turning to Micki, she said, "You keep Bill here company. I'll need some help from you in about half an hour or so."

Micki told Eaton about her life at Michigan State and her golf career before going to help her mother. Eaton mentioned that he, too, enjoyed a round of golf now and then. She seemed pleased by that. Dinner was simple but perfect with the steaks, baked potatoes, vegetables, and a modest salad. When there was a lull in the conversation, Sam asked, "So, Bill, who else have you interviewed, and who's left?"

"Well, there's a former FBI agent named Fred Fry, who knew Bill in his Secret Service days. He lives in St. George, Utah, so I'll fly out there, if he'll meet with me, sometime in March. There was another FBI agent in Washington named Elliott Glenn. He died mysteriously about the same time as Bill. I'm hoping to locate one of his children to see if they have any recollections. There was a witness at Bill's trial named Rita Gray—I'd like to find her, but she must be eighty or so by now, if she's still alive. I'm also hoping to find Bill's children—a boy and a girl—and see if they can provide some insights."

"Whoa," Sam said. "The kids. I know Bill tried to keep track of them, but after Anne remarried it was difficult. As a felon he had no rights, unless his ex was in a good mood. I do know that Sue met them, and they seemed to like her, which pleased Bill a lot."

Then, changing the subject, "But St. George. I hear that's a beautiful place to visit this time of year." Turning to his daughter, "You know, Micki, that's supposed to be an excellent place to play golf."

"Daddy, I know that. Some say it's better than Phoenix."

"Bill, you should take a couple of days, tour some of the parks, and take your clubs."

Eaton drove home that night with a full stomach and a smile on his face. The Starrs were great people, and he was glad to have come to know them. A few nights later, Eaton was at home watching an MSU/Illinois basketball game, when his cell phone rang during halftime. It was Micki Starr.

After some momentary awkwardness, Eaton said, "So, Micki, it's great to hear your voice. What's up?" He was thinking that maybe she was asking him out, but that would be way too much to expect.

"Well, you know, my dad and I were talking last night. He knows I'm bored as hell here in Michigan and thought I might enjoy seeing St. George … maybe with you. You know, play golf, maybe do some sightseeing?"

Eaton was practically speechless. Women didn't make these kinds of proposals, at least not to him. "Let me get this straight, your dad is encouraging you to travel with a practical stranger for an extended weekend across the country?"

"Well, I guess when you put it that way it does sound pretty strange. But Daddy really likes you, and he trusts you. He feels if you were related to Sue Monroe, then you must be a stand-up guy. And, you know, I feel pretty much the same way."

"Yeah, I loved meeting your mom and dad, and, of course, you. I'm still amazed by your call."

"Don't get too many ideas," she said in a light, sexy voice. "Daddy insists that we have separate hotel rooms, and he made me promise that we would not fool around. Jesus Christ, I'm a twenty-four-year-old woman, and he knows that I make my own damned decisions. But on this one, I agree with him. You get too fresh with me, and I'll beat you up," she laughed, adding, "And, you know I can whip you."

"I'm not going to deny that," Eaton said. "And I know you will humiliate me on the golf course, but I think I can handle having my ass kicked by a professional golfer. I've not finalized St. George yet, but I think you've given me an incentive. If we're going to travel somewhere together, maybe we should see a movie this weekend, if you're open."

Micki agreed. Eaton was dumbfounded, but ecstatic.

A couple of days later, Eaton contacted Fred Fry, who was more than happy for a visit and to talk about his friend, Bill Simpson. They agreed on the third weekend in March.

In the meantime, he found one of Elliott Glenn's sons, David, living in Littleton, Colorado, a Denver suburb. Eaton called a number for a David Glenn he found online. A man with an older sounding voice answered.

Eaton quickly introduced himself, adding, "Mr. Glenn, if this is a bad time, I can call back whenever you would like. My name is Bill Eaton. I'm working on a book about a man who died in 1970 and was working with your father on a case at about the same time. I thought you might have some insights on your dad's death, if it's not too painful for you to talk about, and I was hoping we could talk about any memories you have of those days."

There was a pause on the other end. Glenn said, "I'm sorry, who are you writing about?"

"A former Secret Service agent named Bill Simpson; he had at least one meeting with your father and may also have met with your mother."

"Wow, that's a long time ago. God, I was just finishing my sophomore year at Yale when Dad died."

"If you don't mind, do you remember when and how he died?"

"Yeah, sure. Dad was in a serious auto accident and fell into a coma. He never regained consciousness and died in August 1970."

"In the hospital?"

"In mid-July they moved him to a nursing home. It was much closer to our house and made Mom's life a lot easier. He died there."

"Of course. What most do you remember about his death?"

"Really, not much. I was just a kid between my sophomore and junior years in college. He was in a crash, and he died. My mom was shattered and never fully recovered."

"Nothing else comes to mind?"

"No, sir. He was a war hero and had a distinguished career in the FBI. He died before his time. That's about all I can tell you, except that I loved him."

"Sounds great. Listen, if anything comes to mind, please give me a call. I'd really appreciate it."

A few days later, Eaton was watching an old movie on TV when the phone rang. "Mr. Eaton, this is Dave Elliott. Something else came to mind, something I hadn't thought about for years. It probably means nothing, but I thought I'd give you a call anyway."

"Great, go ahead."

"Well, my mother was living in a nursing home near us in the late 1990s. She had dementia, and conversations were difficult. So we often watched TV when we visited her. She liked the History Channel.

So, one night we were watching a documentary on President Kennedy's assassination. The show was about which people might have had an interest in killing the president. Mom was just glued to the show. When it got to the potential of government involvement—it suggested the CIA, the FBI, the military, and even President Johnson might have been involved—Mom got really animated, saying, 'I knew it, I knew it! They're the ones who had your father killed.' We didn't take her seriously; we were just happy she was focusing on something. Still, when I remembered this, I thought I should share it with you. Does it help?"

"Well, maybe. The guy I'm researching definitely thought some of the groups you mentioned might have been involved in the assassinations during the sixties. Thanks for reaching out," Eaton continued. "Oh, if I used your mother's quotes in a potential book, would you have a problem?"

"Probably not, but could you share the language you want to use before any publication?"

"Of course."

A dementia-ridden mind had remembered something from the past. Eaton knew that sometimes people with dementia could clearly remember events from the distant past, but not remember who they had talked to a few minutes earlier. Could this be corroboration, ambiguous as it might be, of Bill Simpson's story?

***

Eaton looked forward to the trip to St. George for many reasons. While he loved living in Michigan, it was always nice to find warmer climates for a long weekend away from the constant cold of winter and the slow warm-up to spring. St. George promised to be a good getaway and a time to begin to close his interviews.

The other big deal was traveling with a woman who was quickly taking a significant role in his life. Micki was smart, gorgeous, and had a great personality. But what made her exceptional was the hard work she put in, both mentally and physically, pursuing her passions.

She also seemed to fully appreciate the work he was doing on his project and respected his professional career. They flew into Las Vegas, rented a car, and made the easy, two-hour drive to St. George, in the southwest corner of Utah. The temperatures that mid-afternoon were in the upper 60s and the surrounding snow-covered mountains were spectacular. The next morning, the pair drove to Fred Fry's condominium. The elderly Fry and his wife, Mary, gave them a warm welcome before Micki was on her way to a driving range at the nearby golf course.

"We are so excited you made the trip—it's good to meet you," Fry said as he led Eaton inside.

After breakfast, Fry and Eaton moved into the family room that overlooked the course, with another spectacular view of the snow-capped mountains in the distance. Fry said, "You know, our golf course is considered pretty nice around here. I'm sure I could get you guys on if you would like to get out."

"I think that's a distinct possibility," Eaton replied.

"Good. I don't want to waste your day here, so let's get down to business. So, you want to talk about Bill Simpson, and you flew across the country just to talk to me. I'm really flattered," Fry said with a smile.

"I'm just happy to be here," Eaton said. "Tell me about Bill Simpson."

"I probably met Bill in late '60 or '61. There were some underworld types pushing bad money. We at the FBI became aware of the situation, and I called Bill. Purely professional, but we got along very well. Over the years, we worked on several cases together. Sometimes we just sought one another out to talk about different issues: office politics, suspected criminal activity, or when the Detroit Lions might put together another championship run. Ha!"

"How did you learn about Bill's Chicago trip in 1963?"

"I remember it well—it damned near destroyed my career. Let's see now, at some point at the very end of October, I think, Bill called me. Now, I knew Bill, but not that well. Still, I always thought he was a good guy. He tells me he's in Chicago and needs some information on a guy. Jesus, I can't quite remember the name of this guy, but he always reminded me of Lee Harvey Oswald."

"Thomas Vallee?"

"Yep, and they used his middle name, like with Oswald."

"Arthur."

"Yeah, that's it. So Bill wants some information on this guy. There were rumors of an assassination plot against President Kennedy, and Bill couldn't raise anyone at the Secret Service offices in DC, so he asks me if I can help. I figure I can use our research office in Washington. It's always open. I made the call and asked them to get whatever info they had on Vallee and send it to Bill in Chicago. I guess they did it, but by then I was out of the loop. I was just connecting one agency with another."

"That was it?" Eaton asked.

"Well, kind of. Somehow the Big Guy—you know, Hoover—finds out. Man, he's pissed that the FBI shared services with the Secret Service without his direct approval. I end up getting demoted and suspended for a couple of weeks. I saw Bill during my suspension. Then, the Kennedy assassination takes place, and I provided some information under the table to Bill about some potentially suspicious activities about Oswald in Ontario. In '64, Bill is up on counterfeiting charges. I never believed them. But after he was convicted, I lost track of him."

"You never talked to him again?"

"Once. He was doing some work for the UAW, investigating Walter Reuther's airplane crash. He called and asked about an FBI agent, senior to me, a guy named Glenn. We agreed to get together, but it never happened."

"You never talked to him around that time about meeting for dinner at the Pontchartrain Wine Cellar?"

"Nope." Fry looked puzzled, but Eaton didn't explain why he'd asked that.

When Eaton was just about through, Fry said, "You know, Bill, if your research shows there were connections between the Kennedys, King, and the Reuther deaths, it could shake this country to its core."

"Yeah, I've thought about that. Even my grandmother thought about that. It just seems to me that if Bill Simpson's journals and the other information can set the record straight, it's worth trying to get it done."

"I appreciate that, but you know, it could be dangerous."

"I've thought about that. But Christ, it's been over fifty years. Don't you think most of these bad guys, whomever they might be, are probably dead or in nursing homes?"

"You're probably right. Still, it's something to think about."

***

Back in Michigan, Eaton spent a solid week and a half trying to locate Rita Gray. He finally took a day off work and went to the McNamara

Federal Building to check records and transcripts of the trial. There was no personal information on the woman of any kind. He did learn that Gray's full name was Rita Elizabeth Gray.

With her full name in tow, he decided to look up marriage licenses, starting with the Wayne County clerk's office. No hits.

He hit pay dirt in Oakland County, though, finding a marriage certificate for a Rita Elizabeth Gray born in 1933. She'd married a man named Benjamin Cutler in 1972 and after some Internet searches, Eaton found she was a widow living in a high-rise condominium in Birmingham, Michigan.

He couldn't locate a phone number, but found an email address and sent an email saying he was working on a book project regarding a trial in the 1960s in which she had been a witness. He asked if he could visit to talk about those days, adding that any conversation was for background only and her identity would never be revealed.

Two days later, he received a brief response saying he could call her that evening between seven and nine. When he called her, she was curt, but seemed enticed by his invitation to talk about her past. Her major concern was privacy, which Eaton said he completely respected. At one point, he said as an aside, "You know, I'm a very nice guy." Her demeanor changed to a more positive tone after that. The result was a meeting to be held at her home the next Saturday.

Gray lived in a five-story condominium on the south side of Birmingham's downtown, between Old Woodward and Woodward avenues. After being cleared by security at the front door, Eaton headed to the top floor, which had just two units. Gray's door opened before he could knock. Standing there was an attractive woman in her eighties, dressed in a comfortable but fashionable dress accenting a fine figure for a woman of her age.

She introduced herself as Liz as she motioned him in. The condo was impeccably decorated, yet looked comfortable. From a wall of window, there was a wonderful view of Woodward and the southern suburbs.

At the table by the windows was a tray of cheese and crackers, along with a bottle of red wine. "Why don't you open the bottle? I thought a little wine might make us more comfortable."

Bill poured the wine.

Gray began: "So, did you read the trial's transcripts?"

"Yes, I did, and I understand why you were so difficult to find."

"Well, of course, that was the idea."

They talked for three hours. Midway through the bottle of wine, Gray became more talkative and trusting. She talked about a difficult childhood and that she was on her own from a young age. She made it clear she had no regrets about the path she took in those early years and the many contacts she made. "But you are here to talk about Bill Simpson."

"That's right."

"It's kind of funny. I only was with Bill a few times really. I could count them on the fingers of my right hand. But, in those few times, he had a significant effect on my life. He was a special guy."

"How so?"

Gray munched on a cracker. "Well, unlike most cops ... hell, most men, he did not try to get me in bed or, more specifically, use his power over me to get me in bed. He was working his case, a counterfeiting case. I actually provided a lead that helped the Secret Service break a significant counterfeiting scheme."

"So I read."

"But it was the second time he came over to my place that stood out. I think he had a crush on me," she said with a laugh, "We flirted with each other, but we both knew it was going nowhere. He told me to get out of the business and to think about my future. It took me a while, but that's exactly what I did."

"When did you see him again, at the trial?"

"After the trial, I felt so goddamned bad. My testimony sent a good man to prison. You know, those bastards from the Secret Service and the US attorney's office forced me to lie at the trial. That hung over me for years. It was when I saw Bill's father's obituary that I really started thinking I had to get my life together. I thought, with the right breaks, I could be good in public relations, and with the auto industry there were a lot of good opportunities. After I started my first job there, I decided I had to get out of my lie. I summoned all my courage and visited Bill's mother. God, that was hard. But she really helped me. She introduced me to some union guys, and they used their influence to get me to talk with the judge."

"Judge Wilson?"

"Yes. He was a crusty old bastard. Anyway, Bill got out of jail. Meanwhile, I was working hard on my new career. I did a little name switch by using my middle name instead of Rita. I was paranoid about anything that might reflect on my old life. So, one night I get a call from Bill. He was trying to be a nice guy, and I gave him the coldest shoulder

I ever gave a human being. I felt bad about that. I just did not want a reminder of my past.

"Then, several months later, I ran into him in a grocery store. He had changed so much. His body had become so lean, his hair long, and his blue jeans. I had only seen him in suits. It was completely different, and I asked him out."

Eaton chuckled. "Really, this guy that you wanted out of your life?"

"Yeah, but you know that connection we had from the old days was still there. Still, as good as he looked, he was such an introvert. It was hard to get anything out of him. I guess it was the prison experience. It made me feel so bad."

Gray told Eaton about the Joni Mitchell concert that led to a night at Simpson's flat. With a smile, she said, "We had a wonderful night. It was magnificent, and I felt good. I knew, if nothing else, I owed him a night of fun and pleasure."

Gray paused, sipped her wine, and looked out the window. "You know, the morning after we were together, we had breakfast at a nearby diner. On our way back to his place, I told him we couldn't have a relationship. I know I hurt him bad, but I had to nip it in the bud."

Gray also talked about Simpson's sweater that she kept for years.

"It was my knock-around-the-house sweater. I wore it all the time. By the early '80s, that sweater was literally falling apart, full of holes, and hanging threads. My husband told me I should get rid of it. My kids agreed. So, I threw it out. God, I loved that sweater. It was so comfortable and just made me feel good. Jesus, I haven't thought of that sweater in years."

She knew Simpson had disappeared under mysterious circumstances, but didn't know any details. By the end of their chat, it was as if she and Eaton had become good friends.

She took his arm and said, "You know, I've had a great life. Two kids and five grandchildren I adore. I had a great marriage to a wonderful man. Still, I've never stopped thinking of Bill Simpson."

***

While he had been looking for Rita Gray, Eaton found leads on Simpson's children. Debbie would have been about sixty and John a few years younger. He could find nothing relevant on either John Simpson or Debbie Simpson. He checked out Anne Simpson and, in the Wayne County Coroner's office found a 2004 death certificate, listing Anne Simpson-Hyland. Bill looked through the Internet using the Hyland name and found an address on Vernier Road in Grosse Pointe Woods.

Without a phone number or email address, he decided to go to the house. For the high-end reputation of the various Grosse Pointe communities, Eaton was surprised by the modest, two-story structure, probably built in the early '40s. As soon as he rang the bell, a dog started barking. He heard a woman quiet the dog before she opened the door. Bill was greeted by a thin, middle-aged woman with short, brown hair. "Can I help you?"

"I hope so, ma'am. My name is Bill Eaton. I'm researching a possible book on your father—"

"My father?" Debbie said, her expression one of shock. "I never knew the man. He's been dead for a long time. To the best of my knowledge, no one cared about him when he was living or dead." She started to close the door.

"Ms. Hyland, please, I need to talk to you. I believe you have memories that might help me understand him better. And, you should know that your father was an amazing man. He devoted much of his life to his country, he was framed for a crime he did not commit, and after your mother divorced him, he completely remade his life."

She paused and gave him a second look. "Alright then, I'll give you five minutes. Come in."

The living room was modest, cluttered, with tables that needed dusting. "I really don't remember much about my father," she said after sitting in an easy chair and he on the couch. A moment later, the thirty-pound mutt joined him on the couch, lying next to his thigh.

Eaton explained about his research and her father's work in the Secret Service, on President Kennedy's detail, and that he was involved in the Chicago investigation before the president had been assassinated.

"I guess I knew he worked for the government and that he was arrested for cheating on my mother, but that's about it," she said, still being very cautious around him.

"Look," Eaton said, "I'm sorry I just barged in on you. I didn't have a phone number, so I thought I could swing by just for a little talk. Would you mind telling me a bit about yourself?"

"Okay," she said, seeming to appreciate his candor. "I was born in Detroit. Like I said, I don't remember too much about my father, but my life didn't seem to begin until my mother married again, to David Hyland. He became the father figure in our lives, but my brother and I didn't give him much peace in his life. He was a lawyer, met my mother at work—I think sometime after my father went away. After they married, we moved to Grosse Pointe into a really big house."

"Do you remember your father at all?"

"Yes, of course. I don't remember him when we lived in Detroit when they were married. I do remember Grandma Jenny; she was so sweet and special. My father started coming into our lives when I was about six or seven. He was out of prison by then. Usually, Grandma was with him. We hardly ever spent time alone."

"What do you remember about him?"

Debbie laughed. "That's easy—his long hair. He looked like an old hippie. Oh, and he was strong. I remember seeing his muscles ripple. I thought he was Superman."

"Was he kind, mean, shy?"

"Well, we didn't see that much of him. I remember we played games and he took us for rides, and he bought us a lot of gifts. As I think about it, there were times when he brought over a woman, a very pretty and nice woman. I don't remember her name."

"Sue?"

"Could be. But then, not long after Sue started coming, he stopped visiting us. It wasn't until I was a teenager that my mother told me he had been killed, shot by some hoodlums." *Shot by hoodlums? Is that what happened or what his wife thought happened? Or just what they told the kids?*

"Did she say your dad was hoodlum?"

"She never said it, but she implied it for sure. She never liked my father and was not shy of reminding us he was an ex-con."

"You should know that when your father died, if that's what happened, he was employed by the UAW to investigate the death of UAW President Walter Reuther."

"You mean, as in the Walter Reuther Freeway?"

"Yeah, that's him. Reuther was an American hero. He helped create the American middle-class."

She shrugged. "Well, I don't know much about that kind of stuff."

Eaton, thinking he had connected with the woman, thought he should focus more on her family members. "So, tell me about your brother. Does he live in the area?"

Her body tensed up. "Johnny's been dead for fourteen years. He overdosed on heroin in Memphis."

"Oh, God. I'm sorry. I had no idea," Eaton replied.

"Of course not."

She took an opened pack of Kool cigarettes from the table in front of her, pulled one out, lit it, and inhaled deeply. Pausing, she said, "I hope you don't mind."

"No, it's fine. It's your house."

She talked about the drug problems she and her brother had while growing up. She became an addict but was now clean and helping other people to sobriety.

As they walked to the door, Debbie said, "Thank you for coming. I think I feel better about my dad. I do remember those times with him and the woman. We had a lot of fun."

"Sue was my grandmother; she died last year."

"Ah, your grandmother. And you are Bill. Did you get your name from my dad?"

"I think so."

"How romantic."

"Yep. Had Bill Simpson lived, they probably would have married. We'd be related."

"That would have been nice."

Debbie smiled.

Just as Eaton was at the door, he suddenly said, "Oh, crap. I almost forgot that I have something for you." He reached into the folder he was carrying and presented Debbie with an 8-by-10 photograph.

"For me?" she said.

"Yep. That's your father talking with President Kennedy in 1962. It was after the president had just played golf, and your dad was part of the Secret Service detail protecting him. I thought you would like it."

She studied it. Her eyes moistened. "This is very thoughtful. Thank you."

As Eaton left, he again noticed that reserved smile.

***

Debbie's smile reminded Eaton of Micki's smile as he started his ninety-minute drive home to Lansing … and that was one overwhelmingly positive thought. In fact, Micki had been taking up more and more of his thoughts recently. Smart, beautiful, compassionate, and confident—this was the type of person that, until now, he had only dreamed about being with. He hoped she felt the same way as he did. She had a bright future, one of being on the road for months at a time, a challenge for her … and for a relationship. But he thought if she were game, though, so was he.

Only a few minutes into his drive, he pressed Micki's name on the car's entertainment screen and dialed her cell just to hear her voice on her voicemail greeting.

Soon after getting back on the road, Eaton focused his thoughts on Bill Simpson. With the material his grandmother provided, the research he completed, and the interviews, he had a lot of intriguing information, though he still didn't know for sure what had happened to Simpson.

Eaton mulled the facts and some possibilities.

Bill Simpson's body was never found, but his car was discovered in the Detroit River. He knew he'd been followed at times. He knew powerful people didn't like him digging into certain things. It could have been a hit, perhaps by the same people Simpson thought may have been involved in those assassinations during the 1960s.

Simpson knew he was in danger. He didn't want his journals to end up in the wrong hands. And Sue ... if he continued contact with her, she could be in danger. So he got her the info before whatever happened to him. Hmmm... Could he have staged his own death and fled the country hoping to return someday? Maybe he started a new life. Who knows?

With all these thoughts, and others, crowding his mind, Eaton formed the probable scenario for Simpson's final hours at the motel, using the final journal entries as his guide. It went like this:

Simpson re-emerged from the hotel room around 11 o'clock or so with his box of files he planned to take to Sue's apartment. He started the car and drove to downtown Birmingham. He parked behind Demery's Department Store and slowly walked to Sue's place, roughly twenty minutes at the pace he'd chosen. He walked close to the smaller, retail storefronts as he moved away from the business district along Woodward.

When he got to Sue's building, he slipped up the steps to her apartment and set the box by her door. He was about to quietly slip away when the thought occurred to him that anybody in the building, worst of all Macalister's people if they showed up, could walk by and take the box. *This stuff is too important to take a chance with.* He thought for a second, then rapped on the Sue's door and quickly took off before she could answer.

There were more cars in the motel parking lot when Simpson returned. He found an out-of-the-way spot and parked. In his room, he glanced at his watch—one-thirty a.m. He sat at a small, laminated table with two plastic chairs.

Simpson knew Sue would be upset and confused when she found the box outside her door and realized he had been there. He hoped the enclosed note would calm her. With any luck, this never-ending night would be over soon. He'd figure out a way to move forward tomorrow after he got to the security of Solidarity House. There, Morris and Mazey could help him. He was sweaty and tired, so he took a quick shower and got ready for bed. He placed one of the chairs against the door, turned the bed down, and stretched out. Before he fell asleep, he reached over to the nightstand for his pistol and placed it under the pillow.

At two-fifteen, Simpson awoke to a commotion outside his door. He instantly reached for his .38. It was a woman's voice, the sound of drunken laughter, with some guy making sounds of encouragement. *Someone's getting lucky.* The guy struggled putting the key into the lock before the pair stumbled inside the room next to his. Drunken laughter turned to loud lovemaking for another half an hour.

Simpson awoke just before seven, feeling hungover from lack of sleep due to the party next door. He took a long, hot shower, dressed, and used his comb to get his long, wet hair to cooperate. As he dressed, he realized the only way out of this mess was to kill Macalister, a cancer on decent society. When things calmed down, he planned to give this strategy greater consideration. Macalister needed to be exposed.

Simpson grabbed his few belongings and left the room. With the state his mind was in, he didn't do his usually methodical job scanning the area for any of Mac's people. But he did look and saw nothing unusual.

Without taking a look around his car as he may have normally done when thinking he might be followed, Simpson unlocked the door, got behind the wheel, and placed the key in the ignition. He heard movement behind him and quickly looked in his review mirror: A face he didn't recognize was looking back at him. *How the hell did they find me?* He felt the pressure of the gun barrel at the base of his skull.

Not a bad ending for a book, thought Eaton, who had at times considered writing as a side career. *Cliffhanger? Sequel? Series? Who knows?*

His grandmother was right about one thing, though—Simpson's journals shed new light on some old stories. They might change the history of the Kennedy assassination, demonstrate that even the highly admired US Secret Service could be corrupt, and possibly help resurrect the reputation of a man who had been dishonored and humiliated.

Eaton also thought it would be beneficial to tell the story of the UAW. Today, the union wasn't the great force it once was. Due to globalization and a glut of auto manufacturers, the union's power was diluted. Unions seemed to be an afterthought and weren't respected by many. He had learned a lot about the UAW and the leadership of Reuther and others. Maybe he could show that the UAW made a difference on many issues, including fighting for justice, even if for just one person, Simpson.

Suddenly, a shiver ran through him.

What if Fred Fry was right and some of the people who killed Simpson were still around? Simpson *was* dead, right? *Probably, even if he survived that night.* Either way, could Eaton be opening a Pandora's box? Was it possible his life could be in danger or his career destroyed? He assumed there were still dark forces in the US government, though to what extent he had no idea. Was it possible he could awaken a dangerous group of people?

He didn't know the answers to these questions. Yet, if some or all of them were true, if his country had truly succumbed to such influences, perhaps, even by a small measure, he might help to turn the tide by telling some hard truths from long ago. It was a battle he decided he was prepared to fight.

Further Reading

This book is a novel; however, it is based on much research. Much of this story evolves from a meeting I had with Paul Schrade in 2015. I met Paul to talk about my 2013 book, *Built in Detroit: A Story of the UAW, a Company, and a Gangster.* During our two-hour conversation we discussed the UAW, the Robert Kennedy assassination, the President Kennedy assassination and much more. As someone who was shot with Senator Kennedy, his insights were fascinating.

Paul strongly recommended I read *JFK and the Unspeakable: Why He Died and Why it Matters*, by James W. Douglass. From this book I learned much about President Kennedy, Lee Harvey Oswald, and the 1963 assassination. It is one of the very best and most realistic books on the assassination of President Kennedy.

My character, Larry McRae, is loosely based on the life of Abraham Bolden, the first African-American Secret Service agent assigned to the Presidential Protection Division. Like my fictitious characters Larry McRae and Bill Simpson, Bolden did go to prison on what many believe was a trumped-up charge by the Secret Service. He is in his late eighties, and in 2022 received a pardon from President Joe Biden. His autobiography, *The Echo from Dealey Plaza* is an excellent read.

About the Author

Lifelong Michigander Bob Morris has spent his entire career involved in public service.

He was a middle school teacher in the Detroit Public Schools before moving to Lansing in 1976 to work for the Michigan House of Representatives. For the next 38 years, he represented public institutions to the state legislature in the pursuit of setting good public policy for Michigan. He also worked for Gov. James Blanchard and the Michigan departments of transportation and education.

During his time with the state, Bob fought for greater funding of Michigan's transportation infrastructure, tougher high school graduation standards, and promoted strong labor policies. In the 1990s, he was assistant county executive for Wayne County Executive Edward McNamara, where he was a key player in establishing the Wayne County Airport Authority Act.

Bob ended his career as a policy advisor to the Southeast Michigan Council of Governments. He is retired and lives in Farmington Hills, Michigan, with his wife, Terry.

He grew up in southeastern Michigan during the 1950s and 1960s at the knees of some of the greatest labor and political leaders in the state. He graduated from Birmingham Seaholm High School and earned a teaching degree and Masters in Public Administration degree from Western Michigan University.

Bob wrote the nonfiction book, *Built in Detroit: A story of the UAW, a Company and a Gangster,* which was published in 2013. For more about Bob and that book, check out www.builtindetroit.net. Books can be purchased at Amazon.com or BarnesAndNoble.com.

Made in the USA
Monee, IL
10 January 2023

24827773R00177